"PIPPA, LET ME SHOW YOU HOW I LOVE YOU," CONRAD SAID.

"I...don't..."

He had unbuttoned my bodice. I put my hands up to stop him, but he took them and began to kiss them. I was afraid and yet overcome by an excitement such as I had never known before. Everything seemed to fade away...the past...the future...everything that frightened me. There was nothing but this moment.

He was kissing me as he took off my bodice.

"What is happening..." I stammered. "I must go now..."

And I heard him laugh softly and then I was in the four-poster bed and he was there with me. All the time he was murmuring endearments and I was shocked and shattered and overwhelmed with delight.

the Judas Kiss

VICTORIA HOLT

FAWCETT CREST • NEW YORK

Contents

Greystone Manor

I was seventeen years old before I discovered that my sister had been murdered. It was then nearly five years since I had seen her, but every day I had thought of her, longed for her bright presence and mourned her departure from my life.

Before she went away, Francine and I had been as close as two people could be. I suppose I, being the younger by five years, had looked to her for protection, and after the death of our parents when we had come to make Greystone Manor our home, I had had great need of it.

That had happened six years before, and when I looked back on those very early days it seemed to me that we had lived in a paradise. Distance enchants the view, Francine used to say to comfort me and so imply that the island of Calypse had not been completely perfect, so perhaps Greystone Manor was not as gloomy as we, newly become its inmates, believed it to be. Although she was as fragile as a piece of Dresden china in looks, I never knew anyone who had a more practical grip on life. She was realistic, resourceful, irrepressible and always optimistic; indeed she seemed unable to visualize failure. I had always believed that whatever Francine decided she would do, she would do successfully. That was why I was so shattered, so overwhelmed with disbelief when I found that newspaper in Aunt Grace's trunk

7

in the attic at Greystone. I knelt there holding the paper in my hand while the words danced before my eyes.

> *"Baron von Gruton Fuchs found murdered in his bed in his hunting lodge in the Grutonian province of Bruxenstein last Wednesday morning. With him was his mistress, a young English woman whose identity is as yet unknown, but it is believed she was his companion for some time at the lodge before the tragedy."*

There was another cutting attached.

> *"The identity of the woman has been discovered. She is Francine Ewell, who has been a 'friend' of the Baron for some time."*

That was all. It was incredible. The Baron was her husband. I remembered so well how she had told me she was going to be married and how I grappled with myself to cast out the desolation of losing her and trying to rejoice in her happiness.

I just knelt there until I realized my limbs were cramped and that my knees were hurting. Then I took the newspaper cuttings and went back to my bedroom, sitting there dazed, thinking back ... to everything she had been to me, until she had gone away.

Those idyllic early years had been spent on the island of Calypse with our adored, adoring and quite unrealistic parents.

They were the beautiful years. They had ended when I was eleven and Francine sixteen, so I suppose I did not really understand a great deal of what was going on around me. I was unaware of the financial difficulties and the anxiety of living through those periods when no visitors came to my father's studio. Not that any of these fears were shown, for Francine was there to manage us all with the skill and energy which we took for granted.

Our father was an artist in stone. He sculpted the most beautiful figures of Cupid and Psyche, Venus rising from the waves, of little mermaids, dancing girls, urns and baskets of flowers; and visitors came and bought them. My mother was his favourite model and next to her, Francine. I posed for him too. They would never have thought of leaving me out, although I had never had that sylph-like quality of Francine and my mother which lent itself so perfectly to stone. They were the beautiful ones. I resembled my father with hair which was rather nondescript in colour and could be called mid-brown, thick, straight and invariably untidy; I had greenish eyes which changed colour with their surroundings and what Francine called a "pert" nose, and a mouth which was rather large. "Generous," Francine called it. She was a great consoler. My mother had a fairylike beauty which she had passed on to Francine—blond and curly-haired, blue, dark-lashed eyes and that extra fraction of an inch on the nose which was sufficient to make it beautiful, and with all this went a shortish upper lip which revealed ever so slightly prominent pearly teeth. Above all there was that air of helpless femininity which made men want to fetch and carry for them and protect them from the hardships of the world. My mother might have been in need of that protection; Francine never was.

There were long, warm days—rowing the boat out to the blue lagoon and swimming there, taking desultory lessons with Antonio Farfalla who was repaid by a piece of sculpture from our father's studio. "It will be worth a fortune one day," Francine assured him. "You only have to wait until my father is recognized." Francine could convey great authority in spite of her fragile looks, and Antonio believed her. He adored Francine. Until we came to Greystone it seemed that everyone adored Francine. She was charmingly protective even of him, and although she joked a great deal about his name, which in Italian meant Butterfly, and he was the most cumbersome man we ever knew, she was always sympathetic when he was distressed by his clumsiness.

It was some time before I began to be worried by my mother's constant illnesses. She used to lie in her hammock, which we had fixed up outside the studio, and there was always someone there talking to her. At first, my father had told me, we had not been accepted very warmly on the island. We were foreigners and they were an insular people. They had lived there for hundreds of years, cultivating the vines and the silkworms and working in the quarry from which came the alabaster and serpentine in which my father worked. But when the people of the island realized that we were just like them, and were ready to live as they did, they finally accepted us. "It was your mother who won them over," he used to say, and I could well imagine that. She looked so beautiful, ethereal, as though the wind would carry her off when the mistral blew. "They gradually came round," my father said. "There would be litttle gifts on the doorstep, and when Francine was born we had a houseful of helpers. The same with you, Pippa. You were made just as welcome as your sister."

They always reminded me of that. There came the time when I began to wonder why it should be necessary.

Francine discovered all she could about our family history. She was always eager to learn everything. Ignorance worried her. She wanted to know the smallest detail—why the silkworm yield was higher or lower; how much Vittoria Guizza's wedding feast cost, and who was the father of Elizabetta Caldori's baby. Everything that went on was of the greatest interest to Francine. She had to know the answer.

"They say," said Antonio, "that those who seek to know all may someday discover that which does not please."

"In England they say, 'Curiosity killed the cat,'" Francine told him. "Well, I am not a cat but I intend to be curious...even if it kills me."

We all laughed at the time, but looking back I remembered that.

Blissful island days they were—the warm sun on my skin, the pungent smell of frangipani and hibiscus; the gentle swish of the blue Mediterranean sea against the shores of the island; long dreamy days lying in the boat after swimming; sitting round the hammock in which our mother gently rocked; watching Francine come into the studio when we had visitors. They came from America and England, but mainly from France and Germany, and over the years Francine and I acquired a fair understanding of these languages. Francine would bring out wine in glasses at the sides of which she had arranged hibiscus flowers. The visitors loved that and they paid high prices for my father's work when Francine talked to them. They were making an investment, she would assure them, for my father was a great artist. He was here on the island because of his wife's health. He should be in his salon in Paris or London. Never mind, it gave these good people an opportunity to acquire works of art at the best possible prices.

They would recognize the beauty of Francine in the statues and they would buy them, and I am sure preserved them and remembered for a long time enchanted afternoons when they were waited on by a beautiful girl who served them wine in a flower-trimmed glass.

So we lived in those long-ago days, never thinking beyond the moment, rising in the morning to the sunshine and going to bed at night deliciously tired out after days of pleasant activities. It was fun, though, to sit in the studio and listen to the rain as it pelted down. "This will bring out the snails," Francine used to say; and when it was over we would go out with our baskets and gather them. Francine was an expert at picking out those which could be sold to Madame Descartes, the Frenchwoman who kept the inn on the waterfront. She would instruct me not to pick those whose shells were soft because they would be too young. "Poor little things, they have had no life yet. Let them live a little longer." It sounded humane, but of course Madame Descartes wanted only those which were edible. We would take them to the inn and receive a little money for them. A few weeks later, when the snails had been taken out of the cage in which they had been kept, Francine and I would go along to the inn and Madame Descartes would give us a taste of them. Francine thought they were delicious cooked with garlic and parsley. I never really fancied them. It was a ritual, however—the end of the snail harvest—and therefore I went solemnly through it with my sister.

Then there was the vine harvest, when we donned wooden shoes like sabots and helped in treading out the grapes. Francine joined in with verve—singing and dancing like a wild dervish, her curls flying, her eyes shining, so that everyone smiled at her and my father said, "Francine is our ambassadress."

Those were the happy days and it never occurred to me that they could change. My mother was growing weaker but somehow she managed to conceal the fact from me. Perhaps she did from my father too, but I wondered whether she did from Francine. But if it did occur to my sister she would have dismissed it as she always did anything she did not want to happen. I sometimes thought that life had bestowed so many gifts on Francine that she believed that the gods were working for her too, so that she only had to say, "I don't want that to happen," and it wouldn't.

I remember the day well. It was September—wine harvest time—and there was that excitement in the air which always heralded it. We would go, Francine and I, and join the young people on the island to begin our stamping on the grapes to the tunes from Verdi's operas which old Umberto would scrape out on his fiddle. We would all sing lustily and the old people would sit and watch, their gnarled hands clasped on their black laps and the light of reminiscence in their rheumy eyes, while we danced until our feet were weary and our voices grew more and more hoarse.

But there was another harvest. One of the poems I liked best was called The Reaper and the Flowers.

> There is a Reaper whose name is Death
> And with his sickle keen
> He reaps the bearded grain at a breath
> And the flowers that grow between.

Francine explained it to me; she was good at explaining things. "It means young people sometimes get in the way of the sickle," she said, "then they get cut down too." It seems significant now that she should have been one of those flowers which grew between. But then it was our mother who died, and she was like a flower. It was not time for her to die; she was too young.

It was terrible when we found her dead. Francine had taken in the glass of milk she had every morning. She was lying quite still and Francine said afterwards that she went on talking for quite a while before she realized my mother was not listening. "Then I went to the bed," said Francine; "I just looked at her and then I knew."

So it had happened. All Francine's magic could not hold it off. Death had come with his sickle and taken the fair flower which grew between.

Our father was as one demented. He was very much the artist and when he worked in his studio making those beautiful women who had a look of my mother or my sister, he had always seemed far away. We always laughed at his absent-mindedness. Francine bustled about the studio keeping us all in order. Our mother, for a long time, had been too ill to do very much; she was just there—a benign presence and an inspiration to us all. She had talked to visitors and made them welcome and they all enjoyed that; and as long as Francine was there everything held together.

Now she was gone, Francine took over completely. She

talked to the visitors and made them feel they were getting bargains. I don't know how we should have got through that year without her. When our mother was laid to rest in the little cemetery close by the olive groves we should have been a desolate household but for Francine. She became in a sense the head of the household, although she was only fifteen years old. She shopped; she cooked; she kept us going. She refused to take any more lessons with the Butterfly, as she called Antonio, but she insisted that I should. Our father lived with his stone but his figures had lost a certain magic which they had had before. He didn't want Francine to pose for him. That brought back too many memories.

The gloomy months began to pass and I felt a change in myself. I was at that time ten years old but I ceased to be a child.

Our father talked to us during that time. It was in the evenings when we would sit on the green slope which ran down to the sea, and as the darkness fell we would watch the sheen of phosphorescence which came from the shoals of fish and were like will of the wisps on the water...eerie and yet comforting in a way.

He talked about his life before he came to the island. Francine had been curious about it for a long time and had gleaned a little information which she had extracted from him or our mother during their unwary moments. We often wondered why they were so reluctant to talk about the past. We were soon to discover. I suppose everyone who had lived in Greystone Manor would want to escape from it and even forget he or she had ever been there. For it was like a prison. That was how our father described it, and later I was to understand.

"It's a fine old house," said my father, "a mansion really. Ewells have lived in it for four hundred years. The first Ewell built it before the reign of Elizabeth. Think of that."

"It must be strong to stand up to all that time," I began, but Francine silenced me with a look, and I knew she meant that we must not remind our father that he was thinking aloud.

"They knew how to build in those days. Their houses might have been uncomfortable, but they could stand up not only to the weather but to attackers."

"Attackers," I cried excitedly, only to be silenced again by Francine.

That was when he said, "It was like a prison. To me it was a prison."

There was a deep silence. Our father was looking back right over the years to when he was a boy, before he had met my mother, before Francine was born. It was hard to imagine a world without Francine.

Our father was frowning. "You children have no idea," he said. "You have been surrounded by love. We have been poor, yes. It has not always been a comfortable life—but love there has been in abundance."

I ran to him and threw myself at him. He held me very tightly in his arms. "Little Pippa," he said, "you have been happy, yes? You must always remember Pippa's song. We named you for that, Pippa.

> 'God's in his heaven—
> All's right with the world.'"

"Yes," I cried. "Yes, yes."

Francine said, "Go and sit down, Pippa. You're interrupting Father. He wants to tell us something."

Our father was silent for a while and then he said, "Your grandfather is a good man. Make no mistake about that. But sometimes good men are uncomfortable to live with—for sinners that is."

Silence again, this time broken by Francine who whispered, "Tell us about our grandfather. Tell us about Greystone Manor."

"He was always proud of the family. We had served our country well. We had been soldiers, politicians, squires, but never artists. Well, there was one...long ago. He was killed in a tavern near Whitehall. His name was never mentioned except with disgust. 'Poetry writing is no life for a man,' said your grandfather. You can imagine what he said when he knew I wanted to be a sculptor."

"Tell us," whispered Francine.

Our father shook his head. "It seemed just impossible. My future was planned for me. I was to follow in his footsteps. I was not to be a soldier, nor a politician. I was the only son of the squire, so I should follow in my father's footsteps. I should learn how to manage the estate and spend the rest of my life trying to be exactly like my father."

"And you couldn't do that," said Francine.

"No—I hated it. I hated everything about Greystone. I hated the house and my father's rule, his attitude towards us all—my mother, my sister Grace and myself. He regarded himself as our master. He wanted obedience in all things. He was a tyrant. And—I met your mother."

"Tell us about that time," said Francine.

"She came to the house to make dresses for your Aunt Grace. She was so gentle, so fragile, so beautiful. It was meeting her that decided me."

"So you ran away from Greystone Manor," said Francine.

"Yes. I broke out of prison. We ran away to freedom—your mother from a life of drudgery with the dressmaking house for which she worked... I from Greystone Manor. We neither of us ever regretted it for a moment."

"Romantic... beautiful," murmured Francine.

"There were hard times at first. In London... in Paris ... trying to make a living. Then we met a man in a café. He had the studio on this island and he offered it to us. So we came. Francine was born here... and so were you, Pippa."

"Didn't he come back to claim the studio?" asked Francine.

"He came back. He stayed with us for a while. You were too young to remember that. Then he went to Paris, where he became quite wealthy. He died some years ago and left me the studio. We have managed to make a living—a poor one, but we have been free."

"We have been very happy, Father," said Francine firmly. "No girls could have been happier."

Then we all embraced one another—we were a demonstrative family—and Francine suddenly became very practical and said it was time we all went to bed.

It was only a few weeks after that conversation that our father was drowned. He had taken the boat out to the blue lagoon as we so often did when a sudden storm blew up and the boat capsized. I wondered afterwards how great an attempt he had made to save himself. Since our mother's death, life had certainly lost its savour for him. He had his two girls, but I think he thought Francine was more capable of looking after herself and me than he was. Besides, he would have guessed the turn events would take, and perhaps he thought it was the best thing for us.

I felt fatalistic, almost as though I knew what was going to happen. I had already come to the conclusion that nothing could be the same after my mother's death. We had tried to regain our old cheerfulness and Francine had managed very well, but even she could not entirely pretend.

We faced each other in the studio on the day he was laid beside my mother near the olive groves. "It was where he wanted to be since she was put there," said Francine.

"What are we going to do?" I said.

She was jaunty almost. "We have each other. There are two of us."

"You'd always be all right and see that I was," I replied.

"That is so," she answered.

Our friends on the island smothered us with kindness. We were fed, caressed and made to feel that we were well loved.

"It's nice for a beginning," commented Francine, "but it won't go on. We have to think."

I was nearly eleven then, Francine sixteen. "Of course," she said, "I could marry Antonio."

"You couldn't. You wouldn't."

"I am fond of the Butterfly, but you are right. I couldn't and I wouldn't."

I looked at her questioningly. She was rarely short of ideas but on this occasion she was. There were dreams in her eyes. "We might go away," she suggested.

"Where to?"

"Somewhere." Then she told me that she had always known that one day she would go away. She could not bear to be shut in, and that was what we were on the island. "It was different when our parents were alive," she said. "It was our home then. It isn't any more, really. Besides, what should we do here?"

Our problem was solved by a letter for Francine.

"Miss Ewell," said the address on the envelope.

"I am that," Francine explained. "You are Miss Philippa Ewell."

As she opened it I saw the excitement in her eyes. "It's from a solicitor," she said. "He's acting for Sir Matthew Ewell. That's our grandfather. In view of the unfortunate circumstances, Sir Matthew wishes us to return at once to England. Our rightful home is Greystone Manor."

I stared at her aghast, but her eyes were shining.

"Oh, Pippa," she said. "We are going to the prison."

There was the excitement of preparing for departure, which was a good thing in a way because it stopped our brooding on our loss, and how great that was we had not yet begun to realize. There was the packing up and disposal of the studio and its contents which Antonio sadly took over from us.

"But it is best for you," he said. "You will live like great ladies. We always knew that Signor Ewell was a grand gentleman."

One of the men from the solicitor's office came to take us to our new home. He wore a black frock coat and a shiny top hat; he looked quite out of place on the island, where he was regarded with great respect. He was a little shy of us at first, but Francine soon put him at his ease. She had become very dignified since our father's death, very much Miss Ewell who was of higher rank than Miss Philippa Ewell. His name was Mr. Counsell and it was clear that he thought the conducting of two girls to England was a very strange task for a man in his position.

We said a sad farewell to our friends and promised to return. I was on the point of inviting them all to England, but Francine gave me one of her warning looks. "Imagine them in the prison," she said. "They would never come," I told her. "They might," she answered.

It was a long journey. We had made the trip to the mainland on several occasions, but it was the first time I had been in a train. I found it absorbingly interesting and I was a little ashamed of myself because I was enjoying it. I was sure Francine was too. People looked at Francine as I realized they always would. Even Mr. Counsell was a little fascinated by her charm and treated her as a beautiful young woman rather than a child. She was, I suppose, in between the two. In some ways she was a very innocent sixteen, in other ways quite mature. She had managed our household, dealt with the customers and taken on the role of guardian of us all. On the other hand, life on the island had been lived simply and I think that at first Francine was inclined to judge everyone by the people she had known all her life so far.

We crossed the English Channel, and to Mr. Counsell's dismay we missed the train which was to take us to Preston Carstairs, the station for Greystone Manor, and were told we had several hours to wait for the next. He took us to an inn near the docks, where we had a meal of roast beef and potatoes in jackets, which seemed exotic and delicious, and while we were eating the innkeeper's wife came to talk to us. When she heard that we had to wait so long she said, "Why don't you see a bit of the countryside while you're waiting? You could take the trap out a little way. Our Jim's got an hour or so to spare."

Mr. Counsell seemed to think it was a good idea, and that was how we came to see Birley Church. Francine had cried out in delight as we were about to pass it by. There was something very interesting about that church. It was Norman, grey stone and, said Francine, exciting when you thought of all the years it had stood there. Mr. Counsell said he did not see why we should not visit the church, so we did. He himself was quite an authority on architecture and he enjoyed passing on information of which he was clearly proud. While he pointed out the interesting features, Francine and I stood in wonder. We didn't care that the pillars and semicircular arches held up the high walls of the clerestory; we were interested in the queer smell of damp and furniture polish and the stained glass windows with the beautiful colours that threw blue and red shadows everywhere; we studied the list of vicars who had held office since the twelfth century.

"When I marry I should like to be married in this church," said Francine.

We sat in the pews. We knelt on the prayer mats. We stood in awe before the altar.

"It's beautiful," said Francine.

Mr. Counsell reminded us of passing time and we went back to the inn and from there to the station, where the train took us to Preston Carstairs.

When we arrived there a carriage was waiting for us. It had an elaborate crest on it. Francine nudged me. "The Ewell crest," she murmured. "Ours."

Relief now sat on Mr. Counsell's homely features. He had delivered his charges safely.

Francine was looking excited, but, just as in my case, the apprehension was beginning to take hold. It was all very well to joke about the prison when it was miles away. It was a different matter when you were within an hour of being incarcerated.

A stern-faced coachman was waiting for us.

"Mr. Counsell, sir," he said, "is these the young ladies?"

"Yes," answered Mr. Counsell.

"The carriage is here, sir."

He was studying us and as was to be expected his eyes rested on Francine. She was wearing a simple grey cloak, which had been our mother's, and on her head was a straw hat with a marguerite in the centre and ribbons under the chin. It was simple attire but Francine could never look anything but enchanting. His eyes scanned me and then he was back to Francine.

"Better get in, young ladies," he said.

The horses' hoofs rang out on the road as we skimmed along past green hedges, through leafy lanes until we came to a wrought-iron gateway. The gates were opened immediately by a boy who touched his forelock to the carriage and then we were bowling up a drive. The carriage stopped before a lawn and we alighted.

We stood together, my sister and I, hand in hand, and I knew that even Francine was overawed. There it stood, the house which our father had spoken of so vehemently as the prison. It was huge and grey stone as its name implied and there were embattled turrets at either end. I noticed the battlements and the lofty archway through which I could see a courtyard. It was very grand, awe-inspiring, and it filled me with apprehension.

Francine pressed my hand firmly, holding it very tightly as though she took courage from the contact, and together we walked across the grass towards a great door which had swung open. A woman in a starched cap was standing there. The coach had gone forward under the archway into the courtyard and the woman stood in the doorway watching us.

"The master is ready to see you as soon as you arrive, Mr. Counsell," she said.

"Come along." Mr. Counsell smiled reassuringly at us and we went forward towards the door.

I shall never forget stepping inside that house. I was quivering with excitement, which was really a mingling of apprehension and curiosity. The ancestral home! I thought. And then: The Prison.

Those thick stone walls, the coolness as we stepped inside, the awesomeness of the great hall with its vaulted roof, the stone floor and walls on which glittered weapons presumably used by long-dead Ewells—they thrilled me and yet made me fearful in some way. Our footsteps sounded noisy so I tried to walk quietly. I saw that Francine had lifted her head and was putting on that bold look which meant that she was a little more apprehensive than she would like people to know.

"The master said you were to go straight to him," the woman repeated. She was rather plump with greying hair very tightly drawn back from her forehead and all but concealed by her white cap. Her eyes were small, her lips tightly shut, like a trap. She seemed to suit the house.

"If you'll step this way, sir," she said to Mr. Counsell.

She turned and we followed her to the grand staircase, which we ascended. Francine was still holding my hand. We went along a gallery and paused before a door. The woman knocked and a voice said, "Enter."

We did so. The scene remained imprinted on my mind forever. I was vaguely aware of a darkish room with heavy draperies and large, dark pieces of furniture, but it was my grandfather who dominated the room. He was seated there in a chair like a throne and he himself looked like a biblical prophet. He was clearly a very big man; his arms were folded across his chest and what struck me immediately was his long, luxuriant beard, which rippled over his chest and concealed the lower part of his face. Beside him sat a woman, middle-aged and colourless. I guessed she was our Aunt Grace. She looked small, ineffectual and modest, but perhaps that was in comparison with the imposing central figure.

"So you have brought my granddaughters, Mr. Counsell," said my grandfather. "Come here."

This last was addressed to us and Francine advanced, taking me with her.

"H'm," said our grandfather, his eyes surveying us intently, giving me the impression that he was trying to find fault with us. What astonished me was that he seemed unimpressed by Francine's charm.

I had thought he might have kissed us or at least taken our hands. Instead he just looked at us as though there was something rather distasteful about us.

"I am your grandfather," he said, "and this is now your home. I hope you will be worthy of it. I doubt not that you will have much to learn. You are now in a civilized community. It will be well for you to remember that."

"We have always been in a civilized community," said Francine.

There was silence. I saw the woman seated beside my grandfather flinch.

"I would disagree with that," he said.

"Then you would be wrong," went on Francine. She was very nervous, I could see, but she sensed in his remarks a slur on our father and she was not going to tolerate that. She had immediately transgressed against the first rule of the house, which was that our grandfather was never wrong, and he was so startled that for a moment he was lost for words.

Then he spoke coldly: "Indeed you have much to learn. I had expected we might have to deal with uncouth manners. Well, we are prepared. Now the first thing to do is to give thanks to our Maker for your safe journey and we will express the hope that those of us in need of humility and gratitude will be granted these virtues, and will follow that course of righteousness which is the only one acceptable in this house.."

We were bewildered. Francine was still smarting with her indignation and I was growing more depressed and afraid every moment.

And there we were, tired, hungry, bewildered and desperately apprehensive, kneeling on the cold floor in that dark room, giving thanks to God for bringing us to this prison and praying for the humility and gratitude which our grandfather expected us to feel to him for the miserable home he was giving us.

It was Aunt Grace who took us to our room. Poor Aunt Grace! When we referred to her it was always *poor* Aunt Grace. She looked drained of life; she was extremely thin and the brown cotton of her dress accentuated the sallowness of her complexion. Her hair, which might have been beautiful, was drawn straight back from her brow and plaited into a rather unwieldy knob in the nape of her neck; her eyes were pleasant, nothing could alter that. They were brown with abundant dark lashes—rather like Francine's except for the colour—only where my sister's sparkled, hers were dull and hopeless. Hopeless! That was the term one immediately applied to Aunt Grace.

We followed her up another staircase and she walked ahead, not speaking. Francine grimaced at me. It was rather a nervous grimace. I guessed that Francine was realizing she would not find it easy to charm such a household.

Aunt Grace opened a door and stepped into a room, standing aside so that we could enter. We did so. It was quite a pleasant room, but the dark curtains which half obscured the windows made it gloomy.

"You are to be together," said Aunt Grace. "Your grandfather thought there was no point in using two rooms."

I felt a sudden surge of pleasure. I should not have relished sleeping alone in that eerie mansion. I remembered Francine's once saying that nothing is all bad—or all good, for that matter; there had to be a little bit of the other, however slight. It was a comforting thought just now.

There were two beds in the room.

"You may choose how you will use them," said Aunt Grace as though, Francine afterwards remarked, she were offering us the kingdoms of the world.

She said, "Thank you, Aunt Grace."

"Now you will want to wash and perhaps change after the journey. We dine in an hour's time. Your grandfather will not tolerate unpunctuality."

"I am sure he will not," said Francine, and there was a note of hysteria in her voice. "It's so dark in here," she went on. "I can't see anything." She went to the windows and pulled back the curtains. "There! That's better. Oh, what a lovely view."

I went to the window and Aunt Grace came and stood immediately behind us.

"That is Rantown Forest down there," she said.

"It looks interesting. Forests always do. How far are we from the sea, Aunt Grace?"

"About ten miles."

Francine had turned to her. "I love the sea. We lived surrounded by it, you see. It makes you love it."

"Yes," said Aunt Grace, "I suppose it must. Now I will have hot water sent up to you."

"Aunt Grace," went on Francine, "you are our father's sister, yet you don't mention him. Don't you want to hear about your brother?"

I saw her face clearly in the light Francine had let in. It twitched and she looked as though she were going to cry. "Your grandfather has forbidden us to mention him," she said.

"Your own brother..."

"He behaved—unforgivably. Your grandfather..."

"He makes the laws here, I see," said Francine.

"I—I don't understand you." Aunt Grace was trying to look severe. "You are young," she went on, "and you have much to learn, and I will give you a piece of advice. Never, never again speak to your grandfather as you did today. You must never say he is wrong. He is—"

"Always right," added Francine. "Omnipotent, omniscient—like God, of course."

Aunt Grace suddenly put out a hand and touched Francine's arm. "*You* will have to be careful," she said almost pleadingly.

"Aunt Grace," I put in—for I thought I had glimpsed something which in her indignation Francine might have missed—and it was in that moment that my aunt became *poor* Aunt Grace for me, "are *you* glad that we have come?"

Her face twitched again, and there was a clouded look in her eyes. She nodded, and said, "I will send the hot water."

Then she was gone.

Francine and I stood looking at each other.

"I hate him," she said. "And our aunt... what is she? A puppet."

Oddly enough, I was the one who could comfort Francine. Perhaps because she was older than I she could see more clearly what our lives would be like here. Perhaps I was clutching at straws for comfort.

"At least we are together," I reminded her.

She nodded and looked round the room.

"It's better now you've let in the light," I added.

"We'll make a vow. We'll never draw those hideous curtains again. I expect *he* ordered them to be put there to shut out the sun. He would hate the sun, wouldn't he? But, Pippa, they are all so dead. That woman who let us in... the coachman... It's like dying. Perhaps we are dead. Perhaps we had an accident on that train and this is Hades. We are waiting while it is decided whether we shall go to heaven or hell."

I laughed. It was good to laugh and soon she was laughing with me.

"Puppets," I said. "They are like puppets, but puppets can be jerked, you know."

"But look who is the puppet master!"

"*We're* not his puppets, Francine."

"Never!" she cried. "Never!"

"I think Aunt Grace is rather nice really. *Poor* Aunt Grace."

"Aunt Grace! She is nothing. 'Never again speak to your grandfather as you did today...'" she mimicked. "I will if I want to!"

"He might turn us away. Where should we go if he did?"

It was a sobering thought and she was at a loss for words.

I put my hand in hers and said, "We have to wait, Francine. We have to wait... and plan."

Plans always excited Francine.

She said slowly, "You're right, Pippa. Yes, you are right. We have to bide our time... and plan."

* * *

We lay in our beds without speaking for a long time. I was reliving that strange evening and I knew that Francine was
doing the same.

We had washed and changed into the dresses of coloured
cotton which we had always worn on the island. That they
would seem incongruous here did not strike us until we joined
our grandfather and aunt. Poor Aunt Grace's look of horror
warned me. I saw our grandfather's cold eyes on us and I prayed
that he would not provoke Francine beyond endurance. I had
a vision of our being turned out, and although I was by no
means enamoured of Greystone Manor and my relations, I realized that there could be worse fates than that which awaited
us here.

We were taken into the dining room, which was large and
should have been bright and colourful. But all that was needed
to make a room mournful was our grandfather's presence. One
single candle lighted the long and intricately carved table, and
I found myself wondering what my father had felt when he had
sat at that table. Because of its size we seemed a long way from
each other. Grandfather was at one end, Aunt Grace at the
other and Francine and I opposite each other.

We made a mistake in the first moment by sitting down
when it was the custom at Greystone Manor to stand and say
grace.

"Are you not prepared to thank your Maker for your food?"
demanded our grandfather in a voice of thunder.

Francine pointed out that we had not had it yet.

"Savages," muttered my grandfather. "On your feet at
once."

Francine looked at me and I thought she was going to refuse,
but she didn't. Grace went on interminably. Our grandfather
apologized to God for our ingratitude and promised this should
not happen again. He gave thanks on our behalf and his voice
went droning on until I felt frantic with hunger, for we had not
eaten for some time.

At last it was over and we sat down. Our grandfather talked
all the time about church affairs, about people on the estate
and the difference our coming to the household would make,
so that we felt we were going to be an encumbrance. Aunt Grace
murmured yes or no at the appropriate moments and all
through the monologue wore an expression of rapt attention.

"It would seem that you are without education. A governess

should be found without delay. Grace, that will be your province."

"Yes, Father."

"I cannot have it said that my granddaughters are ignorant."

"We had a tutor on the island," said Francine. "He was very good. We have fluent Italian, both of us. Some French and quite good German—"

"We speak English here," interrupted my grandfather. "You clearly need to be educated in deportment and general behaviour."

"Our parents brought us up."

Aunt Grace looked so frightened that I threw a beseeching look at Francine, who interpreted it and hesitated.

"Grace," went on our grandfather, "you must take charge of your nieces until the governess arrives. Make them understand that in polite society such as ours, children speak only when they are spoken to. They are seen but not heard."

Even Francine seemed subdued, although she said afterwards that she was too hungry to want to argue with that dreadful old man and all she could think of was the food. Besides she had an idea that he might have some notion that little children should be sent to bed without their supper if they were recalcitrant, so she was playing it carefully . . . just at first.

"Just at first!" That became our watchword in those early days. We would endure it until we discovered how we could escape from it. "But first," said Francine, "we must discover the lie of the land."

So on that first night we lay there silently for a while and then we went over the events of the day, recalling every detail of our encounter with our grandfather.

"He is the most horrible old man I ever met," said Francine. "I hated him from the moment I saw him. I'm not surprised Father said it was a prison and he escaped from it. We shall escape in time, Pippa."

Then she talked about the house. "What a place to explore! And just think, *our* ancestors lived there for hundreds of years. That's something to be proud of, Pippa. We've got to find a way of showing the old man that *we* don't think he is God and if he were I'd be an atheist. He is not the least interested in us. He is just doing his duty. If there is anything I could hate more than that old man it's being a duty to somebody."

"Well," I reminded her, "you've got both your worst hates under one roof."

That made us laugh. How thankful I was then for Francine . . . as never before. I went to sleep thinking that while we were together, nothing was so bad.

The next day we made our discoveries. Hot water was brought by a maid. We were both asleep when it arrived as we had lain awake until late talking. That was when we first saw Daisy.

She was standing between our beds and laughing. I sat up with a start at the same time that Francine did. The realization of where we were came flooding over us and what struck us forcibly was that we were looking at someone who was actually laughing.

"You are a couple of sleepy 'eads," she said.

"Who are you?" asked Francine.

"I'm Daisy," she answered. "Under housemaid. I've been sent up with your wash water."

"Thank you," said Francine and she added in a tone of wonder, "You sound very cheerful."

"Bless you, Miss, ain't no sense in being aught else . . . even in this 'ouse where a smile is thought to be a step along the road to 'ell."

"Daisy," said Francine, sitting up and shaking her fair curls out of her eyes, "how long have you been here?"

"Six months and it seems like twenty. I'll be moving on as soon as my luck turns. My, you're pretty."

"Thank you," said Francine.

"It won't be liked—not in this 'ouse. I'm said to be on the flighty side myself."

"Are you?" asked Francine.

Daisy gave a very pronounced wink which made us laugh.

"I'll tell you one thing," she said, "here's one who's glad you've come. Liven this old place up a bit. I'll tell you something else, there's more fun to be had in the old bone-yard than here." She laughed as though something struck her as very funny. "Yes, 'strue. There's a whole lot of fun to be had in the aforementioned place—that's if you haven't gone there to bury a loved one. Well, there's the living to think of, I always say. The dead has gone and none the worse they'll be thought of for having a bit of fun when they was alive."

This was an extraordinary conversation and Daisy herself seemed to realize it, for she brought it to an abrupt conclusion by saying, "Better look smart. The master don't like latecomers. And breakfast is at eight."

She went out, turning at the door to give us the benefit of that amazing wink.

"I like her," said Francine. "Daisy! I must say I'm surprised to find there is someone in this house whom we can like."

"It seems a good omen," I commented.

Francine laughed. "Come on, get dressed. We have to be at breakfast soon. Remember, our sainted grandfather does not like to be kept waiting. Moreover, he won't tolerate it. I wonder what today will bring forth."

"Let's wait and see."

"A very profound remark, dear sister, because there is simply nothing else we can possibly do."

Francine was back to her old self and that was comforting.

Breakfast was like a repetition of the previous meal with different food. There was plenty of that, which must be because, in spite of his saintliness, Grandfather liked his food. When we arrived he gave us a nod and as there were no complaints, I gathered we were not even a fraction of a second late. Grace was said at some length and then we were allowed to help ourselves from the sideboard after Grandfather and Aunt Grace had done so. There was sizzling bacon, devilled kidneys and eggs in various forms. How different from the fruit and brioche we had had on the island, rising when the mood took us and helping ourselves to whatever there was to eat, sometimes alone, sometimes together, while our father had often worked through the night in the studio to finish some masterpiece and would sleep long into the next day because of it!

This was very different. Here everything ran to order.

As he tackled his food with appreciative gusto, our grandfather barked out orders. Aunt Grace should get into immediate touch with Jenny Brakes. She should be summoned to the Manor without delay to make some suitable garments for his granddaughters. It was clear that on that outlandish island they had run loose like natives. They could scarcely be presented to the neighbourhood until they were suitably accoutred. I caught Francine's eyes and was alarmingly near to giggling. "He made us sound like Roman soldiers going into battle," she said afterwards.

Then Aunt Grace must find a suitable governess.

"Enquire of your friends at the rectory." I thought he spoke rather sneeringly and as Aunt Grace flushed slightly there seemed to be some subtlety in that remark, which I would report to Francine later if she had not noticed.

When Grandfather had finished eating he wiped his hands rather ceremoniously on his table napkin, flung it aside and rose ponderously to his feet. This was the signal for us all to rise. No one lingered at the table after he had decided the meal was terminated. "Like Queen Elizabeth," commented Francine. "Fortunately he appears to be a great trencherman so that gives us an opportunity to tuck a bit away too."

"First," he announced as he rose to his feet, "they should be taken to their grandmother."

We were astonished. We had forgotten that we had a grandmother. As no mention had been made of her, I had presumed she was dead.

Aunt Grace said, "Come with me."

We followed her. As we left we heard our grandfather say to the butler, "The bacon was not crisp enough this morning."

Following Aunt Grace, I thought how easy it would be to get lost in Greystone Manor. There were staircases in unexpected places and numerous long corridors with smaller ones turning off from them. Aunt Grace went on with the practised air of one who was well acquainted with the twists and turns of the house and she brought us at length to a door. She knocked and it was opened by a woman in a white cap and a black bombazine dress.

"Mrs. Warden, I have brought my nieces to see their grandmother."

"Yes. She is already waiting."

The woman looked at us and nodded. She had a serene face. I noticed this particularly because I had been aware of the lack of that quality in the house.

Aunt Grace led us in and there, seated on a chair beside a four-poster bed, was a little old lady in a frilled cap and a gown in which ribbons were threaded. She looked fragile. Aunt Grace went to her and kissed her and I was immediately aware of a different atmosphere in the room from that which prevailed in the rest of the house.

"Are they here?" asked the old lady.

"Yes, Mamma," replied Aunt Grace. "Francine is the elder. She is sixteen years old and Philippa is five years younger."

"Bring them to me."

First Francine was pushed forward. My grandmother lifted her hands and touched my sister's face. "Bless you," she said. "I am glad you have come."

"And this is Philippa." I was brought forward and the fingers gently touched my face.

Francine and I were silent. So she was blind.

"Come, my dears," she said, "sit one on either side of me. Have you stools for them, Agnes?"

Mrs. Warden brought two stools and we sat down. Our grandmother's fingers lingered on our hair. She was smiling. "So you are Edward's girls. Tell me about him. It was a sad day when he left us, but I understand. I hope he always knew I understood."

Francine had recovered from her surprise and began to talk about our father and how happy we had been on the island. I joined in now and then. That hour we spent with our grandmother was such a change from everything else we had found in this house.

Aunt Grace had left us to talk with her. She said she had many things to see to—the dressmaker and finding a governess, for instance. Her departure reminded us of the stern world outside this room. "Like an oasis in a desert," Francine was later to describe it.

Our grandmother was clearly delighted to have us with her, telling her everything she asked. She wanted to hear about our father most of all. The time flew past and once we had recovered from the initial shock her blindness had given us we were completely at home in that room.

"May we come to see you often?" I asked.

"As often as is possible," replied our grandmother. "I hope you will want to come."

Francine said, "Oh, we will. You are the first one who has made us feel that we are wanted here."

"Oh, you *are* wanted here. Your grandfather would not for one moment have considered refusing you a home."

"He would consider it right and our grandfather is always right," said Francine with a hint of mockery. "But we don't want to be taken in because it is right, but because we are wanted and this is our home."

"You are wanted, child, and this is your home. *I* want you and my home is yours."

Francine took the thin white hand and kissed it.

"You've made it all so different," she said.

Mrs. Warden then said that Lady Ewell was a little tired. "She tires easily," she whispered, "and this has been an excitement to her. You must come again and see her often."

"Oh, we will, we will," cried Francine.

We kissed the soft cheek and were ushered out of the room by Agnes Warden.

We were standing in the corridor uncertain which way to turn, and Francine looked at me with sparkling eyes. "Now is our chance to explore the house," she said. "We have lost our way and have to find it, don't we?"

We held hands and ran along the corridor.

"We are very high up," said Francine, "right at the top of the house."

At the end of the corridor there was a window. We went to it and looked out.

"It's beautiful," commented Francine. "Different from the island and the sea... beautiful in a different way. All those trees and the forest over there and the greenness of everything. If our grandfather were like our grandmother I could begin to like it here."

I stood close to my sister, feeling the comfort of her presence. Nothing could be really bad while we could share it.

"Oh look," she cried. "There's a house over there. It looks interesting."

"It's old, I think."

"Tudor, I'd say," said Francine knowledgeably. "All that red brick... and it looks like leaded windows. I like it. We'll have to go and have a look at that."

"I wonder what this governess will be like?"

"They have to find her first. Come on, let's go and explore."

We descended a small spiral staircase and came to a landing. We walked through a door and were in a long room with a spinning wheel at one end.

"This is a voyage of exploration," said Francine. "We are now going to discover all the nooks and crannies, the dark secrets of our ancestral home."

"How do you know there are dark secrets?"

"There are always dark secrets. Besides, you can feel them here. Now this would be called the solarium, I believe, because it gets the sun for most of the day—hence the windows on either side. It's beautiful. There should be parties and balls and lots of people here. If ever I inherit, that is how it shall be."

"*You* inherit? Francine, how could you?"

"I'm in the line of succession surely. Father was the only son. Aunt Grace is not likely to prove fruitful. Perhaps *she* is the crown princess—the heir apparent. I could be the heir presumptive. It depends how they work these things out."

I was laughing aloud and so was she. She could be relied on to bring laughter to most situations.

We went through the solarium and along another corridor, up a staircase similar to that by which we had descended, and found a passage full of bedrooms with the inevitable four-posters and the heavy drapes and dark furniture.

We descended once more and came to a gallery.

"Family portraits," mused Francine, "and look. I am sure that is one of King Charles the First. Charles the Martyr; and those gentlemen who all look rather like him. I bet we were loyal to the monarchy. I wonder if our father is here. Perhaps we shall be—you and I, Pippa."

We heard footsteps and an agitated Aunt Grace burst in on us.

"Oh, there you are. I've been up to your grandmother's room to warn you. I couldn't find you. You'll be late for the service."

"The service?" asked Francine.

"We have three minutes in which to get there. Your grandfather will be most displeased..."

Poor Grace. She would probably be blamed. Francine and I ran with her.

The chapel was reached by a flight of steps from the main hall. It was small, as chapels go, made to accommodate the family and servants, who were all assembled there when, breathless, we arrived.

I saw the curious eyes of the servants on us and was amazed by their number. Seated right at the back was the maid Daisy, who had brought our hot water. Our eyes met and she gave me one of her winks. The rest of them looked very demure, eyes lowered as we were hustled to our seats in the front row.

Our grandfather, already seated, looked neither to the right nor to the left. Aunt Grace sidled in beside him, then Francine and next to her myself.

The service was conducted by a young man who must have been in his middle twenties. He was tall and very thin with restless dark eyes, and hair that looked almost black beside the pallor of his skin.

We sang hymns of praise, and there was a good deal of praying when we stayed on our knees for what seemed an interminable length of time. Then the young man gave an address, during which he reminded everyone of the care of the Almighty who had brought them to Greystone Manor where they found food and shelter and all that was necessary not only for their physical, but for their spiritual comfort.

Our grandfather sat through this with his arms folded and now and then would nod in agreement. Then there was a song of praise, more prayers and the service was over. It had lasted only half an hour but it had seemed endless. The servants all filed out, and we were left with our grandfather, Aunt Grace and the young man—some sort of parson, I imagined.

Our grandfather was not exactly smiling, but he was looking with approval at the young man.

"Arthur," he said, "I wish you to meet your cousins."

"Cousins!" I sensed Francine's surprise. It could not have been greater than mine.

"The Reverend Arthur Ewell," said our grandfather. "Your cousin is in holy orders. You did not meet him last night as he was administering spiritual comfort to a sick neighbour. I am glad you arrived back in time for the service, Arthur."

The Reverend Arthur bowed his head with a sort of smug humility and said that Mrs. Glencorn seemed to have profited from their prayers.

"Arthur, your cousin Francine."

Arthur bowed rather curtly.

"How do you do, Cousin Arthur," said Francine.

"And," went on our grandfather, "this is the younger of your cousins, Philippa."

The dark eyes of Cousin Arthur surveyed me rather briefly, I thought, but I was used to people's greatest interest in my sister.

"Your spiritual welfare will be in good hands," went on our grandfather. "And please remember that the meeting in the chapel takes place every morning at eleven. Everyone in the household attends."

Francine could not suppress her comment: "I can see that our spiritual welfare will receive a great deal of attention."

"We shall make sure of that," said our grandfather. "Arthur, would you like to have a word in private with your cousins? You might wish to discover what religious education they have had. I fear you may receive rather a shock."

Arthur said he thought that would be an excellent idea.

Our grandfather and Aunt Grace went out of the chapel, leaving us to the mercy of Cousin Arthur.

He suggested we sit down and began asking us questions. He was shocked to hear that we had not been to church on the island but perhaps that was as well, as the natives were probably of the Catholic faith—natives often were and worshipped idols.

"Lots of people worship idols," Francine reminded him. "Not necessarily gods of stone, but sets of rules and conventions which sometimes result in the suppression of loving kindness."

Arthur kept looking at her and although his expression was disapproving I saw a gleam in his eyes which I had noticed in people before when they looked at Francine.

We talked to him for a while—at least Francine did. He had little to say to me. I was sure during that time she thoroughly shocked him with what she told him of our upbringing and he would tell our grandfather that intensive instruction would be needed to bring us to grace.

When we escaped from him it was almost time for the midday meal. Afterwards we might like a little exercise, suggested Aunt Grace, and could take a walk in the gardens. It would not be wise for us to stray beyond them, and would we remember to be in by four o'clock when tea was taken in the red drawing room which led off from the hall. She herself was going to the vicarage. There was something of importance she had to see the vicar about. We should be able to go visiting when we had suitable clothes—and that would not be long, for Jenny Brakes would arrive tomorrow morning with materials and the dressmaking session would begin.

"Freedom," cried Francine, when we were alone. "And stay in the garden! Never! We are going to look round, and our first mission shall be to take a closer look at that interesting old house we saw from the window."

"Francine," I said, "I believe you are starting to enjoy this."

It was true, she was. She was fascinated by Greystone Manor and each hour brought fresh revelations. She sensed some sort of battle ahead and it was just what she needed to recover from the shock of our parents' deaths. I knew this because I felt the same myself.

So in a spirit of adventure we set out that afternoon. We had two hours or so to ourselves. We must be back in time for tea, said Francine. It would never do for them to discover that we had been adventuring on our own. "They must believe that we have been meandering through the garden paths," she went on, "admiring the orderliness of everything, for I am sure it is orderly, and exclaiming every now and then on the excellence of our grandfather, who is so holy that I wonder he is not considered too good for this earth."

We were careful until we came through the drive and slipped out by the lodge gate. Fortunately the occupants of the lodge were out of sight. Perhaps the hour of our grandfather's siesta was their only time for relaxation.

We were in a road bounded on either side by high hedges, and when we came to a gate Francine suggested we pass through it and cross the field, for she was sure that was the direction in which the house lay.

This we did, and at the top of the field was a row of four cottages and outside one of these was a woman shaped rather like a cottage loaf, with hair which straggled out of a bun at the back of her head while the light breeze played with the straying strands.

She looked up as we approached. I suppose she did not see many people, for she was obviously surprised.

"Good-day to you," she called, and as we came closer I saw the curiosity in her lively dark eyes, and there was a look of extreme interest and pleasure on her rather plump face. One noticed these things after even such a short time at Greystone Manor, where the general rule was to look solemn and glum.

"Good-day," we answered.

She had been pegging wet clothes on a line, which was fixed to a post at one end and attached to the side of the cottage on the other. Removing a peg from her mouth she said, "You the new young ladies up at Greystone." It was a statement rather than a question.

Francine said we were and how did she know?

"Why, God love you, there's not much I don't know about what goes on up at Greystone. My girl's up there." Her eyes widened as she stared at Francine. "My, you're pretty. Not what you expected up there, was it?"

"We didn't know what to expect," said Francine.

"Well, we knew Mr. Edward. He was a good man, he was— not like...Oh no, he was different, he was...and that lovely young girl he ran off with...Pretty as a picture, and you, Miss, you're the spitting image of her. I reckon I'd have known you anywhere—picked you out I could."

"It's nice that you knew our father and mother," said Francine.

"Dead...both of them. Well, that's life, ain't it? The best often goes...and the rest stays on." She nodded her head, momentarily sad. Then she was smiling again. "You'll know our Daise."

"Daise," we both said simultaneously. "Oh...Daisy."

"Got herself a job up there. Under housemaid. Mind you, I don't know if it will last. Our Daise is a bit of a caution." The woman winked in a way which reminded me of Daisy herself. They must be a winking family, I commented afterwards to Francine.

"Always a bit of a wild one," went on the woman. "I didn't know what to do with her. I say to her, 'You mark my words, Daise, you'll be in trouble one day.' She laughs at that. I don't know. She always liked the boys and the boys liked her. It was the same even when she was in her cradle. I've got six of them. She's the eldest, too. I said to Emms—he's their father, you know—I said, 'Now, Emms, this is enough.' But would you believe it, there's another on the way. What can you do with a man like Emms? But we got Daise to the big house. I thought if this can't make her respectable, nothing can."

"We have met Daise," said Francine. "Just once. She brought us hot water. We liked her."

"She's a good girl...at heart. It's just the boys. Can't seem to stay away from them. I was a bit like that myself at one time. Well, it makes the world go on."

Francine said, "What is the big Tudor house over there?"

"That's Granter's Grange." She began to laugh. "Regular old to-do that caused."

"We thought it looked interesting and we should like to see it closer."

"It was bought by foreigners...that's a year or two ago. Sir Matthew wanted it but he didn't get it. That's upset him. He thinks he owns these parts—and he does in a way. But Granter's Grange...well, the foreigners got in before him."

"Who are the foreigners?"

"Oo...now you're asking! Very high-up foreigners...Grand Dukes and things—but from some outlandish place. They don't count for much round here."

"Grand Dukes," whispered Francine.

"Oh, they're not there now. They're not often there. They come and go. The place is all covered up and left, and then servants come and there's a regular spring clean, then the

Dukes come. It's all very grand—royal stuff. Your grandfather doesn't like it...he doesn't like it at all.

"Is it really any concern of his?" asked Francine.

That made Mrs. Emms roar with laughter and produce one of her winks. "He reckons so. He's the lord of this place. Emms says the Queen herself couldn't be more of a sovereign over all England than Sir Matthew Ewell is over us all here...begging your pardon, he being your grandfather."

"There's no need to ask pardon. I think we agree with you," said Francine, "although we have not seen much yet. Are the Grand Dukes in residence now?"

"Oh, bless you no, and hasn't been these last two months. But they'll be here—oh yes, they'll be here. It makes a bit of excitement. You never know, you see. One day I'll look out of my back windows and I'll see them there. They're just at the back of me so I get the best view."

"Well, we'll go and look at it," said Francine. "We haven't much time. We have to be back by four. So the house is just at the back of you."

"Yes...look. There's a short cut round by the cottages, you can't miss it. Through the hedge and there you are."

"Thank you, Mrs. Emms. We hope we shall see more of you."

She nodded and winked again. Francine said, "Come on, Pippa."

So we came to the house. There was a deep silence everywhere and a great excitement gripped me. I am sure Francine felt the same and I wondered afterwards whether it was a premonition because this house was going to play such an important part in our lives.

There was the gate supported by marble columns and an archway on which we could just make out the date: 1525. We unlatched the gate and went in. I reached for Francine's hand and she gripped mine tightly. We almost tiptoed across the stretch of lawn, which was overgrown and spotted with daisies. We reached the house and I put out a hand to touch the red bricks. They were warm from the sun. Francine was looking in through the window. She gave a little gasp and turned pale.

"What is it?" I cried.

"There's someone...standing there...a ghost...in white."

I began to tremble, but I pressed my face against the glass. I started to laugh. "It's a piece of furniture," I said. "It's covered over with a dust sheet. It does look like someone standing there."

She looked again and then we were rolling about in an excess of mirth which perhaps had a touch of hysteria in it. There was something about the house which affected us deeply.

We walked round it; we looked in through all the lower windows. Everywhere the furniture was covered in dust sheets.

"It must be wonderful," I said, "when the Grand Dukes come."

Francine tried the door. It was of course locked. There was a gargoyle on a sort of knocker which seemed to be jeering at us.

"I'm sure he moved," said Francine.

"This is a place where you could fancy things," I reminded her.

She agreed. "Imagine coming here at night. I'd like to."

I shivered, fearful that she might suggest it. "Let's look at the gardens," I said. We did. The lawns were mostly all in need of attention. There were groves, statues, colonnades and little pathways through the shrubberies.

I said, "We should go back. We're not quite sure of the way and if we're late and they find out we haven't been walking in the gardens—"

"Come on then," she said. "Let's go back past the cottages."

We did with great speed for it was half past three. Daisy's mother was not there, but the line of flapping washing showed that she had completed her task.

We ran all the way back and were punctual at the tea table and as we listened to the usual grace, we were both thinking of the afternoon's adventure.

We saw Daisy next morning when she came in with our hot water. We told her that we had met her mother and she laughed with pleasure.

"Good old Ma," she said. "Was she pleased to get her eldest respectable!"

"Are you respectable then, Daisy?" asked Francine.

"Oh, as near as makes no difference. You've got the dressmaker coming today. Pity. I like your little frocks. They're pretty."

"We don't see you during the day," said Francine.

"Working in the kitchens, that's me."

"It was nice seeing your mother. She told us about Granter's Grange."

"Ah, that's a place I'd like to be at."

"There's no-one there."

"When there is it will be a real sight, I can tell you. Balls and fêtes. They do themselves proud. A lot of people come over from abroad. They say it belongs to a King or something."

"A Grand Duke, your mother said."

"She'd know. Reckon she talks with the servants up there. Foreigners, most of them, but trust Ma."

She winked and went out, and we hastily dressed to be in time for breakfast.

It was very much the same as the previous day. In fact, I was beginning to think that once we had settled into a routine every day was going to be like every other. We visited our grandmother again; Aunt Grace collected us in time to be at the service at the chapel and told us that the rest of the morning would be spent with Jenny Brakes, and we should have dresses which were suitable; we should have a governess who might well arrive within the week and there would be religious instruction from our Cousin Arthur. Our grandfather had said that we must be taught to ride as that was part of a gentlewoman's training. So it seemed our days would be well accounted for.

We got through the chapel service and Francine confided to me that she heartily disliked Cousin Arthur, largely because he looked so virtuous and grandfather clearly had a high opinion of him. Poor little Jenny Brakes was so pale and overeager to please that I felt sorry for her and stood as still as I could while she knelt beside me with a mouthful of pins and adjusted the dark blue serge which I disliked intensely.

So did Francine. "We're going to look as dismal as Greystone Manor," she commented. She was wrong, for she could never look dismal and the navy blue serge of our everyday dresses and the brown poplin of our best ones only accentuated her fair beauty and, by its contrast, her charm. They were not so kind to me. I hated the colours which did not suit my darkness, but I was glad that our new clothes had not spoilt Francine's looks.

That our coming had made a subtle change to the household was obvious to everyone, I think—except perhaps our grandfather. He was so immersed in his own importance and piety that I imagine he rarely thought anything or anyone else of any significance. He wouldn't have known that our grandmother grew quite excited at the prospect of our morning visits. I believe he paid daily visits—as was his duty—and I could imagine what they would be like.

Within a week our governess had arrived. Miss Elton was in her mid-thirties, with brown hair severely parted in the middle and worn in a little knot at the nape of her neck; she wore severe grey gowns on weekdays and a dark-blue one on Sundays, which did honour to the Sabbath by sporting a lace collar. She tested us and found us abysmally ignorant, except in one respect—languages. She spoke fair French herself, but her German was excellent. She told us afterwards that her mother had been German and she had been brought up to speak that language as well as English. She was delighted with our proficiency and said we must aim to perfect it. It would certainly be one of the subjects we studied with enthusiasm. She was obsequious to our grandfather and gently polite to Aunt Grace.

"Subservient," commented Francine slightingly.

"Don't you understand?" I replied warmly. "She wants to keep her post here. She's afraid of losing it. So be kind to her and see her point of view."

Francine looked at me thoughtfully. "Do you know, sister Philippa," she said, "you have a certain wisdom and you can put yourself in other people's places better than most. It's a rare gift."

"Thank you," I replied gratified; and I noticed that she was beginning to respect my judgement more and more. I was quieter than she was, more observant perhaps. I sometimes thought it was because I was more on the edge of things, an observer rather than a main actor. Francine, with her outstanding looks and personality, would always be at the centre of events, and sometimes people like that did not see as clearly as those who were slightly removed from the scene.

However, she accepted my view of the governess and instead of teasing her as she might have done, she became quite a docile pupil and after the first days of strangeness we established a certain rapport with Miss Elton, and lessons went fairly well.

We were now having riding lessons, which we both enjoyed. These were conducted under the supervision of the

coachman who had met us at the station, and usually there
was his son Tom, who worked as a stable-boy and must have
been about eighteen or nineteen years of age. He had to prepare the horses and take them after the lessons. We spent
hours riding round the first paddock on leading reins, then
without. I was proud when he said, "Miss Philippa, you're a
natural. You're going to be a rider, you are." "And what of
me?" Francine asked. "Oh, you'll get by, Miss, I reckon," was
the answer. I couldn't help being thrilled—it was the first
time I had ever excelled over Francine—but almost immediately I felt apologetic and ashamed of my feelings. But I
need not have done. Francine was delighted for me.

One day she took a toss as we were cantering round the
paddock. I was horrified and when I saw her lying on the
ground I realized how very much she meant to me. I was off
my horse and running to her, but Tom was already there.

Francine grimaced at us and got up rather gingerly. She
was moved by my emotion, which I couldn't hide, and she
pretended to laugh at it. "It's what happens to those who are
not naturals," she said.

"Francine, you are all right? You are sure?..."

"I think so."

"You're all right, Miss," said Tom. "You'll feel it tomorrow,
though. You'll want some liniment to put on the bruises.
Reckon you'll have some beauties. Never mind, they'll be
where they don't show. I'll send Daise up with the liniment.
Just one application. No more. It's strong stuff and would
have the skin off you in no time."

"Ought I to get on the brute who threw me and show him
I'm the one in command?"

Tom grinned. "Oh, he knows who that is, Miss, and it ain't
you—not yet, but it will be. I'd go and lie down if I was you.
It's best. Then ride tomorrow."

"Yes," I said. "I'll go up with you and Daisy can come down
at once for the liniment."

I took Francine to our room, still anxious about her.

"Don't look so worried, Pippa," she said. "It'll take more
than that miserable old nag to kill me."

I sent for Daisy and told her to get the liniment. "Tom's
expecting you," I said. "He'll be down in the stables."

"I know where to find Tom," she replied and went off. She
was soon back with the liniment and we applied it to the
bruises, which were already beginning to show.

I insisted that Francine should lie down, although she declared that she felt all right. Daisy came in and said should she take the liniment back and I said she could, as we had finished with it.

Francine lay down and I was standing at the window when I saw Daisy running towards the stables. Tom came out to meet her. They stood for a moment very close. She held out the liniment to him; he took it and with it her arm. He was dragging her towards the stables and she was pretending not to want to go, but I could see that she was laughing. I thought of her mother's remarks: "She's a one for the boys."

"What are you looking at?" asked Francine.

I replied: "Daisy and Tom. They seem to be having a game of some sort."

Francine laughed and Aunt Grace came in then. She was all concern. We must expect the occasional mishap, she said, and hoped no harm was done.

Francine said faintly, "Aunt Grace, I don't feel well enough to come down to dinner tonight. May I have something sent up?"

"Of course."

"And Aunt Grace, could Philippa have hers up here too? In case I..."

"It shall be arranged," said Aunt Grace. "Now you rest. And Philippa, stay with your sister."

"Oh, I will, Aunt Grace."

She left us and when she had gone Francine started to laugh. "Just think. We'll miss one of the appalling meals. Both of us. Out of evil cometh good."

It was almost an hour later when I saw Daisy emerging from the stables. I was sitting in the window talking to Francine, who was still lying down. Daisy's hair was rumpled and she was buttoning up her blouse. She ran swiftly into the house.

Francine was rather more affected than we had first thought, and the next morning the bruises were violently marked. Daisy screamed at the sight of them and said she would go and see Tom at once because he might have something.

However, within a few days they started to subside and Francine was riding again. Cousin Arthur expressed a certain concern and warned Francine that she should pray before she took her lesson. It might be that God would give heed to her safety.

"Oh, I expect He's too busy to bother about that," said Francine flippantly. "Just imagine! When He's contemplating some universal problem, an angel runs in and says it's time for Francine Ewell's riding lesson and You let her fall off the other day. Shall we send out a guardian angel? She has said her prayers."

She enjoyed shocking Cousin Arthur. In fact, she disliked him as much as she did our grandfather, and there was a growing animosity between Francine and the old man. I think that, being quieter and less noticeable, I appeared to be more biddable. He recognized in Francine the rebel—like our father—and he was watchful of her. He probably thought I was more like Aunt Grace. I was determined not to be.

I looked forward to our visits to our grandmother. Her face used to light up when we came in and she would hold out her hands and let her fingers explore our faces. Agnes Warden would hover round while our grandmother talked about the past, and of course we wanted to hear. Although she was old—of a different world from our own—we could talk to her openly. Constantly she asked us questions about the island, and I think within a week she had a clear picture of it. Francine, who was always frank and perhaps spoke before she had considered her words, asked her how she could ever have come to marry our grandfather.

"It was arranged," she said. "It always is with people like us, you know."

"But our father didn't do what his father wanted," Francine pointed out.

"There would always be the rebels, my dear, even in those days. Your father was one. Odd . . . he was a quiet boy. You remind me of him, Philippa. He was purposeful, as I think you would be, if the occasion arose. But I was very young when I married your grandfather. I was sixteen—your age now, Francine. But I seemed much younger. I knew nothing of life."

Francine's face expressed her horror. Married to my grandfather at the same age as herself! I think it was hard for Francine to imagine a worse fate. Francine had not spoken, but it was amazing how sensitive Grandmother was to a mood. She said at once, "Oh, he was different then. He has grown away from the young man he was."

"Poor Grandmother," said Francine, kissing her hand.

"Of course," went on our grandmother, "he ruled the household with his rod of iron right from the first. He was content with the marriage because it joined up the lands, you see, and he has always cared passionately about the family's estate. It has been with the Ewells for so long, it is understandable. We Granters were considered to be something of upstarts by him. We had only been in the Grange for a hundred years or so."

"That's the Tudor house."

"Yes... yes. Oh, there was trouble about that. My brother refused to sell it to your grandfather. He wanted it very much. He could not bear that anything—just anything—in the neighbourhood did not belong to him. You see, he now owns the whole of the Granter's estate—except the Grange. Much of it came with me as my dowry, but there was a larger portion which went to my brother. He wasn't the clever businessman your grandfather was. He lost most of it. He said your grandfather cheated him. It wasn't true, of course, but there was a quarrel and although your grandfather acquired most of the estate, my brother was determined not to let him have the Grange. He sold it to a foreigner—someone from an embassy in some far-away country. I think it was Bruxenstein... or something like that."

"That house fascinated me," said Francine.

"It means something to me," said our grandmother. "It was my old home."

She was silent for a while and I knew Francine was remembering, as I was, how we had peered through the windows and thought we saw a ghost.

"It's not used a great deal," said my grandmother. "Agnes tells me they come here from time to time, and then they go away and it's neglected again. And when they came back, in a flash it's full of life again. A strange way to go on. I heard that when they originally bought it, it was for one of their exiled noblemen and that after he'd been in residence for a month or two there was some coup in the country and he went back again."

"They could have sold the house to our grandfather then," said Francine.

"No, they wanted to keep it. Perhaps they wanted it for another exile. There is always trouble, I believe, in those small German states. We heard that they change their rulers from time to time. Grand Dukes... or Margraves—whatever they call them. However, it is strange to think of those sort of people in my old home."

"Romantic," added Francine, and my grandmother gently ruffled her hair.

I could see that Francine was getting more and more interested in the Grange now that she knew that it had been our grandmother's home; she said she was pleased that the romantic princes or whatever they were had secured it and Grandfather had been outdone for once in his life.

On another occasion our grandmother told us about our father and Aunt Grace. She blossomed when she talked with us, and her great pleasure in our company seemed to have made her younger. I could almost see her as a bride coming to Greystone Manor, a young girl who did not know what marriage was about. We were thankful that we were not ignorant on that score. They had been a passionate race on the island and we had often seen lovers lying on the beaches, wrapped in an embrace; we knew that when some of the girls became pregnant it was due to those embraces and I was fully aware that they had forestalled their marriages. I knew too what Mrs. Emms had meant when she had said Daisy was a one for the boys, and I could guess what had happened when she had gone into the stables with Tom.

But our grandmother's coming to marriage must have been a great shock, and I could not imagine our grandfather as a tender lover. "He was a passionate man in those days," said our grandmother. "He longed for children and was overjoyed when your father was born. He began planning from that day. I was unfortunate in my efforts afterwards, and it was not until five years later that Grace was born. Your grandfather was disappointed because she was a girl. He never cared for her as he did for Edward. He thought Edward was going to be just such another as himself. These plans always go wrong. Then there was Charles Daventry."

"Tell us about him," prompted Francine.

Our grandmother needed no persuasion. "Edward went to Oxford and from that time everything went wrong. Before that, he was interested in the estate. Your grandfather was stern and strict as you can imagine, but there was never any real friction between them until he went to Oxford. It was there that he met Charles. Charles was a sculptor and the two of them had a great deal in common. They became close friends. Edward brought him home during the vacation and your grandfather took an immediate dislike to him. He disliked artists of any sort. He used to say they were dreamers and no good to themselves or to anybody."

"Our father was a great artist," said Francine hotly. "He should have been recognized. I think he will be one day.... All those beautiful things he made...they're scattered all over the world. One day..."

It was the Francine of the studio days who was impressing the customers.

Our grandmother patted her hand. "You loved him dearly," she said. "He was very lovable. Your grandfather said there was no money to be made from chipping stone, but while it was a hobby he was prepared to tolerate it. There was Grace too. She was shy and retiring...but pretty in those days. She was like a young fawn—brown eyes, brown hair; very pretty hair she had in those days. I remember they used to go to the graveyard together, all three of them. They were all interested in the stone statues on the graves. Charles Daventry was a nephew of the present vicar, and the two young men got into touch because of this connection. It was strange how they should both have this taste for sculpting, but I suppose that was why they became great friends."

"I think people should be allowed to do what they want in this life," said Francine hotly.

"Ah yes," agreed our grandmother, "and the strong-willed ones do! Your father made up his mind in the end. I have never seen your grandfather so shocked as he was when he knew that Edward had left. He just could not believe it. You know that your mother came here to sew."

"Yes, we knew that," Francine told her.

"She was exceptionally pretty—dainty as a fairy, and your father loved her from the moment he saw her."

"Until the moment he died," I added quietly.

I felt my grandmother's fingers caressing my hair and I knew that she understood I was near to tears.

"They went off together. Your father did not see your grandfather before he went. He told me though. He said, 'You will understand, Mother, that I cannot talk to Father. That's his tragedy. No-one can talk to him. If only he would listen sometimes...I think he would have been spared a lot of dissatisfaction.' He did suffer when Edward went, though he wouldn't admit it. He raged and stormed and cut him out of his will. I think he was hoping Edward would have a son who would come back here to us."

"And all he had was two daughters!" said Francine.

"Now that I know you, I wouldn't have had it different. After your father had gone, your grandfather turned to Grace. But she had grown fond of Charles Daventry and he was out of the question."

"Why?" asked Francine.

"Well, your grandfather said he was no match for her. He came to live here...I think it was to be near Grace. He has a small place adjoining the vicarage—a sort of yard I suppose you would call it, and there he makes his statues. People buy them for graves and our graveyard is noted for some of the fine figures and effigies he does. He is said to be very clever, but it is a poor living. Fortunately for Charles he can live with his uncle at the vicarage. He does certain jobs in the parish too. He's a delightful man...a bit of a dreamer. He and Grace...well, it's hopeless really. He's not in a position to marry and your grandfather would never hear of it."

"Poor Grace," I said.

"Poor Grace...yes," echoed our grandmother. "She is a good woman. She never complains but I sense a sadness...."

"It's monstrous!" cried Francine. "How dare people interfere with the lives of others!"

"It takes a strong will to go against your grandfather, and Grace always avoided trouble. When she was a little girl she used to hide away until it was over. Your grandfather washed his hands of Grace. He then started to show an interest in his younger brother's boy—your cousin Arthur."

Francine grimaced with distaste.

"He's been Arthur's guardian since the boy was sixteen. That was when Arthur's father was killed in Africa. His mother had gone into a decline some years before. Your grandfather said Arthur was young enough to be moulded. Arthur's father had not left a great deal and your grandfather took over the boy's education. When he heard that he wanted to go into the Church he did not deter him. Your grandfather, as you know, is a very religious man. There was no reason why Arthur should not take holy orders even though he was intended to inherit the estate. One great point in his favour is his name. He's a Ewell and it is very important in your grandfather's eyes to keep the name alive. Francine...how do you like your cousin Arthur?"

"*How* do I like him?" cried Francine. "I don't like him in any way. The answer is, Not at all."

Our grandmother was silent.

"Why are you disturbed?" I asked.

Our grandmother reached out for Francine's hand. "I think I should warn you," she said. "Your grandfather has plans. Arthur is a sort of second cousin to you it is true, but second cousins marry."

"Marry!" cried Francine. "Cousin Arthur!"

"You see, my dear, it would make a neat solution and your grandfather loves neat solutions. You are his granddaughter and your children would be in direct line, but he does not want the name of Ewell to die out. So if you married Arthur, your children would be Ewells and a direct descendant would carry on the family. It won't come for about a year or so, but Francine, my dear, I did not want it to be a shock when it did come."

We were silent with horror. I knew Francine wanted to get away to discuss this fearful possibility.

We had talked it over and over. We had discussed what we should do if it were ever suggested. We should have to get away, said Francine. Where to? We would lie in bed talking about it. Perhaps we could go back to the island. To do what? How could we live? We should have to go and work somewhere. Could she be a governess? Francine wondered. And what of me? What should I do? "You would have to stay here until you were old enough to get away."

But then we should be separated and that must never be.

For a few days the shadow hung over us while Francine's distaste for Cousin Arthur grew. During religious instruction she was curt with him. I was surprised how meekly he took it. Then it occurred to me that she might be having the same effect on him as she had had on many others. In his mild and very proper way he was rather attracted by her. But perhaps this was due to the fact that he knew our grandfather intended them to marry.

It was not like Francine to be depressed for long and after those first few days of gloom she began to recover her spirits. It wouldn't be for a long time. She was only sixteen. It was true our grandmother had been sixteen when she had married, but there was time to start worrying when it was suggested to her. In the meantime she would indicate to Cousin

Arthur that her feelings towards him were very cold indeed, and perhaps his pride would stop him pursuing the matter. Moreover the older she grew the easier it would be to find a solution. So the matter was shelved.

After what we had heard of Aunt Grace's romance our curiosity led us to the yard close to the vicarage and there we made the acquaintance of Charles Daventry. We liked him at once because he reminded us of our father, and because of who we were he was interested in us.

He made tea on an old spirit lamp in his workshop and we sat on stools drinking it and telling him about the island and how we had lived there. He showed us some of his models. I fancied most of the women had a look of Aunt Grace.

He was a sad, quiet man, Francine said of him afterwards. "He makes me impatient. They deserve their fate because they just let life flow over them...tossing them wherever it wants to. They make no effort. That's no way to live. We'll never be like that, Pippa. Our father wasn't, was he? We won't let that old patriarch rule our lives."

Summer had come. The countryside was beautiful—in a different way from that of the island. I realized that there had been a sameness about the blue sea which only changed when the rain came and the mistral blew. Here everything seemed different almost every day and it was wonderful to see the burgeoning of the trees—the forming of the buds and the bursting into flower, the blossoming of the fruit trees, wild roses and strawberries in the hedgerows and mayflies dancing over the water on the ponds, to listen to the cries of birds and try to recognize them, to see the bluebells under the trees and later the foxgloves, the honeysuckle filling the air with its sweet perfume—and the long twilight hour which made one feel that the daylight was reluctant to depart. I had a feeling that I had come home, which was strange when I had been born on the island and had lived most of my life there.

I liked to be alone and lie in the long grass listening to the sound of the grasshoppers and the buzzing of the bees who were marauding the purple buddleia or the sweet-smelling lavender. I thought then: This is peace. And I wanted to hold time still and stay like this for a long while. This was probably because I sensed a menace in the air. We were getting older. Soon our grandfather would be making his wishes known to Francine and she would never obey. What then? Should we be turned away?

I remembered how our father had talked to me when we had sat outside the studio and he had looked over the sea with a kind of nostalgia which all exiles must feel at some time. He quoted to me what he called my song. "Pippa's Song," he would say, "written by a great poet who knew what it was like to long for home."

> The year's at the spring
> And day's at the morn;
> Morning's at seven;
> The hillside's dew-pearled;
> The lark's on the wing;
> The snail's on the thorn:
> God's in his heaven—
> All's right with the world.

I felt it, lying there in the grass. "All's right with the world." And just for that moment I could forget the gathering clouds.

"The clouds pass," my father used to say. "Sometimes you get a drenching. But then the sun shines and afterwards all's right with the world."

Later that day Francine and I took our walk and it led us past Granter's Grange. We hardly ever passed it without taking a look through the windows at the shrouded furniture and Francine wailed as she invariably did, "Oh, Grand Duke, when are you coming to enliven the scene?" I always pointed out that it would make no difference to us whether they came or stayed away, to which she said that it would be nice to have a glimpse of grandeur.

We went to see Charles Daventry. We liked to watch him work. He was glad to see us and liked to tell us stories of the life he and our father had led at Oxford, and how they had had grand plans for sharing a studio in London or Paris and having a sort of salon where artists and the literati assembled.

"You see what tricks life plays," said Charles. "Your father ends up in an island studio and I am here...a sort of stone-mason. What else?"

"It's what you want," Francine pointed out. "If you take what you want, you must take the consequences with it."

"Ah, we have a philosopher here," said Charles.

"As I see it, you have to be bold in life," Francine went on. In her heart she continued to be impatient with him because he was living here alone and Aunt Grace was at Greystone Manor, and neither of them had the courage to defy our grandfather.

Francine leaped up suddenly and said we must go, and as she did so she tipped over a block of stone. She picked herself up and tried to stand, but found she could not do so. She would have fallen if I had not caught her.

"I can't put my foot to the ground," she said.

"It's a sprain, most like," said Charles, kneeling and feeling her ankle.

"I'll have to get back. How?"

"There's only one way."

Charles lifted her up and carried her. When we arrived at the house there was tremendous excitement. Daisy came dashing out, her mouth a round "O" of astonishment when she saw Francine was being carried and when she realized by whom, her excitement increased. She went to get Aunt Grace, who turned red and then white. I learned afterwards that Charles had been forbidden to enter the house and Grace to have any communication with him. My grandfather would have liked to banish Charles from the neighbourhood, but the vicar stood out against him and was not going to turn his nephew away to please him, and they were on bad terms because of this.

Aunt Grace murmured, "Charles!"

"Your niece has had an accident," he said.

I was sure Francine was enjoying the drama even though she was in some pain. Charles said he would carry her to her bed and then go off and ask the doctor to call.

White-faced Aunt Grace, delighted and yet fearfully apprehensive, stammered, "Oh yes...yes please, Charles...and thank you. I am sure Francine is very grateful."

Charles laid her on the bed and Grace was in a fever of impatience to get him out of the house while at the same time she longed to keep him there.

The doctor came. It was a bad sprain and she would have to keep to her bed for a few days, possibly a week, and we were to apply hot and cold poultices. I had instituted myself as my sister's nurse and Aunt Grace sent Daisy up to help.

The pain subsided considerably within the next few hours;

Francine only felt it when she put her weight on her ankle and, as the doctor's orders were that she was not to do this, she hopped everywhere with my help or that of Daisy. She was soon feeling comfortable and congratulating herself for once again escaping those interminable meals, prayers and the company of the odious Arthur.

There followed the most pleasant week we had known since coming to Greystone Manor. We were in our little oasis, as Francine called it, and Daisy was constantly with us. She entertained us with local gossip and showed us how to tighten our dresses so that we showed our figures to advantage.

"Not that you've got one yet, Miss Pip," she said. She called me Miss Pip, which amused Francine and me. "But you will," she added. "As for you, Miss France—" (she had a habit of shortening names) "—well, you've got a figure in a thousand, you have. Curves in the right places, shaped like an hourglass, and no spare flesh to speak of. It's a sin to put you in that blue serge. I once saw some of the grand ladies up at Granter's. Their dresses was all sparkling. It was a ball or something and they was all out of doors. . . . You could hear the music. I was rather friendly with one of the footmen there. Hans . . . or something like that. Funny name for a man, but he was Hans all right. Hands everywhere they shouldn't have been if you ask me—but I shouldn't be talking like this in front of Miss Pip."

"My sister is well aware of your meaning," said Francine, and we were all laughing together.

"Well," went on Daisy, "this Hans got very friendly with me. He used to take me into the kitchens and show me round. Used to give me things to take home. It was before I got a place up at Greystone. We was hoping I'd get a place at Granter's and I would have done if they'd stayed. Let me comb your hair for you, Miss France. I've always wanted to get my hands on that hair. It's what I call real pretty hair."

Francine laughed good-humouredly and let Daisy dress her hair for her. It was amazing what she did with it.

"I've got a real gift. One of these days I'll be a lady's maid, you see. Perhaps when you get married, eh, Miss France?"

The talk of Francine's marrying set a gloom over us.

"Oh, it's that Mr. Arthur, is it?" said Daisy. "He looks a cold fish, but you never know with men. Not your sort at all . . . no more than he would be mine. Not that he'd look at me—well, not with a view to marrying. Some of them has notions though...a quick bit of fun and no more said and the next day looking at you as though he can't remember who you are. I know that sort. But Mr. Arthur is not one of them."

Aunt Grace came up to see us. She had changed and Charles Daventry's coming to the house had had its effect on her. There was an alert look in her eyes. Was it a hopeful look?

Francine said she was proud to have been the means of bringing them to each other's notice again.

"Now," she said, "we will watch for results."

How we revelled in those days of freedom! To be in this ancient house was exciting, as it was to feel its mystery and lure, to laugh, to forget the menace of the future. What pleasure that was! And we lived in the present—Francine and myself—and I fancy Daisy did all the time.

Aunt Grace was the first one to break the spell. She paid daily visits at precisely the same time every afternoon and brought messages from Cousin Arthur. Daisy said he would consider it improper to enter a girl's bedroom unless he were married to her. That sobered us a little. Talk of marriage in the same context as Cousin Arthur always did.

There was a softness about Aunt Grace. I wondered whether she had visited Charles Daventry and came to the conclusion that she had. She looked at Francine with great sympathy in her doe's eyes. "Your grandfather is pleased to hear that you are progressing well. He always asks how you are."

"I am grateful," said Francine with a touch of irony. "It's very gracious of him."

Aunt Grace hesitated. "He will have something to say to you when you come down."

She was looking speculatively at Francine and my heart sank. I knew what our grandfather would have to say. After all, Francine's seventeenth birthday was not far away. Seventeen was a mature age...mature enough for marriage.

What should we do?

Aunt Grace's efforts to make the prospect sound pleasant failed miserably. She knew what it meant to suffer from our grandfather's efforts to rule our lives.

"I won't do it," said Francine emphatically when Aunt Grace had gone. "Nothing could induce me. Now we had better start thinking of a way out."

The subject lay heavily upon us when next day Daisy came in to us in a twitter of excitement.

"I was leaning over the fence down at the cottage with Jenny Brakes when I saw them arriving...."

Jenny Brakes occupied the cottage next to the Emmses'; the other cottages were occupied by gardeners who worked at the Manor.

"You can imagine I was all ears and eyes. They'd all come from the station...just like they did before. I called out to Ma and out she came and we stood there...watching. They all went into Granter's. Some of the servants, they was...and there'll be more coming now. It's all set for the transformation scene, that's what it is. We're in for a bit of fun. High jinks up at the Grange."

We forgot what our grandfather was going to suggest to Francine when she appeared downstairs. We talked excitedly with Daisy and she told us what had happened on other occasions when the exotic inhabitants returned to Granter's Grange.

Strangers
at the Grange

From that time there was change.

Francine could no longer cling to the refuge of our room and must appear at meals. Our grandfather welcomed her with the faintest glow of warmth in his eyes. Cousin Arthur, though restrained, was clearly pleased to see her back. As for Aunt Grace, she still wore that bemused look which had settled on her since Charles Daventry had carried Francine into the hall and I noticed that she wore a rather pretty lace collar on her dress.

The tension was rising and it was most noticeable in our grandfather, who had become almost benign. He was as near affectionate towards Francine as he could possibly be. He came upon her once in the gardens and said he would walk with her and she told me afterwards that he talked all the time about the estate, how vast it was, how profitable and how it had been Ewell land for centuries. One morning he said he wished her to ride with him to see some of the tenants and they went off in his carriage, Cousin Arthur accompanying them; they took wine at the house of Mr. Anderson the agent who, said Francine, was ominously polite to her. "In fact," she said, "the situation is becoming more ominous every day. Soon I shall be presented with the royal command. What *am* I going to do, Pippa?"

54

I had no suggestion to offer, though we had discussed the matter endlessly. Francine was making up her mind that there was only one thing to do and that was run away. That was an easy answer, but the great problem was: Where to?

Our grandmother sensed the growing tension, of which she seemed more aware than sighted people. "Something will turn up, my dear," she said. "Be true to yourself."

Daisy burst into our room one day. She no longer behaved as a servant with us. We were like conspirators. Daisy was no respecter of persons; she was impetuous, affectionate and good-natured. She was resourceful too. Continually in trouble with the housekeeper, Mrs. Greaves, and threatened with dismissal, she was never downcast.

"What is to be, will be," she said with feeling. "And something would always turn up," she added as our grandmother had. She was full of wise sayings and they were all optimistic. "Wait and see. There's something round the corner. The Good Lord will take care of you." I did point out to her once that the only time she mentioned the Good Lord was in his capacity to take care of wayward sinners. "He won't mind," she retorted. "He'll say it's only that Daise."

She was in a state of great excitement. "Hans is back," she told us.

"Hans of the straying hands," asked Francine.

"Oh, he's all that...worse than he ever was, if you ask me. Is he glad to see me!"

"Tom won't be pleased," I said.

"Oh Tom's got nothing to complain of, I promise you."

"Don't promise us, promise him," laughed Francine. And we were all laughing together. We were glad to forget the shadow looming over us, if only temporarily.

"There'll be grand doings up there, Hans says. This Baron's coming. He's ever so important. He's of their branch of the family. The others, of course, are against it."

"What are you talking about, Daisy?" demanded Francine.

"Well, Hans talks a bit about it, you know."

"Don't become involved in Germanic politics, Daisy," said Francine with mock seriousness. "I hear they are very involved."

"Hans says he'll show us over the house. I told him you'd like to see it. That'll be before they arrive. It'll have to be soon. They're due any day."

"It's nice to be able to send out our agents," said Francine.

"You get away with you," retorted Daisy.

A few days later she told us we could go that afternoon because the family was due to arrive the next day. An air of excitement prevailed throughout the morning. I don't know how we got through our lessons without Miss Elton's suspecting that something was afoot. It was necessary to slip out quietly and we met Daisy, as we had arranged, at her mother's cottage.

"We'll have to go round by the stables," she told us. "Hans says most of the servants will be taking a nap at this time. They do, you know." Daisy clicked her tongue. "Foreigners!" she added.

"Some people do here, you know," said Francine, who could never resist stating a truth.

"Well, *they* do regular. And Hans says it's safe. He says even if some of them's about, it don't matter. They know who you are, and they'll like to see you there. Hans says that Miss France is *schön*...or something like that. When I said you wanted to see the house he kissed his hand and threw it out, just as though he meant it for you. He's a one, he is. Are you ready?"

Daisy, like Francine, always liked to add a touch of drama to a situation, and I thought Daisy's attitude to life was just what Francine needed at this time and I was grateful to her.

When we reached the stables at Granter's Grange, Hans was waiting for us. He clicked his heels and bowed from the waist and it was obvious from the way he looked at Francine that he admired her. When she addressed him in German he was delighted. He was very fair, almost whitehaired, and his eyes had a startled look because his eyebrows and lashes were so fair they were scarcely perceptible. His skin was fresh, his teeth good and his smile merry.

"The Baron will be coming," he said. "It's a very important visit."

Daisy insisted that this should be translated for her benefit and Francine asked how long the Baron would stay.

Hans lifted his shoulders. "It is not known," he answered. "So much depends..." he said in English with a strong foreign accent. "We are not sure. There has been..."

"Not another of them coops?" suggested Daisy.

"Oh...a coup...yes. You could say."

"They're always having them," said Daisy, who was enjoying her role.

"Come," went on Hans. We followed and he led the way through a side door. We were in a dark passage and followed him into a large kitchen with tiled floor and benches round two sides, under which were arches in which stood baskets containing vegetables and food of various kinds—all strange to us. On a chair was a fat man fast asleep.

Hans held his hands to his lips and we tiptoed through.

We were in a lofty and beautifully panelled hall. There was an enormous fireplace at one end with seats on either side, and I noticed very fine linenfold around it. In the centre of the hall was a massive oak table on which stood a candelabrum. There were several wooden seats against the wall and on these walls weapons which must have been used by our ancestors, since this was the home of our grandmother and it had obviously been sold furnished to the foreigners. "The great hall," announced Hans.

"It's a lovely old house," remarked Francine. "Very different from Greystone Manor. Do you feel it, Pippa? There isn't that air of gloom."

"It's our dark furniture," I said.

"It's our grandfather," added Francine.

"There is the staircase," Hans went on. "There are steps down to the chapel. We do not use that. So we will go up. Here is the dining salon."

It was a beautiful room with three large leaded windows. On the big table stood a candelabrum similar to that in the hall; there were tapestries on the walls in blues and cream colours and they matched the tapestry on the chairs.

"It's beautiful," breathed Francine.

"I can understand our grandfather's wanting to buy it," I murmured.

"I'm glad he didn't," said Francine vehemently. "He would have made it as gloomy as the Manor. Now it's a wonderful house. Do you sense it, Pippa? Something in the air?"

Dear Francine, she was really very worried. She was looking for some miracle and she was getting so depressed that she was looking in the most unlikely places.

We mounted some more stairs. "It is here that they come to drink the wine."

"It's where the ladies retire after dinner," said Francine, "when they leave the men at the table with their port."

There were stairs leading out of an archway and we were in a corridor. We went along this, past several doors. Hans lifted a finger to warn us to be quiet. Daisy giggled softly and I wanted to do the same. The fact that we were trespassing could only add to the excitement. I was longing to tell my grandmother that we had seen her old home.

We mounted more steps to the solarium, which was not unlike the one at Greystone. There were windows on each side and my imagination peopled it with glamorous men and women in splendid clothes talking excitedly about what was happening in their country. In the solarium was a hole in the wall, and so discreetly did it merge into the stone that I should not have known it was there if Hans had not pointed it out to us.

"From it you can look down into the hall," he explained. "On the other side is another. You can look down onto the chapel. Very good idea. You can see who comes...."

"How fascinating!" cried Francine. "Do you remember, our grandmother talked of the Peeps. That's what she called them. She said they sometimes did not go down to the chapel service but watched from the solarium."

Hans was suddenly alert. He stood very still, his head on one side, and the colour slowly drained away from his face.

"What's wrong?" asked Daisy.

"I can hear carriage wheels. Oh, no—no. This must be—"

He ran swiftly to the window and putting his hands to his head looked as though he were about to tear out his hair.

"Oh, what shall we do? They have come. It is too soon. It should be tomorrow. What shall I do with you?"

"Don't worry about us," said Daisy.

"I must go," cried Hans in desperation. "I must be there. The whole staff is assembling. I must not be missing—"

"What should we do?" asked Francine.

"You stay.... You hide...." He looked about him. "See those curtains? Hide behind them if anyone comes. I will get you out as soon as I can. I will free you. But now...I must go."

"You go," said Daisy soothingly. "We'll be all right. Leave it to us."

Hans nodded and stumbled out of the room.

Daisy was shaking with laughter. "Well, here's a nice kettle of fish!" she said.

"What will they think of us?" said Francine. "We've no right to be here. We shouldn't have come."

"No use crying over spilt milk, Miss France. No good shutting the stable door when the horse is stolen. Hans will get us out. He's clever, Hans is."

The house, which had been quiet before, was now alive with the sound of the bustle of important arrivals. Daisy tiptoed to the Peep and beckoned to us.

The hall was full of people. The fat cook whom we had seen slumbering in the kitchen now wore a splendid white coat and a tall white hat and gloves. He was standing at the head of a line and opposite him was a woman of very proud bearing whose bodice sparkled with black jet.

The door opened and a magnificently attired man came in and shouted something. Then the personages arrived. There were a man and a woman, and the servants who had formed into lines bowed so low that I thought they were going to knock their heads together. The recipients of all this homage were dressed in travelling clothes; with them was a tall, youngish man with very fair hair. Others were coming in— about twenty in all, and among them were a girl and a boy.

The servants began to move away, scuttling in all directions while the arrivals were making their way to the staircase.

"We have to look out now," said Daisy. "We'd better hide behind these curtains. Hans will know where to look for us when he comes."

"They won't come here," I said. "They'll go to their rooms to wash off the stains of travel."

"They might," said Francine. "Come on, let's hide ourselves."

There were sounds of running footsteps on the stairs and a babble of voices. We had hidden ourselves just in time when the door of the solarium was opened. I felt my heart beating wildly as I visualized the outcome of exposure. I imagined our being sent back to the Manor while complaints were made to our grandfather. That we should be in great trouble, I knew.

A girl came into the room. She appeared to be about my age. She was small with blond hair worn in two neat plaits reaching to her waist. She had very pale skin and her light blue eyes were closely set. She stood for a moment looking round while we all held our breath asking ourselves if we were properly hidden. She tiptoed forward and stood still as though listening. Then she said in German, "Who's there?"

I felt sick with shame and horror. Then she said in heavily accented English. "Who is hiding? I know you are there. I see a foot under the curtain."

It was Francine who stepped out. She knew exposure was imminent anyway.

"Who are you?" asked the girl.

"I am Francine Ewell of Greystone Manor," said Francine.

"You are visiting us?"

"Yes," answered Francine.

"And there are others?"

Daisy and I came out then. The girl's eyes rested on me, I supposed because we were of the same age.

"You visit?" she said looking at me.

I decided that the best thing was to tell the truth. "We were being shown over the house," I said. "We were interested because it was our grandmother's old home."

"You know my father...my mother..."

"No," I said.

Francine cut in then. "I have no doubt we shall if they are staying long in the neighbourhood. We are from Greystone Manor. Perhaps we should go now."

"Wait," said the girl. She ran to the door. "*Mutti*," she called.

A woman had come into the room. She was stately and stood looking at us in astonishment. Now we knew we were truly caught.

Francine stepped forward and said in fair German and with dignity, "You must forgive us. We have been guilty of an indiscretion. We were eager to see the house because it was once our grandmother's home and she often talks of it. We did not know that you would be returning and we thought it would be a good opportunity to look over it today...." She trailed off. It was a limp excuse and the woman continued to look at her very curiously.

"What is your name?" she asked.

"Francine Ewell. I live at Greystone Manor with my grandfather. This is my sister Philippa and Daisy our maid."

The woman nodded. Then she smiled slowly. She kept her eyes on Francine who, I must say, looked particularly lovely with the flush in her cheeks and the sparkle in her eyes which the adventure had given her.

The woman said, "We had just arrived. It was good of you to call. You must drink a glass of wine with me."

Daisy had stepped back. I think she was quite speechless with admiration for Francine's skill in extricating us from a delicate situation.

"Come with me," said the woman. "And you—you are?"

"Daisy," said Daisy, for once overawed.

"I shall send—"

At that moment Hans appeared. He was intensely nervous and when he saw who was there he looked as though he was uncertain whether to turn and run or break out into incoherent explanations.

"We have visitors, Hans," said the woman in German which both Francine and I could understand perfectly. "Take...Daisy to the kitchen and give her some wine. And send up more wine to the *Weinzimmer*."

Hans certainly looked astonished. Daisy went over to him and I was sure she gave him one of her winks, though I couldn't see her. She went off with him, and Francine and I followed our hostess down the stairs to the smaller room through which we had recently passed.

"Please to sit," commanded our hostess. "Now tell me. You are from Greystone Manor. It is the Big House here. Bigger than this one. We are just the Grange, eh? It is good of you to call."

Francine said it was hardly a call. It was a piece of impertinence.

"Impertinence?" she cried. "What is this impertinence? An English custom?"

Francine laughed in her infectious way and our hostess was soon joining in.

"You see," Francine explained, "we were very curious."

The woman listened intently as the wine came and with it the girl who had first discovered us.

"Tatiana, what is it you wish?" asked the woman.

The girl said in voluble German that she wished to see the visitors and the woman, whom we presumed to be her mother, chided her. "It is not polite to speak in a language other than that of our guests. You have your lessons in English. Come, you must speak in that language."

Francine said, "We have *some* German. We learned to speak it when we were with our parents. And now we have a governess who is half German and speaks the language with us."

"Ah, that is very good. Language can be a problem. Now

they tell me this room was known as the Punch Room. I said, 'What is this punch?' and they tell me it is a drink—a kind of wine. Then I say, 'This shall be the *Weinzimmer*' ... so here we drink our wine with our guests."

Tatiana sat down and watched us intently. During the conversation our hostess told us that she had had a Russian mother and that her daughter had been named for her. She was the Gräfin von Bindorf and she and the Graf with their family would be staying here for a while.

It was an extraordinary half hour. Here we were being entertained by the Gräfin von Bindorf, sipping the wine which had been brought to us and being treated like honoured guests instead of interlopers. She asked a great many questions about us and we told her how, when our father had died, we had come to Greystone Manor to be with our grandparents. Tatiana asked a few questions, mostly concerning me, and as Francine was talking freely with the Gräfin, I saw no reason why I should not do the same with Tatiana.

At length Francine said we should go, and the Gräfin replied that we must call again. I could see Francine wanted to invite her to Greystone Manor but restrained herself from that folly in time.

We were accompanied to the door where we were joined by Daisy. We were all excited and still marvelling, and talked incoherently all the way home. Daisy said that Hans was amazed at the way it had turned out and he was grateful to us for keeping him out of it.

Francine thought the Gräfin charming. She was dismayed at the prospect of her calling at the Manor.

"It makes you realize," she said, "what restricted lives we lead. It is going to be like that forever?"

I saw by the light in her eyes that she was determined that it should not be.

We did not sleep that night but lay awake talking about the adventure, and Francine came to the conclusion that we might let a week pass and then call again.

Daisy was in a state of great excitement. She and Hans were very friendly again and Tom of the stables was green with jealousy. Daisy was delighted to be the object of so much desire.

Francine's seventeenth birthday was in two weeks' time and as we sat at dinner the night after our adventure our grandfather commented on the fact, and added that he thought it was an occasion which we should celebrate. Aunt Grace nervously fingered her collar and tried to simulate excited interest. She knew all too well what the purpose of this entertainment would be, and being herself a victim of our grandfather's despotic orders she feared for Francine.

Francine said afterwards, "You know what he will do at the party. He will announce the engagement."

I nodded gloomily and waited for some inspiration.

"I'm going to call on the Gräfin," said Francine. "We'll go this afternoon."

"It will be fun," I replied. "But how is that going to help?"

"I don't know," she replied, but there was speculation in her eyes as though she had some scheme in mind.

Boldly we went through the gates; we pulled the bell and heard it clanging through the house. A servant in colourful livery opened the door and we stepped into the hall.

"We have come to call on the Gräfin in response to her invitation," said Francine importantly in German.

The man replied, "The Gräfin is not at home."

"Oh?"

"What about the Lady Tatiana?" I said with sudden inspiration. She had been interested in us, so perhaps she would receive us.

The servant shook his head. It seemed that she was not at home either. So there was nothing to be done but retire crestfallen. The door shut on us and just as we were turning away a man on horseback rode up. He leaped down, looked at us and bowed. He called out and a groom came running to take his horse.

"You look...lost," he said, his eyes on Francine. "Perhaps I can help."

He spoke good English with only the faintest trace of a foreign accent. Francine had brightened considerably. He was extremely handsome, tall, blond and in his early twenties I imagined, with grey eyes and a ready smile.

"We had come to see the Gräfin," Francine explained. "She did ask us to call...and now we find that she is not at home."

"She will be here later today, I believe. I wonder if it would be acceptable for me to take her place? Come, let me offer you tea...is that not what you would take at this hour?"

Francine's cheeks were touched with the delicate rose colour which was so becoming and her blue eyes sparkled with excitement. "That would be most kind," she said.

"Come, then." He pulled the bell and the manservant opened the door. "We have guests," he added.

The servant showed no surprise to see us back again and the young man gave orders in German for tea to be served. Then he ushered us into the room in which we had taken wine on the previous occasion and bade us sit down.

"You must be related to the Gräfin," said Francine.

"No—no. We are not related. Tell me about yourselves."

Francine explained that we lived at Greystone Manor and how we had met the Gräfin. "She did say we might call again," she insisted again.

"She would hope for that. She will be desolate to have missed you. That is unfortunate for her—but fortunate for me."

"You are very gallant," said Francine with a hint of coquetry.

"Who could be aught else in the presence of such beauty?" he answered.

Francine, as always, blossomed under admiration, even though she had always had a great deal of it, and she was soon chatting away telling him about our life on the island and at Greystone Manor, to which he listened very attentively.

"I am so happy that I came when I did," he said. "It has been a great pleasure meeting you and the silent one."

"Oh, Pippa is not usually silent. She generally has plenty to say for herself."

"I shall look forward to discovering what she has to say."

Tea had arrived and with it the most appetising little cakes I had ever seen. They were decorated with whorls of cream and were of various colours.

The young man was looking at Francine. "You must do— what do they say?—the honours? It is the lady's place, is it not?"

Francine settled happily behind the teapot, her fair hair breaking free of the ribbon which tied it back and which she was expected to wear at the Manor, and falling about her face. I had rarely seen her look so lovely.

We discovered the young man's name was Rudolph von Gruton Fuchs and that his home was in a place called Bruxenstein.

"It sounds very grand and far away," said Francine.

"Far away...well yes, perhaps. And grand? Maybe you will visit my country one day and see for yourself."

"I should enjoy that."

"It would be a great joy to welcome you. Just now..." He hesitated and looked at her ruefully. "There are troubles," he added. "There often are."

"It's a troublesome part of the world, I suppose," she said.

"You could call it that. But it is far away, eh, and we are here on this delightful afternoon."

He turned his eyes on me, but I had the impression that he found it hard to tear them away from Francine.

"You must have many adventures," said Francine.

"None," he assured her, "as pleasant as this one is proving to be."

Francine was talking a good deal. She seemed to be intoxicated with the pleasant afternoon. She was determined to enjoy herself in a fever of excitement because she was so dreading what her birthday party would bring forth. Although she swore she would never accept marriage with Cousin Arthur, she was practical enough to wonder what we would do when our grandfather became incensed by her refusal—or, worse still, would not accept it. So for this brief interlude she was determined to enjoy herself. She likes Rudolph, I thought. She likes him as much as he likes her. I could see that she was trying to prolong the afternoon, but eventually and most reluctantly she rose and said we must go.

"So soon?" he asked.

But it was not soon. We had been talking for an hour and a half.

"There is a strict rule in our house," she said. I thought it was rather indiscreet of her to talk about our home in the manner she did.

He said he would walk back with us, but that threw Francine into such a panic that he desisted. But he did walk with us to the gate and there, bowing low, kissed our hands. I noticed that he held Francine's longer than he did mine.

We broke away and started to run across the field to the Manor.

"What an adventure!" said Francine. "I don't think I ever had an adventure like that."

* * *

The invitation came through Hans to Daisy who brought it to Francine. It was from the Gräfin and she asked Francine to visit her that day at three o'clock, as she had a request to make of her. I was not mentioned in the invitation so Francine went alone. I was all agog to hear what had happened and was waiting for her in the field near the cottages.

When she came away about an hour later she looked flushed and more excited than I had seen her for a long time.

"Did you see him?" I asked. "This—er—Rudolph?"

She shook her head. She looked bemused. Had she found another admirer? I wondered.

"It's so exciting," she said. "I saw the Gräfin. What do you think? She has asked me to the ball."

"To a ball! What do you mean?"

"That they are to have a ball and I am invited. It's as simple as that."

"It doesn't sound in the least simple to me. Will Grandfather agree? And you'll need a ball dress."

"I know. I thought of all that. But I said I'd go."

"In blue serge or perhaps your best poplin?"

"Don't be defeatist. I'll have a new dress somehow."

"Somehow is the word."

"What's the matter with you, Pippa? Are you jealous?"

"Never!" I cried. "I want you to go to the dance with Rudolph, but I can't see how you're going to manage it, that's all."

"Pippa," she said—and I have never seen a stronger purpose in anyone's face than I saw in Francine's at that moment—"I *am* going."

All the way back to the house and halfway through the night we discussed it. Rudolph had not been there. She had had tea with the Gräfin who had told her that there was to be this ball and she would be delighted if Francine would attend. She was unsure what she should do about sending an invitation. We must have conveyed very clearly what it was like living at Greystone Manor and she no doubt guessed that to have sent an invitation through our grandfather would have meant an instant refusal. Francine must come, she said. If she did not the ball would not be the same.

In an excess of euphoria and a certain unswerving belief in her powers to achieve the impossible, Francine had promised, sweeping the practical details airily aside. Something would turn up.

"A fairy godmother?" I suggested. "Who'll that be? Perhaps they have them in Bruxenstein. I can't imagine one in the Manor. Shall we be able to find a pumpkin for the carriage? I believe there are a few rats around, so we might be all right for the horses."

"Pippa, stop joking about a serious matter."

It was all rather hopeless but I was glad that temporarily her mind was taken off those impending birthday celebrations.

When we visited our grandmother the next day, with that acute sensibility of hers she immediately realized that something had happened. She knew that Francine had been tense and uneasy because she feared she was about to be forced into marriage with Cousin Arthur, and it was not long before the whole story was drawn out of us. She listened entranced. "So the old Punch Room has become the *Weinzimmer*. I like the sound of the Gräfin and the charming Rudolph." Our grandmother was a very romantic lady and it must have been a terrible tragedy to be married to a man like our grandfather. Miraculously the experience had not soured her; it had made her more gentle and tolerant.

She said, "Francine must go the ball." I listened in amazement. Our grandmother had an answer to everything. The dress? Wait a moment. She believed there was some material in one of her chests. Once she had dreamed she would celebrate the birth of her second child. No, not Grace...the one who had been stillborn. She had bought at the time some beautiful blue silk chiffon embroidered with stars in silver thread. "It was the most beautiful material I ever saw," she said. "But when I lost the child I couldn't bear to look at it. I folded it up and put it away. If the silver stars haven't tarnished...We'll ask Agnes to find it."

Agnes was delighted to see her mistress so happy. She once whispered to me that she had changed since we came. "She was a little like your sister, I imagine, when she was young...but there's more freedom now." Not much more, I thought. It was gratifying that Agnes was an ally, for we needed allies.

We found the material. Francine cried out in delight when she saw it. The stars were as bright as they had been on the day when our grandmother had bought it.

"Take it," she said, smiling as though she could see it clearly, and I was sure she could in her mind. "Go to Jenny and get her working at once. She'll do it well. She makes ball dresses for girls' coming out now and then."

Excitedly we called on Jenny. Daisy came with us, for she considered she was involved in the adventure as it had been through her that we had first come to the Grange and set everything in motion. She herself was deep in an emotional affair of her own. Tom of the stables had discovered her friendship with Hans and, as she said, he was "hopping mad" and threatening all sorts of reprisals. Life was certainly exciting for these two heroines of romance—and I was content to be a looker-on.

Daisy had it from Hans that the Gräfin had been more or less commanded to invite Francine because of the Baron, who was very important. He was in fact the most important of them all. Hans knew why but he wasn't telling even Daisy. "He will...given time," said Daisy confidently. She clearly enjoyed being drawn into this vortex of intrigue and gave us scraps of information about the household. The Gräfin, it seemed, was very ambitious and was already putting out feelers for important marriages for her children. Hans said that back in Bruxenstein she never lost an opportunity.

Jenny Brakes was a little astonished when she saw the material and heard that she was to make it into a ball gown.

"For your birthday party, Miss Francine?" she asked. "Miss Grace has already told me I was to go up to the house. She's got a nice piece of taffeta she tells me for your party dress. It's going to be a very special occasion."

"No," said Francine. "This is to be a very special dress."

"Made in secret," added Daisy.

Jenny looked frightened.

"Come on," said Daisy. "Who's to know?"

"Really...I don't understand, Miss Francine...."

"It's simple," Francine explained. "I want a ball gown made quickly, and you just do not mention that you are making it for me."

"But you're having the taffeta—"

"I'm having this too," said Francine.

Poor Jenny Brakes! I knew how she was feeling. She greatly feared to offend my grandfather. She lived in one of his cottages and if he knew that she was making a ball gown for his granddaughter he would be very angry indeed; and when he was angry he was a man to show no mercy. It was

I who came up with the solution. Jenny need not know at all that it was in secret. The gown was to be made for Francine and as it was needed in a hurry it was simpler for Jenny to make it in her own cottage, as she sometimes did. If we were discovered, Jenny could be proved to be entirely innocent of any intrigue.

At last she agreed and sketched out a design right away. What fun we had making our suggestions! It must be daring; it must be simple; it must be cut to show Francine's swanlike neck. It must accentuate her tiny waist. It must have a billowing skirt.

The excitement was so intense that I thought Francine would betray it. I believe Aunt Grace knew something was in the air but she was too immersed in her own life at the moment, for since Charles Daventry had carried Francine into the house, I believed she was visiting him in secret.

We made a great plan of action. One the night of the ball Francine would slip out of the house and go to the Emms' cottage. Daisy's mother was a willing conspirator, so there could be no blame attached to Jenny. Mrs. Emms would keep the dress in her cottage for Francine to change into. Then she could slip across the lawn to the Grange. Like her daughter, Mrs. Emms was fond of adventure. If she were discovered and my grandfather's wrath was aroused, she would take the consequences. "He would never turn us out," she said. "Not the Emmses. We've been in this cottage too long and my Jim's too useful a man."

So it was all settled.

Daisy reported that this was going to be the most magnificent of all the balls they had had at the Grange. It was in honour of a very important personage—presumably Francine's admirer. "The preparations..." cried Daisy. "All the food...all the flowers and things. It'll be royal, that's what it'll be. I reckon they couldn't do better at Buckingham Palace or that Sandringham where the Prince of Wales enjoys himself so much."

The great day came and we could scarcely contain our excitement. Somehow the hours passed. We were very absentminded at our lessons and Miss Elton remarked on our inattention. I think she knew something was afoot and as the whole household was aware that Francine was destined to marry Cousin Arthur, I was sure that if they knew what it was they would have done their best to shield her.

I went with Francine to the Emms' cottage and there, with Daisy, I helped to dress her. Several little Emmses looked on in wonder, and when she was ready she looked like a fairy princess. Excitement enhanced her beauty and there could not have been a colour which suited her better than the blue silver-spattered chiffon. Of course she needed silver shoes and had only her black satin ones, but they scarcely showed. She looked perfect, I told her.

The arrangement was that I should be watching at our window and when she came home I could creep down and let her in. She would have been to the Emmses first and changed into her day clothes, leaving the gown at the Emms' cottage to be brought back next day by Daisy.

"Such an operation needs careful planning," I had pointed out. "Every detail has to be thought of."

"Philippa is our general," cried Francine with a giggle. "I must obey her commands."

So as everything had been so precisely arranged, I felt that only bad luck could upset our plans. After watching—from a safe distance—Francine enter the Grange with the other guests, I went back to the Manor. I sat at my window, looking out over the lawns. In the distance I could see the towers of the Grange and the lights; I could even hear the faint strains of music. I could see the church, too, and the grey tombstones and I thought of poor Aunt Grace and Charles Daventry who had lacked the courage to make their own lives. Francine would never lack that courage.

"God's in his heaven," I thought, looking up at that black velvet sky, at the glittering stars and the moon that was almost full. What a beautiful sight! I prayed then for Francine's happiness, for a miracle to save her from Cousin Arthur. I remembered the old Spanish proverb my father referred to once. It was something like, "Take what you want," said God. "Take it and pay for it."

One took and one paid. One must never grudge the price. My father had taken a certain way of life which had denied him his patrimony, an old house full of family tradition. My grandfather had taken his own way. He might make others dance to his tune but he was bereft of love. I would not have been my grandfather for all the power in the world.

It was about eleven o'clock when I heard the commotion below. My heart beat so violently that it shook my entire frame. There had been no sign of Francine. She was to have come below my window, and I was to be at my post—which I was. But there was no Francine and surely eleven o'clock was too early to leave a ball.

I went to my door and listened. I could hear my grandfather's voice. "Disgraceful...fornicating...sinful...Go to your room. I shall deal with this as you deserve. I will see you in the morning. You are disgusting. I could not believe my eyes....Under my roof...caught...*in flagrante delicto*."

Someone was moving towards the stairs. I hastily shut my door and leaned against it, waiting. I expected Francine to burst in at any moment.

Nothing happened. Where was she? He had said, "Go to your room." But she did not come and I could not understand what it meant.

I was back at the window. All was quiet down there. I went to my door and listened. There were steps on the stairs. That was my grandfather going to his room.

I was bewildered and dreadfully afraid.

It was about half an hour later when there was a gentle knock on my door. I ran to it and Daisy almost fell into the room. Her hair was tousled and her eyes wide.

"It's that Tom," she said. "That's who it was. He told on us."

"Was it you whom my grandfather was talking to?"

She nodded.

"Oh, Daisy. What happened?"

"We was caught—Hans and me—in the old bone-yard. I always liked it there. It's soft on the grass and it's life, ain't it...life among death."

"You're crazy. I thought it was Francine. Come and sit by the window. I must keep watch for her. She'll still be at the ball."

"For a long time, I reckon."

"Tell me what happened with you."

"Hans said he could slip away at half past ten and I said I'd be near Richard Jones. He had three wives and buried them all with him. It's a lovely stone he had done for himself and the three of them. You can lean against it and there's a beautiful guardian angel over it. It makes you feel kind of safe and happy. Tom liked it there too."

"What were you doing?"

"The usual." She smiled at the recollection. "There's something about Hans, you know. Of course, Tom was hopping mad. Hans wrote a note saying he'd be there by Richard Jones and I lost the note. Tom must have got his hands on it. I never thought he'd tell like that—but you know how it is with jealousy. But you wouldn't, of course, being so young. Sometimes I forget how young you are, Miss Pip. What with me and your sister...well, we're sort of bringing you up fast. So there we were. Your grandfather must have seen us meet. Must have been hiding there. I bet it was behind Thomas Ardley. I never liked that stone. It always gave me the creeps. Then he ups and catches us...right in the act...you might say. He called out to us and there was I with my bodice open and half out of my skirt. And Hans...well. Your grandfather kept saying, 'And in such a place.' Then he took me by the arm and dragged me back. You must have heard him in the hall. 'Up to your room,' he says. 'I'll deal with you in the morning.' It'll be out for me. What'll Ma say? She was dead set on me getting this place and settling down respectable."

"You'll never be respectable, Daisy."

"I reckon you're right," she admitted ruefully. "But I'll be out tomorrow. It'll be the tin box on my shoulder and home to Ma. She'll miss the money. Still, perhaps I'll get a place at the Grange. Hans could speak for me."

We sat on at the window. Midnight struck on the old church clock. I felt wide awake. Daisy would certainly be dismissed. I tried to imagine what it would be like without her, for she had played a big part in our lives.

It was nearly two o'clock when Francine came in. I sped down and drew back the heavy bolt. She was starry-eyed, still living in a wonderful dream as we tiptoed back to our room. Daisy was still there and we hastily told Francine what had happened.

"Daisy, you idiot!" she cried.

"I know," replied Daisy. "But I'll be all right. I'll go and see Hans."

"What was the ball like?" I asked.

She clasped her hands and her ecstatic expression told us all. It had been wonderful. She had danced with the Baron all the evening. Everyone had been charmed by her. They had all been foreigners, of course. "It might have been that the ball was given in my honour. That was how it felt. And the Baron Rudolph...he is perfection. Everything I ever dreamed a man should be."

"Everything that Cousin Arthur is not," I added, and immediately wished I hadn't mentioned him because I feared his name would break the spell.

But it didn't. She scarcely noticed. She was bemused. It was no use trying to talk to her that night.

I told Daisy she should go to her room and get a little sleep. She must remember the ordeal she would have to face the next day. Reluctantly she went and Francine undressed slowly.

"It is something I shall never forget," she said. "No, no matter what happens. He wanted to bring me home so I had to explain and he took me to the Emms' cottage and waited outside while I changed, and when I came out in my old serge he was still there. He brought me right to the edge of the lawn. I told him everything... about Grandfather and Cousin Arthur. He was very understanding."

"It's over now, Francine," I said.

"No," she answered. "It's only just beginning."

The next morning we were all assembled in the chapel for the solemn denunciation. Francine and I sat together in the front row with Aunt Grace. The glow was still on my sister. I could see that, in her thoughts, she was still at the ball. Our grandfather came in with Cousin Arthur and I noticed a look of suppressed excitement in the former's face as though this was not entirely distasteful to him.

He stood up in the pulpit after Cousin Arthur had taken his seat beside Francine. She moved a little closer to me as he did so and I wondered whether he noticed.

Grandfather lifted his hand and said, "This is an occasion of great sorrow to me. I am faced with a situation which fills me with disgust and humiliation. One of my servants—one whom I had harboured under my roof—has behaved in such a manner as to bring disgrace to this house. I cannot express my horror at my discovery."

Yet you are relishing that horror, Grandfather, I thought.

"This wanton creature has behaved in such a manner as decency forbids me to describe. She has been caught in the very act. Feeling it my duty, I forced myself to witness her depravity. She was in my care and I could not believe that a servant of mine could be guilty of such an act. I had to see it with my own eyes. Now she will stand before us all in her sinfulness. Yet I am going to ask God to show mercy to her, to give her an opportunity to repent."

"Magnanimous of him," Francine whispered.

"Let her be brought in," he called.

Mrs. Greaves came in with Daisy, who was wearing a coat over her dark dress, which was not the uniform provided to all the Greystone servants.

"Come here, girl," said my Grandfather. "Let all see you that they may learn the lesson of your folly."

Daisy came forward. She was pale and less sure of herself than I had ever seen her before—slightly defiant, not the chirpy Daisy we knew so well.

"This creature," went on our grandfather, "is so deeply immersed in depravity that not only does she sin but she must do it in a holy place. It may well be that there will be a result of last night's work. The evil that we do lives on to the third and fourth generation. I am going to ask you all to get down on your knees and pray for the soul of this sinner. There is yet time for her to repent her evil ways. I pray God she will do so."

Our grandfather's eyes were glistening as he looked at Daisy and I believe he was imagining her in that position in which he had caught her and revelling in the memory in some strange way. I wondered if he was pleased when people committed sins because it made him appear all the more virtuous. But this was a particular sort of sin which had this effect on him. It was different when someone was caught stealing. One of the men had been dismissed for that and there had not been this ceremony in the chapel. This was like the Puritans I had read about. I wondered he didn't want Daisy to have a scarlet letter sewn on her bodice.

Cousin Arthur preached a short sermon about the wages of sin and then we prayed again, and all the time Daisy was standing there looking rather bewildered. I wanted to go to her and put my arms about her and tell her that whatever she had done in the churchyard wasn't half as bad as what my grandfather was doing to her now.

At length the ceremony was over. My grandfather then said, "Take your box, girl, and go. Never let us see your face here again!"

Francine and I went into the schoolroom. Miss Elton was there, pale and silent.

Francine suddenly burst out, "I hate him. He's a wicked old man. I will not stay here."

She was close to tears and we gripped each other's hands

tightly. I knew I would never forget that horrible scene in the chapel. Miss Elton did not reprove us. She too had been shaken by what she had seen.

Later that day Francine said to me, "I'm going to see Daisy. Are you coming?"

"Of course," I replied, and we made our way to the cottage. Mrs. Emms was there and as usual there were several children running in and out. Daisy was not at home.

"She's up at the Grange," Mrs. Emms told us, "seeing that Hans." Mrs. Emms nodded grimly. "So she's out of the Manor. I thought at first it was all along of you and that ball dress."

"Our grandfather doesn't know anything about that," said Francine.

Mrs. Emms winked. "It would be a case of God 'elp us all if he ever did."

"Somehow now I don't care about him. I hated him this morning...and that smug Arthur. I hate Greystone. I want to get away from it."

"My poor Daise. And all for having a bit of fun in the graveyard. She's not the first, I shouldn't wonder."

"We're worried about Daisy. What will she do?"

"She'll find something. Always able to look after herself, our Daise."

"Do you think she'll be back soon?"

"Who's to say? Her own mistress now, she is."

"Will you tell her we called?" said Francine. "Tell her we hated it all as much as she did. Tell her we thought it was horrible."

"I'll tell her that, Miss. She thinks a powerful lot of you two young ladies."

As we were about to go, Daisy herself came in. She looked quite different from the dejected sinner of the chapel. We flew at her and hugged her. She looked very pleased and Mrs. Emms said, "Well, fancy that."

"Daisy," cried Francine, "we were so worried about you."

"No need," cried Daisy triumphantly. "I've already got myself a situation."

"No!" we cried together.

"Oh yes, Miss. Well, I had half a promise of it before. Hans says, 'Why don't you come up the Grange? I'll speak for you.' Well, there I am. And I've seen the chef there. A very important gentleman—all twirling moustache and fat cheeks.

He gave me a pat and said, 'Start tomorrow.' Kitchen maid! And what a kitchen."

"It's wonderful!" I cried.

Mrs. Emms sat down, legs apart, a hand on each plump knee. She was nodding her head sagely. "What 'appens when they go?" she asked. "They never stay more than a few months."

"Hans says he reckons I could go with them."

The gaiety of the last few moments had faded. We were all thinking of when they were going. Mrs. Emms would not want to lose Daisy. Nor should we. But Francine quite clearly found the prospect of their leaving so depressing that she could not bear to think of it.

Events moved quickly after that. The date of our house party was announced. It was to be the first week in September. Guests would arrive on the Monday; Francine's seventeenth birthday was on the Tuesday; there would be another day of entertainment and the guests would leave on the Thursday.

Jenny Brakes came to the house and made up the taffeta for Francine. It was in a dark red colour; I was to have dark blue—a nice, serviceable colour, said Aunt Grace. Poor Jenny Brakes was a little embarrassed; her recent sin in making the blue chiffon sat heavily upon her, and in view of what had happened to Daisy Emms she was very uneasy. Making up a dress illicitly could not be as great a sin as fornication in a churchyard, but my tyrannical grandfather was greatly feared. Francine pointed out that it would have been the same if Daisy had not had a family nearby to go to; she would have been turned out just the same. "He has no pity," she said. "If that is being a good man, then God preserve me from them."

Her spirits were high during those days of approaching doom because she was going to the Grange every day. Sometimes she would ride out alone. But I knew she did not continue alone and that she was going to some rendezvous with the romantic Baron.

The invitations were sent out to the guests. Great preparations were being made. Mrs. Greaves was delighted and said this was how it should be in a big house. She reckoned that in future there would be a great deal of entertaining. There would be the newlyweds to bring a younger spirit into the house and then they would have to think of a match for Miss Philippa.

I was very apprehensive because Francine was not nearly so disturbed as she should have been and I wondered what that meant.

About two weeks before the party our grandfather sent for Francine. She went to the library with her head held high and I waited in our bedroom terrified of what might happen, for it was perfectly obvious that we were moving towards a crisis.

In half an hour she came to our bedroom, her cheeks slightly flushed, her eyes very bright.

"Francine," I cried. "What happened?"

"He told me I was going to marry Cousin Arthur and that that sainted nephew of his has asked his permission for my hand which he had graciously given. Knowing that it was his wish, he had no doubt that I would accept it with delight."

"What did you say?"

"I have been very clever, Pippa. I have let him believe that I will."

"You mean you've changed your mind?"

She shook her head. "I can't tell you any more yet. I'm going out now."

"Where?"

She shook her head. "I promise I'll tell you. Before I do anything I'll let you know."

It was the first time I had not been completely in her confidence, and I was apprehensive. I felt that everything was changing about me. Daisy had gone. And what had Francine meant? Was she going to do what our grandfather wished and marry Cousin Arthur? Or else what?

Miss Elton asked me where she was and when I said I did not know she did not pursue the matter. Miss Elton had always seemed a colourless person, but I think she understood a good deal of what was going on; everyone in the household must have realized that Francine and Cousin Arthur were just about as unsuited to each other as two people could be.

I went up to our grandmother. We had told her about the ball and she had sat there smiling and holding our hands as she liked to. She had been alarmed for Francine and believed that if Francine married Cousin Arthur her life would be intolerable. "I would die happy if I knew you two girls were all right," she had said. "And by all right, I mean leading worthwhile lives which might not always be lived in perfect bliss...that would be asking too much...but lives you have made for yourselves. Your grandfather made my life what it was...empty...not mine at all. He has done the same for Grace. He tried to with your father. You must strike out boldly to live your own life. Take it...live it...and do not regret the consequences, because it is what you have chosen."

I knew she was right. I told her about Daisy.

She said, "He would call himself just. He has set up a code of morals which do not always add up to morality. Daisy is a girl who will always have men. She may well find herself in trouble through it. But she will work her way out. And his unkindness, his harshness, his revelling in that so-called justice which brings hardship to others, is a greater sin than any Daisy could commit in the graveyard. Dear child, this seems strange coming from me. In the old days I would not have said it...would not have thought it. It was only when blindness descended on me and I knew my life was virtually finished that I looked back over everything more clearly than I ever had when I could see with my eyes."

"What do you think is happening at the Grange?" I asked.

"We can only guess. Perhaps there is an avenue of escape. She must not marry where she does not love. She must not become your grandfather's victim."

Soon after I left my grandmother, Francine came back. I had never seen her so excited. "I am leaving Greystone," she said. She threw herself into my arms and we clung together.

"Going away..." I stammered. "I shall be left...."

"I will send for you. I promise."

"Francine when...how?"

"Rudolph and I are going to be married. We are leaving at once. It is all very complicated."

"You are leaving England?"

"Yes. I shall go to his country. Pippa, I am so happy.....It's all very involved. I shall learn about it. Pippa, I am so happy...except for one thing...leaving you."

I had known that it was inevitable. She would never have married Cousin Arthur. This was escape and she was in love at the same time. I tried to think of her happiness, but I could only think of myself and the terrible loneliness of being without her.

"Cheer up, Pippa," she said. "It won't be for long. Rudolph says you can come to us...but not yet. He has to leave rather quickly. He is very important in his country and there are all sorts of intrigues and that sort of thing. We can't do without each other... we both know that. So I'm going with him. We're leaving tonight. Help me get a few things together. Not much. I shall have everything new. I shall take my starry ball dress. I'll get that from the Emms' cottage. Daisy is helping. Oh, Pippa, don't look so frightened. Don't look so lost. I'll send for you."

I helped her get a few things together. She was so excited she could hardly speak coherently. I said, "You must see our grandmother before you go. You must tell her."

"She'll understand," said Francine.

It was a strange evening. We dined as usual. Grandfather was in a benign mood because he believed everything was going to be as he wished. Cousin Arthur looked smug, so I presumed he had heard that Francine would favour his suit. Aunt Grace said very little as usual, but I think she was rather sad. Perhaps she had hoped Francine would not submit as she had had to. Perhaps she was planning rebellion herself and wanted the support of another rebel.

Francine was unnaturally bright, but no one seemed to notice it. Our grandfather looked at her with something like affection—or as near to that emotion as he could get.

As soon as the meal was over we retired to our room. Francine was leaving at ten o'clock and at a quarter before the hour she slipped out of the house with my help. I carried her cloak so that if we were seen she would not be dressed for outdoors.

We stood there, facing each other for a few moments. The night was still—not the slightest breeze to ruffle the leaves. Francine laughed on a high note. Then she reached for me and held me tightly.

"Oh, little Pippa," she said, "I wish you could come with me. If only I could take you I'd be perfectly happy. But soon... soon. I promise you."

"Goodbye, Francine. Write to me. Let me know all that happens."

"I promise. Goodbye."

She was gone.

I stood there for some minutes listening. I visualized her at the Emms' cottage. Daisy would be there.

I remained there...listening. There was no sound at all. Then I turned and crept back to the quiet house, a feeling of desolation creeping over me such as I had never before known in the whole of my life.

Visits
to a Vestry

Four years had passed since that night when Francine ran away and I had not seen her since. She wrote to me by the way of the Emmses, feeling that if her letters were sent to Greystone Manor they might have been kept from me.

I never want again to live through such a time as that which followed her departure. My sense of loss was heartbreaking, so much so that my grandfather's wrath passed over me without affecting me in the least. I could only know that my beloved sister had gone. I had even lost Daisy. A few weeks after Francine's flight, the Graf and Gräfin with their household left the Grange, and Daisy, as a member of the staff, went with them.

On the morning after Francine had left the storm broke. Her absence at breakfast naturally meant that I was questioned. When I said I did not know where she was, it was presumed at first that she had taken an early morning walk and forgotten the time. I did not say that her bed had not been slept in, for I did not know how far she had gone by that time and I had visions of my grandfather's going after her. In his new mood of tolerance towards my sister—for he was convinced she was going to fall in readily with his plans—he allowed her absence at breakfast to pass. Although Miss Elton knew when she did not appear at lessons and Aunt Grace was aware of her absence, the news did not reach my grandfather until midday.

Then the storm broke. I was questioned and blamed for not reporting that she had left the night before. I faced him defiantly, too wretched to care what happened to me.

"She has gone away to be married to a Baron," I said.

I was shouted at and shaken. I had been wicked. I should be severely punished. I had known what was happening and done nothing to prevent it. His granddaughter was disgraced and dishonoured.

I took refuge with my grandmother and she kept me with her all day. My grandfather came up to her room and started shouting. She lifted her hand and raised her sightless eyes and said, "Not here in this room, Matthew. This is my refuge. The child shall not be blamed. Pray leave her to me."

I was surprised that he obeyed. She comforted me, stroking my hair. "Your sister will lead the life she has chosen," she said. "She had to go. She could not have stayed here under your grandfather's rule. She has chosen the right way. As for you, little Pippa, you are desolate because you have lost your dearest companion, but your time will come. You will see."

But she could not comfort me because there was no comfort. Perhaps somewhere within my innermost thoughts I knew that I had lost Francine forever. In the meantime I was at Greystone Manor—at the mercy of my grandfather.

After the Graf and his household had left the Grange we seemed to settle down to normal—the household, that was. Nothing could be as it had been for me without Francine. My grandfather ceased to mention my sister's name. He had announced in the beginning that she would never cross his threshold again, but he implied that he would still do his duty by me.

There was even stricter supervision than there had been before. Miss Elton was to go with me when I went out, so that I was never alone. My religious instruction was to be intensified. It was quite clear that my beginnings in that heathen island had had a bad effect if the behaviour of my sister was anything to go by.

Miss Elton was sympathetic and that was a great help. She had been fond of Francine, as almost everyone had been, and she hoped that everything would go well with her. So when I was with Miss Elton I was allowed to call at the Emms' cottage and Daisy would meet me there. "I promised your sister I would keep an eye on you," she told me. "Poor little Miss Pip. Not much fun up there with that old ogre, as Miss France used to call him."

When the Grange was empty again and Daisy had gone I was at my lowest ebb. Once I persuaded Miss Elton to let me run and look through the windows. When I saw the dust-sheeted furniture and the tallboy which looked like a human figure I wanted to fling myself to the ground and weep. I never went to peer in again. It was too heartbreaking.

I disliked Cousin Arthur as much as Francine had done. I hated the lessons I took with him. He was very fond of praying and would keep me on my knees for a long time while he exhorted the Almighty to make me a good woman obedient to my guardian, and full to overflowing with gratitude towards him.

I would find my thoughts straying to Francine and wondering what it would have been like if she had married Cousin Arthur instead of her Baron.

At least, I thought, she would be here.

Poor Aunt Grace was sympathetic but too much in awe of my grandfather to let it be known. My only solace in those days was my grandmother. She was the only real friend I had. Agnes Warden encouraged me to visit her often. I think she loved my grandmother dearly.

They say time heals all, and although that is not entirely true it certainly numbs the pain.

A whole year passed—the most melancholy of my life—and my only interest was the constant hope of news from Francine.

One day when I was in the garden I saw one of the Emms children staring at me.

"Miss Pippa," he called.

I turned to him and he looked about him to see if we were being watched. "My mum's got something for you."

"Thank you," I said.

"Says will you go along and get it?"

"Tell her I'll be there as soon as I can."

I had to go carefully. The order was that I was not to go out alone, so when I walked out with Miss Elton I said I wished to call at the Emms' cottage and she waited for me in the field while I went.

Mrs. Emms took a letter out of a drawer.

"Reckon it's that sister of yours," she said. "It come here.

And there's one from our Daise. Jenny Brakes read it to me.
Doing well, our Daise is. Oh, talk about high society. You
can read Daise's. She got Hans to help her. Not much with
a pen, our Daise. But I reckon you'll want to see what your
sister's writ."

"I'll take it home and read it there and I'll come back and
see Daisy's letter tomorrow."

Mrs. Emms nodded and I ran out to Miss Elton. She did
not ask what it was I had but I think she guessed, for when
I reached Greystone Manor I went straight up to my room.
My fingers were trembling as I opened the letter.

It was written on thick white paper almost like parchment,
and there was a heavy gold crest on it.

My dearest Pippa,

    *I am taking the first opportunity to write to you. So much
is happening here and I am very happy. Rudolph is everything I ever wanted a husband to be. We were married in
Birley Church. Do you remember that church we looked at
and liked so much? It caused some delay but Rudolph had
arranged it before we left because we had to get away as
quickly as possible. Rudolph is very important in his own
country. I can't tell you how important.*

    *We are surrounded by intrigue and have our enemies
who are trying to rob him of his inheritance. Oh, it is
hard to understand when you think of the way we have
lived—the island and then Greystone. We didn't know
a thing about the outside world, did we? Certainly not
a place like Bruxenstein. There are several dukedoms
here. There are margraves and barons, and they all want
to be the chief one. But I am digressing. It is no use my
trying to explain their politics to you because I don't
understand them myself. But it does mean that we live
rather dangerously. You want to hear about my adventures, though.*

    *Well, Rudolph said we should be married before we
reached Bruxenstein. It must be a* fait accompli *because
there would be people who would try to prevent it. So we
were married and I became Baroness von Gruton Fuchs.
Fancy me with such a grand name. I call myself Mrs.
Fox-Fuchs, you see. It's much easier and it amused Rudolph.*

    So we were married and crossed the Channel and

then we travelled right through France to Germany, finally reaching Bruxenstein. I wish you could see it, but you will. You are coming as soon as everything is settled. Rudolph says that I must not bring you here yet. It would cause trouble. You see he is what is called a great parti which means he is the most eligible man here. He's a sort of heir to the crown . . . only it is not a kingdom . . . and they wanted him to marry someone else . . . someone they had chosen for him. These people will interfere . . . just like our grandfather. So it is a little awkward. I know you'll understand. Rudolph has to go carefully.

Well, I have the most wonderful clothes. We stopped a few days in Paris where they were made for me. I kept the blue starry dress. Rudolph said he will always love that one because I wore it on that night you remember. But my things are truly magnificent now. I have a kind of tiara which I wear sometimes.

It would be such fun if you were here. Rudolph says it won't be long. They're afraid of what Daisy always used to call a 'coop.' Remember? They're always having these upheavals . . . it's jealousy between the rival members of the family. Some seem to want what others have got.

Now I have a secret to tell you. It's going to make a lot of difference if it's a boy. Yes, Pippa, I'm pregnant. Isn't that wonderful? Just fancy, you'll be an aunt. I tell Rudolph that I can't do without you and he keeps saying soon. He indulges me. I'm so happy. I wish they would stop their stupid quarrels though. I have to keep away from the castle, particularly now I'm pregnant. Rudolph is afraid for me. You see, if I have a son . . . But I'm talking their silly old politics again.

Dear Pippa, be ready at any time. One day you're going to find there is a bustle of preparations at the Grange. Then the army of servants will arrive and I shall be there . . . and next time, Pippa, dearest little sister, you are coming with me.

I love you more than ever.

Francine.

I read and reread the letter. I carried it inside my bodice so that I could feel it against my skin. It livened my days and when I was feeling particularly unhappy I read it once more.

The hope that one day when I went past the Grange I should see signs of activity there sustained me through the difficult times.

The days went past more quickly after the first few months. It was the same routine every day: breakfast with my grandfather, Aunt Grace and Cousin Arthur, prayers, lessons and riding with Miss Elton, visits to my grandmother and religious instruction from Cousin Arthur. I hated it and it would have been unendurable but for the long rides I took through the countryside, for by this time I had become an accomplished horsewoman. Then, of course, there were the sessions with my grandmother when we talked about Francine and imagined what was happening to her.

A whole year elapsed before I heard from Francine again. Once more the letter came through Mrs. Emms.

"Dearest Pippa," she wrote.

> *Don't think for a moment that I have forgotten you. Everything has changed so much since I last wrote. Then I was making plans for you to come here. Alas, they have all foundered. We had to move about a great deal and now we are living in a sort of exile. If you wrote to me I never received your letter and it may be that you did not get mine either. I expect it is still that dreary routine. Poor Pippa. As soon as everything is all right again you are coming here. I have told Rudolph that I must have my little sister with me. He agrees. He thought you were a darling—although he always says he hadn't eyes for anyone but me. But he wants you to come. He really does.*
>
> *Now I must tell you about the Great Event. Yes, I am a mother. I have a son, Pippa. Think of that. The most adorable being you could ever imagine. He is fair with blue eyes. I think he is like Rudolph but Rudolph says he is the image of me. He has a grand name: Rudolph (after his father) Otto Friederich von Gruton Fuchs. I call him my little Cub. Fox-cub, you see. I have no need to tell you that Cubby is the most miraculous child that ever was born. From the moment he arrived he showed an amazing grasp of affairs. But what would you expect of my child? I'd love you to see him. Oh you must. We will think of something.*

I wish these wretched old troubles would stop. We have to be so careful. It's all quarrelling between the various branches of the family. This one should have the margravate ... or that one should. It is very tiresome and disrupting. Rudolph is always deeply involved. There are secret meetings and comings and goings at the hunting lodge at which we are now staying. Don't imagine it is some poor broken-down place. Nothing of the sort. These margraves and counts and grafs and barons knew how to look after themselves very well. We live in magnificent style but we have to be careful. Rudolph chafes against it. He says that as soon as we are back in the castle I may send for you. I can't wait. I tell Cubby about you. He just stares at me but I swear he is taking it all in because he looks so wise.

My love to you, dear sister. I think of you a great deal. Never fear. I am going to rescue you from Greystone Manor.

Francine, the Baroness (Mrs. Fox).

After receiving the letter I lived in a state of euphoria for some weeks. I was constantly going past the Grange, looking for signs of activity. There was none. I called on Mrs. Emms often.

"No letters?" I would ask, and she would shake her head dolefully.

"There's one from Daise. All chuffed up she is. She's married that Hans. She's not with your sister though. She has to be with Hans, you see. She says they're all afraid of some coup or other."

Then I began to be alarmed. I felt so frustrated. This talk of coups and life in a world far removed from the quiet peace of our Victorian England was hard to imagine. Everything about the Grange and its inhabitants had seemed to belong to a highly coloured romantic world where the strangest adventures were possible. It was something I could have imagined and talked of with Francine, but the unreality of it all had come too close and Francine was drawn into it.

I prayed for her safety every night. That was a new element now. Fear for her safety.

There was another letter. This time it was all about the child. It was more than three years since Francine had left and her little Cubby must be eighteen months old now. He was beginning to talk and she could hardly bear him out of her sight. She talked to him about his Aunty Pippa.

> *He likes the word Pippa and keeps saying it. It's strange how they like some words, and Pippa is a word which certainly appeals. He has a funny little toy. They call it a troll here. This troll goes to bed with him and he sucks its ear. He won't go to sleep without it. He calls it Pippa. There you are, sister. There is a troll named after you.*
>
> *You would love my baby. He is perfect.*
>
> Your sister Francine.

That was the last letter I had had for a long time and I was very anxious. Mrs. Emms said there was no news from Daisy either.

I was getting older too, and those clouds which had seemed merely shadows on the horizon were beginning to gather overhead.

I had been only twelve when Francine had gone, and now I was approaching my sixteenth birthday. There were ominous signs. My grandfather was taking an interest in me. He invited me to ride round the estate with him and I remembered how he had taken Francine. He was more affable to me. When I went riding with him, Cousin Arthur came with us. Gradually I began to grasp the significance of this.

He had washed his hands of Francine, but he had another granddaughter and in a short time she would be of a marriageable age.

My sixteenth birthday was celebrated with a dinner party to which several of the surrounding families were invited. Jenny Brakes made a taffeta dress for me in a rather grownup style and Miss Elton told me that my grandfather had expressed the wish—no, command—that I put my hair up for the occasion.

This was done and I looked quite grown-up. I had an inkling of what was planned for my seventeenth birthday.

When I sat side by side with Cousin Arthur, he would place his hand on my knee and I would feel my whole being recoil from him. I tried not to show my repugnance and for the first time since Francine had left I became obsessed with my own problem. I hated Cousin Arthur's cold flabby hands for I could guess what he was thinking.

I was able to talk to my grandmother of my fears.

"Yes," she agreed, "it is coming and you might as well realize it. Your grandfather is going to insist that you marry your Cousin Arthur."

"I will not," I replied, as firmly as Francine had said it in the past.

"He will insist, I fear. I don't know what he will do, but it will be impossible for you to stay here if you do not agree."

"What can I do?"

"We must think," she said.

I talked it over with Miss Elton. She was rather anxious herself because she could see her post coming to an end. My grandmother said that the only way out, as far as she could see, was for me to take some post and she thought that I should be looking around for something, for such situations were not easy to find and my grandfather might try to force me into an engagement at any time now. The wedding would probably be planned for my seventeenth birthday, but I would have to be prepared before that.

I had not felt so depressed since the first months after Francine's departure. I was worried about her because there were no more letters, but my personal problem was so acute.... As far as I could see, my only way out was to take some post and I gave a good deal of thought to that prospect.

Miss Elton told me that there were certain posts advertised in the papers and she would get those papers and we would look together, for she had made up her mind that she was not going to be caught either.

We looked through the advertisements. "Your age is against you," she said. "Who would look at a girl of sixteen as a governess or a companion? You will have to pretend you are older."

"I shall be seventeen next year."

"Even seventeen is very young. I think you might just pass as eighteen if you draw your hair right back from your face. If you had a pair of spectacles... wait a moment." She went to a drawer and brought out a pair of glasses. "Try these on." I did and she laughed. "Yes, that would do the trick and with your hair back you look quite severe... all of twenty... perhaps twenty-one or two."

"I can't see a thing through them."

"They can be obtained with plain glass. One thing I am certain of. Your obvious youth would debar you from getting anything. You can't possibly hope to do that for two years at least."

"Two years! But I am sure he is planning my wedding for my seventeenth birthday."

I was able to laugh at my appearance in Miss Elton's cloak, with scraped-back hair and glasses.

Miss Elton then said she would get the glasses for me. She would say someone at the house wanted them just as a shield against the winds, which gave her a headache. She had become very sympathetic to me since Francine left, and that had drawn us close together.

She did manage to acquire the glasses, and when I put them on I thought how Francine would have laughed to see me.

Miss Elton looked for posts and found several that might suit her. She was, after all, an experienced governess of mature age. The more we talked, the more I began to see the hopelessness of my situation and laughed at myself derisively for thinking that a pair of spectacles would make up for a lack of experience.

It wasn't going to work, I knew, and even Miss Elton's will to proceed in her own search flagged a little.

"Perhaps it is early days yet," she said. "Perhaps something will turn up."

While we were thinking of all this a major event took place in Greystone Manor. Aunt Grace eloped with Charles Daventry. Perhaps if I had not been so involved in my own affairs I should have seen it coming. There had been a marked change in Aunt Grace ever since Francine had gone. There had been rebellion in the air and although it had taken her some years to come to the decision, Aunt Grace had finally broken the shackles with which her father had bound her. I was delighted for her.

She just walked out one day and there was a note for my grandfather saying that she had at last decided to live her own life and would soon be Mrs. Charles Daventry which was what she should have been ten years before.

My grandmother had been in on the secret of course, and I wondered how strongly she had urged Grace to act as she did.

My grandfather was incensed. There was another meeting

in the chapel at which he denounced Aunt Grace. She was an ungrateful child, such as the Lord abhorred. Had He not said "Honour thy father and thy mother?" She had bitten the hand that had fed her and the Almighty would not turn a blind eye to such dishonouring of her obligations.

I said to Cousin Arthur afterwards: "I think my grandfather sees God as a sort of ally. Why does he presume that God is always on his side? Who knows? He might be for Aunt Grace."

"You must not talk like that, Philippa," he replied sombrely.

"Why should I not say what I feel? What has God given me a tongue for?"

"To praise Him and honour your betters."

"You mean my grandfather and perhaps...you, Cousin Arthur?"

"You should have a respect for your grandfather. He took you in. He gave you shelter. You must never forget that."

"Grandfather doesn't, and he is certainly determined that I shall not either."

"Philippa, I will not mention what you have said to your grandfather, but if you continue to talk in this vein you would compel me to."

"Poor Cousin Arthur, you are indeed my grandfather's man. You are the Holy Trinity—you, my grandfather and God."

"Philippa!"

I looked at him scornfully. Now you really have something to tell my grandfather.

He did not, in fact. Instead he became rather gentle towards me, and my distaste for him grew in proportion to the passing of time.

I went to see Aunt Grace in the shack near the graveyard. She was visibly happy and did not look like the same grey woman who had inhabited Greystone Manor.

I embraced her and she looked at me apologetically. "I wanted to tell you, Philippa," she said, "but I was afraid to tell anybody...except Mamma. Oh, my dear, I am sure if you and your sister hadn't come I should never have had the courage. But ever since Francine went I have been thinking of this. Charles has been urging me for years, but somehow I could never quite make up my mind to...and then when Francine went I suddenly thought, Enough is enough...and then what seemed impossible gradually began to seem quite easy. I only had to do it."

Charles kissed me and said, "I have to be grateful to you and your sister. How do you think Grace is looking?"

"Like a new woman," I answered.

Aunt Grace was full of plans. They had Charles's room in the vicarage and they must live in that for a while. It meant that my grandfather would be furious, but he had no jurisdiction over the vicar. The living was a matter for the Bishop and the Bishop had never—"only don't mention a word of this," begged Aunt Grace—liked our grandfather. They had been at school together and there had been a feud between them. As for the vicar he had never been on very good terms with Greystone Manor, and with the Bishop's backing he didn't have to be.

Grace babbled on excitedly and I was so happy for her.

"I shan't be able to see my mother," she said, "because I have been forbidden the house and she can't come out, but you'll take messages for us, won't you, and you'll tell her how happy I am."

I promised I would.

It was a pleasant afternoon sitting among the stone figures and drinking tea which Charles brewed for us. In Grace's happiness I forgot briefly my own difficulties and when I did remember them the realization that I could talk to Aunt Grace comforted me.

"Yes," she agreed, "he is going to try to marry you to Cousin Arthur."

"I will never marry him," I said. "Francine was determined not to and so am I."

Her face clouded when I mentioned Francine. I went on: "I do worry about her. I haven't heard from her for so long. I can't understand why she doesn't write."

Aunt Grace was silent.

"It is strange," I went on. "Of course I always knew it might be difficult to get the letters... she being so far away."

"How long is it since you heard?" asked Aunt Grace.

"It's more than a year now."

Aunt Grace was still silent but after a while she said: "Philippa, I wonder if you would bring some of my things for me. You'll have to smuggle them out of the house. I expect you'll be forbidden to see me."

"I will disobey those orders," I promised.

"Be careful. Your grandfather can be a very harsh man. You cannot stand on your own yet, Philippa."

"I'm going to have to, Aunt Grace. I may try and find some post where I can earn my living. Miss Elton is helping me."

"Oh...has it gone as far as that?"

"It has to—because of Cousin Arthur."

"It's the best thing. You have to start a new life. I used to think of taking a post myself, but I always lacked the courage. You want to put the past behind you, everything...just everything, Philippa. Then perhaps you will find some good man. That would be the best. Forget everything...and start again."

"I would never forget Francine and our life together."

"You will find the way. And Philippa, there is something I want you to bring to me. It is my commonplace book. It is in the brown trunk in the first of the attics. There are newspaper cuttings and all sorts of things in it. It's a red book. You'll see my name written on the fly-leaf. I should like to have it. Do go and look for it. You cannot fail to find it."

The earnestness in her eyes, the manner in which her hand shook and the sudden darkening of that glow which her newly found happiness had brought her...all that might have warned me that I would find something startling in the commonplace book.

As soon as I returned to the house I went up to the attic. I opened the trunk and there was the book for which she had asked. I opened it. Her name was written inside just as she had said, but it was the newspaper cutting which caught my eye. The words formed themselves into sentences and they made terrible pictures for me.

Baron Rudolph von Gruton Fuchs was found murdered in his bed in his hunting lodge in the Grutonian province of Bruxenstein last Wednesday morning. With him was his mistress, a young English woman whose identity is as yet unknown, but it is believed that she had been his companion at the lodge for some time before the tragedy.

I looked at the date of the paper. It was over a year old. There was another cutting.

The identity of the woman has been discovered. She is

*Francine Ewell, who had been a "friend" of the Baron
for some time.*

The paper slipped from my hands. I just rocked there on
my knees while my mind conjured up pictures of a bedroom
in a hunting lodge. Rather grand, she had described it. There
would be many servants. I pictured her lying in a bed with
the handsome lover beside her...and there would be blood
everywhere...my beloved sister's blood.

So this was why I had not heard. They had not told me,
and there had been no mourning for her; my dear, beautiful,
incomparable sister might never have existed.

Dead! Murdered! Francine, the companion of my happy
days. The months of anxiety had culminated in this. Always
before there had been hope. No longer could I call at the
Emms' cottage to be bitterly disappointed because there was
no news. How could there be news...ever again?

They had said she was his mistress. But she was his wife.
They had been married at Birley Church before they had
crossed the Channel. She had written to tell me that. They
had a son. Cubby. Where was Cubby? There was no mention
of him.

"Oh Francine," I murmured, "I shall never see you again.
Why did you go? It would have been better to have stayed
here...to have married Cousin Arthur...any-
thing...anything rather than this. We could have gone away
together. Where? How? Anywhere...anything rather than
this."

I tried not to believe it. It must be someone else. But it
was his name...and hers. Had she told me the truth about
the marriage? Had she thought that I would want it to be
respectable and proper, conventional and right? Yes, I should
have done. But she need not have lied to me. She could have
omitted to mention the ceremony. And then there was the
child. What had become of the child? Why didn't the paper
mention him? It was such a brief cutting, as it would be in
the English papers. Just a little of the usual trouble that
cropped up in those turbulent Germanic states remote from
peaceful England. The only reason it was mentioned at all
was because the woman involved was English.

Was that all I was to know? Where could I find out more?

Clutching the red commonplace book under my arm, I ran
to the vicarage. Aunt Grace was waiting for me among the

statues. She must have known that I would come. I just held the book out, looking at her.

"I didn't tell you," she stammered. "I thought it would upset you too much. But now...I thought...she is older. She ought to know."

"All this time I have been waiting to hear from her...."

Aunt Grace's lips trembled. "It's terrible," she said. "She should never have gone."

"Is there anything else I should know, Aunt Grace? Are there more cuttings...more reports...?"

She shook her head. "Nothing. That was all. I read it and cut it out. I didn't show it to anyone. I was afraid someone would see it. Your grandfather perhaps. But people don't take much notice of foreign news."

"She was married to him," I said.

Aunt Grace looked at me piteously.

"She was," I insisted. "She wrote and told me so. Francine would not lie to me."

"It must have been a mock marriage. Those sort of people do things like that."

"But there was a child," I cried. "What of the child? There is no mention of a child."

Aunt Grace murmured, "I should never have let you know. I just thought it would be best."

"I had to know," I cried. "I want to know all about her. And all this time I have been in the dark...."

I could think of nothing but Francine. I could not shut out the thought of her lying dead in that bed...murdered. Francine...so full of life. I could not imagine it. I would rather have believed she had forgotten me, that her life was so full and varied that she had no time to remember a drab little sister. But Francine would never have been like that. The bond between us was too strong and had been forever...until death parted us. Death. Irrevocable...violent...shocking death!

Never to see her again! Francine and that handsome young man whom I had met briefly and who had been all that a romantic hero should be—a fitting husband for the most beautiful of girls. But they had lived dangerously of course.

There was no-one to whom I could talk but my grandmother. She had learned of Francine's death recently, for Aunt Grace had told her.

"I should have been told," I cried passionately.

"We should have told you...in time," she said. "But we knew of your devotion to each other and we thought you were so young. We wanted to wait until your sister had become a remote memory. It would have softened the blow."

"She would never have become a remote memory."

"But it was better, my child, that you should have thought she had forgotten you in the excitement of her new life than that you should know that she was dead...just at first, that was."

"It happened a year ago."

"Yes, but it was better to wait until now. Grace acted on the spur of the moment. She is a changed woman now. All her life she hesitated...."

"They say Francine was not married. Grandmother, I *know* she was."

"Well, my dear, look at it like this. He was someone of very high rank in his country. Marriages are arranged for people like that. If they marry outside the laws..."

"It says she was his mistress. Francine was his wife. She told me."

"She would tell you that. Of course she would. She thought of herself as his wife."

"She said they were married in church. I've been to the church. We saw it the very day we arrived in England. We went there because we had time to spare when we were waiting for the train at Dover. I remember it well. Francine said at the time it would be a nice church to be married in, and she was."

My grandmother was silent and I went on: "What of the child?" for I could not stop thinking about him.

"He will be taken good care of."

"Where? How?"

"It would have been arranged."

"She was so proud of him. She loved him so much."

My grandmother nodded.

I cried out: "I want to know what happened."

"My dear child, you must forget about it."

"Forget Francine! As if I ever would. I should like to go there...to find out everything."

"My dear child, you have problems of your own."

I was silent for a moment. The sudden discovery had wiped everything from my mind. My problem did remain though. Even as I sat there, my mind full of pictures of Francine...ones that I remembered and imaginary ones, chief of all that of a bedroom in a hunting lodge...I could almost feel Cousin Arthur's flabby hands on me; I could see the bridal suite at Greystone, a dismal room with heavy grey velvet curtains and a high four-poster bed; I could see myself lying there and Cousin Arthur coming to me; I could picture his kneeling by the bed praying God to bless our union before he set about the practical means of bringing it into action. I could never never endure that.

And yet I could not think of that for long. All I could see was Francine lying in that bloodstained bed with her lover dead beside her.

I went to the Grange and looked at it. Sadly I passed the Emms' cottage. I often saw Mrs. Emms hanging out the washing; she seemed to be washing clothes interminably. I supposed she would be, with a large family, and yet they did not give an impression of excessive cleanliness. I stopped and talked to her.

"Never hear from Daise these days," she said. "I often wonder what's happening to her with that there Hans. Well, they go to foreign parts and it seems you've lost them. No news from your sister either?"

I shook my head. I did not want to talk about the tragedy with Mrs. Emms.

Yet I could not stop myself looking at the house. I felt so frustrated. I railed against my youth. Something could and must be done.

Miss Elton had heard from her cousin who was working somewhere in the Midlands as a children's nurse. She said they would shortly be needing a governess and she had spoken for Miss Elton. The position was hers if she could wait for three months when they would be ready to take her.

Miss Elton was settled. She had had an interview with my grandfather when she explained that she believed I would soon not be needing a governess and that she had this offer of a post in three months' time. He graciously commended her wisdom in looking ahead and said he would be very happy to retain her services for another three months when, as she rightly divined, I should not longer be in need of a governess.

There was something irrevocable about that. My grandfather looked complacent. I was sure he thought he would not have the same difficulty with me as he had with my sister.

Then, to my great excitement, there was acitvity at the
Grange. Young Tom Emms told me when he came to help his
father in the garden. He sought me out and I was sure Mrs.
Emms had ordered him to tell me.

"There's people up at the house," he whispered conspiratorially.

"The Grange!" I cried.

He nodded.

It was all I needed. As soon as the midday meal was over
I was off.

Mrs. Emms was waiting for me. When she wasn't hanging
up clothes she was in her garden watching.

She was at her door as soon as I approached. "Only the
servants, so far," she said.

"I'm going to call," I told her.

She nodded. "I went over to ask about our Daise. I thought
she might be there."

"And she's not?"

Mrs. Emms shook her head. "I got quite the cold shoulder.
No, Daise wasn't there. Nor was Hans. They're not the same
lot as before. Funny way of going on I must say."

I was not going to be put off and I left her and made for
the Grange. My heart was beating wildly as I went up the
drive. I lifted the gargoyle knocker and the sounds echoed
through the house.

At length I heard footsteps coming and a man opened the
door.

We stood for a moment looking at each other. He raised
his eyes interrogatively and I said: "I have come to call. I am
from Greystone Manor."

He said, "Not at home. No-one here."

He was about to shut the door but I had stepped forward
so that he could not do so without forcing me out.

"When will the Gräfin arrive?" I asked.

He lifted his shoulders.

"Please tell me. I met her some years ago. My name is
Philippa Ewell."

He looked at me oddly. "I do not know when they will
come. Perhaps not at all. We are here because the house has
been left so long. Good day."

I could only step back defeated.

But I was in a fever of impatience. The arrival of the
servants had in the past meant that the house would be oc-

cupied in due course, and surely someone there would be able to give me some information about Francine.

A strange thing happened soon after my call at the house. There was a man whom I seemed to meet constantly. He was of heavy build with a thick, short neck, and there was a Teutonic look about him which stamped him as a foreigner. I fancied he must be a tourist who was staying at the Three Tuns Inn close to the river, where occasionally people came for the trout fishing. What was strange was that I met him so often. He never spoke to me; in fact he never seemed aware of me. He just seemed to be frequently there.

Miss Elton, whose own future was now secure, was becoming very sympathetic towards me and genuinely anxious on my behalf. The time was passing. In six months I should be seventeen. She knew that I loathed the thought of marrying Cousin Arthur. Yet what alternative had I?

She said, "You should have a plan of action."

"Such as?" I asked.

"You're so listless about yourself. You're obsessed by what happened to your sister. She is dead. You are living and you have to go on living."

"I wish I could go to that place, Bruxenstein. I'm sure there is some mystery to be cleared up."

"It is all simple, really. She was bewitched by him. She went away with him. He promised marriage..."

"He *did* marry her. It was in the church we visited once." I was hit by an idea. "Don't they have registers and things in churches? Well, if she was married there...there would be an account of it, wouldn't there? And wouldn't it be in the church?"

Miss Elton was looking at me intently. "You're right," she said.

"Oh, Miss Elton. I must go to that church. I must see it for myself. If it was there, that record of their marriage...it would prove part of that report was wrong, wouldn't it?"

Miss Elton was nodding slowly.

"I'm going then...somehow. Will you come with me?"

She was silent for a while. "Your grandfather would want to know."

"Am I going to be his slave all my life?" I asked.

"Yes, if you don't take some action now."

"I will take action, and my first will be to go to Birley Church to see if there is any record of my sister's marriage."

"And if there is?"

"Then I must do something. It makes a difference, don't you see? I want to find out why my sister was murdered. And there is something else. I want to find her son. What of that little boy? He must be three years old now. Where is he? Who is looking after him? He is Francine's child. Don't you see? I can't just sit here and do nothing."

"I can't see what you can do, apart from prove whether your sister was married or not. And how is that going to help?"

"I'm not sure. But it would ease my mind a little. It will show that she was telling the truth if that record is there. She said she was the Baroness. She called herself Mrs. Fox. One of his names was *Fuchs,* you see."

"She always was rather frivolous."

"She was the loveliest person I have ever known and I can't bear it."

"Now, don't get upset again. If you're set on going to that place—near Dover, is it? We could go there and back in one day. That makes it easy."

"You'll come with me, Miss Elton."

"I will, of course. You can't tell your grandfather what we are going to do, can you? How would it be if I told him that our lessons have been touching on the ancient churches of England and there is a particularly interesting Norman one near Dover which I should very much like you to see."

"Oh, Miss Elton. You are so good."

"He is inclined to be a little less severe with us now. Perhaps because I shall soon be going and he thinks you are going to be a docile granddaughter and obey his wishes."

"I don't care what he thinks. I want to go to that church and look at the records."

She was right about my grandfather. He graciously agreed to the outing and we set out early in the morning from the station at Preston Carstairs. We could catch the three o'clock train back. It was strange that just as we were getting into the station the mysterious man from the Three Tuns came hurrying onto the train. He did not look at us at all, but the thought crossed my mind that it was strange that he should be there once more—and travelling on the very same train that we were; but I was so excited by the prospect ahead that I had soon dismissed him from my mind. He was very likely on holiday and seeing something of the countryside, and as the town of Dover and its environs were of outstanding historical interest, it was natural that he should wish to visit it.

It was a fairly long journey and to my impatient mood we seemed to chuff along at a very leisurely pace. I looked out at green meadows, oast houses, the ripening hops and the fruit-laden trees of the orchards which were a feature of this part of the country. Everything was green and pleasant, but I was so anxious to reach the church.

As we came into Dover I saw the castle at the top of the hill and the fantastic view of white cliffs and sea; but I could only think of what I was going to find—for I had no doubt that it would be there.

We alighted from the train and made our way out of the station.

"The church is not very far," I said. "Francine, Mr. Counsell and I went there in a trap and the people from the inn drove us there."

"Could you find the inn?"

"I am sure I could."

"Then we'll go there and have what they have to offer us to eat and then we can enquire about the trap to take us to Birley Church."

"I never felt less like eating."

"We need something. Besides, it will give us a chance to talk to the innkeeper."

We found the inn easily, and we were offered hot bread straight from the oven with cheddar cheese, sweet pickle and cider. It would have been tasty if I had been in the mood for eating.

"I have been here before," I told the innkeeper's wife.

"We get so many," she answered, apologizing for not remembering me.

"When I was here before, I visited Birley Church."

"We should really like to see it again," said Miss Elton. "How far is it?"

"Oh, some three miles or so from the edge of the town."

"Last time we drove there in a trap," I explained. "The trap was one of yours. Is it possible to take us again?"

She lifted her shoulders and looked faintly dubious. "I'll ask," she said.

"Oh, please arrange it," I begged. "It is so very important to me."

"I'll see what I can do."

"We shall have to pay her," I said when she had gone.

"Your grandfather gave me some money for this educational jaunt," said Miss Elton comfortingly. "And it won't be so very much surely."

The woman came back and said that the trap would be ready in half an hour. I was so impatient, it was hard to wait and as I sat there longing for the time to pass I saw a figure walk quickly past the window. I was sure it was the man I had seen getting on the train. So he had even arrived at this inn!

When the half hour was up, there was the trap waiting for us and I then saw the man again. He was examining one of the horses belonging to the inn and striking a bargain for it.

I immediately forgot him as we rattled along, for my mind was taken back so poignantly to when Francine and I had sat so close together as we drove along this road, and were so apprehensive of what awaited us at our grandfather's house.

We came to the church—small, grey and ancient—and made our way across the graveyard where many of the tombstones were brown with age and the engraving on them almost illegible. I remembered how Francine had read some of them aloud and I could hear her high laughter at the sentiments expressed. We went into the porch and I smelt that odour indigenous to churches of this kind—damp age and some sort of furniture polish used for the pews. I stood facing the altar; the light flickering through the stained glass windows shone on the brass lectern and the gilded fringe of the altar cloth. There was silence everywhere.

Miss Elton at length broke it. "I suppose we should go to the vicarage," she said.

"Yes, of course. We must see the vicar."

We turned to go and as we did so the door creaked and a man came into the church. He looked curiously at us and asked if he could help.

"I'm the churchwarden here," he said. "Are you interested in the church? It's Norman, you know, and a very fine example for its size. It's been restored recently and we have had to repair a great deal of the tower. People don't come to see it very often, but that's because it's a bit off the map."

Miss Elton said, "We have a purpose other than to see the

architecture. We wanted to know if it is possible to see the records. We want to make sure that a wedding took place here."

"Well, if you have the dates and the names of the parties that should not be an impossibility. Our vicar is away until the week-end. That's why I'm looking in, you see. If I can be of any help...."

"Could you show us the records?" I asked eagerly.

"I could do that. They're kept in the vestry. I'll have to get the keys. Was it very long ago?"

"No. Four years," I said.

"Well, there should be no problem there. People usually want to see a hundred years back. They're chasing their ancestors. There's a lot of that done nowadays. I'll just pop into the vicarage. I'll be back with you shortly."

When he had gone we looked at each other triumphantly. "I do hope you find what you want," said Miss Elton.

True to his promise, the churchwarden soon returned with the keys, and tingling with excitement I followed him into the vestry.

"Now..." he said. "What date did you say? Ah yes...Here it is."

I looked. It was true. There it was. Their names as clear as I could wish.

I gave a cry of triumph and turned to Miss Elton. "There!" I shouted. "There is no doubt. It's proved."

I was possessed by a great excitement for I knew that having proved Francine had been married, I was not going to leave it at that. I had to find out more of what happened. Moreover I had begun to be haunted by the thought of that little boy, the child who had liked to say my name and had called his troll after me.

As we came out of the church I thought I saw a figure lurking among the tombstones. It was a man. He was stooping over a grave and seemed to be reading the inscription on the stone.

I took no further notice. I was so elated by what I had seen that I could think of nothing else all the way home.

I could not wait to see my grandmother. I sat on the stool at her feet and told her what I had seen in the church register.

She listened intently. "I'm glad," she said. "So Francine was speaking the truth."

"But why should they say that she was his mistress?"

"I suppose it was because he was a man who was in an important position. It may be that he already had a wife."

"I don't believe it. Francine was so happy."

"My dear Philippa, you must stop thinking about it. Whatever happened, it's over and done with. You have your own life to think of. Soon you will be seventeen. What are you going to do?"

"I wish I could go to Bruxenstein. I wish I could find out what it was all about."

"You could not do that. Now if I were younger...if I had my sight—"

"You would go with me, wouldn't you, Grandmother?"

"I should be tempted to do so...but just as it is impossible for me to do that, so is it for you. Dear child, what are you going to do about this matter nearer home? I have been thinking that if your grandfather insists that you marry your cousin, you might go and stay with Grace."

"How could I? They have only one room in the vicarage."

"It would be difficult I know. I am just trying to find a solution. You are clutching at straws, my dear child. You have immersed yourself in this mystery which you cannot solve, and even if you did, that would not bring your sister back. Meanwhile you yourself are in danger."

She was right, of course. Perhaps I should try to find a post as Miss Elton and I had at first thought I should. But who would employ me? When I considered that, the whole scheme seemed ridiculous.

The next day there was a dinner party. The guests were the Glencorns with their daughter Sophia. "Just a small, intimate dinner party," my grandfather had said, looking at me with the satisfaction he was beginning to show towards me. "Six is a pleasant number," he added.

I dressed disconsolately in the brown taffeta which Jenny Brakes had made for me. It didn't suit me. Brown was not my colour. I needed reds and emerald greens. Not that I was the least interested in clothes or how I looked now. My thoughts were far away with Francine's little boy. I felt I knew him. Fair-haired, blue-eyed, a miniature Francine holding a troll. What did a troll look like? I imagined some sort of Scandinavian dwarf. A troll whom he had named Pippa after me.

He was somewhere far away...unless they had murdered

him too. Perhaps they had, and being a child he did not rate a mention in the English papers.

I piled my hair on top of my head. It gave me height and took away that look of extreme youth. Now I looked like a person who might be able to defend herself.

I hated the thought of the dinner party. I had met the Glencorns once or twice. They lived in a big house on the edge of my grandfather's estate. I gathered he had bought land from the Glencorns who had reluctantly sold it because, as my grandfather remarked gleefully, they had no help for it. Sir Edward Glencorn had never been able to manage the estate he had inherited. He was a fool, said my grandfather. He despised fools, but the Glencorns were neighbours and when their property came on the market, which he was sure it must within the next few years, he wanted to get the first chance of acquiring it. Acquisition was the aim of my grandfather's life, which was why he had been so angry when the Grange had passed out of his orbit. Land and people—he had a desire to possess them all, to make them work for him, to fulfil his plans. He was like an earthly God creating his own universe. So although he despised Sir Edward Glencorn he liked to be in his company, which naturally gave him an even greater sense of his superiority.

Dinner was an ordeal, as all meals were, and I found it hard to concentrate on the conversation. Being in the company of Cousin Arthur was making my flesh crawl more than ever. I knew the time was getting nearer when I should have to accept him or find myself alone and destitute.

At a gathering such as this it was hard to put all that behind me, and as I was still in a state of shock over Francine's fate, I was to say the least absentminded.

Sophia was a quiet girl, although I had always had the feeling that one could never really know her. Often I would find her watching me intently as though she were trying to read my innermost thoughts. If Francine had been with me and this terrible fear and uncertainty had not been hanging over me, I realized we should have been rather interested in Sophia Glencorn.

Sir Edward was complimenting me on my looks—quite conventionally, I was sure, for I knew that the brown taffeta suited neither my skin nor my colouring, and I must surely show some sign of my anxieties. Moreover he had been talking to me for some time and I couldn't remember what I had answered, so he must be thinking me half-witted.

"No longer the little girl, eh? Quite the young lady."

My grandfather was looking almost benign. "Yes, it is surprising how quickly Philippa has seemed to grow up."

Ominous words. I could see the plans in his eyes. The wedding...the birth...the heir, the little Ewell who would be moulded by my grandfather.

"Philippa is taking a great interest in the estate," added Cousin Arthur.

Was I? I hadn't noticed it. I cared nothing for the estate. My thoughts were entirely occupied with my own affairs and my sister.

My grandfather nodded, looking down at his plate. "One has to consider all the time," he said. "One inherits lands, possessions, and with them responsibilities."

How amused Francine would have been.

"Philippa is taking an interest in architecture also," went on Cousin Arthur.

How I wished they would not talk about me as though I weren't there.

"Miss Elton has groomed her in the subject," went on my grandfather. "What was that church you visited recently?"

I said it was Birley Church...not far from Dover.

"Quite a way to go to see a bit of stone," commented Lady Glencorn.

Grandfather gave her an indulgent but rather contemptuous smile.

"Norman, wasn't it?" he said. "I believe the most interesting feature of Norman architecture is the way they built the roofs—timber boarding in the roof-trusses to make tunnel-shaped ceilings. Is that so, Philippa?"

I was only vaguely aware of what he was talking about, for Miss Elton and I had not thought of architecture until I wanted to go to Birley Church.

"Oh yes, yes," I said. "Miss Elton is rather sad because she will be leaving us so soon."

My grandfather could not hide his contentment. "Philippa is getting too grown up for a governess now. She will have other matters with which to concern herself."

It was strange, really, for I had never felt so important. But it only meant that I was now quite a significant piece on the chess-board to be moved this way and that at his pleasure.

I was glad when the meal was over and we went into the solarium where after-dinner wines and liqueurs were served when we had guests. Sophia was invited to play for us on the piano. She had quite a strong voice and she sang some of the old songs like "Cherry Ripe" and "Drink to me Only with Thine Eyes." This last she sang very soulfully while Arthur stood beside her and turned the leaves of the music as she sang. I noticed that when he leaned over and turned the page, his hand rested on her shoulder and lingered there for quite a while.

I had always watched Cousin Arthur's hands with a sort of repellent horror because I hated it when he touched me; and he was rather fond of physical contact I noticed. I had thought this was reserved for myself, but it seemed it was a habit of his. I noticed him do it again and again with Sophia at the piano and it comforted me in an odd way. It did mean that it was not specially for me.

The evening was over at last and the Glencorns left in their carriage. Grandfather, Cousin Arthur and I saw them off and when they had gone grandfather sighed with satisfaction.

"It would not surprise me," he said, "if old Glencorn were not on the edge of bankruptcy."

Each day seemed long in passing, yet looking back one week had gone and we were halfway through another. I knew I was fast approaching a precipice. Miss Elton had only one month to go, for we were now well into February. My grandfather's ultimatum was about to burst upon me and I was still dreaming impossible dreams about getting to that remote country which was only a name to me. I had looked at it many times on the atlas—a little pink spot very small and insignificant compared with the mass of America, Africa and Europe, with our little island flung out on the side. But then there were all those red pieces which were British—that Empire on which the sun never set. But the place that I longed to see and to know more about was that little pink spot in the midst of all those brown mountain ranges.

In despair I decided to call at the Grange once more. I started across the lawn, and as I did so a man came towards me.

I was startled for a moment because I thought he was

Francine's lover. I caught my breath and must have turned pale.

"Is anything wrong?" he asked.

"No.... I just came to call on...er..."

"To call on?" he repeated encouragingly.

"I met the Gräfin when she was here some years ago. She was kind enough to invite me to...call again."

"She is not here, I'm afraid." He spoke impeccable English with only the faintest trace of a foreign accent. "Can I be of any help?"

"You are...?"

"Oh, I am just here to see that things are well with the house. It is some time since it was lived in. That is not good for houses. May I know your name?"

"It is Philippa Ewell."

He was alert. A picture of those newspaper lines flashed into my mind. "We know the identity of the English woman. She is Francine Ewell...."

He would have recognized the surname, but all he said was: "How do you do?" and added, "Would you like to come into the house?"

"You say the family is not at home?"

He laughed. "I am sure the Gräfin would not wish me to be inhospitable. I will welcome you on her behalf."

"Are you a sort of—what do you call it? a major-domo?"

"That is a good description."

I had the position clearly. He was a servant but a very superior one. He had come to make sure that all was well with the house. That sounded very reasonable.

"I suppose you are getting the house ready for them?"

"That could well be," he said. "Come in and I will refresh you. You drink tea at this hour, do you not?"

"Yes, we do."

"I believe we could have tea."

"Is that in order, do you think?" I asked dubiously.

"I don't really see why not."

I remember how Hans had shown us round and how embarrassing that had been. Still, I was certainly not going to refuse such an offer. I was tremendously excited. I could feel my cheeks beginning to burn as they did on such occasions. Francine had said: "Don't worry about it. It makes you quite pretty."

He opened the door and we went in. I remembered it so

well—the dining hall, the stairs, the small room where we had been entertained by the Gräfin.

Tea was brought by a serving maid who did not seem in the least surprised. He smiled at me. "You would perhaps, as I believe they say, do the honours, yes?"

I poured out the tea and said, "I—I wonder if you ever met my sister."

He raised his eyebrows. "I have been very little in England lately. I spent some years in my youth...for my education."

"Oh," I said, "this was four or five years ago. She met someone in this house. She was married and then...she died."

"I think I know to what you refer," he said slowly. "It was a big scandal at the time. Yes...I remember the name of the Baron's friend."

"My sister was his wife."

He lifted his shoulders slightly. Then he said: "I knew there was a friendship...a liaison."

I felt myself growing hot with indignation. "That was not true," I said shrilly. "I know the account in the press mentioned her as his mistress. I tell you she was his wife."

"You must not get angry," he said. "I know how you feel, of course. But the Baron could not have married your sister. His marriage was of the utmost importance to the country because he was heir to the ruling house."

"Do you mean my sister would not have been considered good enough for him?"

"Not necessarily so, but he would have married someone of his own nationality...someone chosen for him. He would not have married outside that."

"I must assure you that my sister was worthy to marry anyone."

"I am sure she was, but you see it is not a matter of worthiness. It is a matter of politics, you understand?"

"I know that my sister was married to him."

He shook his head. "She was his mistress," he said. "It is what will happen, you know. She would not have been the first or the last...had he lived."

"I find these comments most offensive."

"You must not find the truth offensive. You must be a realist."

I stood up. "I will not stay here to hear my sister being

insulted." I felt the tears in my eyes and I was enraged with him for making me show my emotion.

"Now come, please," he said gently. "Talk reasonably. You must look at this as a woman of the world. They met romantically, I suspect. They loved. Well, that is charming. But marriage for a man in his position with someone who...oh, I am sure she was beautiful and charming, I am sure she was worthy in every way...but it was simply not suitable. A man in his position must consider his liabilities...and he always did that."

"I tell you they *were* married."

He smiled at me and his calmness angered me more than anything else. That he could talk of this tragedy almost as though it were an everyday occurrence wounded me so deeply that I felt I should lose control of myself completely if I stayed any longer and had to look at that unruffled, smiling face.

"If you will excuse me..." I said.

He stood up and bowed.

"I must go," I said. "You are talking nonsense and telling lies...I think you are aware of it. Goodbye."

With that I turned and ran out of the house. I was just in time for the tears were now running down my cheeks and the last thing I should have wanted was for him to see them.

I hurried into the house and up to that room which I had once shared with Francine. I threw myself on my bed and for the first time since I had seen those horrible newspaper cuttings, I wept uncontrollably.

I didn't want to go to the Grange after that. I found it hard to understand why he had upset me so. Perhaps it was because he had reminded me a little of Francine's Baron. This man was a servant, I told myself, and wanted everyone to know that although he was a servant he was a very superior one. Rudolph had worn his royalty—or whatever it was these Grafs and Barons had—very lightly. Everyone had known he was the Baron and he did not have to remind them. Perhaps I was being rather unfair to the man, just because he had been so sure that Francine had not been married.

Anyway I did not want to see him again. But perhaps that was foolish, for he might know something. He might be aware of what happened to the child.

Already I was beginning to regret my hasty departure. Why should I have cared if he saw my grief?

I saw him again next day. I think he was waiting to catch me, for when I went out for my afternoon walk he must have seen me leave the house. I went towards the woods at a fast pace but he followed me.

Inside the wood I sat down under a tree and waited for him to come up.

"Good afternoon," he said. "So...we meet again."

Since I was sure he had waited for me and knew he had followed me this seemed, to say the least, deceitful.

"How do you do?" I said coldly.

"May I?" he said and sat down beside me. He was smiling at me.

"I am glad you are no longer angry with me," he said.

"I was rather foolish, I'm afraid."

"No...no." He leaned towards me and put his hand over mine for a moment. "It was natural that you should be upset. It was a terrible thing that happened to your sister."

"It was wicked. I wish I knew....I wish I could find her murderers."

"It was not possible to find them," he said. "There was a search, of course. Nothing came to light and it therefore remains a mystery."

"Will you please tell me all that you know about it? There was a child. What happened to the boy?"

"A child! There was no child."

"My sister had a son. She wrote and told me so."

"That is impossible."

"Why should it be impossible for two people to have a child?"

"It is not an impossibility in the way you suggest, but in view of Rudolph's position."

"His position had nothing to do with it. He married my sister and it is the most natural thing in the world that they should have a child."

"This is something you do not understand."

"I should be pleased if you would not treat me as a child, and a half-witted one at that."

"Oh, I do not consider you a child and I am sure that you are in full possession of your wits. I know too that you are a very fiery young lady."

"This is something which is very important to me. My sister is dead but I will not allow her memory to be desecrated."

"You use strong words, my dear young lady."

He had leaned towards me and tried to take my hand which I firmly removed. "I am not your dear young lady."

"Well..." He put his head on one side and regarded me. "You are young. You are a lady..."

"Of a family not worthy to marry with foreigners who honour our country by visiting it occasionally."

He laughed aloud. I noticed the firm line of his jaw and the gleam of strong white teeth. I thought: He reminds me of Arthur...by the very contrast.

"Worthy...worthy indeed," he said. "But because of certain political commitments, such marriages cannot take place."

"Do you think that a girl like my sister would condescend to become the mistress of this high and mighty potentate?"

He looked at me solemnly and nodded.

"You are talking nonsense," I said.

"Where I was wrong," he went on, looking at me in an odd, intent sort of way, "was to call you *my* dear young lady. You are not mine."

"I find this an absurd conversation. We were talking about a very serious matter and you have introduced this light and frivolous note."

"It is often wise when talking of serious matters to introduce a light-hearted note. It prevents tempers rising."

"It does not prevent mine."

"Ah, but you are a very hot-tempered lady."

"Listen to me," I said. "If you are not prepared to talk seriously about this matter, there is no point in our talking at all."

"Oh, do you feel like that? I'm sorry. I have been thinking that there is a great deal of point in talking on any subject. I should very much like to know you better and I hope you feel some curiosity about me."

"I have to find out what happened to my sister and why. And I want to be assured that her child is being cared for."

"You are asking a great deal. The police were not able to solve the mystery of what happened that night in the hunting lodge. As for the non-existent child—"

"I will not listen to any more."

He did not speak, but sat still, glancing sideways at me. My impulse was to get up and leave him and I should have done so if I had not wanted more than anything to learn the truth.

I did start to move away but he reached out and, taking my hand, looked at me appealingly. I felt myself flushing. There was something about him which stirred me. I disliked his arrogance and his assumption that Francine's Baron could never have stooped to marry her. In fact his implication that Francine and I were romancing about the whole matter infuriated me, and yet—I could not say what it was, because I had had too little experience of the world; and yet to be near him brought me such a feeling of excitement ad I did not remember ever feeling before. I could tell myself that it was because I was on the verge of discovering something and was actually in the presence of someone who had known Baron Rudolph. Somehow this man gave me the impression that he was aware of more than he was letting me know, and I told myself that whatever effect he had on me I had to see him as much as possible.

I don't know how long we were like that—he holding my hand, myself making a half-hearted effort to break away from him while he watched me with a rather mischievous smile, as though he could read my thoughts and, moreover, knew my vulnerability.

"Please sit down," he said. "We obviously have a great deal to say to each other."

I sat down. I said: "In the first place, you know who I am. My sister and I lived at Greystone Manor until she went to this unfortunate ball."

"Where she met her lover."

"She had met him before and the Gräfin invited her. It wasn't easy. Do not imagine that we at Greystone Manor thought it such an honour. My sister had to go to all sorts of subterfuge in order to attend that ball."

"Deceit?" he asked.

"You are determined to be offensive."

"Certainly not. But I must insist that if we are to discover anything we must look facts straight in the face. Your sister slipped out of the house in her ball gown and went to the Grange. Her family—with the exception of her little sister who was in on the secret—knew nothing about it. Is that right?"

"Yes...more or less."

"And there she and the Baron fell in love. They eloped.
She travelled as his wife...to placate conventions."

"She *was* his wife."

"Now we are right back at the beginning. The marriage
could not have taken place."

"But it did. I know it did."

"Let me explain to you. Rudoloph's country is a small one.
It is always fighting to preserve its autonomy. That is why
there must be no stepping aside from conventions. There are
neighbouring states always casting greedy eyes on it, always
seeking to aggrandize themselves, to make themselves more
powerful. One day they will all band together into one state
and that will doubtless be a good thing, but at the moment
there are these petty states—dukedoms, margravates, principalities, and so on; Bruxenstein is one of them. Rudolph's
father is an old man. Rudolph was his only son. He was to
marry the daughter of a ruler of a neighbouring state. He
would never have made this *mésalliance*. Too much was at
stake."

"Nevertheless he did."

"Do you really believe that possible?"

"Yes. He was in love."

"Very charming, but love is a different thing from politics
and duty. The lives of thousands are involved....It is the
difference between war and peace."

"He must have loved my sister dearly. I can understand.
She was the most attractive person I have ever met. Oh, I
can see you are cynical. You don't believe me."

"I believe she was all you say she was. I have seen her
sister and that makes it easy to imagine."

"You are laughing at me. I know that I am plain and quite
unlike Francine."

He took my hand and kissed it. "You must not think that,"
he said. "I am sure you have as much charm as your sister
but perhaps in a different way."

Once again I firmly removed my hand. "You must not
tease me," I said. "You don't want to talk of this, do you?"

"There is nothing really to say. Your sister and Rudolph
were murdered in the hunting lodge. It was a political murder, in my view. It was someone who wanted the heir out of
the way."

"Well, who would inherit this dukedom...or principality...or
whatever it is? Perhaps he is the murderer."

"It's not as simple as that. The next in line was not in the country at the time."

"Well, those sort of people have agents, don't they?"

"There was a thorough investigation."

"It could not have been so very thorough. I expect they are not very efficient in that little place."

He laughed. "They are, you know. There was a detailed enquiry but nothing could be brought to light."

"I suppose my sister was killed because she happened to be there."

"It looks like it. I am so sorry. What a pity she ever left Greystone Manor."

"If she hadn't, she might have been married to Cousin Arthur...but she never would have done that."

"So...there was another suitor."

"My grandfather wanted the match. I suppose it is rather like your Bruxenstein. He hasn't a dukedom or a principality, but he has a fine old house which has been in the family for generations and he is very rich, I believe."

"So you have the same problems as we have in Bruxenstein."

"Problems created by people's pride. There should be no problems at all. No-one should attempt to choose people's husbands for them. If people love, they should be allowed to marry."

"Well spoken," he cried. "Do you know, we have at last found agreement."

I said, "I shall have to go now. Miss Elton will be looking for me."

"Who is Miss Elton?"

"My governess. She is leaving very shortly. I am considered to be no longer in need of one."

"Almost a woman," he commented.

He was beside me and he laid his hands on my shoulders. I wished he would not touch me; when he did so an incomprehensible desire to stay with him came to me. It was the opposite effect of that which Arthur's flabby hands had on me, but it did occur to me that they both had a habit of using them a good deal.

He drew me to him and kissed me very lightly on the forehead.

"Why did you do that?" I demanded, hastily drawing back and flushing scarlet.

"Because I wanted to."

"People do not kiss strangers."

"We are hardly that. We have met before. We have drunk tea together. I thought that was an English ceremony. If you take tea you are immediately friends."

"You obviously know nothing of English ceremonies. One can take tea with one's bitterest enemies."

"Then I musjudged the situation and you will forgive me."

"I forgive you for that but not for your attitude towards my sister. I know she was married. I have evidence that she was, but it is no use trying to convince you so I will not attempt to do so."

"Evidence?" he said sharply. "What evidence?"

"Letters. Her letters, for one thing."

"Letters to you? In which she insists she was married."

"She didn't insist. She didn't have to. She only had to tell me."

"May I see...these letters?"

I hesitated.

"You have to convince me, you know."

"All right then...."

"Shall we meet here...or would you care to come to the Grange?"

"Here," I answered.

"Tomorrow I shall be here."

I ran out of the wood. When I reached the edge of it I looked back and saw him standing among the trees. There was a strange smile on his lips.

I was in a bemused state for the rest of the day. Miss Elton, who was in the midst of packing, did not notice my abstraction. She would be leaving in a few days and I knew that she was anxious about me, but could really see no practical way out of my difficulties. I wondered whether to tell my grandmother about this man, but for some reason I was reluctant to do so. I did not even know his name. He was over-familiar. How dared he kiss me! What did he think? That all girls here could be lightly kissed and engaged in intimate relationships without marriage?

I stayed up late that night reading the letters. It was all so clear: her ecstasy and her marriage. Hadn't I seen the entry in the register? I should have told that man about this piece of irrefutable evidence. Why hadn't I? Perhaps I had deliberately held it back so that when I did tell him and prove him to be wrong he would be made to feel very humble indeed. Of course Francine had been married. There was her talk of the baby—dear little Cubby. Even suppose she had told me of the marriage because she thought she ought to be, she would never have invented the child. Francine was not the most maternal of women, I was sure; but once she had a child she had loved him and that came over in the letters.

The next day I was early at our meeting place but he was already there.

My heart started to beat faster at the sight of him. I wished that he did not have this effect on me because it made me feel at a disadvantage. He came forward; he bowed, I thought with a certain mockery, and clicking his heels took my hand and kissed it.

"There is no need to stand on ceremony with me," I said.

"Ceremony! This is no ceremony. An ordinary form of greeting in my country. Of course, with elderly ladies and children we often kiss the cheek instead of the hand."

"As I am neither you can at least dispense with that."

"Somewhat regrettably," he said.

But I was determined that I would not allow this rather offensive bantering to intrude on the seriousness of the occasion.

"I have brought the letters to show you," I said. "When you read them you will accept the truth. You will have to."

"Shall we sit down. The ground is a little hard and this is not the most comfortable place for a consultation. You should have come to the house."

"I hardly think that would be right while your employers are away."

"Perhaps not," he said. "Now . . . may I see the letters?"

He took them and began to read them.

I watched him. I suppose it was that excessive masculinity which was affecting. It must have been something like that which happened to Francine. Oh no, that was absurd. She had fallen violently in love. My feelings were quite different. I felt antagonistic towards this man, although I was intensely excited in his presence. I had known few men. One could not count Antonio and the people on the island. I had been far too young then. But few people came to my grandfather's house and I supposed I judged everyone by Cousin Arthur, which meant that they all must seem devastatingly attractive.

I started suddenly. I had the feeling that we were being overlooked. I turned sharply. Did I see a movement among the trees? It must have been imagination. I was in a state of excitement, I realized that. I had been ever since I had met this man...solely because I thought I had fitted in a few more pieces in the jigsaw of mystery concerning the murder in the hunting lodge. A crackle of dry bracken, the sudden flutter of a bird as though it had been disturbed had given me this strange uncanny feeling of being overlooked.

"I fancy someone is nearby watching us," I said.

"Watching us? Why?"

"People do...."

He put down the letters and sprang to his feet. "Where?" he cried. "In which direction?" I was sure then that I heard the sound of hastening footsteps.

"Over there," I said, and he ran off in the direction I had indicated. After a few minutes he came back.

"No sign of anyone," he said.

"Yet, I was sure..."

He smiled at me and, sitting down, picked up the letters. When he had read them he handed them back solemnly to me.

"Your sister thought she would set your mind at rest by telling you she was married."

Now was the moment. "There is something you don't know," I told him triumphantly. "I have definite proof. I have seen the church register."

"What!" That moment had been worth waiting for. He was completely taken aback.

"Oh yes," I went on. "It is there as plain as it could be. So you see you have been absolutely wrong."

"Where?" he asked tersely.

"In Birley Church. Miss Elton and I went to look for it and found it."

"I cannot credit Rudolph for behaving so..."

"It is not for you to credit or discredit. The marriage took place. I can prove it."

"Why did you not tell me before?"

"Because you were so pigheadedly cocksure."

"I see," he said slowly. "Where is this place?"

"At Birley, not far from Dover. You should go there. See it with your own eyes...then perhaps you'll believe it."

"Very well," he said. "I will."

"You can take the train to Dover. It is quite simple. You can get a horse and trap to take you out to Birley. It's about three miles from Dover."

"I will most certainly go."

"And when you have seen it you will come back and apologize to me."

"Abjectly."

He folded up the letters and began, as though absent-mindedly, to put them in his pocket.

"They are mine, remember."

"So they are." He gave them back to me.

I said: "I don't know your name."

"Conrad," he told me.

"Conrad...what?"

"Don't bother with the rest. You would find it unpronounceable."

"I might be able to manage it."

"Never mind now. I should like to be just Conrad to you."

"When will you go to Birley, Conrad?"

"Tomorrow, I think."

"And will you meet me here on the following day?"

"With the greatest pleasure."

I tucked the letters into my bodice.

"I believe," he said, "that you suspect me of planning to steal them."

"Why should I?"

"You are rather suspicious by nature and particularly of me."

He moved towards me and put his hand on the neck of my bodice. I cried out in alarm and he dropped his hand.

"Only teasing," he said. "You have put them in a rather—shall I say tempting spot."

"I think you are impertinent."

"I fear you are right," he said. "Remember I come from that outlandish place of which you had never heard until your sister went there."

My eyes clouded and I started to think of her as she had been on the night she left. He saw it at once and his hands were on my shoulders.

"Forgive me," he said. "I am clumsy as well as impertinent. I know your feelings for your sister. Believe me, I admire them tremendously. I will see you the day after tomorrow.

I shall come prepared, I assure you, to eat humble pie—that is what you call it, is it not?—if you can prove me wrong."

"Then you had better start preparing for that dish immediately. I warn you I shall want abject apologies."

"If you can prove your case you can have them. That's better. You are smiling now...satisfied...complacent. You know you are right, don't you?"

"I do. Goodbye."

"*Au revoir. Auf Wiedersehen.* Not goodbye. I don't like that. It's too final. I should be at all pleased if it were goodbye between us."

I turned and ran off. I was already a little sad because a day must elapse before I saw him again. But the day after tomorrow I should have the satisfaction of seeing his dismay and that would be worth waiting for.

As soon as I entered the house I decided to go and see my grandmother. She would have awakened from her afternoon sleep and would probably be having a cup of tea. I must tell her about Conrad, but I would be careful not to betray to her the effect he had on me. I was being rather silly about that. It merely meant that he was the first man with whom I had ever been on such terms and, as Miss Elton would probably have commented if she had noticed my abstracted state, it was going to my head. That was the case. I was lonely. No one had paid any attention to me except Cousin Arthur, who was acting on my grandfather's instructions, and here was an attractive man attempting to carry on in a rather flirtatious manner with me. Sometimes I felt he was in earnest and really liked me; at others I thought he was laughing at me. Perhaps it was a little of each.

I knocked at my grandmother's door and Agnes Warden came out.

"Oh, it's Miss Philippa," she said. "Your grandmother is sleeping."

"Still? Isn't she having her tea?"

"She had a bit of a turn this afternoon. She's sleeping it off."

"A turn?"

"Well, her heart's not good, you know. She has these turns now and then. They leave her very tired and the only thing is rest after them."

I was disappointed.

I went back to my room and met Miss Elton coming into the corridor.

"I want to leave tomorrow if possible," she said, "instead of waiting until the end of the week. My cousin can meet me and she says we could have a week's holiday before going to our employers. She has arranged for us to stay with a friend of hers. Do you think your grandfather would agree to my leaving tomorrow?"

"I'm sure he would. In any case, you have really ceased to be employed by him."

"But I wouldn't want to upset him. I have my reference to think of."

"I should go to him at once. I am sure it will be all right."

"I will."

She came to my room about ten minutes later looking flushed and pleased.

"He has agreed that I shall go. Oh, Philippa, it is all so exciting, and of course my cousin says it is an easy house and the children are delightful."

"A little different from Greystone. My grandfather is not the best of employers."

"But I had you two girls. I don't think I shall ever feel the same about other pupils."

"About Francine, of course." I felt the sadness overwhelming me again. Miss Elton put her arm about me.

"You too...just as much," she said. "I grew very fond of you both. That is why I am so concerned for you now."

"I shall miss you."

"Philippa, what have you decided? Very soon now..."

"I know. I know....I just cannot think for a moment. I will though. I'll think of something."

"There's so little time."

"Please, Miss Elton, don't worry about me. I have a dream sometimes that I go to that place and find out what's really happened. There's the child, you know."

"You would best forget it. You need to get away from here—unless you are going to agree to your grandfather's wishes."

"Never...never!" I said emphatically. Since I had met Conrad the thought of Cousin Arthur's flabby hands groping for me had become something of a nightmare.

Miss Elton shook her head. I could see she believed that in the end I would accept my fate. Normally I should have talked to her, but because my thoughts were full of Conrad I did not wish to. I did not understand, myself, but somewhere at the back of my mind was the thought that he would provide some sort of solution—just as his fellow countryman had for Francine.

"Well," said Miss Elton, "tomorrow I must say goodbye. It is always hard leaving one's pupils, but this is the hardest wrench."

When she had left me I looked at the bed which had been Francine's and a desolation swept over me. My grandmother was ill; Miss Elton would be gone; I should be alone.

I realized then how I depended on those two.

And yet I could not stop thinking of Conrad.

The next morning Miss Elton left. I clung to her for a last farewell and she was very emotional.

"May everything go right with you," she said fervently.

"And for you," I replied.

Then she was gone.

I went up to see my grandmother. Agnes met me at the door. "You should not stay long," she said. "She is very weak."

I sat by her bed and she smiled at me rather wanly. I longed to tell her about Conrad and the strange feelings he aroused in me. I wanted to discover for myself whether it was due to him or merely because he came from that place where Francine had met her death. But I realized that my grandmother was not quite sure who it was who sat by her bed, and at moments was confusing me with Grace, and as I left her my desolation increased.

I could scarcely wait for Conrad's return. I was in the woods before the appointed time, waiting. He was on time and my heart leaped with excitement as he came striding towards me.

He took both my hands and bowed before he kissed first one and then the other.

"So?" I said.

"I went as we arranged I should," he said. "It's not a bad journey."

"And you saw it?"

He looked at me steadily. "I found the church. The vicar was helpful."

"He was away when Miss Elton and I went. We saw the churchwarden."

He looked at me intently. "You mustn't mind this," he said. "I know you thought you saw this entry—"

"*Thought* I saw it—I did see it! What are you talking about?"

He shook his head. "The vicar showed me the register. There was no entry."

"This is the most absurd nonsense. I saw it. I tell you I saw it."

"No," he insisted. "It was not there. I had the right date. There was no doubt of it. There was no entry."

"You are provoking me."

"I wish I were. I'm sorry to upset you in this way."

"Sorry! You're glad. Besides, it's a lie. You can't say this. I tell you I saw it with my own eyes."

"I'll tell you what I think," he said soothingly. "You wanted to see it. So you imagined it."

"In other words I suffer from delusions and I'm mad. Are you suggesting that?"

He looked at me sadly. "My dear, dear Philippa, I am sorry. Believe me, I wanted to see it. I wanted you to be right."

"I shall go there myself. I'll go again. I'll find it. You must have been looking in the wrong place."

"No. I had the correct date. The date you gave me. If they had been married it would have been there. It is not there, Philippa. It is definitely not there."

"I am going there. I shall lose no time."

"When?" he asked.

"Tomorrow."

"I will come with you. I will show you that you have made a mistake."

"And I will show you that I have not," I said vehemently.

He took my arm but I shook him off.

"Don't take this to heart," he said. "It's over and done with now. Whether she was married or not . . . what difference does it make?"

"It makes a difference to me . . . and the child."

"There was no child," he said. "No marriage . . . no child."

"How dare you suggest my sister was a liar or that I am mad? Go away. . . . Go back to your own country!"

"I fear I shall have to . . . very soon. But first you and I will go there . . . tomorrow."

"Yes," I said determinedly, "tomorrow."

* * *

I had not thought how I was to get away. It had been different when I had gone before. But I was reckless. I could think of nothing but proving Conrad wrong. I told Mrs. Greaves that I was going to look at an old church and was not sure how long I should be away.

"Your grandfather would not want you to go without someone with you," she said.

"I shall have someone with me."

"Who will that be? Miss Sohpia Glencorn?"

I nodded. It was the only way. I did not want a hue and cry before I started.

Conrad was at the station as we had arranged.

As I sat opposite him I thought how pleasant it could have been if we were just taking a trip somewhere together. I studied his face as he sat, his arms folded, his eyes on me.

It was a strong face with firm features and deeply set bluish grey eyes. It was a Nordic face. The blond hair grew back strongly from a high forehead. I could imagine his coming to our shores in one of the tall ships, a Viking conqueror.

"Well," he said, "are you summing me up?"

"Just casually observing," I replied.

"I hope I meet with your approval."

"Does it matter?"

"Enormously."

"You are bantering again. It is because you know what we are going to find when we get to the church. You're trying to make a joke of it. I think it's a very poor joke."

He leaned forward and laid his hand on my knee. "I would not dream of joking about a subject which is so near to your heart," he said seriously. "I don't want you to feel too badly when..."

"Shall we talk of something else?"

"The weather? It is quite a pleasant day for the time of the year. Now in my country it is not so warm in the winter. I believe it is because you are singularly blessed by the Gulf Stream, one of God's gifts to the English."

"I think it would be better to be silent."

"Just as you wish. My great desire is to please you now as always...and forever."

I closed my eyes. His words touched a deep chord in me. Always and forever. It sounded as though our relationship was not the transient one that I had thought it to be and the idea lifted my spirits considerably.

As we chuffed along in silence his eyes remained on me. I looked out of the window but I scarcely noticed the passing scenery. At length I smelt the tang of the sea and there was the approach to the town...the white cliffs again, the view of the castle which medieval kings had called the gateway to England.

We made our way to the inn, for he insisted that we have some food.

"It's necessary if we take the trap," he said. "Besides you need a little refreshment."

"I could eat nothing," I said.

"But I could," he replied, "and you will."

We had the bread and cheese again with cider. I did manage to eat a little.

"There, you see," he commented. "I know what is good for you."

"How soon can we start?" I asked.

"Patience," he retorted. "Do you know, in different circumstances I should be enjoying this thoroughly. Perhaps you and I can take some trips round the countryside. What do you say?"

"My grandfather would never allow it."

"Has he allowed this?"

"There was a little...subterfuge."

"Oh, you are capable of intrigue then?"

"I had to come," I said. "I would not have stayed away for anything."

"You are so vehement. I like it. In fact, Miss Philippa, there is so much I like about you. I feel I know very little, though, and there is so much more to know. It would be a glorious voyage of discovery."

"I am afraid you would find it rather dull."

"What a woman for contradictions you are! One minute you are raging against me for not having a high opinion of your mental powers and then next you are telling me how unworthy you are for study. Now what am I to make of you?"

"I should give up the study if I were you."

"But I am so intrigued."

"Do you think we have finished now?"

"Such impatience!" he murmured.

We went out to the trap and I could scarcely contain my impatience as we approached Birley Church.

"We'll go first to the vicarage and find that charming

vicar," he said. "He was so helpful to me. I shall have to give a large donation to the upkeep of the church."

We went to the vicarage which was almost as old as the church. A woman who was obviously the vicar's wife came to the door and said we were lucky. The vicar had just come in.

We went into a drawing room—shabby but cosy. The vicar greeted Conrad warmly.

"It is a pleasure to see you again," he said.

"I have another request," replied Conrad. "We want to look at that register again."

"That's no problem. Did you have the wrong date?"

My heart was beating fast. I knew there had been a mistake somewhere and I believed I was on the verge of discovering what it was.

"I'm not sure," said Conrad. "It might have been. This is Miss Ewell, who is particularly interested. She has been here before."

"I didn't see you then," I said to the vicar. "You were away. I saw your churchwarden."

"Oh yes, Thomas Borton. I was away for a while. That is not so long ago. Well, if you come into the church you can see what you want."

We made our way to the church. There was the familiar smell of damp, old hymn books and that unusual furniture polish.

We went into the vestry and when the register was produced eagerly I turned the pages. I stared. It was not there. There had been no wedding on that date.

I stammered: "There is a mistake..."

Conrad was beside me. He had slipped his arm through mine but I threw him off impatiently. I looked from him to the vicar.

"But I saw it," I went on. "It was here....It was in the book—"

"No," said the vicar. "That could not be. There is a mistake in the date, I think. Are you sure you have the right year?"

"I know I have. I know when it happened. The bride was my sister."

The vicar looked shaken.

I went on: "You must remember it. It would have been a rather hasty wedding—"

"I was not here at the time. I took over the living only two years ago."

"It *was* here," I could only insist. "I saw it.... It was for anyone to read."

"There must be some mistake. You will find you have the wrong date."

"Yes," said Conrad, close to me. "It's a mistake. I'm sorry. But you insisted on seeing for yourself."

"The churchwarden brought us here," I cried. "He would remember. He showed us the book. He was here while we found it. Where is the churchwarden? I must see him. He will remember."

"There's no need for that," said Conrad. "It's not here. It was a mistake. You thought you saw it..."

"One does not think one sees things! I saw it, I tell you. I want to see the churchwarden."

"I am sure that is possible," the vicar told us. "He lives in the village. His house is number six, the Street. There is only one street worthy of the name in the village."

"We will go and see him at once," I said.

Conrad turned to the vicar. "You have been most helpful," he said.

"I am sorry there has been this upset."

I turned back to the register and looked again. I was trying to conjure up what I had seen on that day with Miss Elton. It was no good. It was simply not there.

Conrad put two sovereigns into the offertory box in the porch as we went out and the vicar was most grateful.

"You'll find Tom Borton in his garden, I daresay. He's a great gardener."

It was not difficult to find him. He came out to see us, looking mildly curious.

"The vicar gave us your address," Conrad told him. "Miss Ewell here is very anxious to see you."

As he turned to me there was no recognition in his eyes.

I said, "You remember I came to see you not long ago. There was a lady with me."

He wrinkled his eyes and flicked a fly off the sleeve of his coat.

"You must remember," I persisted. "We looked at the records in the vestry. You showed us...and I found what I wanted."

"We get people now and then to look at the records.... Not often...but now and then."

"So you do remember. The vicar was away...and we saw you in the church..."

He shook his head. "I can't say as how I remember."

"But you must. You were there. You *must* remember."

"I'm afraid I can't remember anything about it."

"I recognized you at once."

He smiled. "I can't say as I remember ever seeing you before Miss...er, Ewell, did you say?"

"Well," put in Conrad, "we're sorry we troubled you."

"Oh, that's all right sir. Sorry I couldn't have been better help. I think the young lady's thinking of something else. I reckon I never saw her before in all my life."

I was led away feeling bewildered. I felt that I was living in some sort of nightmare from which I must soon wake up.

"Come, we must get our train," said Conrad.

With five minutes to spare, we sat in the station. He had taken my arm and was holding it tightly. "You mustn't be too upset," he said.

"I am upset. How can I help it? I saw it clearly and that man was lying. Why? He must have remembered seeing me. He said himself that not many people come to look at the registers."

"Listen, Philippa, strange things happen to us all at times. What happened to you was a sort of hallucination."

"How dare you say that?"

"What other explanation is there?"

"I don't know. But I'm going to find out."

The train came in and we got into it. We had a carriage to ourselves for which I was grateful. I felt exhausted with emotion and a certain fear. I was almost beginning to believe that I had imagined the whole thing. Miss Elton had gone so I could not ask her. She had looked at the register with me. But had she actually seen the entry? I wasn't sure. All I remembered was seeing it myself and calling out in triumph. I tried to reconstruct the scene. I could not remember her actually standing beside me and looking at the book.

But the churchwarden had said he had never seen me before, yet he showed the register rarely. Surely he *must* have remembered.

Conrad came and sat beside me and put an arm about me. I was amazed that I could find some comfort from the action.

He said, "Listen to me, Philippa. The entry is not there. It's all over now. Your sister is dead. If you had found that entry it would not have brought her back to life. It is a sad episode, but it is over now. You have your own life to live."

I was not listening to him. I just felt the comfort of his being near me and I did not want to move away.

When we left the station he brought me as far as the woods. I would not let him come any nearer. There would be a great deal of explaining to do if I were seen with a man.

As I went into the Manor, Mrs. Greaves was standing at the top of the staircase.

"Is that you, Miss Philippa?" she said. "You are back. What a relief. Your grandmother was taken very ill this afternoon."

She was looking at me steadily.

I said, "She's dead, isn't she?"

And she nodded.

Suspected
of Murder

I was in a bewildered state. I had schooled myself to offer some explanation for my absence, but it was not needed. My grandmother's death had meant that I had not been missed.

"She slipped away quietly in her sleep," Mrs. Greaves told me.

It must have been just at the time when I was coming face to face with the blank register.

"She didn't ask for me?" I said.

"Why, Miss, she has not been conscious at all through the day."

I left her and went up to my bedroom. I stood in the middle of the room and let the desolation sweep over me. It was a feeling of utter loneliness. I was losing everyone. Francine, Daisy, Miss Elton and now my grandmother. It was as though a cruel fate was robbing me of everyone I cared for.

The thought of Conrad suddenly came to me. He had been kind. I was sure he had been really sorry that we could not find the entry.

We met at dinner that night—myself, my grandfather and Cousin Arthur.

My grandfather discussed funeral arrangements and said the family vault would be opened. Cousin Arthur should go to see the vicar. Our grandfather couldn't endure the man. Besides, he might meet Grace or her husband.

Cousin Arthur said, "I am only too happy to be of assistance to you, Uncle."

"You are always that, Arthur," replied my grandfather.

Arthur lowered his head and looked as pleased as the circumstances and his overwhelming humility would let him.

"It's a great blow to us all," went on my grandfather, "but life has to go on. The last thing she would have wished would be for us to upset the lives of those who have to go on living. We must think of what she would wish."

I thought that it would be the first time he had ever done that. Did people have to be dead to get some consideration?

The coffin had been brought to the house—a magnificent affair of polished mahogany and lots of ornamental brass; it was placed in the room next to my grandfather's. She was closer to him there than she had been for many years. The funeral was to take place in five days' time. Meanwhile she lay there, and all the servants went one by one to pay their last respects.

All through the night candles burned in that room. There were three at the head of the coffin and three at the foot.

I went in to see her. The smell of the wood and the memory of that room of death would remain with me forever. There was nothing eerie about it. She lay there—just her face visible, and a starched cap hid her hair. She looked young and beautiful. She must have been something like that when she first came to Greystone Manor as a bride.... One could not be afraid even though the room was full of shadows cast by the flickering candle-light. She had been so good and kind in her life, how could anyone fear her in death?

There was just a terrible desolation—a frightening sense of loss, and the understanding, as never before, how very much alone I was in the world.

Two days later I went to the woods. I sat under a tree hoping that Conrad would come. This was the hour when I took my walk. Would he think enough of me to come?

It seemed that he did, and my spirits lifted when I saw him coming towards me.

He threw himself down beside me and, taking my hand, kissed it. "How are you feeling?" he asked.

I said: "When I reached home I learned that my grandmother had died."

"Was it unexpected?"

"I suppose not. She was old and an invalid and she had been very unwell for some days. But it was a great shock, particularly as..."

"Tell me," he said gently.

"Everyone has gone," I said. "There was my sister and Daisy the maid, who was a friend too. Then Miss Elton and now my grandmother. There is no-one left."

"My dear little girl..."

For once I did not mind being called a little girl. He went on softly: "How old are you?"

"I shall soon be seventeen."

"So young...and so troubled," he murmured.

"If my parents had not died everything would have been different. We should have stayed on the island. We were happy there. Francine would never have died. I should not be here alone...without anyone."

"What about your grandfather?"

I laughed bitterly. "He will force me to marry Cousin Arthur."

"Force you! You do not seem to me the sort of person who would be forced."

"I have always said I wouldn't be, but I should have done something. Miss Elton said I should. I should have found some post. But who would employ someone of my age?"

"You are certainly young," he agreed. "And of course you are not exactly fond of Cousin Arthur."

"I hate Cousin Arthur."

"Why?"

"If you saw him you would understand. Francine hated him. She was to marry him. She was the elder, you see, but she married Rudolph. They *did* marry, I know they did."

"Let us consider your problem. It really is of the greater importance."

"When I am seventeen my grandfather wants me to marry Cousin Arthur, and I shall soon be seventeen. Then it will be a case of 'Marry Arthur or get out.' I'd like to get out, but where would I go? I shall have to take a post. If only I were say—two years older... You see what I mean?"

"I do indeed."

"My grandmother was kind and good and understanding. I could talk to her. Now there is no-one."

"Well, I'm here," he said.

"You!"

"Yes. My poor little girl, I don't like to see you unhappy. I like you full of fire raging against me...yes. Though I should prefer to see you tender, perhaps. But I do not like to see you in despair."

"I am in despair. I wanted to talk to my grandmother. I wanted to tell her about the register. There is no-one to talk to now. I am all alone."

He put his arms round me and held me tightly. He rocked me gently and kissed my forehead, the tip of my nose and then my lips. I was almost happy in those moments.

I drew back from him a little, afraid of my emotions. It was extraordinary that I could feel thus towards someone who had just proved me wrong on a matter so near my heart.

I was confused, not knowing which way to turn.

He said gently, "You are not alone, you know. I am here. I am your friend."

"My friend!" I cried. "Why, you have tried to destroy my belief in my sanity."

"You are not being fair. All I did was confront you with the truth. The truth must always be looked at...straight in the face...even when it is unpleasant."

"That was not the truth. There's some explanation. I wish I knew what it was."

"I can tell you this, my dear Philippa. You are so concerned with the past that you are letting the dangers of the present creep up on you. What are you going to do about Cousin Arthur?"

"I will never marry him."

"Then...when your grandfather turns you out...what then?"

"While I have been sitting here it has occurred to me that my grandmother's death will delay matters a little. There could not be a wedding following so close on a funeral, could there? My grandfather would always observe the conventions."

"So you think the evil day is postponed."

"It will give me time to find a way out. My Aunt Grace would help me. She escaped from Greystone Manor and is very happy now. Perhaps I could stay a while at the vicarage."

"A ray of hope," he said. "And how do you think you will enjoy going into some strange household with the status of a servant after the way in which you have lived?"

"I have not lived so happily at Greystone Manor. I have always felt something of a captive here. Francine felt it too. So I have not such a glorious past to look back on. Besides, I might be a governess. They are not servants...exactly."

"Somewhere in between," he said. "Poor, poor Philippa. It's a grim prospect which lies before you."

I shivered and he held me closer.

"I have to tell you," he went on, "that I am leaving England tomorrow."

I was completely shattered and unable to speak. I just stared wretchedly ahead of me. Everyone was going. I should be left to the mercy of my grandfather and Cousin Arthur.

"Do I discern that you are a little sorry that I am going?"

"It has been comforting talking to you."

"And I am forgiven for the part I played in that disastrous register affair?"

"It wasn't your fault. I don't blame you."

"I thought you hated me for it."

"I am not quite as foolish as that."

"And you promise me that you are going to forget it? You are going to stop looking back?"

"I couldn't stop myself wanting to know. She is my sister."

"I know. I understand perfectly. Dear Philippa, don't despair. Something will turn up for you. I'm sorry I have to go. It's vital that I should."

"I suppose you have been called back by your employers?"

"That's the idea. But I have one more day. We'll meet tomorrow. I'm going to try to come up with a solution to your troubles."

"How could you possibly do that?"

"I'm something of a magician," he said. "Didn't you guess that? I'm not quite what I seem?"

I gave a forced laugh. I was really miserable because he was going and I did not want him to know how deeply I felt about it.

"I'm going to save you from the arms of Cousin Arthur, Philippa...if you'll let me."

"I don't think you have enough magic for that."

"We'll see. Will you trust me?" He rose to his feet. "I have to go now."

He held out a hand and pulled me up. We stood close to each other. Then his arms were round me. His kisses had changed. They were bewildering, a little frightening, and I wanted them to go on.

When he released me he was laughing. "I think you are a little more kindly disposed towards me now," he said.

"I don't know what I feel...."

"There is a little time left to us," he replied. "Will you trust me?"

"What a strange question. Should I?"

"No," he answered. "Never trust anyone. Particularly people you know nothing about."

"You are warning me?"

He nodded. "Preparing you, perhaps."

"You do sound mysterious. At one moment you are going to help me and the next you are warning me against you."

"Life is full of contradictions. Will you meet me here tomorrow? I may have a solution. It will of course depend on you."

"I will be here tomorrow."

He took my chin in his hands and said: *"Nil desperandum."* Then he kissed me lightly and walked with me to the edge of the wood where we parted.

I went into the house past the chamber of death up to my bedroom and threw myself on Francine's bed, which seemed to bring her nearer to me.

There was no doubt about it. Conrad excited me, and I wanted to be with him. When I was, I could forget almost everything else.

I could not bear to be in that house of death and yet the sense of loneliness had lifted a little. Conrad would meet me tomorrow and he had said he would find a solution. I could not believe this was possible and yet it was a comforting thought. Being with him was a sort of opiate and I was in such a desperate state that I was ready to grasp at anything.

I could not endure to stay in the house so I went out into the garden, and while I was there one of the Emms boys came to me.

He said: "I was told to give you this when no one was looking, Miss."

I seized it.

"Who...?" I began.

"From the Grange, Miss."

"Thank you," I said.

I slit the envelope and took out a thick white paper with a golden crest at the top. Grange paper, I thought; and then I was reading what had been written.

Philippa,
I have to leave early tomorrow morning. I must see you before I go. Please come this evening, can you, at ten o'clock. I'll be waiting for you in the Grange shrubbery.

C.

My hands were trembling. So he was going tomorrow. He had said he would find a solution for me. Could it be possible?

I should have to slip out of the house and leave the door unlocked. No. That might be discovered. There was a window in the courtyard which was low. If I left that unlatched I could easily get through it . . . just in case when I returned the door had been locked.

I must see him.

I don't know how I lived through the rest of that day. I pleaded a headache and did not join my grandfather and cousin for dinner. It seemed a reasonable enough excuse, for the normal routine of the household was naturally somewhat disrupted on account of my grandmother's death and the preparations for the funeral.

I had tested the courtyard window. People rarely went past it, so it should be safe enough.

At a quarter to ten I was on my way. He was waiting for me in the shrubbery and when he saw me he caught me in his arms and held me against him.

"We'll go into the house," he said.

"Should we?" I asked.

"Why not?"

"It isn't your house. You're only the equerry."

"Shall we say I'm in charge. Come along."

We walked into the Grange, and as we passed through the hall I looked up anxiously at the high holes in the wall which I knew could be peered through in the solarium.

"No one will see us," he whispered. "They are all asleep. They have had a busy day preparing for departure."

"Are they all going tomorrow?"

"They'll be leaving in a day or so."

We went up the stairs. "Where are we going?" I asked. "To the *Weinzimmer?*"

"You'll see."

He threw open a door and we entered a room in which a fire was burning. It was a large room with heavy velvet curtains. I noticed the alcove in which was a four-poster bed.

"Whose room is this?" I asked quickly.

"Mine," he answered. "We're safe here."

"I don't understand."

"You will. Come and sit down. I have some excellent wine here. I want you to try it."

"I know nothing of wine."

"Surely you drink it at Greystone Manor?"

"My grandfather always decides what it shall be and everyone else has to drink it and like it."

"A despot, your grandfather."

"What is it you have to say to me?"

"I am going away. I thought I had to see you."

"Yes," I said, "you told me."

He took my hand and, sitting down in a large thronelike chair, he drew me down to him so that I was sitting on his knees.

"You should not be afraid," he said quietly. "There is nothing to fear. Your welfare will be my greatest concern from now on."

"You say the most extraordinary things. I thought I had come here to say goodbye to you."

"I am hoping you won't do that."

"How could it be otherwise?"

"The difficulties are not insurmountable."

His hands were on my neck, caressing it gently. I was beginning to feel that I wanted to stay in this room forever.

"How do you feel about me?" he asked.

I tried to free myself from his searching hands.

"We hardly know each other," I stammered. "You're not...English."

"Is that a great handicap?"

"Of course not, but it means—"

"What?"

"That we probably think differently about everything. I would rather sit on a chair and hear what it is you have to say to me."

"But I would rather you stayed here...near me. Philippa, you must know that I am falling in love with you."

I felt dizzy with sudden happiness, as though I were slipping into a deep pool of contentment, but I was conscious of warning voices within me. It was a dangerous pool.

"Philippa," he went on. "It's rather a dignified name." He repeated it. "Philippa."

I said, "My family always called me Pippa."

"Pippa. Short for Philippa. I like it. It recalls a poem called 'Pippa's Song'...or 'Pippa Passes.' You see, I may not be English but I was educated here. I know my Browning. 'God's in his Heaven—All's right with the world.' That's Pippa's Song. Is it true for you?"

"You know very well that it is far from being so."

"So perhaps I could make it so. I should be very happy if I could. 'All's right with the world.' I want you to tell me that that is the case."

"Yet you are going away and I shall not see you after tonight."

"That is what I have to talk to you about, because whether you continue to see me or not depends on you."

"I don't understand you."

"It's simple. I could take you with me."

"Take me to—"

"That's right. Take you back with me."

"How could that possibly be?"

"Quite easily. We meet tomorrow at the station. We do not go to Dover as we did before. We go to London and from there to Harwich. We take ship and after our journey across the sea we take another train in due course we come to my home. What do you say?"

"You are teasing me."

"I swear I'm not. I want you with me. Don't you understand I have fallen in love with you?"

"But...how could I possibly come with you?"

"How could you not?"

"My grandfather would never agree."

"I thought we were going to outwit Grandfather and Cousin Arthur. So we don't need the agreement of either of them. Pippa, let me show you how I love you."

"I...don't..."

"Then let me teach you," he said.

He had unbuttoned my bodice. I put my hands up to stop

him, but he took them and began to kiss them. I was afraid and yet overcome by an excitement such as I had never known before. Everything seemed to fade away...the past...the future...everything that frightened me. There was nothing but this moment. He was kissing me as he took off my bodice.

"What is happening..." I stammered. "I must go...."

But I made no attempt to. I was overwhelmed by an irresistible longing.

He kept telling me that he loved me, that I had nothing to fear. We were going to be together forever and ever. I could forget my grandfather, forget Cousin Arthur. They were in the past. There was nothing else that mattered except this wonderful love of ours.

The contrast to all I had felt since Francine had gone was so great that I had to shut out everything but this moment. There was one part of me that was trying to reason, but I wouldn't listen.

"I must go now..." I began; and I heard him laugh softly and then I was in the four-poster bed and he was there with me. All the time he was murmuring endearments and I was shocked and shattered and overwhelmed with delight.

Afterwards he just lay still, holding me. I was trembling and very happy and in an odd way defiant, telling myself that I wouldn't have it different if I had a chance to go back.

He stroked my hair and told me I was beautiful, adorable and that he would love me forever.

"Nothing like this has ever happened to me before," I said.

"I know," he answered. "Is it not wonderful to be together like this? Come, little Pippa, tell me the truth?"

I told him it was.

"And you have no regrets?"

"No," I said firmly. "No."

Then he kissed me and made love to me again, and this time it was different; the shock was gone and there was a different kind of ecstasy. I realized that my cheeks were wet, so I must have wept, for he kissed my tears away and said he had never been so happy in his life.

He got up and put on a silk robe of blue with gold figures on it. The blue matched his eyes and he looked like one of the Norse gods.

"Are you mortal?" I asked, "or are you Thor or Odin or one of the gods or perhaps heroes of the Norsemen?"

"You know something of our mythology, I see."

"Francine and I used to read of it with Miss Elton."

"Who would you like me to be—Sigurd? I always thought he was a bit foolish to drink the potion and marry Gudrun when his true love was Brunhild, didn't you?"

"Yes," I answered. "Very foolish."

"Oh, little Pippa, we are going to be so very happy." He went to the table and poured out more wine. "Refreshment after our exertions," he said. "It will give us strength to renew them."

I laughed. Something was happening to me. I drank the wine. He seemed to grow taller than ever and I felt a little dizzy.

I said: "It's the wine."

Then his arms were round me and we were caught up again in our love.

That was a night of awakening for me. I was no longer a child, no longer a virgin. I slept a little and when I awoke the effect of the wine was no longer with me.

I sat up hastily and looked at Conrad. He stirred and reached for me. As though to warn that the magic night was over, the church clock struck four. Four o'clock in the morning and I had been out since ten!

I touched my naked body in dismay. My clothes were lying on the floor.

I cried out, "I must go!"

He was wide awake now. He put his arms round me.

"There's nothing to be afraid of. You are coming with me."

I said, "Where shall we be married...in a church like Francine?"

He was looking at me in silence. Then he smiled and drew me to him. "Pippa," he said, "there can't be a marriage any more than there could be for Francine."

"But we have..."

My eyes took in the disorder of the bed and the man naked beside me. There were memories of the night we had spent together, the empty wine bottle, the ashes in the fireplace.

He smiled gently.

"I love you," he said. "I will take you with me. I will care for you always. We will have children perhaps. Oh, you will have a wonderful life, Pippa. You will lack for nothing."

"But we *must* marry," I said foolishly. "I thought that was what you meant when you said you loved me."

He smiled, still tender but just faintly cynically I thought. "Love and marriage don't always go together."

"But I cannot be...with you like this...if I am not your wife."

"But you can and you have proved it, for you have."

— "But—it is impossible."

"In the world of Greystone Manor perhaps. We are leaving that behind us and everything will be different now. I would to God I could marry you. That would make me very happy. But I am already as good as married."

"You mean you have a wife?"

He nodded. "You could say that. That is how it is in my country. Wives are chosen for us and we go through a ceremony which is tantamount to marriage."

"Then you should never have deceived me into thinking that we should be married."

"I did not deceive you. Marriage was not mentioned."

"But I thought that we were going to be. I thought that was what it all *meant*.... You said you would take me away with you."

"Everything I have said I would do, I will do. The one thing I cannot do is marry you."

"Then what are you proposing? That I should be your mistress?"

"Some would say this is what you already are."

I covered my face with my hands. Then I was off the bed and searching for my clothes.

"Pippa," he said, "be sensible. I love you. I want you with me all the time. Please, dearest Pippa, you must understand."

"Yes, I do understand. You do this sort of thing because it amuses you. You do not love me. I am just a light o' love. I believe that is what they call it."

"A rather old-fashioned expression, I believe."

"Please do not joke. I see I have been foolish again. You enjoy making me seem so. First the entry. It wasn't the right register, was it? You arranged that."

"I assure you I did no such thing."

"You planned this. You gave me that wine...and now—you have ruined me."

"My dear child, you talk like a character in a cheap melodrama."

"I am cheap perhaps...cheaply come by. I succumbed very

readily, did I not? And you took advantage of that ... and now you say you have a wife. I don't believe you."

"Once again I assure you it is true. Pippa, you must believe that if this had not been so I should have asked you to marry me. I am sure you must see that what is between us will grow and grow.... It will be the sort of love which is the most worthwhile thing in the whole world."

I was so miserable. My puritanical upbringing at Greystone made me see myself as ruined, a fallen woman.

"Listen to me," he said. "Come away with me. I will show you a new life. There is more to relationships between two people than signing a name in a register. I love you. We can have a wonderful life together."

"And your wife?"

"That is something apart."

"You are cruel and cynical."

"I am realistic. I was involved in this marriage for family reasons. It is a marriage of convenience. That is accepted. It is not meant to prevent my loving someone else—someone who could become dearer to me than anyone on earth. You don't believe me, do you?"

"No," I replied. "I have heard of men like you. I did not think of that in the beginning. I was carried away."

His arms were round me once more. He said, "You are adorable. You love me, you see. You wanted me. You did not say then, 'When are you going to marry me?' That did not come into your head."

"I realize I know very little about the ways of the world."

"Then come with me and learn. Customs are made for men and women, not men and women for customs."

"I could not take your view of life."

I had started to dress. He said, "What are you going to do? Will you be at the station this morning?"

"How could I? It would be wrong."

"So you will let me go ... alone?"

"What alternative have I?"

"Come live with me and be my love, and we will all the pleasures prove! Another of your English poets. You see, I know them well. Oh, little Pippa, you are a child still ... in spite of the fact that I have made a woman of you. You have so much to learn. If you do not come with me today you will regret it all your life."

"I could regret it if I came."

"That is a chance we must take in life. Pippa, take your chance. Do what you want to do."

"But I know it would be wrong."

"Throw away your conventions, Pippa. Throw them away and learn to live."

"I must go back," I said.

"I will take you back."

"No..."

"But I will. Give me a moment."

I stood there watching him and there were wild doubts in my heart. I was seeing myself setting out for the station. He would be there. We would board the train together...to love and adventure. It was like Francine's story repeating itself.

"Come." He slipped his arm through mine and as he did so he kissed me tenderly. "My darling," he went on, "I promise you you will never regret."

It seemed that Francine was very close to me then. And what of the entry in the register? Had I really seen it? Had Francine had to face the same dilemma? I felt lost and bewildered and very inexperienced.

We came out into the cool air of the early morning.

"You should go," I said. "You should not be seen with me."

"Let us hope no one sees you returning at this hour of the morning."

He was holding my hand firmly against him. "This morning," he said. "Ten o'clock at the station. Be careful. We'll get on the train separately. I shall have your ticket."

I drew myself away and ran. My heart was beating wildly as I came into the courtyard. By good fortune the window was as I had left it. I scrambled through and closed it, and hurrying through into the hall started up the stairs.

Suddenly I felt myself go cold with apprehension. Mrs. Greaves was standing on the top stair watching me. She was in dressing gown and slippers and her hair was in iron curlers.

She cried out, "Oh, Miss Philippa. You gave me a shock, you did. I thought I heard someone. Wherever have you been?"

"I—I couldn't rest. I went for a little walk in the gardens."

She looked disbelievingly at my tousled hair. I was sure I must have appeared rather strange.

I sped past her as she stood aside and once in my room I sank onto my bed. I felt bruised and bewildered and was trying not to look ahead to what the future held.

* * *

I think I must have slept at last, for I was physically and mentally exhausted. I awoke startled and saw that it was nine o'clock. I lay in bed thinking of the events of last night and I longed to be with him. I wanted to forget my scruples and go with him. I wouldn't care if it was wrong, if it was not all against my upbringing. I just wanted to be with him.

It was all I could do to restrain myself from throwing a few things together and running to the station. What did it matter if we could not marry? I had already been a wife to him. If only Francine could have been with me! She would have said, "You must go with him!" Francine would have gone. Hadn't she gone with Rudolph? Was it similar? Had her assertions that she had married been a fabrication, a sop to the conventions? Had I imagined I had seen that entry in the register? Life was becoming like a fantastic dream.

If Miss Elton had been here she would have brought a certain sanity to the situation. I could imagine her folding her hands together and saying, "Of course you cannot go and live with a man who will not marry you." And I know I should have felt that was not only right but the only possible answer.

Oh, but I wanted to go. How desperately I wanted to!

It was nine-thirty. Too late now.

There was a knock on the door. It was one of the maids. "Miss Philippa, are you not well?"

"I have such a headache," I replied.

"I thought you had. I told Sir Matthew that you weren't feeling well. He looked quite concerned."

"Thank you, Amy."

"Would you like something brought up, miss?"

"Nothing thanks. I'll get up later."

Twenty more minutes to ten o'clock. Yes, it was too late. I could never get there in time. I pictured him at the station, waiting for me, hoping, longing perhaps. He was fond of me. I was sure of that.

And when the train left and I had not joined him? Perhaps he would shrug his shoulders. "A pity," he would say. "I liked her. I could have enjoyed teaching her to be a woman. But she did not come. She lacked the courage. She's a conventional little mouse, that's all. It is a pity—but that is how it is."

All I would be to him was an episode in his life.

As equerry to the Grand Duke or the Margrave or something like that he would live a romantic life among the mountains, attending ceremonial occasions in some old *schloss*.

I wanted to be with him so much.

Ten o'clock struck stridently, it seemed, triumphantly. Too late. Virtue had prevailed.

I went through the day in a bemused state. At dinner my grandfather was quite solicitous and I had never known him to be so gracious before. He enquired about my headache and said he was glad to see that I had obviously recovered. After dinner he would like a word with me in his study.

Oddly enough my thoughts were so very much with Conrad that it did not immediately occur to me that the moment I had been dreading for so long had come, and even when he received me in the study as graciously as he had at dinner, I did not think of it. He was smiling kindly, not dreaming for a moment that he would find any obstruction to his plans.

He stood up, his hands in his pockets rather as though he were addressing a public meeting.

"This house is sadly bereaved," he said. "Your poor grandmother lies in her coffin and there is a great sadness on us all. But she would be the last to expect life to stand still merely because she had left it. She would be the first to wish us to go on with our lives and perhaps bring a little lightness into the gloom which is so dark at this time."

I was scarcely listening to him. My thoughts were still with Conrad.

"I had planned a great celebration for your seventeenth birthday, your passing into womanhood."

I wanted to shout: I am already there, Grandfather. I spent a glorious night in the Grange with the most wonderful lover, and now he has gone and I never felt so desolate in my life...not even when Francine went.

"That will not be seemly in the circumstances," my grandfather was going on. "Your grandmother's death"—he sounded a little peevish as though it were most inconsiderate of her to die at such a time—"yes, your grandmother's death precludes that. Still, I thought on the occasion we would have a dinner party with friends...and the announcement could be made then."

"The announcement!"

"You know what my wishes are for you and your Cousin Arthur. His coincide with mine as I am sure yours will. I see no reason for a delay just because we have a death in the family. Of course the ceremonies will have to be conducted more quietly than I had at first thought...but there is no reason why we should delay. We shall announce the engagement on your seventeenth birthday. I always believed long engagements were a mistake. You can be married within three months, say. That will give everyone the time they need for preparations."

I heard myself speaking then and it was as though my voice was disembodied and didn't belong to me.

"You are making a mistake, Grandfather, if you think I am going to marry Cousin Arthur."

"What?" he cried.

"I said I have no intention of marrying Cousin Arthur."

"You have gone mad."

"No. I never intended to marry him any more than my sister did."

"Don't talk about your sister to me. She was a harlot and we are well rid of her. I should not have wished her to be the mother of my heirs."

"She was no harlot," I retorted vehemently. "She was a woman who would not be forced into marriage...any more than I will."

"I tell you," he cried, and he was so incensed that he was shouting at me, "you will do as I say or you will not continue to live under my roof."

"Then if that is so," I said wearily, "I must leave here."

"All this time I have nurtured a viper in my bosom!"

I could not stop myself laughing hysterically. The cliché hardly fitted the case and the idea of my grandfather nursing anything in his bosom seemed hilariously funny.

"You brazen girl," he shouted. "How dare you! I think you have taken leave of your senses. Let me tell you you will regret this. I had made plans for you. I had left you well provided for in my will when you married Arthur. I shall send for my lawyers tomorrow morning. Not a penny shall you have. You are throwing away everything, do you understand? This house...a fine husband..."

"Not everything, Grandfather," I said. "I shall have my freedom."

"Freedom? Freedom to do what? Starve? Or take some menial post. For that is the choice you will have, my girl. You will not stay under my roof, living a life of luxury. I had brought you here from a savage place... I have educated you... fed you..."

"I *am* your granddaughter, remember."

"It is something I wish to forget." His voice was raised and I wondered who was listening. I was sure the servants could hear it all."

His mood changed suddenly. He was almost placating. "Now perhaps you have not given enough thought to this prospect... a glorious one. Perhaps you have spoken rather hastily...."

"No," I said firmly. "That is not so. I have known what was in your mind and have given much thought to the matter. In no circumstances will I marry Cousin Arthur."

"Get out!" he cried. "Get out... before I do you an injury. You will leave here tomorrow. I shall see my lawyer at once to make sure that you never benefit from anything of mine... ever. You will be penniless... penniless I tell you. I shall make sure of that."

I turned to the door and went out, my head high, my eyes blazing. As I came into the corridor I heard a scuffle and a rustling so I knew that we had been overheard.

I went to the stairs and mounted them. So it had come. Everything was happening at once. I was alone and tomorrow I should be homeless. I had no notion of where I should go or what I should do.

I opened the door of the room next to my grandfather's bedroom and in which the body of my grandmother lay in her coffin. The candles had been freshly lighted. They would all be replenished before the household retired and would burn through the night.

I stood on the threshold and looked at that peaceful face and I murmured: "Oh, Grandmother dear, why did you not live to talk to me, to advise me what to do? Why did you leave me alone and desolate? Help me. Please help me. Tell me what I should do."

How still it was in that room, and yet somehow I did feel a certain peace. I could almost believe that the cold lips smiled at me reassuringly.

I awoke from my sleep. It was dark and I wondered what had awakened me. When I had retured for the night I had lain awake for a long time wondering what the next day would bring, and where I should go when I left Greystone Manor.

Then, from very exhaustion, I must have fallen into a heavy sleep.

Now I sat up in bed. I could smell something strange and I heard a sound which I did not immediately recognize.

I listened intently—and then I was out of bed.

It was fire!

I thrust my feet into my slippers and ran.

My grandfather's room was at the end of the corridor and next to it was that one in which my grandmother had lain in her coffin. Then as I stood there I saw the tongue of flame creeping along the top of the door.

"Fire!" I shouted. "Fire!"

I ran towards my grandfather's room and as I did so Cousin Arthur appeared.

"What is it?" he cried; and then, realizing: "Oh—God help us."

"There is a fire in my grandfather's room," I called to him.

By this time several of the servants were on the scene. Cousin Arthur had opened the door of my grandfather's room and as he did so the flames burst out.

"Give the alarm!" shouted Cousin Arthur. "Keep away from the room. It's ablaze. The room next to it too."

One of the footmen was already making his way through the smoke and flames. He had disappeared into my grandfather's room and when he came out he was dragging my grandfather along the floor.

Cousin Arthur was calling out: "Get water...quickly. Douse the fire. The whole place will be ablaze. These timbers are as dry as straw."

Everyone was rushing about. I went over to Cousin Arthur, who was leaning over my grandfather.

"Send one of the servants for the doctor—quickly," he said.

I ran downstairs and found one of the grooms who had heard the commotion and seen the fire from his rooms over the stables.

He was off without a word and I went back again. There was water everywhere and the smoke was choking me, but I could see that they were getting the fire under control.

It appeared to have started in the room in which my grandmother lay.

Cousin Arthur said: "I never thought it safe to have those candles burning all night."

It was a shock to see my grandfather lying in the corridor,

a pillow under his head and blankets covering him. He looked quite unlike the man who a few hours before had thundered at me in his study; he looked forlorn, vulnerable, with his beard completely burned and burns on what I could see of his face and neck. He must be in terrible pain, I thought, but no sound came from him.

When the doctor arrived I was still standing there. The fire had been put out and the danger was past.

The doctor took one look at my grandfather and said, "Sir Matthew is dead."

A strange night...with the smell of the fumes still in my nostrils and my grandfather, who but a short time before had been screaming abuse at me—dead.

I try to piece together the events of that night but it is not easy.

I remember Cousin Arthur in a long brown dressing gown offering me something to drink. He seemed kinder than he ever had before, less self-righteous, more humane. He was clearly very shaken by what had happened. His benefactor was dead. He looked as if he couldn't believe it.

"You must not upset yourself, Philippa," he said. "I know you had a bit of trouble with him tonight."

I was silent.

He patted my hand. "Don't fret," he said. "I understand."

The doctor was looking grave. He wanted to have a few words with Cousin Arthur. He was disconcerted and uneasy. He did not think my grandather's death was due to suffocation. There was a cut on the back of his head.

"He must have fallen down," said Cousin Arthur.

"It could have been so," replied the doctor dubiously.

"This has been a terrible night for my cousin," went on Cousin Arthur. "I wonder if you could give her a sedative." He looked at me with such compassion that I wondered if I had ever really known him before. Moreover he was acting with a new authority as though he were already master of the house. Summoning one of the maids he told her to take me to my room.

I allowed her to lead me away and back in my bedroom I fell onto my bed. I could not believe this was really happening. My life had taken an unexpected turn. For so long it had gone along uneventfully, and now one dramatic event was following on another.

I took the drink which the maid brought up to me and which she said had been given to her by the doctor. Soon I had fallen into a heavy sleep.

The next morning the nightmare continued. The house was in turmoil and there were strangers everywhere.

Cousin Arthur asked me to come to my grandfather's study and there he told me that they had taken my grandfather's body away because they were not satisfied about the way in which he had died. There would be an inquest. "He said something about a blow on the back of his head."

"Do you mean he fell down and struck his head?"

"It could have been that he became aware that there was a fire and in rushing to get out of his room, he fell. It seems one of the candles round your grandmother's coffin must have fallen over and perhaps set the rug alight. The coffin was on that side of the room which was in immediate proximity to your grandfather's bedroom. As you know, there is a communicating door between the two rooms and there were cracks in the side of the door through which the flames could penetrate. I am not sure, of course. I am surmising...but the fact is...those two rooms are the only ones which are damaged—and your grandfather's bedroom is more so than the room in which the coffin lay. Fires start in all sorts of ways."

I nodded.

"I know how you will be feeling, Philippa, because of that altercation last night."

"I had to tell him how I felt," I said.

"I know. And I am aware of the subject you discussed. I want you to understand that I am your friend, Philippa. Your grandfather's wish was that we should marry, but you did not want that. It is a disappointment to me, but I don't want you to think for one moment that I hold it against you."

One of the most bewildering aspects of this situation was the change in Cousin Arthur. He had taken on a new stature with the passing of my grandfather. Gone was the humble, grateful relation, so eager to ingratiate himself. He was now behaving like the head of the house; he was even being kind and understanding to me.

He smiled ruefully. "We cannot force our affections where they will not go," he said. "Your grandfather wanted to provide for you and use you to continue the direct line. Well, he is dead now, and I would not wish you to be forced into a marriage distasteful to you. On the other hand I want you to regard this house as your home...for as long as you wish."

"Oh Cousin Arthur, that is good of you, for now I suppose all this will belong to you."

"Your grandfather always said I should inherit. Perhaps I am being a bit premature in talking thus. What I should say is that if it worked out as we have been led to believe it will—then this is your home for as long as you wish."

"I couldn't stay here," I said, "knowing that he had turned me out. I shall make some plans but I am relieved by your kind offer to allow me to stay until I do so."

He smiled at me affectionately. "Then that little matter is settled. There will be anxious days ahead. I do not want to add to your anxieties. There may be some unpleasantness. That blow on the head...Well, obviously he fell, but you must not reproach yourself, Philippa."

"I don't. I had to tell him the truth. I would do exactly the same again. I could not allow him to force me..."

"No, of course not. There is one other matter. Your grandmother's coffin has been scarred by the fire, but it is intact and I think the best thing we can do is to carry on as far as her funeral is concerned as though this had not happened. She will be buried tomorrow, and we will follow all the usual arrangements. Do you agree that is the best thing to do?"

I did agree.

"All right," he said, patting my shoulder. "That is how it will be."

Of course he too had been under the dominating sway of my grandfather. He had no more wanted to be forced into marriage than I had. The difference in us was that he was prepared to go to great lengths to please my grandfather and get his inheritance, whereas I was not. I supposed that Arthur would have been turned out penniless into a harsh world if he had not obeyed my grandfather, and I have no doubt that being some low-paid curate did not appeal to him. I could understand that and I was even liking him a little now.

My grandmother's funeral took place the next day. Aunt Grace came to the house with Charles Daventry and we talked together. Aunt Grace was very upset at the death of her mother and that she had not been allowed to visit her at the end. She was shocked by the death of her father, but if we were absolutely honest we would have to admit that it was a relief to us all.

We stood round the grave and as the scarred coffin was lowered into the earth and we listened to the clods being thrown onto it, I was thinking of our talks and all that Grandmother had done for us during those first difficult days at the Manor. She had been a kind of anchor to two bewildered young people. I was going to miss her sadly.

But everything would be changed. I must begin to find a post. At least I should soon be seventeen, which was a landmark to maturity. If I explained that I had suddenly fallen into poverty after having lived at Greystone Manor with my grandfather, perhaps I could now get by.

We went back to the house and in my grandfather's study, over biscuits and port wine, we assembled to hear the reading of the will.

We were astonished to learn that my grandmother had had a considerable estate, unknown to my grandfather. I was sure he would have wished to deal with it had he known how rich she was in her own right, and I have no doubt would have taken control of it so that it would no longer have been hers. I had always known that she was a strong-minded woman; her gentleness was misleading. She was kindly too, but once having been forced into marriage, she had been determined not to be completely dominated by her husband. So she had kept her secrets and this was one of them.

The disposal of the money was an even greater surprise to me. Agnes Warden must have been in on the secret because she admitted afterwards that she had brought the lawyer to my grandmother. Agnes herself was left a legacy to provide an annuity; there were one or two other bequests, but the bulk of it was split between her daughter Grace and her granddaughter Philippa "to enable them to live independent lives."

I was stunned.

The great problem which had lain before me had been pushed aside by this gesture of my grandmother's. I was to be comparatively rich. I need not worry about finding that post. I could go from this house as a rich woman of independent means.

"To lead independent lives!" I looked at Grace. She was crying quietly.

The following day the inquest on my grandfather took place. That day stands out in my memory as the strangest of my life. I sat there with Cousin Arthur and Grace and Charles and listened to the doctor's evidence. The heat of the room, the drone of the voices, the ritual of it all was awe-inspiring. I tried to grasp the significance of what the doctor was saying. Sir Matthew Ewell's death was not due to suffocation or the result of burns, and while this might have been caused when he fell and struck his head on the edge of a fender or some piece of furniture, on the other hand there was a possibility that it could have come through a blow administered by some person or persons unknown. It was likely that he had awakened from his sleep to become aware of the fire which had come through from the room next to his. He could have stumbled out of bed in a hurry and fallen. But this was conjecture and it was not possible to prove because the body had been dragged out of the room and it was not known what position it had been in at the time of death.

There was a great deal of discussion about this and at length the inquest was adjourned until the following week.

"What does it mean?" asked Aunt Grace of Charles.

Charles said it meant they were not entirely satisfied with the findings.

It was a strange week which followed. I went about the house in a kind of daze. I longed to get away...right away.

"You can't make plans until this wretched business is over," said Cousin Arthur.

I noticed the servants were looking at me strangely. I read suspicion in their looks. It could mean only one thing. They had heard my quarrel with my grandfather and they knew that he was threatening to turn me out. And now this talk about his having been struck by someone...I knew the implication. Someone had struck him, killed him, and then started the fire to cover up the deed.

I couldn't believe it. Did those dark looks implicate me? Could they possibly think that *I* had done this?

I began to be frightened.

I noticed Mrs. Greaves particularly. She watched me closely. It was ridiculous. It was such nonsense. As if I would kill my own grandfather!

Agnes Warden was kind to me; so were Aunt Grace and Charles.

"I can't think what they want to make all this fuss about," said Charles. "It is quite obvious that Sir Matthew fell and killed himself."

"There is always this sort of enquiry in cases of sudden death," added Cousin Arthur.

My grandfather's will was read. Arthur had inherited the estate and the house. I was mentioned. There was to be a settlement on the occasion of my marriage to Arthur and there would be a small income for me for life, to be increased on the birth of every child I should have.

This was what he had planned to change when the lawyer would have been summoned. He had clearly wanted it to be definitely understood that in view of my ingratitude I should never have a penny of his money.

Arthur took charge of the household and I continued to be astonished by his consideration to me.

"I think," said Grace, "he is hoping you will change your mind and it will all work out as my father wished."

"That could never be," I told her. "I am grateful for Cousin Arthur's consideration, but I could never marry him."

Grace nodded. Secure in her new life with Charles, she felt she knew a great deal about love and marriage.

Mrs. Greaves' manner towards me became so cool that one day I asked her if anything was wrong.

She looked at me steadily. She had a hard, even a cruel face. I had always thought that long years of service in my grandfather's household had made her like that.

"I think that is a question you should ask yourself, Miss," she said severely.

"What do you mean, Mrs. Greaves?"

"I think you know well enough."

"No," I replied. "I don't."

"Well, there's a lot of speculation as to how that poor gentleman died . . . and it's thought that someone in this house might be able to throw a little light on that."

"Do you mean *I* could?"

"Ask yourself, Miss. We heard the quarrel that went on on the last night of my master's life. I was not far off—ac-cidentally—I couldn't help hearing."

"It must have been a great distress to you to have been forced to listen, Mrs. Greaves."

"If you'll forgive my saying so, Miss, that's the sort of thing I'd expect to hear from you. I heard it because I was there and I saw you go into your grandmother's room after."

"What did you think I did? Set the place on fire and let

it burn slowly for hours before I guided it into my grandfather's room?"

"No. The fire was started later."

"Was started, Mrs. Greaves? You mean it began. Nobody started it."

"Who's to say, and I fancy some of them people at the inquest has got their own opinions."

"What are you trying to say? And why don't you say it outright?"

"Well, it seems to be a bit of a mystery, Miss. But mysteries get cleared up and all I can say is some people are not what they seem. I don't forget, Miss, that I saw you coming in in the early morning hours—and that not so long ago. I just wondered what you were up to. It only goes to show that you can never tell what people will do, can you?"

I was terribly shaken that she should refer to that night with Conrad. I felt angry and hurt. Why did I not run away with him? Why did I let my foolish puritanical conscience stand in my way? If I had gone I should not have been here when my grandfather died. There would never have been that scene in the study.

Mrs. Greaves had seen how her words affected me. I heard her give a slight snigger as she turned and went silently away.

It occurred to me then that I was in a very dangerous situation.

I think I was too bemused by everything that had happened so suddenly to realize the extent of that danger, which was perhaps fortunate.

Arthur was so kind to me—almost tender; and I wondered vaguely whether Grace was right and he was trying to make me change my mind towards him.

"If they should ask you questions," he said, "all you have to do is tell the truth. If you do that no harm can come. One must never tell a lie in court for if one is discovered one is never believed on a single thing. You'll be all right, Philippa. We shall all be there."

I had never visualized anything like this—the court with all its dignitaries. And it was only a coroner's court. No-one was accused. This was only to decide whether my grandfather had died by accident or design. If the latter was decided then there would be accusations... and perhaps a trial.

I just could not believe that this was really happening to me. All I could tell myself was that if I had obeyed the instincts of my heart I would now be happy in some vaguely foreign land with the man whom I realized now I undoubtedly loved.

People gave evidence. The doctors who had examined my grandfather's body confirmed that he had not died of asphyxiation but from the blow on the head, which could have occurred an hour or so before the fire was discovered. There could be an explanation of this. He could have smelt the smouldering rug, risen from his bed and fallen and killed himself. The fire was clearly slow burning for the room in which my grandmother lay had not been so badly burned as had my grandfather's room. Experts agreed that it was possible for the rug to have smouldered for the best part of an hour before bursting into flames, and this would account for the lapse of time between my grandfather's receiving the blow and the presence of the fire being discovered by other members of the household.

People were put in the witness box after the doctors. Cousin Arthur first. He told how he had heard the cry of "Fire" and had rushed to the spot. He had immediately gone to my grandfather's room where one of the servants was dragging out the body. He had thought my grandfather was alive and had sent for the doctor. Had there been a quarrel between Sir Matthew and a member of the household on the previous night? he was asked.

Cousin Arthur, obviously reluctant, said that there had been a disagreement between Sir Matthew and his granddaughter Philippa.

Did he know what it was about?

Cousin Arthur thought that Sir Matthew had expressed his wish that there should be a match between himself and Sir Matthew's granddaughter and that she had refused to agree to this.

"Did he threaten her at all to your knowledge?"

"I was not present," said Cousin Arthur evasively. "But Sir Matthew was a man who could lose his temper easily if crossed." He believed he had shouted a little.

"To what effect? That he would cut her out of his will? That she would have to leave the house?"

"It may have been so."

"Was Philippa Ewell upset by this?"

"I did not see her at the time."

"When did you next see her after the argument?"

"On the landing outside the rooms which were on fire."

"Did she sleep in the corridor?"

"Yes, several bedrooms were there."

"Was yours?"

"Yes."

"And the servants?"

"They were on the floors above."

Arthur left the box and Mrs. Greaves was called. She said she had overheard the quarrel between my grandfather and me.

"Did he threaten to turn her out of the house and cut her out of his will?"

"He did," said Mrs. Greaves readily.

"You have very good hearing, Mrs. Greaves?"

"The best."

"Very useful in your position. Did you see Miss Philippa Ewell after the interview?"

"Yes. I saw her go to the room where her grandmother lay in her coffin."

"And did you see her later?"

"No, I didn't. But that did not mean that she stayed in her room all the night."

"We are not asking for your opinions, Mrs. Greaves, only for facts."

"Yes, sir, but I think I ought to say that Miss Ewell did have strange habits. She did roam about at night."

"That night?"

"I didn't see her that night. But I saw her one early morning. I had heard a noise—"

"Your excellent hearing again, Mrs. Greaves?"

"I thought it my duty to go and see who was prowling about. I have to look after the maids and make sure they behave, sir."

"Another excellent quality! And on this occasion..."

"I saw Miss Philippa coming into the house. It must have been five o'clock in the morning. She was fully dressed and her hair was loose."

"And what conclusion did you come to?"

"That she had been out all night."

"Did she tell you this?"

"She said she had been for a walk in the gardens."

"I see no reason why Miss Ewell should not take an early morning walk if she wishes to, nor should I expect her to dress her hair before doing so."

It was clear that Mrs. Greaves was not making the impression she intended, but the reference to that morning shocked me deeply. I wondered what I could say if asked about it.

Should I tell them that I had spent the night with a lover? I should be condemned if I did so. There were many people who would think loose morals—for that was what I should be accused of—was as great a crime as murder. I had never felt so frightened in my life.

Then it was my turn.

"Miss Ewell, your grandfather wished you to marry your cousin and you refused to do this."

"Yes."

"And your refusal angered him?"

"Yes, it did."

"He threatened to turn you out of the house and cut you out of his will."

"He did."

"What did you say to that?"

"I said: 'I cannot marry someone I do not love and I will leave the house as soon as possible.'"

"And you would have done that the following day? Where would you have gone to?"

"I had thought I might go to my Aunt Grace or to one of the cottages until I had found a suitable home."

"And after this stormy interview what did you do?"

"I went into my grandmother's room to take a look at her in her coffin. We had been very fond of each other."

There was a nod of sympathy. I had a feeling that the questioner liked me and believed me and I felt, also, that he had disliked Mrs. Greaves and suspected her of malice. That gave me a certain courage.

"What happened in your grandmother's room?"

"I just looked at her and wished that she were alive to help me."

"Were the candles burning when you went into her room?"

"Yes. There had been candles burning since her death."

"Did you notice any insecurity about them?"

"No."

"I believe your grandmother has left you money with the wish that you may live an independent life. Was she of the opinion that your grandfather made harsh demands upon you?"

"Yes."

"You may step down, Miss Ewell."

It had been easier than I had thought it possibly could be and I was so relieved because there had been no mention of that early morning encounter with Mrs. Greaves.

After that it seemed that it went on for a long time. There was a great deal of discussion and I sat there limply waiting. Cousin Arthur reached for my hand and pressed, and for once I did not want to reject his hands.

Then the verdict: Accidental death. In the coroner's view there was insufficient evidence to say how the blow had been inflicted, and he was of the opinion that Sir Matthew had fallen and struck his head against the sharp edge of a fender—for there was evidence of such a fender surrounding the fireplace in his bedroom.

So we were free. The fearful menace which I had only half understood was lifted.

As I left the court with Cousin Arthur, Aunt Grace and her husband, I thought I saw someone I vaguely recognized. I couldn't think who it was for the moment, but it came to me later in a flash. It was the man whom I had seen when Miss Elton and I had gone to Dover to look at the register, the man whom I had assumed to be staying at the local inn and exploring the countryside.

I dismissed him from my thoughts. There was so much else to occupy me.

I was free now to make my plans.

I did not want to stay in Greystone Manor. There was a horrible atmosphere of suspicion there, instigated I was sure by Mrs. Greaves. I noticed the servants watching me furtively, and if I looked up and caught them suddenly they would look embarrassed and turn away.

Cousin Arthur continued to be extremely kind. "You must stay here as long as you like," he said. "In fact, you can regard Greystone Manor as your home."

"I certainly couldn't do that. My grandfather ordered me out and I shall go."

"It belongs to me now, you know."

"It's kind of you in view of everything, but I must go quickly."

It was Aunt Grace who came to my immediate rescue. "You must come and stay with Charles and me," she said. "Stay as long as you like, my dear. We have the money now to buy a house for ourselves and there is one not very far away from the vicarage, Wisteria Cottage. Do you remember it? Charles thinks it would suit us beautifully, and there is a big garden where he can have his workshop and display his statues. Come and help us to make the move."

It was good of her. She was delighted to have the money that had been left to her and to have the approval of her marriage which her mother had implied. In death my grandmother had given us both the help we needed.

So I left Greystone Manor and went with her. The vicarage was a roomy house and the vicar kindly let me have a room until the move to Wisteria Cottage could be arranged.

Aunt Grace did a lot for me in those weeks. She and Charles talked to me a great deal and we planned what I should do. There was no need for me to take some uncongenial post now. I was a free woman and I needed time, said Aunt Grace, to decide how I should live.

Fate decided for me.

I was in Charles's shed sorting out some books for him when I heard footsteps outside. I went to the door, and to my amazement and delight there stood Daisy.

She had changed since I last saw her; she had grown plumper, but her cheeks were as rosy as ever and the mischief still sparkled in her eyes. As though to show her pleasure and that it was an extremely happy occasion, she favoured me with one of the winks I remembered so well.

"Miss Pip!" she said.

"Oh, Daisy!" I cried and we hugged each other fiercely. "So you've come home...at last."

"Only on a visit. The servants are up at the Grange—preparing it like they always do. I came with them. Hans isn't with me, but he let me come with them. He said I deserved to see my own folks and it was only right for me to. He's had to stay behind. He's got an important job now. I'm married, you know. Frau Schmidt, that's me. What do you think of that? Hans made an honest woman of me...when young Hans was born. I'm a mother now. Think of that, Miss

Pip. You never saw a little man like my Hansie. He's a regular tartar, I can tell you."

"Daisy, when are you going to stop for breath? Do you mean to say they're opening up the Grange?"

"Somebody will be coming over soon. Not sure when, but it has to be all ready and prepared."

"And you..."

"Oh, I'm not one of the servants now. Frau Schmidt, that's me. I'll stay here till some of the servants go back, and I'll go back with them. But first tell me—what about you? And that old man...dead now. Well, I don't think he'll get quite the welcome he's expecting from the angels."

"You heard about it, did you?"

"Haven't heard of anything else."

"Daisy, they suspect me."

"Not my Ma don't. Nor Pa. They said that old tartar got out of bed in a rage and got what he deserved. Mind you, you mustn't speak ill of the dead, they say, but in his case I reckon it's allowed. I won't ever forget standing in that chapel in what he called my shame...and all for having a bit of fun in the churchyard. But that's all done with. What about you, Miss Pip? How many years is it since I saw you?"

"Too many. It must be five. I was twelve when you and Francine went away, and I'm seventeen now."

"I'd hardly have known you. Quite grown up, you are. Just a little shaver you was then."

"Daisy, what do you know about Francine?"

"Oh." Her face was solemn momentarily. "That was a bit of a scandal, that was. I cried myself to sleep when I heard of it. I used to think she was the most beautiful girl I'd ever seen—or ever likely to—and to think of her getting murdered..."

"I want to know what happened, Daisy."

"Well, it was in this shooting lodge. That's where they were at the time. It was never cleared up. Who killed them we don't know. It wasn't anything to do with Miss Francine. She was just there with him...when they came to kill him...and because she was with him they killed her too."

"Who could have done it?"

"Now you're asking me. If *they* don't know, how could I?"

"Who's they?"

"All the army...and the reigning family and the police...all of them."

"It's been such a mystery to me and I want you to tell me all you know. Come into the shed. There's no one here. My aunt and her husband are at Wisteria Cottage getting ready to move in."

"Oh, I heard about that. What a change-about eh? Miss Grace getting married and all. She ought to have done it years ago."

"I'm glad she did before she got the money. She had to break away, as I did. But sit down, Daisy, and tell me all you know about my sister."

"Well, she went off, didn't she?"

"Yes, yes," I said impatiently.

"And the Gräfin and Graf and her household went off and I got my job with them . . . so off I goes. It's a wonderful place if you like that sort of thing. The trees and mountains . . . oh, it's beautiful. I get a bit homesick at times though for the fields and the hedges and the lanes and the buttercups and daisies. But Hans was there, and me and Hans—well, we get on together a treat. It's funny. He laughs at me—the way I try to say their words—but I can laugh at him for saying ours. We like it."

"So you are happily married. I am so pleased. And you have that adorable little Hans. But what do you know about my sister?"

"Only that she came over with the Baron. I didn't know who he was then. I knew he was important, of course, but not that important. Hans told me. He said this Baron Rudolph is the only son of this Grand Duke or something, and this Grand Duke is a sort of King. Not like our Queen, of course, but the ruler of this dukedom, or whatever it is. But it's different over there. It's like a lot of little countries all with their own kings and though they seem little to us, they're thought to be pretty big over there."

"I understand, Daisy."

"Well, I'm glad you do, Miss Pip, because it's more than I do. But what I'm telling you is that when Rudolph came back with your sister there was a regular to-do. You see, he's the heir and he's supposed to marry some sort of grand lady from one of those other places and there could be war if he didn't. There's always going to be war . . . and they're afraid of that. So Baron Rudolph is supposed to marry this lady. That means having Miss France there he had to keep her out of the way."

"He was married to my sister so how could he possibly marry this grand lady?"

"Well, it seems he wasn't exactly *married....*"

"He was. They were married near Dover before they left the country."

"Well, they said she was his mistress. That was all right with them. He'd had them before...and all Grand Dukes had. But with marriage it was different...if you understand me."

"Listen, Daisy, my sister was married to him in Birley Church. I saw—"

I stopped. I *had* seen that entry, hadn't I? In view of everything that had happened I was beginning to doubt it.

"I reckon it had to be one of them mock marriages," said Daisy. "It would be the only way and Baron Rudolph would have known it. He had to keep her out of the way...or he should have done. But there was one part of the country where he was very popular...and I believe he was there with her."

"You never saw her, Daisy?"

"Oh no. I was in the Graf's slosh."

"Where?"

"The slosh. They have a lot of them over there. They're very pretty. Like castles."

"Oh I see—a *schloss.*"

"That's it. No, they didn't come to our slosh. The Graf was very loyal to the Grand Duke and he and the Gräfin thought that Rudolph ought to settle down and learn how to rule the country, which he would have to do when the Grand Duke dies, and they thought he ought to do all he could to stop this war they were all worried about, which would come if he didn't marry this one they'd got for him."

"So all this time you never saw her. What about the child?"

"Child? What child is this you mean, Miss Pip?"

"My sister had a little boy. A son. She was very proud of him."

"I never heard nothing of that."

"Oh, Daisy, I wish I knew what happened."

"You know she was killed in that shooting lodge."

"Where exactly was the lodge?"

"It's not far from the slosh. Right in the middle of the pine forest, it is. It was an awful shock when it happened. The town went into mourning for a whole month. They said it nearly broke the Grand Duke's heart...his only son, you see.

They looked for the murderers. High and low they searched. But they couldn't find them. They said it was political. You see, there's a nephew. He's to be the next Grand Duke when the old man dies."

"Do they think *he* killed them?"

"They don't dare go as far as to say that. But this Baron Sigmund...you see he's a son of the old man's brother and next in line, which is because of Rudolph's death...if you get my meaning. So if anybody wanted Rudolph out of the way it could be Sigmund...though Hans thinks it could be someone who just wanted Rudolph out of the way, he being not what they considered right to be the next Grand Duke."

"So someone who wanted Rudolph out of the way murdered him in the shooting lodge...and just because Francine was with him she was shot too."

"That's about it. It's the general view. Nobody can be sure..."

"But what about the child? Where was he at the time?"

"Nobody's ever said nothing about a child, Miss Pip."

"It's a great mystery to me. I am sure Francine was truly married and I am sure there was a child. I want to *know*, Daisy. It's the only thing I really care about now."

"Oh, you wouldn't want to get muddled up in all that, Miss Pip. You ought to settle down and marry some nice young man. You haven't got to worry about money now, have you? Get married and have babies. I can tell you this...there's nothing I can think of better than holding your own little baby in your arms...."

"Oh, Daisy, it's lovely to think of you as a mother."

"You ought to see my little Hansie."

"I wish I could." I was looking straight at her. "Daisy," I went on, "why shouldn't I?"

The idea had come and it would not be dismissed. It excited me as I had not been excited for a long time. It would give me a reason for living; it would get me away from the atmosphere of furtive suspicion from which I could not escape. At the back of my mind was the thought that I might see Conrad again.

During the last weeks the possibility that there might be results from my encounter with him had occurred to me. Somehow I had rather hoped there would be. It would add very much to the complications of my life, but I think the joy it would have brought me would have compensated for that. It would have put me in a desperate situation...but to have had a child, a living memory of the hours I had spent with Conrad, filled me with longing.

It was a strange mingling of relief and disappointment when I knew that I had definitely not become pregnant, and I felt I had to give myself a reason for living. And now that Daisy had appeared she had, in a way, opened a door for me.

"Daisy," I said, "how would it be if I came back with you?"

"You, Miss Pip! Back with me?"

"I have money now. I am free, thanks to my grandmother. I want to find that child of Francine's. He exists, I know. Sometimes I feel he is calling for me. He would be nearly four years old by now. If he's there I should like to see him. I want to make sure that he is well looked after."

"Well, as I said, I never heard nothing about no child, and I reckon there'd have been plenty of people to find out if there was one. They're very fond of a bit of gossip over there, just as they are everywhere."

"I am convinced that there *is* a child and that my sister was married. This is what I want to settle, Daisy."

"All right then. When do you want to go?"

"When do you leave?"

"I was to stay till one or two of the others went back, but I don't really want to wait that long. I'm missing my two Hanses very much, I can tell you."

"Could you come back with me? We could travel together. You'd be such a help to me as you've done it before. Could we go together?"

Daisy's eyes were sparkling. "I reckon we could manage that. How long would you want to wait?"

"I want to leave as soon as I can."

"I see no reason why we shouldn't go when you're ready."

"I could go to the town and stay in an inn somewhere while I look round."

"There are inns all right. But I'll tell you what. Why couldn't you stay with me until you got sorted out? You see, I've got a cottage, a lovely little place in the valley just below the slosh. We had it when I was going to have the baby. That was when Hans didn't want me to work no more. The Gräfin is very good to her servants and she and Miss Tatiana gave me things to furnish it with. So you could stay with me till you found what you wanted."

"Oh, Daisy, that would be wonderful. That would help me a lot. I could then look round and find out what I ought to do. I want to do this. I want to do it so much. It needs thinking about though. I am going there and I am going to find out who killed my sister. I'm going to find her baby."

Daisy smiled at me indulgently. "Well, if you can do better than the Grand Duke's police and guards you are a bit of a marvel. Don't you think they tried to find the murderer?"

"Perhaps they didn't try hard enough. This is my sister...my own flesh and blood."

"So you're going to be like one of them detectives, are you?"

"Yes, I am."

I was so excited. Life had taken on real meaning for me. I was as near happy as I had been since Conrad had gone. I felt I was emerging from the slough of despond at last.

I talked a great deal about my project with Grace, with Charles and of course with Daisy. Aunt Grace thought it was preposterous, but Charles said a little travel would do me no harm and if I could go back with Daisy I would have company, for travelling alone would have been impossible.

I let them talk about the difficulties. Aunt Grace tried to dissuade me. There was a home for me at Wisteria Cottage and I knew she was thinking of a husband for me in the not too distant future.

Cousin Arthur called at Wisteria Cottage. He was very affable, and being squire suited him. He was quite dignified when the old subservience dropped from him. He listened thoughtfully to my plans for travelling back with Daisy and was surprisingly understanding. "It will do you the world of good," he said. "It will get you away from here and that is what you need. My dear cousin, perhaps when you come back we can be the good friends I always hoped we should be."

He was looking at me rather wistfully and I was wondering what meaning lay behind his words. He was helpful in a practical way. He thought that travelling so far and through several countries I might be in need of some papers, a passport. He made enquiries and even conducted me to London to acquire these.

I said, "I should never have thought of it but for you, Cousin Arthur."

"I am very glad to be able to offer you some assistance," he answered.

"Cousin Arthur, is all going well at Greystone?"

"Oh yes. We are very quiet at the moment. I am not entertaining at all. Only the Glencorns have been once or twice, but they are such old friends. I do hope that when you come back you will visit me often. As you know, there would always be a home for you at Greystone Manor."

"It is good of you, Cousin Arthur. I don't know what my plans will be. I want to get this—er—holiday over first and then see how I feel."

"All very natural, dear Philippa. You have been through a trying time. Get right away and forget it, eh?"

"I will try."

I helped Aunt Grace move into Wisteria Cottage while I was making my preparations. I saw a great deal of Daisy for there were so many plans to be made. She described the country to me and something of the life she lived. She was very happy in her cottage in the valley close to what she persisted in calling the "slosh," and she told me that Hans came home every evening so that it was all very cosy and life had turned out romantically and happily for her.

"Of course," she commented, "some would have said I was a bad and wicked girl to go off with Hans. I never thought I was. I reckon if you love it's all right. After all, it's better than marrying someone for money...or so it seems to me. Well, all's well that ends well, as they say, and Hans and me is very well, thank the Lord."

She didn't know how close I had come to doing what she had done, and I often wondered how different my life might have been if I had obeyed my natural impulses on that night.

However, as Daisy herself would be the first to admit, what was done was done, and we had to go on from there. It was a favourite expression of hers.

The more I thought of my decision the more it seemed like a miracle that I was able to do what in my heart I had always wanted to. I was going over there...to Conrad's country. Would I see him again? What if there should be another chance? I should have to wait and see what life had to offer me. Perhaps he would not want to renew our acquaintance. That he was a man who must have had many love affairs I could readily believe, but I did think that his sense of chivalry would have stopped his casually seducing a young virgin. I liked to think that it was only because he had been carried away by his passion that he had done so, and that he had really intended that we should be together. Oh yes, I really did believe that he had cared for me.

"I tell you what you're going to be," said Daisy gleefully, "some sort of detective, that's what. Now there's something that's struck me. You're the same name as your sister and there was quite a bit about her in the papers. They called her 'the woman Ewell.' You see what I mean. Some people might remember the name. It might stop them telling you things if they thought you was snooping around. Do you follow me?"

I did follow her.

"You could call yourself something else," suggested Daisy. "I reckon that would be best."

"You're right. It is clever of you to have thought of this."

"When they was over here you came to the Grange, didn't you. Some of them saw you. Well if they was to see you again and heard you was Philippa Ewell, they'd remember right away. Twelve you was then. You're different now ... five years older. . . . And that makes a lot of difference. If you called yourself something else, they'd never guess who you were."

"I tell you what I'll do. I'll call myself by my mother's name before she was married. That was Ayres. I'll be Philippa Ayres."

"There's still the Philippa."

"Well, what about Anne Ayres? Anne is my second name."

"That sounds all right to me. Nobody's going to compare Anne Ayres with Philippa Ewell if you ask me."

That day when I was preparing my clothes for departure I came across the spectacles with the blank glass in them which Miss Elton had procured for me when we were talking about my seeking a post. I put them on. They certainly were effective. Then I took my rather heavy hair and pulled it back from my forehead. I screwed it into a bun on the top of my head. The effect was startling. I really did look like another person.

When Daisy came to see me I received her wearing the glasses and my new hairstyle. She stared at me, not recognizing me for a few moments.

"Oh, Miss Pip," she cried. "You look so funny. Not like you at all."

"It's my disguise, Daisy."

"You're not going to travel like that, are you?"

"No, but I shall take the glasses with me for use if the need arises."

The time was passing now. We were ready to leave—and so I set out for Conrad's country with Daisy as my guide.

The Hunting
Lodge

Our journey was long but never tedious, for I was in a
state of great excitement from the outset. It was the most
wonderful piece of luck that Daisy had come to England at
this time. She was a very resourceful young woman and liked
to imagine herself the seasoned traveller.

I had insisted that we travel first-class and that I should
pay for Daisy as she was going to be my companion and guide.
As we took the train to Harwich and I sat back in the first
compartment looking at a very complacent Daisy, I knew
that Cousin Arthur had been right when he had said this
was the best thing I could do. I was starting a new life and
I was glad to escape from the last weeks which had become
almost intolerable.

I was convinced that from now on my life would be ad-
venturous. I had an important project in mind and I felt as
though I were setting out to seek my fortune.

The crossing from Harwich to the Hook of Holland was
uneventful, and after staying the night at an inn we boarded
a train and travelled for miles across the flattest country I
have ever seen.

"Never mind," said Daisy, "you'll have mountains and forests enough when you get to Bruxenstein. Perhaps you'll be
wishing for a bit of flat there."

"I can't wait to arrive," I said.

"You've got a long way to go yet, Miss Pip."

How right she was! Once again I had reason to be grateful to Cousin Arthur, who had made the arrangements for us with a company in London that looked after such matters, so we knew exactly which way we had to go. We were to spend a night at Utrecht before taking the train to Bavaria, and the journey was beginning to be so interesting that had I not been so eager to reach my destination, I should have liked to linger longer over every detail of it.

The first-class carriages had four seats in front and four behind, and each carriage was subdivided into two sections by a central door, just as in our first-class carriages at home. But there was a more formal atmosphere here. One was conscious of a display of discipline, and the attendants wore cocked hats and carried swords so that they looked almost military.

"We're a bit like that in Bruxenstein," Daisy explained. "All that clicking heels and bowing from the waist...It sometimes makes me want to laugh."

At Arnheim two men and a woman joined our carriage. They looked pleasant and smiled in our direction. I explained that we were English, and they thereupon began to talk to us in our own tongue although they only had a fair command of it, and my German, thanks to Miss Elton and my early grounding, was better than their English.

Were we going beyond Utrecht, they wanted to know? I told them we were travelling to Bruxenstein.

"Is that indeed so," said the man. "Interesting place, Bruxenstein...at the moment."

"Why do you say at the moment?" I asked. "Is there some reason why it is now so?"

"Things have been a little...what do you call it...in the boiling pot since the death of the Baron Rudolph."

My heart began to beat faster. Daisy sat demurely beside me, like the quiet little maid she had said everyone would think she was, because she looked the part and I looked like the mistress.

"Wasn't there some scandal—?" I began.

"Scandal indeed. He was shot dead in his hunting lodge. There was a woman with him and she was killed too."

"I heard of it."

"So the news travelled to England."

The woman said, "That was probably because the lady in the case was English."

"That may be," said the man, "but in any case the country has been a little uneasy since."

"Mind you," put in the other man, "there is always something going on in these little states. It's time they were all joined up and became part of the Germanic Empire."

"Being a Prussian, you would say that, Otto," said the other with a smile.

"Do you know what really happened about this shooting matter?" I asked.

"No-one really knows, but one can guess. There are theories...many of them. Perhaps the lady had another lover who was jealous. That's one of the theories. But I don't think that's the answer. No. Someone did not want Rudolph ruling over the province, so that person—or persons—put a bullet through him. Probably someone from the other side."

"You mean he has a rival?"

"There is always someone next in the line of succession. There's this nephew of the reigning duke. What's his name, Otto?"

"Baron Sigmund."

"Yes, son of a younger brother of the Grand Duke. Isn't that so?"

"Exactly. Some seem to think he'd suit the part better and that it is not such a bad thing that Rudolph is out of the way."

"Murder is rather a drastic way of settling these matters!" I said.

"Still," went on Otto, "it is better that one—or two—should die than that thousands should be submitted to tyranny."

"Was this Rudolph a tyrant, then?"

"Far from it. I've heard that he was something of a sybarite, a young man too fond of pleasure to make a good ruler. That kind always get surrounded by the wrong people who rule for them. The present Grand Duke has been a good ruler. It's a pity he's so old. I gather he was old when Rudolph was born. He married twice, the first time being unfruitful. His brother was killed fighting in one of the rebellions of wars...and that left Sigmund heir after Rudolph."

"You know a great deal about the family."

"It's common knowledge. It's a small principality—or

dukedom rather—and the royal family lives close to the people. Different from in your country, Miss er..."

I hesitated and then said quickly, "Ayres. Anne Ayres."

"Very different, Miss Ayres, although I suppose your Queen's private life is not exactly a closed book to your people."

"It is so exemplary," I replied, "that there is no need for it to be. If there are differences and family friction, I suppose there would be a tendency to keep that secret."

"How right you are! And I daresay there is very much the people of Bruxenstein do not know about their ruling family. Do you intend to spend any time in Utrecht?"

"Only an hour or so...possibly a morning...as we have to wait for trains."

"You'll enjoy it. It's one of the most interesting of the Dutch cities, I always thought. Tremendous history. The Romans built a fortress there to guard the river, one of the branches of the Rhine, you know, where it is joined by the Vecht. You must see the remains of the great cathedral..."

I was scarcely listening. My thoughts were with Francine lying dead on that bed in the hunting lodge.

We said goodbye to our travelling companions at Utrecht and continued our journey, and as we crossed the border into Germany my excitement increased. Those fir-covered mountains, those little streams, the glorious river with its castles looking down almost scornfully, it seemed, on the scene below, the little villages which seemed to have come straight out of stories by the brothers Grimm which Miss Elton used to read to us in the original...all this seemed to me the stuff of legend. This was the land of goblins and elves, of trolls and giants, of mountain kings and snow queens and children lost in enchanted woods where wolves roamed and there were gingerbread houses. It was the land of the Norse gods—Odin, Thor and Baldur the beautiful and mischievous Loki. It was in the air...I could sense it—in Hollenthal Gorge, called the Valley of Hell, in the glorious forests of the Schwarzwald, the Thuringian Wald, and the Odenwald...vine-covered hill slopes. There were miles and miles of trees—oaks, beeches, but mainly the firs and pines of the forest. It was the romantic land—Conrad's land, and the farther I penetrated, the more I thought of him.

The journey had taken us several days, as it had been the

advice of those who planned it that we should take it comfortably. I realized that they were right, and although I longed to be in Bruxenstein where I was beginning to believe the answer to the mystery would be found, I did feel that I was getting an understanding of the country and even the people, through those I met on the journey.

In due course we arrived at the town of Bruxburg which was, I gathered, the capital city of Bruxenstein, and we were able to take a trap out to the cottage which was the home of Daisy and Hans, and in this we rode through the town. It was quite large, but on that occasion I saw very little of it beyond the square with the town hall and a few impressive buildings. But I noticed immediately the castle on the incline presiding, as it were, over the town, and looking very much like those I had seen throughout our journey through the country. It looked impressive and very beautiful, I thought, with its towers and grey stone walls.

"We're right below it," said Daisy. "It's easy to get up to the slosh. There's a road runs from our cottage right up to it."

"Daisy," I said, "what are you going to tell Hans about me?"

"About you! What do you mean?"

"He'll know me."

"I shouldn't think so."

"But don't you think some of the servants... when they come back from the Grange...?"

"They'll never recognize you now. You've changed a lot from that little twelve-year-old. I'll tell Hans all about it and we'll explain that as your name is Ewell and there was that scandal about your sister, you've decided to call yourself Anne Ayres. Hans will see the point. We'll let it be known that you came out with me. Miss Ayres is someone I knew in England and as she was coming out I said why didn't she stay. A sort of paying guest, you see."

So she lulled my fears.

The trap deposited us with our luggage—mostly mine—at the cottage, and Hans came out to meet us. He and Daisy were immediately caught up in a delighted embrace; then he turned to greet me. I remembered him well. He clicked his heels and bowed while Daisy began explaining the situation to him in rather a breathless manner. I was going to be their paying guest until I decided what to do. I wanted to see something of the country. She knew it was all right. And how was her darling little Hans?

Little Hans was well. Frau Wurtzer had looked after him well and Hans had seen him almost every day while Daisy had been away.

"I'll be off first thing in the morning to get that young fellow," said Daisy.

I went into the cottage, which was spotlessly clean. I later discovered that there were two bedrooms and a sort of box-room upstairs and two downstairs with a kitchen. It was delightfully fresh and I could smell the pines of the nearby forest.

Hans welcomed me warmly and I wondered whether this was due to natural politeness or whether in fact he resented my presence in this rather small house.

As we went in a round faced woman appeared from the kitchen. She was in a large, very clean print apron and her sleeves were rolled up; she carried a ladle in her hands.

Daisy flew at her. "Gisela!" she cried.

"Daisy..."

Daisy turned to me. "This is my good friend, Gisela Wurtzer, who has been looking after Hansie for me."

The woman smiled and looked conspiratorially at Hans.

"He's here!" cried Daisy. "My little Hans is here."

She flew up the stairs and Hans looked at me and smiled. "She missed her baby," he said, "but I thought she should take the opportunity to see her mother and her father. There is a duty to the parents when they are getting old, eh?"

I agreed that this was so and Gisela nodded to imply that that was her opinion also. Daisy came down the stairs holding a sturdy boy who was rubbing his eyes and looking a little cross because he had obviously been wakened from his sleep.

"Look at him, Miss—" She had been going to say Pip and stopped herself in time. "Now tell me, did you ever see a more beautiful boy?"

"Never!" I cried.

She kissed him fervently and now, fully awake, he regarded me from a pair of light-blue eyes.

I took his fat little hand and kissed it.

"He likes you," said Gisela.

"It's true," agreed Daisy. "He's a very sharp young fellow. How's he been, Gisela? Missing his mum?"

Hans had to translate most of Daisy's words, which were

spoken in English, and as Gisela had no English, conversation was a little difficult. But the rapport between the two women was obvious.

"Tell her how good it was of her to bring him so that I didn't have to wait," commanded Daisy.

Gisela smiled when she heard. "But of course I brought him," she said.

I had to hear of all the wonderful qualities of young Hans, which I did in English from Daisy and in German from Gisela and Hans.

"Gisela knows," said Hans, "for she is especially good with children."

"I should be," replied Gisela. "I have six of my own. Numbers help. The big ones look after the little ones."

Young Hans showed signs of wanting to return to his bed, so Daisy took him upstairs and Gisela, who had set the table, said that food was ready. We partook of a soup of a rather mysterious but delicious flavour with rye bread, after which there was cold pork with vegetables and to follow, a pie containing apples. It was a good meal and Gisela was clearly proud of it. She served it and ate with us while we talked of the journey, and then she said she must get back because Arnulf did not like to be left too long to look after the children.

Hans walked home with her.

"Now you see, Miss Pip," said Daisy when we were alone, "what a nice little situation I've got myself into."

"I do, Daisy," I replied. "But shouldn't you stop calling me Miss Pip?"

"I must. Miss Ayres sounds so funny. Not a bit like you. Miss Pip is just right. It won't matter much if I get a slip of the tongue. That's what is so good about this. You say something you shouldn't and you just blame the language. It helps the wheels go round."

"Oh, Daisy, how happy you must be. Hans is so good and the baby such a darling."

"Well, as I say, Miss P—I mean Miss Ayres—I reckon I've done pretty well for myself."

"You deserve all the good luck in the world."

"Well, come to think of it, you could use a bit yourself and by rights you ought to have it."

She showed me my room. It was very small with chintz curtains, a bed, a chair and a cupboard . . . very little else, but I was grateful for it.

"We don't use it often," she said apologetically. "It's to be for young Hans when he gets a little older. In the meantime his bed's in the very small room next to ours and that'll be all right for a few months more."

"I shall be gone by then."

"Don't talk about going. You've only just come." Daisy had turned to me, her eyes shining. "It's ever so exciting, you coming here like this. I reckon we'll make a fine pair of detectives, you and me." She paused. "You know Gisela ... well, she was caretaker at the lodge.... Still keeps an eye on it, you know."

"Daisy!" I cried. "Well then she might know—"

"Don't you think we've talked? She doesn't know any more than anyone else. I haven't found out anything from her because she doesn't know."

"No one ... however friendly ... must know why I'm here."

"Trust me," said Daisy. "Silent as the grave, that's me."

Hans returned and Daisy reckoned it was time we had a good night's sleep.

"We can talk in the morning," she added.

And we all agreed with her.

The next day I decided to explore the town. Daisy could not accompany me because she had her son to look after. When she went into the town one of the servants from the *schloss* would bring down a pony carriage which they used for short journeys and take her in. They did this twice a week so that she could shop. Hans, it seemed, now held quite an important position in the Graf's household which entitled him to such privileges.

It was a beautiful morning. The sun was shining on the green and red roofs of the houses and the grey walls of the *schloss*. Here and there the sharp flint edges twinkled like diamonds where the sun caught them.

I was in a mood of exultation. I had accomplished so much and I was certain that something tremendous would happen soon. I wondered what I should do if I came upon Conrad sauntering through the town. I knew so little of him. I did not even know his surname. He was simply Conrad to me. I must have been in a bemused state not to ask him more questions and to be so easily put off with evasions. Equerry to a nobleman! I wondered if that could be the Graf, as he had been staying at the Grange, although the house was used by several families, I believed. But if the Graf were his employer he might at this very moment be within those grey stone walls.

How wonderful it would be to see him again. I tried to imagine our greeting. Would he be surprised? Delighted? Had he perhaps dismissed me from his mind as the sort of woman a man meets, makes love to and rides away from... forgotten in a few months... even weeks... just one of the women who amused him for a while?

I could see the bluish grey stream of the river winding its way through the town to where the slopes on either side were covered with pines and fir trees, and away in the distance the vines were growing in abundance. I was again transported to those days when Miss Elton read to us. There in the forest I knew I should hear the cowbells ringing through the mist. Miss Elton had told us of her visits to such places when she was taken to see her mother's people. There the gods roamed and the valkyries rode. I could sense it all. In that square I could see the mayor and his corporation sitting in dismayed discussion; I could see the Pied Piper playing his magic pipes and luring the rats into the river and the children into the mountainside. It moved me deeply. I was aware of much of the past. I pictured Francine coming here with Rudolph. I wondered how she had felt, whether she had been aware from the beginning that her liaison—I had ceased to call it a marriage in my thoughts—was to be kept a secret.

There were several large houses with oriel windows projecting from the façades and carved woodwork at these windows. It appeared to be a prosperous town. There was the minster with its pointed spire and around it streets of small houses. I guessed that many of the people who were not employed in the big houses worked in the vineyards. I passed a forge and a mill... and then I was really in the town.

I wandered through the market, where dairy produce and vegetables were for sale. Some people looked at me rather curiously. They would know at once that I was a stranger and I guessed that they did not get a great many tourists here.

At length I came to an inn over which a sign creaked in the wind. It proclaimed itself to be the Grand Duke's Tavern. I saw stables which contained horses, and at the back of the inn there was a garden in which tables and chairs had been set up. I sat down at one of these and a plump smiling woman came out to ask what I should like.

I guessed it was one of the *biergartens* of which I had heard and I asked her for a tankard of beer, wondering as I did so whether women did this sort of thing here or whether I was acting strangely.

She brought me a goblet of beer and seemed inclined to talk.

"You are travelling through our town, Fräulein?"

"I am staying for a visit," I told her.

"That is very good. It is a beautiful town, eh?"

I agreed that it was. An idea had occurred to me. "I see you have horses here. It is not always easy to go round on foot. Do you hire out your horses?"

"There is not much call for it. But I think my husband might."

"I want to see something of the country. I ride a great deal at home in England. If I could hire a horse—"

"Where do you stay, if I may ask, Fräulein?"

"I am staying in a cottage. It belongs to Herr Schmidt. I am a friend of his wife."

"Ah!" A smile broke out on her face. "You speak of the good Hans. He is a very proud man. He has an English wife and a fine little boy."

"Oh yes... young Hans."

"His wife—she is very nice."

"Very nice."

"And you are from the same country... come to see your friend?"

"To see her and the baby and your beautiful country."

"Oh, it is very beautiful. You could see much on horseback. You are an experienced rider, Fräulein?"

"Yes, indeed. I ride a great deal at home."

"It will be arranged. There must be a charge."

"But of course."

"When you have drunk your beer you must see my husband."

"I will."

"He will be in the inn."

She seemed reluctant to leave me and I think she may have been a little fascinated by my foreign appearance and perhaps by my speech, for although I was fluent enough I guessed that my accent might betray my country of origin.

"Such nice places to visit," she went on. "You can go to the old ruined *schloss* which was the home of the Grand Dukes years ago. You can go to the shooting lodge ... Oh, but perhaps not."

"The shooting lodge?"

"Yes, it is the Grand Duke's lodge. You cannot see his *schloss*. No, it is not that one you see on the hill. That is the *schloss* of the Graf von Bindorf. The Grand Duke's can only be seen from the other side of the town. You cannot go in, of course, but there is a good view and that is worth seeing."

I said, "What about the shooting lodge?"

She lifted her shoulders. "There was a tragedy there," she said.

"You mean the one where the Baron was murdered?"

She nodded. "It was a few years ago."

"Is it near here?" I asked quickly.

"It is about a mile and a half from Herr Schmidt's cottage. You would not want to see it. It's dismal now. At one time ... oh, but there it is. No, you would not want to visit it now."

I did not reply. I was going to get that horse and see that shooting lodge just as soon as I possibly could.

I went to see the innkeeper before I left. Then I walked back to Daisy's cottage, having booked a horse for the next day. I was making progress. I was about to visit the scene of the crime.

I did not mention even to Daisy that I was about to visit the hunting lodge. I merely told her that I had been to the Grand Duke's Tavern and seen horses there and had decided to hire one to help me around to see the countryside. She was pleased because looking after the cottage and young Hans was really as much as she could find time for.

So accordingly, on the next day, I went into the town, and was soon riding back the way I had come, past Daisy's cottage, for the innkeeper's wife had said the lodge was a mile and a half from that spot.

I had known that Daisy's cottage was on the edge of the forest, so I was not surprised to find that after I had left it a little way behind, the trees grew closer together. There was only one path through them so I took it.

It was a beautiful morning. I made my way through the trees. Except for the occasional oak and birch, they were chiefly fir and pine and the resinous smell was strong in the air. I could not rid myself of the feeling that I had stepped into one of Miss Elton's fairy tales of the forest.

After I had ridden some way, I came to a cottage and I wondered if it was Gisela's. I was about to stop and ask, but I was anxious that no one should guess that I was unduly interested in the lodge...even a friend of Daisy's.

The door of the cottage was shut, but it had a little garden and in this was a child's wheelbarrow. I passed it and went on up the path. I must have gone for about half a mile when I saw it. It was bigger than I had thought it would be. A hunting lodge suggests something rather small—a place where people stayed for a night or two when hunting in the forest. But of course this was a royal hunting lodge, so naturally it would be more grand.

My heart was beating fast. I pictured Francine coming here through the forest with her lover. How had it been with them? This would have been her home. She had stayed here because her lover was so important that he could not admit to marrying someone quite unsuitable. The idea of Francine's being considered unsuitable for anyone because of her unworthiness made me feel really angry. I told myself not to be foolish. If I were going to get foolishly emotional I should soon betray myself.

The hunting lodge was in grey stone and looked like a miniature *schloss*. It had two towers—one at either side—and an arched porch. There were several windows in the front. There could be no doubt that this was the place. I dismounted and tethered my horse to a post which I found and which was obviously meant for that purpose. There was an eeriness about the scene. Was it because I knew that a murder had taken place here or because the trees grew so close together, making it dark and full of shadows, and because the faint breeze stirring the leaves sounded like whispering voices?

My heart was beating wildly as I went uneasily forward, picking my way through the long grass scattered with pine cones.

I approached the porch, tingling with excitement. I stood on the porch and listened. There was a bell on the side of it with a long chain. I pulled this and the sound which broke the silence was deafening.

I held my breath, listening. I noticed a shutter in the door which could be pulled back to allow someone on the inside to look out and see who was standing there. I stared at it. Nothing happened. And then I heard an almost imperceptible sound and it came from within. It was as though someone was creeping towards the door.

I stood very still and my heart seemed as though it would leap from my body. I was already forming in my mind what I would say if I was confronted by someone who demanded my business here. I was a stranger. I was lost in the forest. I wanted to know my way back to the Schmidts' cottage where I was staying during my visit to Bruxenstein.

I stood there waiting, and then I began to wonder whether the sounds I heard were merely the wild beating of my own heart. No, surely not. There was the sound of something being dragged along the floor. I waited in trepidation, but nothing happened. Of one thing I was certain. There was someone inside the hunting lodge.

I stood there for some minutes. There was complete silence, but I knew that someone was on the other side of the door.

I rang the bell again and the sound burst out loud and clanging. I listened, keeping my eye on the shutter. But nothing happened.

I walked away and as I did so I heard a faint noise behind me. The shutter had moved. Oh yes, I was right. Someone was in the house, someone who would not answer my ringing. Why? I wondered.

It was all rather uncanny.

I walked along to one of the windows and looked in. Dust sheets covered the furniture. I walked round to the back.

"Oh, Francine," I murmured, "what happened? Someone is in there. Is it some human? Or is it ghosts?"

I had come to the back of the lodge. I could hear a bird singing somewhere in the forest. A gentle breeze ruffled the pine trees and their scent seemed stronger than ever. There was a door at the back and I went to it and rapped loudly on it and while I stood there I heard movement behind me. I turned sharply. My eyes went immediately to a clump of bushes, for I thought I detected movement there.

"Who is there?" I called out. "Come out and tell me the way. I'm lost."

I heard a soft laugh, more like a giggle. I went towards the bushes.

They stood before me with wide blue eyes and tousled hair.

They were both dressed in dark blue jerkins and blue skirts. One was slightly taller than the other, but I guessed them to be of the same age, which could not have been more than four or five years old.

"Who are you?" I asked in German.

"The twins," they answered simultaneously.

"What are you doing in this place?"

"Playing."

"Have you been watching me?"

They started to laugh and nodded.

"Where have you come from?"

One of them pointed vaguely.

"Are you a long way from home?"

The same one nodded.

"What are your names?"

One pointed to the blue jerkin and said "Carl." The other did likewise and said "Gretchen."

"So you're a little girl and you're a little boy."

They nodded, laughing.

"Is anyone in there?" I asked, pointing to the lodge.

Again they giggled and nodded.

"Who?"

They hunched their shoulders and looked at each other.

"Won't you tell me?" I asked.

"No," said the one named Carl. "You've got a horse."

"Yes. Would you like to come and see it?"

They both nodded with enthusiasm. As we walked round to the front of the lodge I looked towards the porch and so did they. I guessed they knew who was in the house and I promised myself that I would get it out of them.

The children were delighted with my horse. "Don't go too near him," I warned and obediently they stood back.

I turned my head sharply. The shutter was open and we were being observed.

"Can you take me into the lodge?" I asked the twins.

They looked at each other without answering.

"Come on," I said. "Let's go and look. How do you get in?"

Still they did not speak, and as we stood there a boy appeared. He must have come round from the back of the lodge. He called out, "Carl! Gretchen! What are you doing?" He looked rather flushed and defiant.

"Hello," I said. "Where have you come from?"

He didn't answer and I went on. "I'm lost in the forest. I saw this place and thought you would tell me the way."

I fancied he looked relieved.

"Was it you in the house?" I asked. "Did you look at me through the shutter?"

He didn't answer. Instead he said, "Where did you want to go? The town is in that direction." He pointed to the way I had come.

"Thank you," I said. "What an interesting place this is."

"There was a murder here once," he told me.

"Was that really so?"

"Yes. It was the heir to the throne."

"How did you get in?"

"I have a key," he said rather importantly, and the twins looked at him with undisguised admiration.

"How did you get the key?"

He was silent, shutting his lips firmly.

"I wouldn't tell tales," I promised him. "I'm a stranger here...just someone who's lost her way in the forest. I'd love to look inside that place. I've never seen where a murder was committed."

He looked at me pityingly. I guessed him to be about eleven years old.

I went on, "What's your name?"

He said, "What's yours?"

"I'm Anne Ayres."

"You're a foreigner."

"That's right. I'm here looking at the country. It's very beautiful but most of all I'd like to see a place where a murder was committed."

"It was in the big bedroom," he said. "It's all covered up. Nobody comes now. People wouldn't want to sleep in a place where there had been a murder, would they?"

"I should think not. Are there ghosts here?"

"I don't know," he said.

"Do you come often?"

"We have the key," he said importantly again.

"Why do you have the key?"

"So that my mother can go in and clean it."

Now I was sure who the children were.

"I see. Would you take me in?" He hesitated and I said, "Take me in and I'll give you a ride on my horse."

I saw the sparkle in his eyes and now it was my turn to receive the awed glances of the twins.

"All right," he said.

"Come on then."

We walked round to the porch, and I said to him, "You heard me ring, didn't you?"

He nodded.

"And you looked through the shutter at me. And you had to pull something up to see through it."

"Next year I'll be tall enough."

"I am sure you will be."

Proudly he opened the door. There was a creaking sound as he did so. We were in a hall with wooden floors and oak walls. There was a large table in the centre and on the walls were spears and lances. Everything was covered up with dust sheets. The door shut and the twins, hand in hand, walked behind us.

"By the way, what is your name?" I asked the boy. "I know the twins are Carl and Gretchen."

"Arnulf," he said.

"Well, Arnulf, it is good of you to show me round."

He seemed suddenly to lose his suspicion of me. He said, "I'm not supposed to come here."

"Oh, I see. That's why you didn't open the door."

He nodded.

"Gisela was coming with me."

"Who is Gisela?"

"My sister. She wouldn't come. She was afraid of ghosts. She said I wouldn't dare go alone."

"And you wanted to show her that you would."

He looked disparagingly at the twins. "*They* follow me everywhere."

The twins looked at each other and smiled as though they had done something clever.

"I wouldn't let them come in, though. I made them wait outside. I thought that if there were ghosts they might not like the twins in here, giggling. They're always giggling."

"You didn't think the ghosts would mind you?"

"Well, they're such babies. And they never go anywhere without each other."

"Twins are often like that," I said sympathetically.

He started up the stairs. "I'll show you the bedroom," he said. "It's where it happened, you know."

"The murder," I whispered.

He threw open the door with the gesture of a showman who is about to reveal his masterpiece.

Now I was actually there...where Francine had been murdered.

The bed was partially covered in dust sheets, but the four posts with their elaborate red hangings were visible. I was overcome by my emotion. Face to face with the scene of the crime, I could picture it so clearly. My beautiful sister in that bed with her handsome, romantic but oh so dangerous lover. I wanted to throw myself on those dust sheets, to touch the soft velvet of the draperies and just release the bitter tears I had tried so hard to hold back...to weep for the sadness of it all.

"Are you all right?" asked Arnulf.

"Yes...yes. It's a big bed."

"It had to be. There were two of them."

My voice shook a little. I said, "What do you know of them? Why were they killed?"

"Because they didn't want him to be Grand Duke and because she was there and saw it." He dismissed the cause as though it were of little importance. "My father is the care-taker," he added proudly. "And my mother comes in to clean."

"I see. That explains everything. Do you come here often?"

He hunched his shoulders and did not answer. Then he said, "We've got to go now."

I was torn between my desire to stay in that room and a desperate need to get away if I were going to control my feelings. I said quickly, "May I take a look at the rest of it?"

"Quick then," he said.

"Then you show me."

He enjoyed showing me. He liked best the kitchens where, he told me, venison was cooked on the great spits and in the cauldrons, relics of a previous age and yet they had been used until recently. There were several bedrooms for servants and huntsmen, I guessed, and there was one room that was full of guns.

I looked out of a back-room window and saw the stables, which were empty now.

"Come on," said Arnulf. "It's getting late."

"Perhaps another time you'll show me some more," I said. "I want you to have this." I gave him a coin which he looked at in amazement. "Guides are always paid," I told him.

"Am I a guide, then?"

"You have been this morning."

He looked at the coin almost disbelievingly, and the twins came closer to inspect it. It was clear that they had a very high opinion of their brother.

"Arnulf is a guide," said Carl to Gretchen.

She nodded and they kept repeating the word: Guide.

"So," I said, "if I should wish to see it again..."

Arnulf smiled at me.

"Tell me where you live," I said. "Is it far from here?"

He shook his head.

"I'll take you home," I said. "I tell you what, you can all ride on my horse and I'll walk beside you. How's that?"

They all nodded gleefully. Arnulf carefully put back the bench he had drawn to the door in order that he might look through the shutter, and we went out and he locked the door.

The three children sat on my horse and we were on our way. I was not surprised when Gisela came to the door of the cottage, but she was. "Why," she cried, "it's Fräulein Ayres."

Arnulf suffered a moment's apprehension when he realized I knew his mother.

I said quickly, "Well, fancy the children's mother being you. We met in the forest. We talked and I offered them a ride home."

Her plump face was creased in smiles.

"Well, you have had a good morning," she said. "And the twins too."

I lifted them down. Arnulf showed his superiority by needing no help.

"I think," said Gisela, "that we must ask Fräulein Ayres if she would care to have some refreshment."

"Oh yes please, *Mutti*," cried Arnulf, and the twins nodded vigorously. It was pleasant to know that they had taken a fancy to me as I had to them.

I tethered the horse and we went into the cottage, which was small but exceptionally clean. We sat at a table and Gisela poured some soup into platters. It was rather like that which I had sampled on my arrival at Daisy's house and we ate rye bread with it.

I said, "This is very good of you. I was wondering whether I should return to the town and go to the inn for something to eat."

"Did you see the hunting lodge?" she asked. "This is the road to it, you know."

There was a moment's silence at the table while three pairs of eyes watched me anxiously to see if their owners would be betrayed.

"It's the rather palatial place about half a mile from here, is it not?"

"That's it. This is in the nature of being the lodge cottage. Part of the royal estate. Arnulf and I had to look after the place. Those duties go with the cottage."

"Arnulf is my father," the young Arnulf explained. "It's not me. I'm named after him."

"I see," I said.

Gisela smiled at Arnulf and at me. She was a very motherly woman and I liked her more than ever.

"You took the twins with you," she said to Arnulf. "Where are the others?"

"Gisela wouldn't come with us."

"And the others are with her, I suppose." She smiled at me. "They love playing in the forest and Gisela won't let them go too far. Arnulf, go and call in the others."

Arnulf went out and the twins followed him rather reluctantly, I thought. They were torn between the habit of following their elder brother and staying to study the stranger.

Gisela said, "They keep me busy, but when the elder ones look after the small ones it makes life easier."

"You must have a great deal to do...your own house...your children...and the hunting lodge."

"I only go there two or three times a week now. In the old days it was different. There were people there then. They would have parties too. It was one of the Baron's favourite places."

"The one who was murdered?"

"That's right."

"He was there with..."

"Yes, his lady friend. She was a very beautiful young woman."

"Did you know her?"

"Why yes, I was up there...looking after the place, and when there was all that trouble she was living there. He used to come when he could. They were very much in love. It was such a shame."

"Was she there very long?"

"Quite a long time. You see, he couldn't very well set her up in the town. The Grand Duke would not have allowed that."

"But if they were married—"

"Oh, there was nothing of that. Rudolph had had his ladies before...but this one seemed..."

"Seemed what?"

"Well, rather different. She was a lovely lady, kind to the servants, always laughing. We all liked her and it was a blow to us when it happened. There's a lot of rivalry here among the various noble houses, you know."

I was growing tremendously excited. This had been a rewarding morning. Not only had I visited the scene of the crime but I was actually talking to someone who had known Francine well.

"I did hear there was a child," I began tentatively.

She stared at me in amazed horror. "Where on earth could you have heard such a tale!"

"I—er—heard it," I replied lamely.

"Since you have been here?"

"N-no. There was something about the murder in the English papers."

"Did they mention a child then?"

"It was some time ago..."

"Yes, a few years. But a child! I'm surprised about that."

"Well, you would know...living here."

"Oh yes, I should have known. I must say I'd rather we didn't have to look after the place now. It always seems a bit ghostly nowadays. Of course it was always dark and rather damp in the heart of the forest as it is, and now being shut up."

"Do you think it will be used again?"

"In time, I daresay. In a while all this will be forgotten. I reckon when the Grand Duke dies and Sigmund takes his place, there will be changes."

"Do you think that will be a good thing?"

"We should all be sorry to see the old Grand Duke go. He's been good for the country. Sigmund...? Well, he's a bit of a puzzle at the moment. He has a certain fascination...well, Rudolph had that. They've got good looks and charm, the whole family. There's no doubt about that. When Sigmund marries the young Countess I should think he will probably settle down."

I wasn't interested in the future. It was the past which obsessed me. I took my leave with many thanks and Gisela requested that I call again and meet the rest of her family very soon.

I said I would.

Eventually I took the horse back to the inn with the promise that I would hire it again.

I was extremely satisfied. It had been a rewarding day.

After having made such a good start and got, as I thought, so far within a few days of my arrival, I was due for a disappointment.

I told Daisy about my encounter in the forest and how I had found the lodge and Gisela's cottage. Yes, she said, Gisela had what they called the hunting cottage and she kept an eye on the hunting lodge. She was a busy woman and they didn't have a lot of time to see each other, but they did whenever they could.

I said, "Daisy, you must have seen my sister when you visited Gisela."

"No, I didn't visit her when your sister was here. It was only when young Hans was born that we got the cottage and became neighbours. Before that I was up at the slosh and that's a good way from the forest."

"Two or three miles, I suppose."

"That would be about it, and there wasn't much call for me to go her way or her to come mine. It's only since I've lived here."

"It was strange that I should meet the children like that."

"A bit of luck, though. I daresay Gisela would have shown you round if she'd been there. I can see it's upset you, seeing all that. What good does it do? Come to think of it, what good is it going to do if you find out who murdered her?"

"There are two things I want to discover, Daisy. And those are: Was she really married and the whereabouts of her child."

Daisy shook her head. "These barons don't marry like that. It's all arranged and there was no mention of a child."

"But Daisy, Francine *told* me in her letters. She told me she was married and where the ceremony had taken place. I went to the church and saw the entry in the register . . . and then when I went again it wasn't there. She told me she had a little boy, Rudolph. She wouldn't have made that up."

Daisy was thoughtful: "She might," she said. "Think of the shock it would be to her, for I reckon she *thought* he was going to marry her and then when she found he couldn't, she started to dream up what might have been. You know Miss France. She was one to look on the bright side of things, and if it didn't work out right she'd want to believe it did."

"But I tell you I saw the entry."

"But when you went again you didn't see it."

I realized she thought I was a little like Francine. If things were not what I wanted, I imagined they were so strongly that I believed what I wanted to.

A week passed, and I had got no further. I had hired the horse on several days and ridden into the forest. It was no use just looking at the hunting lodge. That would not get me very far. I explored the town; I sat in the *Biergarten*. People talked to me now and then because I was a stranger, I supposed. They gave me directions as to how to see the best of the country. There was one subject I wanted to discuss but I dared not do that too frequently. The information I gleaned was always the same. Rudolph had been murdered by some political enemy and his mistress with him because she happened to be on the spot. There was never a mention of a child.

I visited the hunting cottage and gave the children rides on the horse. I talked to Gisela over rye bread and hot soup, for there always seemed to be a cauldron of it bubbling on the open fire in the living room. I met the other children: Gisela, Jacob and Max. Max was the baby and about two years old. Jacob was older than the twins and came somewhere in between Arnulf and Gisela. It was interesting and enjoyable, but I had a sole purpose and I was getting restive.

Daisy noticed it.

"Well, I don't know what you think you're going to find out," she said. "I reckon the secret's in higher circles than you'll find here. It's not in the forest, that's for sure. It's up there somewhere, I reckon. The answer will be with them up at the slosh."

"I do wish I could find out."

"Well, you won't get an invitation to the slosh by telling them you're Miss Philippa Ewell, sister of the dead lady, who's come to sort out the mystery. That's for sure."

She was right and the thought depressed me.

Then, just as I was beginning to despair and to feel that

I had been foolish to hope just because of my initial success, I had an amazing stroke of luck.

It came through Hans.

I was sitting in the little garden with Daisy, and young Hans was running round on the small patch of lawn, taking water from a bucket and attempting to water the flowers which grew round the border. Daisy and I were laughing at his antics, for Hans himself got more water than the flowers, but he was so delighted with his work that we couldn't help joining in the merriment. Hans the elder was suddenly coming towards us.

"I thought I'd come home to tell you," he said, and he was looking directly at me. "It's like this. It's the Countess Freya..."

"Who is she?" I asked.

"She is betrothed to Sigmund, the heir, and she is at the Grand Schloss, being brought up in the Grand Duke's household. She has been there ever since she was betrothed. It is the custom that these brides are brought up with their future husband's family. It is supposed to get them used to the ways and habits of their future homes."

"Yes, Hans, we know she's there," said Daisy impatiently.

"Miss Philippa didn't."

"No, that's true, and she's Miss Ayres while she's here, remember."

"Yes," said Hans. "I'm sorry. Well, what I've heard is that the Countess Freya has to improve her English. Her present governess has taught her something of the language but they reckon her accent is wrong, and they want an Englishwoman to put her right."

I was staring wildly at Hans as a hundred possibilities crossed my mind.

He nodded, smiling at me. "That's what I thought," he said. "If you got inside the *schloss* you'd be able to find out if there is anything in all this talk."

"Teaching English to the Countess," I murmured.

"What's this?" cried Daisy, and when it was translated for her she was as wildly excited as I was. "It's the very thing. You're getting tired of being here with nothing happening....You'll be going away soon unless something does pretty quick. But to go there...to the slosh, wouldn't that be a lark!"

"Oh Daisy, it would be so exciting."

"Now listen to me," said Hans, "if you thought you'd like to do it I'll go along to the comptroller of the Grand Duke's household. He's a friend of mine and a recommendation from me would go a long way. But you see, if they knew you were Miss Francine's sister—"

"Why should they?" demanded Daisy. "Oh, how right you were to come here as Miss Ayres."

"If you were found out I should say I knew nothing about it," said Hans quickly. "I'd say you were someone my wife knew and she'd heard you wanted to stay for a little, and as we could do with a little extra, you became a paying guest."

"That's right," said Daisy. "That fits the book."

"But, Daisy, *you* couldn't very well say you didn't know who I was."

"Let's cross that stile if ever we get to it. When I'm asked awkward questions I always say I don't speak the language."

"It's the great opportunity," I cried. "It's manna from heaven. I was just beginning to think how hopeless everything was and that I should never get anywhere... and now this."

"So you're going to do it," said Daisy.

"Yes. Please Hans, will you speak for me?"

Hans was a cautious man, and I could see that he did not wish to be involved in anything that could bring him trouble.

"Why should you know who I am?" I persisted. "You had hardly ever seen me in England. I am here as Anne Ayres. Even Daisy hadn't seen me for five years. If I'm found out I'll say I knew Daisy was here and I came as Anne Ayres. But I really don't see why my true identity should be discovered."

"Of course it won't be." Daisy supported me. I could see she was as excited as I was.

Finally we agreed that I should try for the post. Hans went off to speak to the comptroller of the Grand Duke's household, and within a few days I was making my way to what was known as the Grand Schloss to be interviewed by the comptroller and the mistress of the household for the important task of instructing the august young lady in English.

A carriage had been sent to convey me to the *schloss* and when it arrived at the cottage Daisy and I regarded it with something like awe. Engraved on the side were the royal arms of Bruxenstein—crossed swords under a crown and the words which translated were "Advance to Victory."

I had debated with Daisy for a long time how I should

dress, and we had decided that I should wear my plainest clothes and that my hair—which was rather unmanageable, yet at the same time was my only real claim to beauty because it was fine and very abundant—should be taken right off my face and gathered into a knot at the nape of my neck, which enabled my dark-blue straw hat to sit on top of my head in a demure fashion.

I wore a dark blue skirt and coat with a white blouse, and I thought I looked capable and as though I had never even heard there was such a thing in the world as frivolity.

Daisy clapped her hands when she saw me and I felt I had left Philippa Ewell behind me and taken on a new personality: Miss Anne Ayres.

A liveried footman helped me into the carriage and jumped up at the back of it, while the driver of the two fine bays whipped them up and we were off. I knew that Daisy would be watching us from the top window of the cottage, as excited as I was, for Daisy had often said, "I can't bear nothing to happen. I'd almost as soon have *any*thing . . . rather than nothing."

As we gambolled through the town a few people stopped to stare at the royal carriage, which they immediately recognized, and I fancied one or two of them, who were able to catch a glimpse of its occupant, were wondering who this plainly dressed and rather prim young woman could be.

We went past the guards at the gate of the *schloss,* who looked very splendid in their light blue uniforms and splendid helmets with the pale red feathers in them, and their swords clanked at their sides as they saluted the royal coach.

We came into a courtyard, where we alighted, and I was conducted into a hall a good deal larger than the one in the hunting lodge, but built on the same lines with the vaulted roof and the thick stone walls into which stone benches had been cut.

A liveried servant appeared and told me to follow him. I did so into a small room which led from the hall.

"You will please to wait for a moment," he said.

I nodded and sat down.

Some five minutes elapsed before I heard footsteps in the hall and the door was opened. A man and woman came in.

I rose and inclined my head. They inclined theirs.

"You are Fräulein Ayres?" the man asked. "I am Herr Frutschen and this is Frau Strelitz."

I wished them good day, which greeting they returned in a most courteous manner.

I knew that Herr Frutschen was the comptroller of the household and the friend of Hans and I gathered that Frau Strelitz was the mistress of the household, and that she was the one I should have to impress if I were to get the post.

"You are from England?" she asked.

I agreed that I was.

"And you are seeking a post here?"

"I was not looking for a post, but I heard of this through Herr Schmidt and I thought I should like to do it."

"You are not a governess."

"No, I have never worked in such a post."

"You are very young."

My heart sank. Could it be that my demure hair style had not done for me what I had hoped it would?

"I am nearly eighteen years old."

"And you came to visit this country?"

"My grandmother left me money and I thought it would be a good idea to realize a long-standing ambition to see the world."

"So you intended to go on and your stay here was temporary?"

"I had no definite plans. I thought this would be interesting."

The comptroller looked at Frau Strelitz. She nodded almost imperceptibly.

"Your task would be to teach a young lady to speak English fluently. She has learned the language but has difficulty with the accent."

"I understand exactly."

The woman hesitated. "It would only be for a year...no more. Until the Countess marries."

"I understand that."

"That will be in about a year's time. She is fifteen years old at the moment. The ceremony will very likely take place when she is sixteen."

I nodded.

"You have been well educated, I believe."

"I was educated by a governess who was half German, which I think accounts for my own command of the language."

"It is good, good," put in the comptroller, who clearly

wanted me to be given the post because of his friendship with Hans.

"Yes," agreed Frau Strelitz, "it is good."

"Fräulein Ayres is a very well-educated lady," said the comptroller. "That is important for the right accent."

"This is a very important post," went on the woman. "You must understand, Fräulein Ayres, that your pupil will one day be the first lady in the land. She is to marry the Grand Duke's heir. That is why we have to be so careful."

"Of course," I said. "I understand perfectly."

"Your references from a previous employer—"

"I have no previous employer."

"Is there anyone who could vouch for you?"

I hesitated. I thought of Charles Daventry and the vicar. But they had never heard of Anne Ayres. There was Cousin Arthur. I wondered if I could explain to them.

I said, "At home, yes. I have friends...and the vicar, if you wished...."

"We shall leave you for a moment," said Frau Strelitz. "Please excuse us."

"Certainly."

They went out, shutting the door behind them. I was in a fever of impatience. Something told me that I must get this post, that if I did not there could be nothing to do but admit defeat and go home.

Good luck was with me. In ten minutes they came back. The comptroller was beaming.

The woman said, "We have decided to give you a trial, Fräulein Ayres. I hope you do not think we are being impolite. It is such an important post because of the young lady involved. She herself must be happy in our choice. We will give you a week's trial...and then three weeks after that. If at the end of that time we find you suitable, then..."

"Of course," I cried. "I understand."

"We have decided not to write to England for references," said the comptroller. "My friend, Herr Schmidt, tells us that you are a lady from a good family. That is what we want— in view of the rank of our young lady. Nor do we want someone who is looking for a more permanent post. So if you would care to start at the beginning of next week, that would be good. Now, shall we discuss remuneration?"

I knew there would be no difficulty about that. All I wanted was to get into the royal *schloss*.

I was driven back in the royal carriage. I rushed into the kitchen where Daisy was bending over the stove.

"I've got it!" I shouted. "Behold the English governess of the most important lady in the land!"

We danced round the kitchen and young Hans toddled out and seeing our gaiety joined in. We were breathless with laughter.

"This is the beginning," I said.

The English
Governess

On the following Monday the carriage came to collect me and my travelling bag. I was leaving some of my things at Daisy's and was in a fever of excitement when I presented myself at the *schloss* and was taken to the same small room in which I had been interviewed. It was not long before I was joined by Frau Strelitz.

"Ah, Fräulein Ayres," she said, "the Countess is very eager to meet you. Her apartments are on the third floor. There is a schoolroom there and you will have a room in her apartments. She has a governess. You will work out with her the time of her studies, but the Grand Duke has stressed that her English must be improved. That is the most important of her studies at this time. The Baron, her future husband, who will be our ruler in due course when the Grand Duke dies—but that, God willing, will not be for some time yet—I was saying that the Baron speaks good English and she must do the same. When he visits her he will expect improvements."

"You may rest assured that I will do my best to see that this is brought about."

"I am sure you will. You may have some difficulty with Countess Freya. She is a high-spirited girl and naturally her awareness of her position has made her somewhat—well, expecting to have her own way. It is a great responsibility which is yours, Fräulein Ayres, and you do not seem a great deal older than the Countess."

She was looking at me dubiously. Perhaps my hair was not quite so severely controlled. I could feel it beginning to work out of its confinement.

"I have travelled, Frau Strelitz, and I am sure that a lady of the world such as yourself will understand that the acquisition of knowledge is not necessarily a matter of age."

"You are right in that, Fräulein. Well, I wish you good fortune. I must tell you that if the Countess does not take to you she would make it very difficult for you to continue here."

"I suppose that situation arises with any governess."

"And it is not as though you are dependent on this post for your livelihood."

"I shall pursue it with all the more zeal," I said. "With me it will be a labour of love rather than necessity."

I think I impressed her a little, for her manner warmed towards me.

"Very well," she said. "If you will follow me I will show you your room and introduce you to your pupil."

The Grand Schloss was worthy of its name. It was built on a hill overlooking the town, of which it commanded a good view from all its windows. There were liveried servants everywhere, it seemed to me, and I was taken through galleries past rooms at which the guards were stationed and finally to the apartments of the Countess.

"The Countess has occupied these since she came from Kollenitz. That was, of course, after the death of Baron Rudolph when she became affianced to Baron Sigmund."

I nodded. "It was then, of course, that she became so important," went on Frau Strelitz, "for both the Margrave of Kollenitz and the Grand Duke are eager to unite the margravate and the Duchy by this marriage."

Frau Strelitz paused and knocked at a door. A voice called, "Enter!" and we went in. A middle-aged woman rose and came towards us.

"Fräulein Kratz," said Frau Strelitz, "this is Fräulein Ayres."

Fräulein Kratz had a pale lined face and a rather harassed look. I felt sorry for her at once and could see that she was surprised by my youth.

A young girl had risen from the table and she came towards me somewhat imperiously.

"Your Highness," said Frau Strelitz, "may I present Fräulein Ayres, your English governess?"

I bowed and said in English, "I am delighted to make your acquaintance, Countess."

She replied in German, "So you have come to teach me to speak English as the English do."

"Which is, of course, the best way to speak it," I continued in English.

She was very fair—so fair in fact that her eyelashes and eyebrows were scarcely perceptible. Her eyes were light blue, not large enough for beauty, particularly as she lacked the darker lashes which would have enhanced them; the very lightness of these gave her a look of perpetual surprise which I found rather endearing. She had a long, somewhat aquiline nose and a very firm mouth. Her thick fair hair was worn in braids and she looked rather like a petulant schoolgirl. I was wondering what effect I had on her.

"I hope you will be a good pupil," I went on.

She laughed, for she understood my English very well. "I expect I shall be a bad one. I am often—am I not, Kratzkin?"

"The Countess is really very bright," said Fräulein Kratz.

The Countess laughed. "You spoilt it with the 'really,' didn't she Fräulein Ayres? That gives it all away."

"Well, Fräulein Ayres," put in Frau Strelitz, "you and Fräulein Kratz will make your arrangements about lessons. Shall I take you to your room, and later you can settle things between you."

"*I* shall take Fräulein Ayres to her room," announced the Countess.

"Your Highness..."

"My Highness," mimicked the Countess, "will have it so. Come, Fräulein, we have to get to know each other, do we not, if we are to converse in your abominable language."

"You mean my beautiful language, of course, Countess," I said.

She laughed. "I am going to take her. Class is dismissed. Kratzkin and Frau Strelitz, you may leave us."

I was somewhat appalled by the imperious manner of my pupil, but I felt my spirits rising. I could see that we were going to have some interesting encounters.

"Have her bags sent up at once," ordered the Countess. "I want to see what she has brought." She laughed at me.

"I come from Kollenitz where they are rough and ready in their manners. We are not as cultivated as they are here in Bruxenstein. Have you gathered that, Fräulein Ayres?"

"I am beginning to."

That made her laugh.

"Come on," she said. "I have to talk to you, don't I?"

"In English," I said, "and I see no reason why we should not begin right away."

"Well, I do. You are merely a governess. I am the Countess, the Grand Duchess Elect. So you had better take care."

"On the contrary, it is you who have to take care."

"What do you mean by that?"

"I am a lady of independent means. I do not need to stay here. I am doing it because the idea appeals to me. It is not a case of earning my living. I think I should make that clear from the start."

She stared at me. Then she began to laugh again.

The two women were still hovering in the doorway and she cried out, "You heard me tell you to go. Leave at once. I will look after the English governess."

I smiled apologetically at Frau Strelitz. "It is good that we should talk together," I said. "I shall refuse to speak to the Countess except in English, as I have decided that that is a rule of paramount importance."

The young girl was too surprised to argue with me and I felt I had won the first round. I had also won the admiration of poor harassed Kratzkin and the approval of Frau Strelitz. But it was the Countess with whom I had to deal.

"This is your room," she said, flinging open a door. "I am at the end of this corridor. I have finer apartments, of course, but this is not bad for a governess."

"I daresay I shall find it adequate."

"Far better than you are accustomed to, no doubt," she said.

"In fact no. I was brought up in a large manor house which I think on the whole was every bit as luxurious as your *schloss*."

"And you really are doing all this...for fun?"

"You could call it that."

"You are not very old, are you?"

"I am experienced in the ways of the world."

"Are you? I wish I were. I'm not nearly as experienced as I should like to be."

"It comes with the years."

"How old are you?"

"I shall be eighteen in April."

"I am fifteen. There is not much difference."

"Actually there is a great deal. The next four years will be some of the most important of your life."

"Why?"

"Because one grows out of girlhood into womanhood."

"I shall be married next year."

"So I gathered."

"People talk about us a lot, don't they?"

"They know certain facts."

"I wish you wouldn't keep talking in English."

"It is what I am here for."

"It restricts the conversation. I want to know so much about you and I can't always understand as I want to if you will speak in English."

"It will be an incentive for you to master the language."

"You talk just like a governess. I have had quite a number but they never stay very long. I'm a difficult person. I've never had one like you."

"It will be a change for you."

"I don't suppose you'll stay long."

"Only while you need me, of course."

"I daresay you'll leave before that. I am not easy, you know."

"I have gathered that."

"Poor Kratzkin is terrified of me. Frau Strelitz is a bit, too."

"I don't think you should look so smug about that."

"Why not?"

"The fact that you make things uncomfortable for them should not make you glow with satisfaction. It is easy, is it not, to score over those who cannot reply?"

"Why don't they reply then?"

"Because they are employed here."

"Shall I score over you?"

"Most definitely not."

"Why not?"

"Because I am not dependent on pleasing you. If you don't like me you can tell me to get out, and if I don't like you I can go with equal ease."

She looked at me in astonishment. Then she smiled slowly.

"What's your name?"

"Fräulein Ayres."

"I mean your first name."

"Anne."

"I shall call you that."

"What is yours?"

"You know. Everybody knows. I'm the Countess Freya of Kollenitz."

"Freya. That's one of the goddesses."

"The goddess of beauty," she said complacently. "Did you know that when Thor lost his hammer the giant, Thrym, would only give it back if Freya came to the land of the giants as his bride?"

"I did. And Thor dressed as Freya and went to the land of the giants and got his hammer back. Those legends used to be told to me by my governess. She went often to the Black Forest for her holidays. She had a German mother."

"So you had a governess too. Was she nice? Did you like her?"

"She was very nice and I liked her."

"You were a good girl, I expect."

"Not always. But we were always well-mannered."

"Who were *we?*"

"My sister and I." I felt myself flush a little and she was quick to notice.

"Where is your sister now?"

"She died."

"That makes you sad, doesn't it?"

"Very sad."

"Tell me about your governess."

I told her all I could remember of Miss Elton and her family.

She was very interested but I noticed that her mind flitted from one thing to another very quickly. She had seen my bags. "Are you going to unpack?" she asked.

"Yes," I said.

"I'll watch you."

And she did, as I took my clothes out and hung them up. She made comments on them as I did so. "That's ugly. That's not so bad."

I said: "I see what you mean about Kollenitz manners!" which sent her into peals of laughter. There was a book lying on the top of my case and she seized it. She read slowly with a strong German accent, "The Poems of Robert Browning."

I said: "I can see that we shall have to work hard on your accent."

The book opened naturally at a certain page and there was a reason for it, for I had often turned to that particular poem.

"Pippa's Song," she read out slowly.

"'The year's at the spring
And day's at the morn—'

"Oh, I can't read this. Poetry's very difficult."

I took the book from her and read the poem aloud. There was a slight tremor in my voice when I reached the last lines.

"'God's in his Heaven—
All's right with the world.'"

I shut the book. She was looking at me intently. Then I smiled slowly and she returned the smile.

I thought: It's going to be all right. I'm going to like my little Countess.

The next few days were crowded with new impressions. To the surprise of the servants, the Countess and I got on remarkably well. I think this may have been due to a certain aloofness I was able to display, which was the result of my independence and the fact that I could, at any moment, leave if I wished without any financial considerations—which affected my manner and hers. I interested her as she interested me. She liked to be with me and wanted to neglect her other studies for the sake, as she rather unctuously said, of 'improving my English.' It was not difficult for me because there were no lessons to prepare. She had been grounded in the language and it was only conversation that she needed, so we were able to talk on various subjects, and when she made a mistake I would point it out to her.

Sometimes I would say to her, "Shouldn't you be with Fräulein Kratz?"

She would grimace. "Oh, I want to get on with my English. That is the most important. Who cares about mathematics—silly stuff anyway. Who cares about history? What does it matter what kings and queens did years ago? I can't change that, can I? I really do feel that I need to get on with my English."

I replied to that, "You forget that I must have my free times. You are encroaching on them."

I think it was rare for her to consider anyone but herself, but she did become thoughtful and went back to the schoolroom rather subdued.

I was flattered. When I visited Daisy I heard that Hans had been told by the comptroller of the household that they were amazed by my success with the Countess. It was very gratifying.

So we were together a great deal and I think, in a way, becoming friends. Life in the royal household was not exactly what I had expected. We were very much segregated and although two weeks had passed since my arrival, I had never once had a glimpse of the Grand Duke. The turret in which we had our apartments was quite separate from the royal apartments, and although there was much arriving and departing of emissaries and such like, this affected us not at all. It was like living in the wing of a country house—part of the main residence and yet completely cut off from it.

Freya and I walked in the grounds of the *schloss;* we rode together; she was a good horsewoman but I could compare favourably with her.

Once she said with a grudging admiration, "You can do everything."

She was always soberly dressed when she rode out and we always had to take two grooms with us, which irked her. I remarked that they were very discreet and kept their distance. "They had better," she said, her eyes flashing.

We rode through the forest together and she told me stories which had been passed down through the ages. She showed me an old ruined *schloss* where some baroness was said to have walled up her husband's mistress. "She said she wanted a new room added, and when the workmen were making it, she brought this beautiful girl to them and made them wall her in. They say you can still hear the girl's screams on certain nights."

She showed me the Klingen Rock with the ravine far below. "They used to take people out there and invite them to throw themselves over—to avoid a worse fate."

"You have some very pleasant customs in Bruxenstein."

"All people have them," retorted Freya. "They don't talk about them, though, and this was long ago."

"Klingen Schloss once belonged to a robber baron who used to waylay travellers, capture them and hold them to ransom. He used to chop off their fingers one by one and send them to their relatives, and with each finger the ransom was increased, and if the ransom wasn't paid they would be thrown from the rock...to get rid of them."

"It's horrible."

"The gods are nicer," admitted Freya, and her eyes glowed when she talked of Thor. "He was strong...the god of thunder." He was her favourite among the gods. "He had red hair and a red beard. He was the strongest of them all and very gentle, but when he was angry sparks flew out of his eyes."

"I hope he did not get angry often. Getting angry is foolish. It never helps."

"Don't you ever get angry, Fräulein Anne?"

"Oh yes—now and then. Fortunately I am not Thor, so you have no need to fear the sparks."

She laughed. She was constantly laughing in my company. I noticed how the servants would look at us when they heard her, and there was no doubt that I was getting a reputation for knowing how to handle the Countess.

I did understand that she had lived in a rarefied atmosphere and that her position had set her apart; she had known few other children and she had never had a playmate. All she had was her royalty, which manifested itself in her power over others. She had exerted it because it was all she had.

I was beginning to feel rather sorry for my arrogant little Countess. I encouraged her to talk. She had little to tell of her daily life; she lived in a world of her own, populated by gods and heroes. She talked constantly of Freya, which was natural enough as she had been called after that goddess.

"She was golden-haired and blue-eyed," she told me on one occasion, looking complacently at her reflection in the glass as she spoke, "and she was considered to be the personification of Earth because she was so beautiful. She married Odur, who was a symbol of the summer sun, and she had two daughters who were as beautiful as herself...well, not quite, but almost. She loved them dearly, but she loved her husband more. He was a wanderer, though, and could not be content at home. I wonder whether Sigmund will be a wanderer. I think he will be. He is hardly ever here. He is travelling now. Perhaps he doesn't want to be where I am."

I said, "You must not think that life is going to be for you just as it was for this goddess. We live in modern times."

She looked at me intently and said with a flash of wisdom: "But people don't change much, do they...whenever they lived they are much the same. They marry...and are unfaithful and they go wandering."

"It will be your task to see that Sigmund does not go wandering."

"Now you are talking like Kratzkin. Oh, please don't be like her. Be like yourself. I couldn't bear it if you became like someone else."

"I hope I shall always be myself, and I should imagine that this Freya who was so beautiful should have let her husband go wandering and not have bothered about him."

"She was so unhappy. She wept and when her tears fell into the sea they turned into amber."

"I hardly think that is the scientific explanation of that substance."

She laughed again and I was glad to see her merriment because I sensed beneath these conversations her preoccupation with her coming marriage to Sigmund, and I realized she was apprehensive. I hoped in time she would confide her feelings to me.

"She went in search of him and she wept so much that where she wept gold was found later."

"Many people must be grateful to the lachrymose lady," I said.

"Well, it all seems hard to believe now, but I'm glad they called me Freya. Though Freya did not marry Sigmund. He married Borghild...but she was wicked and he put her from him. Then he took a new wife in her place. She was Hjördis. You see, she wasn't Freya either."

"You have lived too much with these old legends," I told her. "They are not always meant to be taken so seriously. In any case your Sigmund was one of the heroes, wasn't he? I know you regard yourself as a goddess, but I should remember if I were you that Sigmund is a man. And you are a woman. And if you want to live together happily you must not forget this."

"You make it all sound so easy, Fräulein Anne. Is it always so easy for you?"

"No," I said firmly, "it is not."

"I want to tell you something."

"Yes?"

"I'm glad you came here."

It was remarkable progress, and that after two weeks!

She told me about life in Kollenitz. "It was much less

formal than here," she said. "Of course my father, the Margrave, governs only a little place... but it is important. That is the point. It is where Kollenitz is situated—not our power or our welath or anything like that. Bruxenstein needs to be friends with Kollenitz so that Kollenitz can be what they call a buffer state. Do you understand?"

"Yes."

"Well, how would you like to be a buffer?"

She looked at me questioningly and I replied on impulse, "I think it would depend on Sigmund."

That made her laugh yet again. "Sigmund is tall and handsome. I think the hero Sigmund must have been rather like him. But perhaps he is more like Sigurd. I always liked him better really. He was my favourite among all the heroes."

"You must get away from all those myths. Tell me about Kollenitz."

"I was the only child. It's a great blow when they don't have sons. They seem to blame it on you."

"I'm sure they don't."

"I am sure they do and please don't talk like Kratzkin."

"All right. Shall we say then that they feel a little resentful towards a female child?"

"That's better," she said.

"But it was no fault of yours, you should not allow it to upset you."

"It didn't, much. But... perhaps it did a little. It made it difficult for them—nurses, governesses, I wanted them to know that even if I was a girl I was also important—the heiress. Well, then I was betrothed to Sigmund and that was after Rudolph was murdered."

"What do you know about that?" I asked eagerly.

"About Rudolph? He was with his mistress in the hunting lodge and someone came in and killed them with one of the guns from the gun room there. I didn't hear about it until after, though if he had lived I should have married Rudolph."

"*You* would?"

"Yes, because of Kollenitz being the buffer. They want Kollenitz allied with Bruxenstein."

"What happened then?"

"It was a long time ago and I was very young at the time. I used to hear them whispering together, but they always shut up when they saw me. Then I heard I was going to be betrothed to Sigmund. I couldn't understand it at first because

they had always told me before that Rudolph was going to
be my husband."

"When did you learn that he had died?"

"When I was betrothed to Sigmund. They had to tell me
then that it was not going to be Rudolph and why. I didn't
go through any ceremony with Rudolph. It was all in treaties,
but there was a betrothal ceremony in the *schloss-kirche* here
and Sigmund and I made our vows. It wasn't a marriage...it
was just a betrothal; but it does mean that we are promised
to each other. We couldn't marry anyone else now without
a dispensation and that would never be given because my
father and the Grand Duke would never allow it."

"I see what an important person you are."

"A buffer," she answered.

I laid my hands on her shoulders. "Countess," I said, "I see
that you are going to be very happy."

"Where do you see it?"

"In your stars."

"Can you tell?"

"I can tell you that this will be so."

"I wonder why Sigmund stays away so long. Do you think
it is because he doesn't like me?"

"Certainly not. It is because he is arranging treaties and
such like with foreign powers."

She laughed. Then she was serious. "Perhaps it is," she
said. "You see, it was only when Rudolph died that he became
important. Before that, he was only the son of the Grand
Duke's younger brother."

"It must have made a lot of difference to his life."

"Of course. He'll be the Grand Duke when this one dies.
Oh, I do hope he's not going wandering like Freya's husband."

"He won't, and you won't go crying after him, even if it
does add to the world's supply of amber and gold."

"Oh, Fräulein Anne, I do like you. It's because you are
funny, I think. I am going to call you just Anne, not Fräulein
any more, because that makes you seem like any old governess."

"I can see we are making rapid strides. Your manners are
improving with your English accent. You ask my permission.
Dear Countess, I should like you to call me...just Anne."

"And will you call me Freya?"

"When we are alone," I said. "But before others it might
be wise to stand on a little ceremony."

She kissed me then and I was deeply moved. We were indeed becoming friends.

I had been with Freya for nearly a month when she said she wished to go to the mausoleum because this was the anniversary of her great-grandmother's death and she was buried there. I wanted to know how this came about and she told me that her great-grandmother had made a second marriage into Bruxenstein and had lived the last years of her life there, though the children of her first marriage had remained in Kollenitz.

I was very eager to see anything connected with the family and I greatly looked forward to the visit.

It was necessary to get the key to the mausoleum from the comptroller of the household and he greeted me with smiles. Like everyone else he knew of the success I was having with the young Countess, and he regarded himself as responsible for this happy appointment. He had even been congratulated by the Grand Duke himself, he told me, for the Grand Duke had had an account from Frau Strelitz and others.

I told him that I was enjoying the work and that the Countess was making excellent progress.

"It is said that she is so interested in her English studies that she is inclined to neglect others," he said complacently.

"Fräulein Kratz and I try to keep an even balance."

The comptroller beamed and gave me the key to the mausoleum, asking that when the visit was over I should return it to him.

This I promised to do and Freya and I set out on foot, for the church was adjoining the *schloss*. It was beautifully situated, high up with magnificent views of the town below. Some of the graves had been made quite recently and fresh flowers and wreaths lay on them.

The mausoleum was imposing and quite grand. Freya whispered to me that it had been there for many years and had been designed by one of the greatest architects.

She opened the door and descended a few steps. The floor was of marble, as was the chapel; and there were side galleries in which the sarcophagi had been placed.

"How quiet it is!" I said.

"Quiet as the grave," agreed Freya. "Anne, are you just a little bit frightened?"

"What is there to be afraid of?"

"Ghosts?" suggested Freya.

"The dead cannot harm the living."

"Some people think so. What if they have been murdered? They say that if people have died violently they can't rest."

"Who says?"

"*They.*"

"I never believe *them.* They are always so vague and it is as though they are afraid to say their names."

"This is the coffin of my great-grandmother. I always wonder about her when I come here. She came from Kollenitz to Bruxenstein...just as I did. But she was older than I and had been married before...so she knew something about it. I say a little prayer and hope that she is happy in heaven. I saw a picture of her once. They say she was like me."

"*They* again. They seem to be everywhere."

She laughed out loud and then put her fingers to her lips. "Perhaps we shouldn't laugh in here."

"Why not?"

"They might not like it."

"Here *they* come again."

She was serious. "I mean the ghosts this time," she whispered.

"Well," I said loudly, "we have nothing to fear from them or they from us."

"Come and look at this," she said, and she led me to the coffin which lay on one of the ledges. "Can you read it?"

I leaned forward. "Rudolph Wilhelm Otto Baron von Gruton Fuchs. Aged twenty-three years..."

"Yes," she interrupted. "It's the one who was murdered. I wonder if he rests in peace?"

I stared in shocked silence, stunned, although I should have realized that he would be buried here. My mind had gone back over the years to the day when I had first seen him coming to the Grange and taking Francine away.

Then suddenly I realized that I was alone. I turned sharply and heard the key turning in the lock. I was startled and then deeply shocked. Freya had locked me in.

I stared at the door. Then I went to it and said sternly, "Open this immediately."

There was no response. I banged with my fists but that made little impression.

I did not know what to do. This was not serious. I should soon be missed and they would know where I was because the comptroller had given me the key to the mausoleum, and if Freya returned without me they would come immediately and release me. But my first feelings were disappointment that Freya could have done this. I knew she was trying to break through my calm and frighten me, to show that I possessed the same weaknesses that she did; but to be locked in a mausoleum with no company but the dead was a terrifying experience and of this she would be very much aware, and yet in spite of our friendship she had subjected me to it.

It was indeed eerie in this place. I looked at the sarcophagi on the side galleries and thought of the dead—Rudolph among them. If he could but come alive and tell me the truth of what happened, I would be ready to face anything for that.

I sat on the steps and stared ahead of me. "Oh, Rudolph..." I murmured to myself, "come to me now, I won't be afraid. I want so much to know...."

And then suddenly...I was aware of a presence...close to me. I fancied I heard the sound of suppressed laughter.

I turned sharply and the silence was broken by Freya's merriment. She had quietly opened the door and was standing behind me.

"Were you frightened?" she asked.

"When you foolishly locked me in, shall we say I was very surprised."

"Why?"

"That you could do something so—"

"Childish?"

"No. That would have been forgivable."

"Are you angry then? Aren't you going to forgive me? Will you go away?"

I turned to her and said, "Freya, some people might have been very frightened indeed to be locked in such a place."

"You wouldn't."

"How did you know?"

"You are not frightened of anything."

"Good heavens! Have I given you that impression?"

She nodded.

"It was cruel of you," I continued. "You should never do a thing like that to anybody."

"I know. I got frightened as soon as I'd done it. I thought your hair would turn white in a minute. Some people's do when they're frightened. I thought you might die of shock. Then I told myself you'd be all right. Then I got frightened that you would be so angry that you would go away. So I opened the door... and there you were just sitting there talking to yourself."

"Give me the key," I said. "Did you take it out of my pocket?"

She nodded.

"It was all rather silly," I commented.

"It wasn't in a way," she argued, "because it shows me that you really are very brave and just as I thought you were. You didn't scream or shout. You just sat there and waited because you knew I would be sorry almost at once."

I led her firmly out of the mausoleum and locked the door. As we made our way back to the *schloss* she said, "I know another grave. I'll show you if you like?"

"What grave?"

"It's rather a special one. It's a secret. I'll take you tomorrow. I do like you, Anne. I'm sorry I took the key and locked you in. But you were not frightened, were you? I don't think you ever would be. I think you've got special powers."

"Now please don't confuse me with your gods and heroes. I'm not one of them."

"What are you, Anne?"

"The long-suffering English governess."

It was a pleasant trait in Freya's character that she was really penitent about locking me into the mausoleum and tried very hard to make up for her conduct.

I dismissed it all as of little importance and pointed out that as she had so quickly repented we could forget it.

She was determined to please me, though, and only the next day suggested that we take a ride into the forest. We set out with two grooms riding behind us at a safe distance, and I was amazed to find that we were making our way towards the hunting lodge. We passed the cottage. None of the children was visible.

I said: "I have friends in that cottage."

"The lodge people?" she asked.

"Yes, I met them once. They have some charming children."

"Oh, they're the people who looked after the hunting lodge when it happened."

"Yes."

We fell into silence for a while, then she said, "We shall come to it in a minute."

And there it was, looking more imposing than ever. Freya had pulled up and, to my astonishment, dismounted.

"We are going in there?" I asked, and I hoped she did not notice the excitement in my voice.

She shook her head. "There's nothing in there," she told me. "Nobody goes there now. Well, would you want to? Where a murder had been committed?"

I shivered.

"You looked really scared, Anne." She was regarding me intently. "You look more frightened than you did in the mausoleum. Well, not exactly frightened...but odd somehow."

"I assure you I'm not frightened."

"All right then. Come on."

"Where are we going?"

"I told you. I promised to show you something."

My excitement was increasing. I felt that I was on the verge of a discovery, and that it should come through the Countess was amazing.

She called to the grooms, who were following at a discreet distance, "We are going to walk round the lodge. Stay there with the horses. Come on," she went on to me. "This way."

I followed her, wondering whether Arnulf, the twins or one of the other children were close by. But there was no sign of life anywhere.

She led me round to the back of the house, not pausing but going straight on until we came to a gate which opened out into a part of the forest which had been shut in with green palings. There was a gate made of the same palings and Freya went to this.

"Can you guess what's in here?" she asked.

"No."

"It's a grave." She opened the gate and we went through. There was a mound in the centre of the patch and on it someone had planted a rose-bush; the surrounding grass had been neatly cut.

I knelt and read the inscription on the plate, which was almost hidden by the rose-bush.

"Francine Ewell," I read. And there was the date of her death.

I was overcome with emotion. This was the last thing I had expected. I wanted to throw myself on that earth and weep for her, my dear, beautiful and beloved sister. Now she lay there under this earth. At least I had found her grave.

I was aware of Freya beside me. "That is...the woman," she whispered.

I did not answer. I could not have spoken then.

"They must have buried her here...near the lodge where she died," went on Freya.

I stood up and she continued: "That's what I wanted to show you. I thought you'd be interested...because you are, aren't you? You like hearing about the murder." She was studying me intently. "Are you all right, Anne?"

"Yes, thank you. I'm quite all right."

"You look a bit odd."

"It's the light here...all these trees. They make you look pale too."

"Well, that's what I wanted to show you. It's interesting, isn't it?"

I agreed that it was.

I tried to appear normal, but I kept thinking of Francine's body being taken out of the lodge and buried close by.

As we rode home the thought struck me. Somebody tends her grave. Who would that be?

I longed to return there...alone. That seemed impossible, for I could not absent myself long enough. Then I told Frau Strelitz that I should like half a day's freedom as I wished to visit Frau Schmidt with whom I had lodged before I came to the *schloss*.

"But of course, Fräulein," she said. "We don't want you to think of yourself as a prisoner. You must take free time often. You and the Countess have become almost like friends and it did not occur to me that you wished to go off alone."

It was not so easy with Freya. She could not understand why she could not come with me.

"It would be embarrassing for my friends. They are not accustomed to entertaining personages in their tiny cottage."

"*I* should not mind."

"That is not the point. *They* would."

"It's Herr Schmidt's wife, isn't it? He works for the Graf von Bindorf."

"So you know that."

"I like to know *all* about you, Anne." She laughed aloud. "Why, you looked scared for a moment. I believe you have a secret. Oh, have you...? Have you?"

"Now you are going off into your wild imaginings."

I turned the matter off as lightly as I could and I wondered if I deceived her. She was very astute.

However I did have my free afternoon and rode over to Daisy, who was delighted to see me and told me she had heard from Hans that I was making a great success at the post and that the Countess was spending a great deal of time with me.

"Well," she said, "it's natural. You was brought up at the Manor and I reckon a real English lady is as good as any foreign Countess."

"Don't let anyone hear you say that. I am sure they wouldn't agree."

"We'll keep it to ourselves," said Daisy with a wink. "Now let me get you a glass of wine. I've got some good wine cakes too. I keep them for Hans's friends when they drop in."

I sipped the wine and told her that I had seen Francine's grave.

She was startled.

"The strange thing is," I said, "that someone is looking after it."

"I wonder who that could be?"

"Daisy, it must be someone who knew her."

"It might not be. People do look after graves. It's a sort of respect for the dead."

"I want to go and look at it again."

"Why now?"

"It's an opportunity and they are not easy to get."

"I've heard what a fancy the Countess has taken to you. Poor little thing. Rushed into marriage. Rudolph was for her. All right. He's murdered so it's Sigmund instead."

"Rudolph could never have married her," I said firmly, "because he was married to Francine."

Daisy said nothing. She did not want to contradict me over a matter on which I felt so strongly. "I'll see you on the way back," she said.

I think she was rather disappointed that I did not stay with her, but she did understand my burning desire to have another look at the grave.

I rode off with all speed and in a short time had passed Gisela's cottage. I glimpsed the twins playing in the garden. They noticed me and called after me. I turned and waved and went on.

I came to the lodge, dismounted, tethered my horse to the

mounting block and made my way round to the back of the house. I found the grave and went through the green paling gate. I knelt beside it and thought of Francine.

I wished that I had brought some flowers to put on her grave. Would that be foolish? Would someone notice? Would they say why does this strange Englishwoman visit the grave?

I shouldn't have come perhaps. I might already have betrayed my emotion to Freya. What if someone found me here?

I stood up. I felt as though eyes watched me, that someone was peering through the forest trees. I fancied I could hear whispering voices, but it was only the wind murmuring through the pine trees.

I must not be found here. I had been discovered at the hunting lodge by the children. If it were known that I had returned, what would they think? Surely they would begin to wonder at my apparent morbid interest in a crime which had been committed some time ago.

I hurried to my horse and rode away. When I came to the cottage Gisela was at the door, a young child in her arms. I gathered this was Max.

She called good-day to me. "How are you? Frau Schmidt was telling me about your post up at the Grand Schloss."

"Yes, I am enjoying it. The Countess is charming."

"And she is a good pupil?"

"Very good...with her English."

"Have you been to the lodge?"

"I passed it." I hesitated, then I rushed on, "By the way, what is that little enclosure with the palings round it—at the back of the lodge?"

She looked puzzled for a moment and then she said, "Oh...I think what you mean is a grave."

"It's a strange place for a grave."

"I suppose there were reasons."

"It looks as though someone looks after it...a friend, I suppose, of the person buried there."

"Oh...did you go and look?"

"I had dismounted so I went through the little gate. It seems to be well tended. I wonder who does it?"

"I tidy it up a bit now and then. It's so near the lodge and as I was seeing to that..."

"Who is buried there? Do you know?"

She hesitated and said: "It was the young woman in the shooting case."

"Strange that they should bury her there. Why not in an ordinary cemetery?"

"I heard it said they buried her quickly. They didn't want to make a ceremony of it. So few people come out here.... But I don't know. I'm guessing."

"Well," I said, "it was a long time ago."

"Yes, a long, long time ago."

I took my leave and rode thoughtfully back to Daisy's. I was disappointed. I had hoped to find someone who had tended her grave lovingly, someone who had known her in life. If there had been such a person he or she could have told me a good deal.

I stayed talking with Daisy, mainly about my life at the Grand Schloss, which interested her very much.

"You've not found out anything yet?" she asked anxiously.

I shook my head and told her that I had seen Gisela who had said she tidied up my sister's grave.

"She would, Gisela would. She'd want to tidy up the place. She's got the German passion for tidiness."

"It looked more than just tidying up," I said. "It looked as if someone tended it with care."

I said goodbye to Daisy and rode back through the town to the Grand Schloss. As soon as I came near the gates I was aware that something had happened. A man on horseback was riding out as I came up to it, and he passed me as though he were in a great hurry.

The guards were about to challenge me and then, recognizing me, they let me pass. As I entered the hall one of the servants hurried to me.

"Frau Strelitz would like to see you in her room without delay."

I went there in some trepidation, wondering what could have happened.

She was waiting for me.

"Ah, Fräulein Ayres, I am glad you are back. The Grand Duke has had a seizure."

"Is he—"

"No, no, but dangerously ill. He has had this sort of thing before. But if he should die, Baron Sigmund would become Grand Duke immediately. As you can imagine, this could cause trouble. Because of this unfortunate death of Rudolph, who was the undoubted son of the Grand Duke assuring the accepted succession, it is not quite so straightforward. There are some who feel that another has prior claim. He is called Otto the Bastard because he claims to be the illegitimate son of the Grand Duke. Our great desire is to keep the Grand Duke alive...but we must make sure that he does not die before Sigmund arrives."

"Where is the elusive Sigmund? I hear so much about him."

"He is travelling abroad. It is his duty to meet the heads of state in various countries. We have sent couriers to him at once. He'll have to come back now. The only thing is he must do so because if the Grand Duke dies... You understand. We don't want to be plunged into war."

"So that is why there is this change. I sensed it as soon as I passed the gate."

"It may be necessary for you to take the Countess away from the Grand Schloss for a while. We are not quite sure yet what is going to happen. But I wanted you to be prepared. We must pray for the recovery of the Grand Duke."

I went to find Freya. She was waiting for me.

"You see what happens when you go away," she said. "Now the Grand Duke is ill."

"That has nothing to do with my going out for the afternoon."

She narrowed her eyes and looked at me steadily. "I think it might," she said. "Fräulein Anne, you are not what you seem."

"What do you mean?" I asked sharply.

She pointed her finger at me. "You're not a witch, are you? You're one of the goddesses returned to earth. You can assume which shape you like..."

"Stop this nonsense," I said. "You know this is very serious. The Grand Duke is very ill."

"I know. He is going to die and I can only think of one thing. Anne, Sigmund is coming home."

Frau Strelitz sent for me the next day.

She told me at once that the Grand Duke was a little better. The doctors were with him and they had made an announcement. He had had a seizure like this before and had recovered. There was every hope that he would do so again.

His ministers had been talking through the night, she told

me. "They eagerly await the return of the heir. In the meantime they consider that the Countess Freya should not be in the Grand Schloss...in case of trouble. So we have decided that she should leave with you and Fräulein Kratz and a few of her servants."

"I understand. When do we leave?"

"Tomorrow. The Grand Duke's ministers think the sooner the better—just in case, of course. We have every hope of the Grand Duke's recovery. It is thought that she should not be too far away. The Margrave of Kollenitz would be very suspicious if we moved her away from the capital, so we have arranged that she shall go to the *schloss* on the other side of the river, and the Graf von Bindorf has offered you all hospitality until the situation is clarified."

I felt as though the room were spinning round me. I was to go into the household of the Graf and Gräfin von Bindorf. Some members of that household had seen me before, including the Gräfin and her daughter Tatiana. Would they recognize me? And if so, what would happen? I was sure that my coming here under an assumed name in order to attempt to uncover a mystery involving my sister would not be regarded with any great pleasure.

I was in my bedroom getting my things together when Freya came in and sat on my bed. I was holding the glasses which Miss Elton had procured for me and considering whether I should wear them on entering the von Bindorf *schloss*.

"What have you got there," demanded Freya. "Oh...spectacles. You don't wear them, do you?"

"Sometimes..."

"Have you got weak eyes? Oh, you poor Anne! All that reading you have to do. Do your eyes get tired? Do they make your head ache?"

"I suppose I should wear them more," I said.

"Put them on and let's have a look at you."

I did so and she laughed. "You look different," she said.

I was glad to hear that.

"You look severe," she went on. "Just like a governess. You look quite alarming."

"Then I should certainly wear them more."

"You're prettier without them."

"There are things more important than looks."

"I think you're just wearing them for a reason."

She alarmed me. Sometimes she seemed to see right into my mind. She was now looking at me slyly, teasing me as she loved to do.

"What reason?" I said sharply.

"What reason could there be but to try to make me afraid of you?"

I laughed with relief. But sometimes her comments shook me.

As we prepared to leave for the von Bindorf *schloss,* I kept remembering fragments from that long ago meeting. Could the Gräfin remember anything about me? I had been young then, a schoolgirl, nondescript, like so many other girls of my age. I had grown several inches taller because I had shot up rather suddenly, and from being a small girl had become a fairly tall young woman. I supposed that anyone who had known me would have recognized me, but the Gräfin had seen me for only a short time and then she had obviously been so much more interested in Francine.

The spectacles might well be useful. I would wear them when there could be a need to do so, and I did not believe that Freya had any real suspicions about them. I was over nervous. I had nothing to fear. It was hardly likely that the Gräfin would take much notice of her important guest's English governess.

The next day the carriage drove us over to the *schloss.* There were little knots of people in the streets and quite a crowd outside the Grand Schloss. The comptroller of the household had attached a bulletin of the Grand Duke's condition on the gate and there was a crowd reading it. I noticed the faces of the people as we passed through. They gave a little cheer for the Countess, who acknowledged it with the grace and solemnity which the occasion demanded.

I thought: She will make a good duchess when the time arises.

Fräulein Kratz and I sat well back in the carriage as we went through the town and across the bridge to that other *schloss.* I thought: I shall be nearer Daisy, and Hans will be under the same roof. It was a comforting thought.

We went under a kind of portcullis and into a courtyard where the Gräfin and the Graf were waiting to greet the Countess. On either side of them stood a young man and a young woman. The young woman looked vaguely familiar and I immediately thought: Oh yes, Tatiana. And again I was touched by a shiver of apprehension. I had to escape detection not only by the Gräfin but by her daughter, and casting my mind back it occurred to me that Tatiana would have been interested in one of her own age. I should have put on the glasses.

Freya was helped out of the carriage by one of the footmen and she went straight to the Graf and Gräfin who bowed and then embraced her.

Fräulein Kratz stepped out of the carriage and moved to one side. I followed her, head lowered. She had taken up her stand on the edge of the group; I kept close to her, and I was relieved that everyone seemed intent on watching Freya and that I did not receive more than a cursory glance.

I watched Tatiana greet Freya, and the young man clicked his heels and bowed. Freya smiled graciously and the Gräfin took her by the hand and led her into the *schloss*.

I mingled with a group of people. Those, I thought, who are of little importance; and I thanked heaven for them.

I saw Hans suddenly. He was looking for me, I guessed, and he came over and spoke to me.

"I will take you to the apartments which have been assigned to you and Fräulein Kratz," he said. "They are next to those of the Countess."

I smiled my appreciation and with Fräulein Kratz slipped away from those surrounding the main party. We were conducted through a narrow passage and up a stone staircase—the spiral kind, each step being built into the wall at one end and consequently very narrow and much wider at the other end. There was a thick rope hand-rail.

"Your apartments can be reached by the main staircase," Hans told me, "but on this occasion it is better to use this one."

I was grateful to him. He must have guessed that I would be apprehensive.

He showed us a suite of rooms. Fräulein Kratz and I were next to each other, and there was a large room which could be used for a schoolroom. On the other side of this were those apartments allotted to the Countess.

Fräulein Kratz nervously said that she hoped the Grand Duke would soon recover.

"They say it is almost certain that he will," Hans told her.

"I feel quite exhausted," she said.

"Have a little rest," I suggested.

"I must settle in first," she said, and went into her room, which left me alone with Hans.

I looked at him questioningly.

"They'll never recognize you," he said. "You look quite different. I didn't know you again when I saw you after all that time. They hardly ever look at people unless they are grand dukes or counts. It will be all right."

"Hans, if I am discovered, I hope it doesn't make trouble for you."

"I shall disclaim all knowledge. Daisy will come up with something. You can trust Daisy."

He tried to restore my spirits by giving me an imitation of one of Daisy's winks, which looked so grotesque on him that it made me smile.

"I reckon you won't be here long," he said. "As soon as the Grand Duke's better you'll be going back. And he will recover. He has before."

I was in my room when I heard the Countess being brought up to hers. There was a great deal of conversation and I could detect Freya's high-pitched voice.

Then I heard her say: "Gräfin, you must meet my very good friend, Fräulein Ayres. She's an English lady and teaches me English...just for fun."

I felt suddenly sick with fear. I put on the glasses and pretended to be looking at the view as the door opened and Freya came in with the Gräfin. I stood with my back to the light.

When I turned I saw that Tatiana and the young man were with them.

"Fräulein Ayres," said Freya, very much on her dignity, "I want to present you to the Gräfin von Bindorf and to Count Günther and the Countess Tatiana."

I bowed low.

The Gräfin's eyes momentarily swept over me and, I thought, dismissed me. As for Tatiana I could only faintly recognize in her the girl whom I had seen at the Grange. Her blond hair was elegantly dressed and piled high on her head, and although she had grown considerably, she was far from tall. She could have been a beauty but for those too closely set eyes, and her rather tight lips made her appear somewhat forbidding.

Günther was quite different. Though as blond as she was with similar closely set eyes, there were laughter lines about

his, and his pleasant expression implied that he looked upon
life as something of a joke. Tatiana repelled me, but I immediately liked her brother.

"Welcome," he said. "I hope you will be happy here."

"Oh, we shall be," said Freya. "Fräulein Ayres and I are
always happy. We love our English chatter, do we not?"

I tried to look governess-like. I said: "The Countess is
making excellent progress."

The Gräfin turned away with the air of one who has hu-
moured the whim of a child. She laid her hand on Freya's
arm and said: "Come, dear Countess, we have much to talk
of."

As they went out, Tatiana threw a backward glance at
me.

I had lowered my eyes and turned away.

They had no idea who I was, I was sure.

During the next few days I saw less of Freya. She deplored
this. She said they were always making demands on her. The
Gräfin was determined to honour her. "She is looking to the
future when I shall be Grand Duchess," said Freya. "I don't
know what it is...but she looks down her nose at me when
she thinks I don't see her and is always flattering me to my
face. I don't think she likes me one little bit, although she
pretends to admire me. I wish we were back at the Grand
Schloss. Günther's nice, though. He's different from the others and I think he is really pleased that I am here."

The bulletins of the Grand Duke continued to be favourable and it now seemed certain that he was going to recover
after all.

My fears were lulled. It was quite clear that I was going
to see very little of the Gräfin and her daughter and if ever
I was summoned to their presence, I would make sure that
I was wearing my glasses and that my hair was more severely
dressed than usual.

There seemed little fear that I should be and I felt im-
mensely relieved. Our stay here would be short, since the
Grand Duke was improving every day, and as long as I could
remain in obscurity no one would think of connecting me
with Francine. It occurred to me once again how wise I was
to have come as Anne Ayres. My own name would have betrayed me immediately.

It was three days after our arrival when Freya burst into my room.

"Hello, Anne," she cried. "We see so little of each other, I don't like it. I'll be glad when we go back. But you know that, don't you? Now I'll tell you something you don't know."

"Well?"

"Sigmund is coming tomorrow."

"Oh, it's about time, isn't it?"

"They had to let him know and then he had to travel back. He will go to the Grand Schloss first to see the Grand Duke and then he will come here. It will be evening when he arrives and the Gräfin would like to make a grand occasion of it, but of course it can't be all that grand because of the Grand Duke's illness."

"Just an intimate dinner party, I suppose."

"More than that. You see, the Duke is so much better. He has actually been sitting up in bed taking nourishment."

"That is good news. Sigmund need not have interrupted his pleasure."

"He should be here. State duties and all that. He'll be a sort of Regent. Besides, he has to woo me."

"Poor man! What a task!"

"Anne, it is good to be with you. The others are all so serious. They never laugh and what I like best is laughing."

"It shows a happy temperament," I said.

"Anne, listen. There's to be a sort of minor ball."

"What on earth is that?"

"A ball... but not a grand ball, of course. Fewer people... less fuss... less ceremony... but a ball all the same."

"And I can see the sparkle in your eyes. Is that for the ball or the laggard Sigmund?"

"Why do you call him a laggard?"

"Because he has delayed so long. He's a laggard in love. I hope not a dastard in war."

"Are you quoting poetry again?"

"I admit it."

"You do love it, don't you? I am to have a new dress for this ball and I am going to Madame Chabris who has set up in the town as the court dressmaker. She is from Paris and you know all the best fashions come from there."

"I have heard it," I replied. "When do we go to Madame Chabris?"

"Immediately."

"Will there be time to make this dress by tomorrow?"

"Madame Chabris is a marvel. She knows my size. She has made dresses for me before. She knew that Sigmund would be coming home and that I should be needing an exquisite gown. It would not surprise me if Madame Chabris had the very thing waiting for me."

"She sounds as though she is very clever."

"But the good news is this. You are coming too, Anne."

"I!"

"I insisted. I don't deny it was hard. The Gräfin said, 'A governess!' I explained that you were a very special sort of governess. You have been brought up almost as nobly as we have. You are only doing this because you are seeing the world and doing the grand tour and finding it all rather boring travelling aimlessly. You could leave us at any minute which *I* should not like at all, and I should never forgive anyone who made you feel like a servant in any way. Tatiana didn't like it either, but I don't like Tatiana in any case. Günther thought it was all right. He said, 'What harm will it do, Mamma? Let the English lady come. She will be swallowed up among the guests.' How do you like the thought of being swallowed up?"

"Wait a moment. Do you really mean that *I* am to come to the ball?"

"Cinderella, yes. I am your fairy godmother. I shall wave my magic wand."

"It's impossible. I have no dress."

"Isn't that just what Cinderella said? I will arrange that with Madame Chabris, of course."

"There is no time."

"We are going to Madame Chabris this morning and I'll wager—"

"Please do not talk of laying wagers. It is unseemly. And as the Gräfin quite clearly does not approve of my going, I shall most certainly not."

"Wait a minute. You *are* coming, Anne Ayres. To please me you are coming. I want you to come. I am the Countess...Grand Duchess to be...and unless you want to offend me, which will be at your peril, you will come."

"You forget I shall not be one of your subjects. I can leave here and go home when I wish."

"Oh dear, dear Anne, you would not disappoint me. I have worked so hard to make them agree and the reason is I am really frightened. I have to meet this Sigmund...and I need to know you are there."

"What nonsense," I said. "He is not a stranger to you."

"No. But I need your support. You must come. Oh, promise ...*promise*...."

I hesitated. I felt a tremendous excitement creeping over me. I was making very slow progress. Who knew what I might discover if I mingled with people who in all probability actually had known Rudolph?

"Get on your cloak," she urged. "I have ordered the carriage. We are leaving at once for the salon of Madame Chabris."

It was a revelation to see myself gowned by Madame Chabris. Her salon was beautiful. I said, "It's almost as grand as I imagine the hall of mirrors at Versailles to be."

"Well, she is French," Freya reminded me.

We were given a very warm welcome. Madame Chabris herself, elegant in the extreme, perfectly coiffured and shod as well as exquisitely gowned, greeted us.

She had the very dress which Freya needed. She admitted that she sometimes designed dresses to suit people whom she admired, so it was not to be marvelled at that she had just the right thing for the Countess Freya. As for myself, I had a good figure, she commented, and naturally she had the very dress that would suit me.

Freya tried on her dress and pirouetted in front of the mirrors, seeing herself reflected all round the room.

"It's beautiful," she cried. "Oh, Madame Chabris, you are a marvel."

Madame Chabris looked quietly pleased as though such hyperbole was commonplace to one of her genius.

Then it was my turn. The dress was deep blue and there was a vein of gold running through it.

"I call it my lapis lazuli," said Madame Chabris. "It is beautiful...a little expensive alas."

"Fräulein Ayres is a lady of independent means," said Freya quickly. "She works only because she wishes to. We are good friends, so I know."

"Then I am sure she will consider the price a minor matter when she sees how the lapis will bring out the glow of her skin."

I tried it on. Madame Chabris was right. That dress did a great deal for me.

"The alterations are infinitesimal," said Madame Chabris airily. "My work girls will do them in two hours. You are very slender, Fräulein. You have the beautiful figure—but if I may say, you have not yet realized it. The lapis will show you. Step in here, please, and I will send a fitter."

I went into a small cubicle and was soon joined by a middle-aged woman with a pocketful of pins.

I had to admit the transformation was miraculous.

When I had been pinned, the dress fitted me perfectly. There was a gold-coloured girdle to match the veins in the material and the effect was startling.

Freya clapped her hands and danced round in an ecstasy of joy when she saw me.

"The Fräulein's hair will need attention," said Madame Chabris warningly.

"It will receive it," promised Freya.

She had suddenly remembered that she was the future Grand Duchess and became somewhat imperious.

"You will have the dress, Fräulein. Madame Chabris, you will make the alterations and deliver tomorrow morning early. That will give Fräulein Ayres time to try it on and make sure all is well."

"It shall be done, Countess," said Madame Chabris.

Freya laughed all the way back to the *schloss*.

She kept saying: "Oh, Fräulein Anne, I do like being with you. We laugh a lot, don't we?"

So I was to go to the ball. I was greatly excited and knew instinctively that I was walking into danger, but I did not care. I had to do this, I reminded myself, if I were to discover anything.

My dress arrived and I tried it on. Fräulein Kratz, who saw me in it, stared in astonishment.

"The Countess insisted," I said.

"And the Gräfin has agreed?"

I nodded.

"The Countess is very wayward."

"She is charming," I insisted. "She has a strong character and will make a very good Grand Duchess."

"I wish she were a little more...orthodox."

"Oh come, she is an individualist. That is far more interesting than following the crowd."

"When one is in her position it is often better to follow the crowd," retorted Fräulein Kratz. "As for you, Fräulein Ayres, aren't you terrified? I should be."

"Terrified? Why should I be?" I spoke sharply. Sometimes, I thought I must give away the fact that I have something to hide.

"Well, I should be," she said lightly. "The last thing I should want is to go to one of their balls."

"I am looking forward to it," I said firmly and she turned away, shrugging her shoulders.

I was living in the clouds for the rest of that day. I had never been to a ball before. Grandfather had never entertained in that style at Greystone Manor. The most he had had was a dinner party. But I supposed I should be very much in the background.

Freya gave me an indication of what was likely to happen. Sigmund would arrive and be greeted by herself and the Graf, the Gräfin, Tatiana and Günther. Then they would come into the great hall where people would be assembled. "Everyone there will form into two lines. You'll be somewhere at the end, I'm afraid, Anne."

"But of course," I replied.

"Then Sigmund will take my hand and we shall walk in between the two lines. Sigmund will say something to the important ones. Not you, Anne."

"Indeed not."

"You have to curtsy as we come through."

"I think I can manage that very well."

"That's all there is to it. Then we shall dance...rather discreetly...and then we shall all go to supper and it will end at midnight out of respect for the Grand Duke."

So I dressed in the most beautiful and becoming gown I had ever possessed. I was amazed at the transformation. While I was struggling with my hair, Freya came in with a small dark woman who carried combs and pins on her head.

"This is the Gräfin's lady's maid," she announced. "She has done my hair. Is she not clever? Now she is going to do yours."

"Oh, but—" I began.

"It needs it," retorted Freya. "And *I* have said she shall."

"You are good to me," I said suddenly.

Freya's lips twitched slightly, and I was deeply touched

as always by these signs of her unselfishness. She really was a very charming girl.

So my hair was dressed and I went to the ball in some trepidation. I joined some men and women who were gathered at one end of the hall. They smiled at me rather nervously, I thought, and I guessed they were the poor relations of some noble house and were slightly overawed in the assembled company. I had a feeling that my place was with them. It occurred to me that it might be from such people that I could discover something which would help me unravel the mystery.

Freya was not present. I knew she was with the Graf and Gräfin, Tatiana and Günther, and from the sounds without it appeared that the great Sigmund had arrived. The company began forming into two lines as, with the sound of trumpets, a group of men in uniforms of blue, with plumes in their helmets and swords at their sides, came into the room.

In their midst was a man slightly taller than the rest. I could not see him clearly for my view was obscured by people in the line.

Now the party was moving towards us. I noticed that everyone was standing very still, their eyes cast down; so I did the same.

They were moving along...the Graf on one side of this illustrious personage and Freya on the other.

I began to feel a little dizzy. There was something very unreal about this. I thought: I must be dreaming. This is not really happening.

For there he was, standing before me. Conrad...my lover. Conrad whom I had never forgotten although I had tried to deceive myself into thinking that I had.

"This is Fräulein Ayres, who teaches me such good English." Freya was beaming, proud of me...proud of him...her face alight with joy.

I curtsied as I had seen the others do.

"Fräulein Ayres," he murmured. It was all there, the voice, the look, all that I remembered. His bewilderment was as great...perhaps even greater...than my own.

"You are English," he said. He had taken my hand. Mine was trembling. He was staring at me. "I understand that you are a very good teacher."

Then he passed on. I felt as though I were going to faint. I must recover myself. Vaguely I heard him speaking to someone else along the line.

I wanted to get away. I wanted to escape from this room and think over what I had just discovered.

When he reached the end of the line, he took Freya's hand and they went into the centre of the hall to lead the dance. People started to fall in behind them.

Someone was at my elbow. It was Günther.

I stammered: "Count Günther..."

"Countess Freya asked me to keep an eye on you."

"She is such a dear girl," I replied. "But perhaps I should not speak so of the Countess."

"It is true," he said. "She speaks highly of you too, and she is anxious about you. She told me that she insisted that you come to the ball. May I have the pleasure of this dance?"

"I don't really know your dances, but thank you."

"This is easy. Come... just a few steps and then twirl."

"Did the Countess tell you you must ask me to dance?"

He admitted it.

"Well, then you have done your duty."

"Not duty," he replied with a charming smile, "a pleasure."

"I think I should retire after this. It was so good of the Countess Freya to insist on my coming... but I really feel I should not be here."

He had drawn me onto the floor and I found I was dancing easily.

"You are doing splendidly," he said. "Look at Countess Freya. She will make a charming Grand Duchess, do you not think so?"

"I do. When will the marriage celebrations take place?"

"Not for a year, now the Duke is recovering. At least I hope." He looked a little wistful and it occurred to me that he was quite taken with my young Countess.

I wondered whether Conrad was too.

Why had he given me a false name? He must have decided that he did not want to betray his identity. Why had he pretended to be the Graf's equerry? Had he? Had I assumed that? He had not contradicted it. I felt very uneasy and suddenly terribly sad.

I wanted to get away from this ball now. I could not bear to see him there. People surrounded him. Of course they did. He was the heir to the dukedom, the most important man here. This gathering was in his honour, although it was only a small ball because of the Grand Duke's illness, but there must be a celebration of some sort because the Duke's heir was coming.

He would ignore me, of course. I hoped he would. How could I face him in this room?

I must get away quickly.

I chose my opportunity. It was not difficult. I slipped away, but as I did so I saw him glance my way. He was smiling and talking and went on doing so.

I felt heartsick. What a fool I had been to fall in love with the first man who crossed my path! I should have had more sense. And how easily I had fallen into the trap he had laid for me! Easily come by and therefore not valued over much.

But what a man he was! He was like the hero of a legend. I remembered I had thought of him as Sigurd when I had first met him. A Norseman. A Viking commander. That was what he had looked like then. Now in his uniform he looked more than ever like a hero of legend. He was outstanding among all the people there. He was everything that I had tried to shut out of my mind.

I should never have come here. It was a foolish thing to have done. What could I do now? I must go away—that was clear. I must forget why I had come here. I must go back to England. I could stay with Aunt Grace. I must live quietly and unadventurously. It was the only way not to get hurt more desperately than I had already been.

I sat down by my open window. I could see the lights of the town, the bridge and the river winding like a black snake through the town. I had grown to love the place; I had grown to love Freya. I would never forget it and there would always be an ache in my heart when I thought of it.

And him? Would I ever forget him? I had told myself that I had forgotten him. I would not allow myself to think of him. I had tried to forget that interlude, to tell myself it had never really happened; I had refused to admit even to myself that he was constantly in my mind and that I could not rid myself of those flashes of memory when I saw so vividly scenes from that time we had spent together. Secretly I had always known that I should never forget him. Conrad the deceiver, Sigmund the heir to a troubled dukedom, betrothed to my little Freya.

They would marry in due course. That was irrevocable. They were bound together. That was what he had meant when he had said he could not marry me.

There was a footstep in the corridor. Someone was at the door. The handle was slowly turning.

And there he was, looking at me.

"Pippa," he said. "Pippa!"

I tried not to look at him. I said: "I am Anne Ayres."

"What *is* this? What does it mean?"

I retorted: "What are you doing in my room, er—What do I call you, Baron?"

"You call me Conrad."

"What of the great lord Sigmund?"

"My ceremonial name. Sigmund, Conrad, Wilhelm, Otto. They gave me a large supply. But, Pippa, names are unimportant. What of you?"

He had come across the room and taken my hands. He had pulled me to my feet and held me against him. I felt my resistance slipping.

I could only say: "Go away. Go away, please. This is no place for you."

He had taken my chin in his hands and was looking into my face. "I searched for you," he said. "I have been in England. I came back for you. I was going to take you away with me . . . by force if necessary. I couldn't find you . . . and then in desperation I came back here . . . and here you are. You came to find me, did you not? While I was searching for you, you were searching for me."

"No—no. I did not come here for you."

"You are lying, Pippa. You came for me, and now we have found each other we shall never part again."

"You are wrong. I shall not see you again. I shall go back to England. I know who you are now and that you are betrothed to the Countess Freya and that your betrothal is tantamount to marriage. You cannot escape it. I have learned something of your problems here. There is Kollenitz, the buffer state. You need its help and you have to marry Freya because you could never deny the marriage, but you know all this and you know now that I shall have to go home."

"This will be home to you now. Listen, Pippa, you are here. We have found each other . . . never to part again. We'll be together. I'll find some place where we can make our home."

"There is an unoccupied lodge in the forest nearby," I said with a touch of bitterness.

"Don't speak of it. It won't be like that. I love you, Pippa. Nothing can change that. As soon as I had gone I knew how much. I should not have left when you did not come to the station. I should have come back for you and made you come with me. It is the only way for us. But you came to me. It was clever of you to change your name. Better for no one to know that you are Francine's sister. But you came here.... My dear, clever Pippa. This is different from anything that has ever happened to either of us. You know that as well as I do. We are going to be together now...no matter what happens."

"You have taken me by surprise."

"As you have taken me, my love," he answered and he was kissing me fiercely, and in my thoughts I was at once transported back to that firelit room in the Grange. I wished I were there at that moment. I wished I could forget his involvement with Freya. I wanted so much to be with him.

"The most wonderful surprise of my life," he said. "You here...my own Pippa...and never, never going to leave me again."

I was aware of the intensity of his passion and how ready I was to meet it. I remembered so much from that other occasion. Instinctively I knew that he was a man who had never learned to deny himself. There was so much I knew about him. And I loved him. It was no use trying to convince myself otherwise now that he was here...close to me...holding me in his arms....I could never forget him. I was a fool, for I realized the hopelessness of our situation. I was terrified that here, now, my resistance would melt away as it had on that other occasion. I had to try to think of Freya. Suppose she came in and found him here? She might not notice my absence but she would notice his. Everyone would notice it. What if she came to look for him? She would never look for him in *my* room, of course. But what if she came to me...what if she found me in the arms of her future husband?

The situation was dangerous and impossible.

I drew away from him and said as coolly as I could, "You will be missed in the ballroom."

"I care nothing for that."

"Do you not? The heir to all this.... Of course you care. It is your duty to care. You must go back and we must not see each other again."

"You suggest the impossible."

"What use can it be?"

"I have plans."

"I can guess the nature of those plans."

"Pippa, if I go now will you promise me something?"

"What is it?"

"We meet tomorrow. In the forest, shall we say? Please, Pippa, I must talk to you. Where? Where?"

"There is only one spot I know in the forest."

"Then we shall meet there."

"The hunting lodge," I said.

"We'll meet there and we'll talk and we'll talk."

"There is no more to be said. I was misled. Perhaps it was my fault. I did not ask enough questions. I accepted you as some equerry... some servant of the Graf... and you did not attempt to enlighten me... and you must have known that I had no idea who you really were."

"It seemed of no consequence."

I laughed rather bitterly. "No, I suppose not. You proposed to amuse yourself during your brief stay in England. I understand that perfectly."

"You do not understand. You do not understand at all."

I was alert, listening. "The music has stopped," I said. "They will have noticed the absence of the guest of honour. Please go now."

He had taken my hands and was kissing them with passion. "Tomorrow..." he said, "at the hunting lodge. At ten o'clock."

"I cannot be sure. It is not easy for me to leave. You must remember that I am employed here."

"The Countess said that you came as a sort of favour and that she had to please you or you would leave."

"She exaggerated. Remember, I may not be able to come."

"You will," he said. "And I shall be there... waiting."

I drew myself away from him, but he caught me again and held me fast. He kissed my lips and throat. It was so like that other time that I feared for myself.

Then he had gone.

I turned to the window and looked over the town.

I remained at my window for a long time without noticing the passing of time. I was back at the Grange, living through those hours I had spent with him, and which I had deceived myself into thinking I had erased from my mind. Then suddenly I heard the town clock strike midnight. That would be the end of the ball, because it was to finish at that hour on account of the Grand Duke's illness. I could hear the commotion below which signified that the guests were leaving. Ceremony would accompany him wherever he went, except of course when he was away from home, living incognito.

I must change my plans. I must abandon all hope of staying here and unravelling the mystery surrounding my sister's death. And at the back of my mind was the thought that somewhere—probably near here—her child was living. I could never be at peace until I knew what had become of that little boy...and yet, how could I stay here? My position with Freya had become untenable.

I was still sitting there in my lapis lazuli dress when there was a knock on my door and it was abruptly opened before I had time to give permission for whoever was there to enter.

As I expected, it was Freya. Her face was flushed, her eyes dancing and she looked very pretty in her Chabris dress.

"Anne," she cried. "You ran away. I looked for you. I sent Günther to look for you and we couldn't find you anywhere."

I shivered inwardly, wondering what would have happened if she had come upon her betrothed in my bedroom.

"I should never have been at the ball," I said quietly.

"What happened?"

"Well...I came away."

"I mean *something* happened. You look..." She was eyeing me suspiciously.

I said quickly—too quickly, "What do you mean? How do I look?"

"Strange...exalted...shining in a way. Did you meet Prince Charming?"

"Really Freya," I said rather primly.

"Well, we did say you were like Cinderella. She did meet Prince Charming, didn't she, and she ran away and dropped her slipper."

She looked down at my feet and in spite of everything I could not help smiling at her childishness.

"I can assure you I retained *both* my slippers. I did not have to leave on the stroke of twelve, and there was no Prince Charming for me. He...was for you."

"What did you think of Sigmund? He spoke to you, didn't he?"

"Yes," I answered.

"I hope you liked him. Did you? Did you? Why don't you answer?"

"It is difficult for me to answer that."

She threw back her head and laughed. "Oh, Anne, you are funny. You are going to say that you don't make decisions about people on a slight acquaintance. I am not asking for an assessment of your conclusions on his character."

"That is wise of you, for you won't get it."

"I just meant did he make a favourable impression?"

"Why yes, of course."

"And you think he'll be a good husband?"

"That is for you to discover in due course."

"Oh, cautious, cautious! He is handsome, is he not?"

"Yes, I think he would be called that."

"He has such an air. He is a man of the world. That is what you would call him, wouldn't you?"

"I have told you that I..."

"I know you only spoke to him once in line. Günther danced with you, didn't he? I saw him. I told him to, you know."

"I know you did. It was sweet of you, but you need not have done so. I didn't expect it. However, he did his duty nobly."

"He is rather nice, Günther, don't you think?"

"Yes, I do."

"Oh, you can be definite enough about him. Of course, he's not really so devastatingly attractive as Sigmund is. I'm a bit in awe of Sigmund. He seems well...too worldly. Is that the right word?"

"I think it may well be exactly the right word."

"I am sure he has had a host of mistresses. He's the sort of man who would. They all do...particularly the Fuchses. They are very much like that, you know...lusty and amorous."

"Freya," I said solemnly, "do you want to marry this man?"

She was thoughtful for a moment. Then she said, "I want to be the Grand Duchess."

I said then that it was time we went to bed and I was ready if she was not.

"Good night then, Anne...dear Anne. When I'm married I shan't want you to go. You can stay and comfort me when Sigmund is unfaithful with all his mistresses."

"If you feel so sure of his future infidelities, you should not marry him."

She jumped up and gave a mock salute. "Bruxenstein," she cried. "For Kollenitz! Good night, Anne," she went on. "At least it is all rather exciting, isn't it?"

I admitted that, at least, it was.

* * *

I rose early next morning. I looked in on Freya, who was fast asleep. I was glad. It would give me a chance to get out. I drank a cup of coffee and managed to eat one of the bread rolls spattered with caraway seeds which I had enjoyed since I had arrived in Bruxenstein. I did not taste it on this morning. Then I went into the stables and saddled a horse.

In less than half an hour I was at the hunting lodge. He was already there, impatiently waiting. He had tethered his horse by the mounting block and helped me to dismount. He held out his arms as I did so and I slid into them. He held me tightly, kissing me.

I said, "It is no use."

"You're wrong," he contradicted. "Let's walk and talk. I have lots to say to you."

He put an arm about me and we walked into the forest, away from the lodge.

"I have been thinking about us all night," he said. "You're here and you are going to stay. I am in this position—thrust into it by an accident of birth—but I am not one to accept a fate which is thrust on me and give up what I could never live without. I have to go through with this marriage. I have to do my duty to my country and my family...but at the same time I am determined to live my own life. It is not an unusual situation. It has happened to so many of us. It is the only way in which we can do what we have to. My family life...the life I want and am determined to have...and the path of duty. I can manage them both."

"As Rudolph did?"

"He and your sister could have been happy. Rudolph was careless. He always was. He was killed because someone...some members of a party, were determined that he should not rule. It was purely a political murder. Unfortunately for your sister, she was with him."

"It could happen to you," I said, and I wondered whether he noticed the tremor of fear in my voice.

"How do any of us know what will happen to us from one moment to another? Death can come unexpectedly to the most lowly peasant. I know that Rudolph would not have been a popular successor to his father. He was too weak, too pleasure-loving. There were factions working against him."

"And you?"

"I was not concerned in it. The last thing I wanted was to be where I am today."

"You could refuse to accept your position, could you not?"

"There is no one to take my place. There would be chaos in the country; our enemies would step in. Our country needs a ruler. My uncle has been a strong one. I hope to God he will go on living, for while he does we have security. I have to preserve that security."

"And you can?"

"I know I can...providing our allies support us."

"Such as Kollenitz?"

He nodded. He went on: "I was betrothed to the child, Freya, as soon as Rudolph died. This special betrothal commitment is tantamount to marriage in all but the consummation. On her sixteenth birthday there will be an official marriage ceremony. Then we must produce an heir. Therein lies my duty, my inescapable duty. But I have my own life to lead. This is my public life; but I shall have my private one."

"Which you plan to share with me?"

"Which I am going to share with you. I could not live without it. One cannot be a puppet all one's life, moving in the way which is ordained. No! I will not do that. I wish I could give it all up and go off quietly with you...and live in peace somewhere. But what would happen if I did? Chaos. War. I don't know where it would end."

"You must do your duty," I said.

"And you and I—"

"I shall go back to England. I can see that it is impossible to live the life you suggest."

"Why?"

"Because it would not work. I should be an encumbrance."

"The most adored and loved encumbrance that ever was."

"An encumbrance nevertheless. I sometimes think that Rudolph's involvement with my sister may have been the cause of his death. It might be that I should be the cause of yours."

"I'd be prepared to risk that."

"And children?" I said. "What of children?"

"They should have everything a child could desire."

"My sister had a child. I wonder where that child is now? Imagine it. A little boy. I know it was a boy because she told me. What happened to him? Where did he go when they killed his father and his mother? You talk of our being together, having children. In secret, I suppose. And Freya, what about her part in this?"

"Freya would understand. She knows ours is an arranged marriage. I should make her understand."

"I know her very well. I doubt she would understand ... and that *I* should be the one ... that would be insupportable. I can see the impossibility of it all and that I must get away quickly."

"No," he cried. "No! Promise me this: You will not run away and hide yourself. You will tell me before you do anything."

He had stopped and put his hands on my shoulders. I wished that he would not look at me in that way, because it was harder when I faced him and I felt all my resolutions melting away.

"Of course I will tell you when I am going," I said.

He smiled confidently. "In time I will make you see. Tell me ... what did you feel when you saw me?"

"I thought I was dreaming."

"I too. I have dreamed of it often ... coming face to face with you ... finding you suddenly. I always knew I should find you. I intended to. And to think that I might still be in England ... searching ..."

"What did you do? Whom did you ask?"

"I went to the stonemason's place. I knew that you were friendly. He was no longer there. The vicar was away. There was someone doing his duties in his absence. He told me that your aunt and her husband had moved away, but he did not know where. There was no-one at Greystone Manor except servants."

"Surely my cousin was there."

"They said he was away on his honeymoon."

"Honeymoon! Oh no. That could not be."

"That's what I was told. It was like a conspiracy against me. I did hear of your grandfather's death."

"What did you hear about that?"

"That he had died in a fire."

"Did you hear anything about ... my connection with that?"

He frowned. "There was some innuendo. I didn't understand what it meant. It was oblique comments. I stayed at the inn. They didn't seem to want to talk very much."

I said, "On the night my grandfather died I quarrelled with him. People in the house heard it because he was shouting at me. He was insisting that I marry my Cousin Arthur and he threatened to turn me out if I didn't."

"How I wish I had been there!"

"That night he died. His room and the one next to it were burned out. The fire was confined to those two rooms. My grandfather was dead when they brought him out...but it was not asphyxiation. He had had a blow on the head. They thought he might have fallen...but on the other hand he might not."

"You mean they thought it was foul play?"

"They were unsure. The verdict at the inquest was 'Accidental Death.' But several people had heard the quarrel between us."

"Good God! My poor Pippa. If I had been there..."

"If only you had! I had my Aunt Grace. She was good to me and Cousin Arthur was kind...and my grandmother left me money which enabled me to get away...to come here."

He held me tightly against him. "My dearest Pippa," he said. "I shall look after you from now on."

For a moment I lay against him, letting him believe it could be possible—and perhaps deluding myself.

He said: "That's all over now. It must have been a nightmare. I should have been there. I hesitated on that platform. I was coming back to get you and then I thought, How can I if she does not want to come?"

"I did want to come. I did. I did."

"Dear, dear Pippa, if only you had!"

"Where to? To this hideaway you are planning? A hunting lodge in the forest. It is like a pattern repeating itself. Francine and myself. We were always close...like one person. Sometimes I think I am reliving her life. We were always together until she loved so unwisely...and now it seems I have done the same."

He was looking at me earnestly. "It is going to be the wisest thing you ever did—to love me."

I shook my head. "I wish you were an ordinary person—an equerry perhaps, as I first thought you to be. I wish you were anything but what you are...with those commitments ...and particularly Freya."

"We are going to rise above all that. I am going to show you the place I will find for you. Our home. I want to give you everything I have."

"But you can't. You can't ever give me your name."

"I can give you my devoted love...all of it, Pippa."

"You must think of your marriage. I have grown fond of Freya. She is a child yet...and charming. She will lure you to love her."

"I am not to be lured away from my Pippa. Oh, Pippa, dearest Pippa, listen to the birds singing. 'The lark's on the wing...All's right with the world.' Remember that? It is Pippa's song. All must be right with the world while you and I are together."

"I must go back. I shall be missed. You too, I daresay."

"We shall meet again...tomorrow. I will find somewhere where we can be together. It has to be. It is no use fighting against it. From the moment we met, it was clear to me. I said, 'This is the one out of the whole world and no-one else will do.'"

I shook my head. I was hovering between ecstasy and despair. I knew I was going to weaken. I knew that I had to take what I could get.

He was aware of it, too. I had betrayed my emotions too readily.

"Tomorrow. Tomorrow, Pippa. Promise. Here."

So I promised, and we went back to our horses. When he had helped me to mount he took my hand and looked at me beseechingly and I loved him so much that I knew in my heart that I would do anything he asked of me.

I withdrew my hand, for I was very much afraid of my emotions, and I said as coolly as I could: "We must not ride away together. We might be seen. Please go ahead."

"We'll go together."

"No. I prefer it this way. It might be difficult for me to get away freely if we were seen together."

He bowed his head and accepted the wisdom of that. "Perhaps for a while we should be careful," he said. He kissed my hand fervently and rode away.

I remained there for some moments looking at the lodge. I was in no mood to go back to the *schloss* immediately. I was forming excuses for my absence. Freya would want to know where I had been, and I decided to tell her that I had felt the need for fresh air and exercise after the previous night, and had taken it in the forest.

Suddenly I had the desire to dismount and go and look at Francine's grave. I felt as close to her as I ever had. I tethered the horse and walked round the lodge.

As I approached the grave I had the uncanny feeling that

I was not alone. At first I thought that I was being followed by someone who had seen my meeting with Conrad. I felt cold with terror. Why is it that one can sense the presence of another person? Was it due to some sound I had heard? Was it instinct?

I had reached the enclosure. I saw a movement... a flash of colour. Then I realized that there was someone at the graveside.

I drew back, not wishing to make my presence known, for I guessed it must be Gisela. I stood very still, holding my breath. Then a figure rose. She had a trowel in her hand and had been planting something.

It was not Gisela. This was a young woman, taller, fairer than Gisela. She stood still for a moment, looking down at her handiwork. Then suddenly she spoke. "Rudi," she called. "Come here, Rudi."

Then I saw the child. He must have been about four or five years old. His hair was like sunshine, fair and curly.

"Come here, Rudi. Look at the pretty flowers."

I watched, while the child went and stood beside her.

"Now, we must go," she went on. "But first..."

I was amazed because they knelt down together. I saw the child, his eyes closed, the palms of his hands pressed closely together, his lips murmuring. I could not hear what was said.

They stood up. The woman was holding a basket in which was the trowel in one hand, with the other she took that of the child.

I drew back in the shadow of the bushes which grew in clumps in this spot, and I watched them come through the gate and walk away into the forest.

My heart was beating fast, my mind racing.

Who was she? Who was the child? And I had stood there, numb, watching them. I should have spoken to her, discovered why she was tending my sister's grave.

But I had not lost her. I could at least follow her and see where she went.

I kept them in sight. It was not difficult for me to remain hidden because of the trees which provided me with good cover. And after all, if I was seen why should I not be someone who was taking a walk in the forest?

We had come to a house—small but pleasant. She released the child's hand and he ran on ahead of her up the path to the door. He danced up and down on the porch, waiting for her. She came along and let herself and him in, while I stood there watching.

I felt amazed by what I had seen. Why had she tended Francine's grave? Who was she? More important still, who was the child?

I was not sure how to act. Could I knock on the door, ask the way and engage her in conversation?

It was already late. I should find it difficult to explain my absence. Another day? I thought. I'll come back. I shall have time to think how is the best way to tackle this.

With my mind whirling through what I had seen and my meeting with Conrad, I was bemused and uncertain, wondering what would happen next, and telling myself that I must be prepared for anything.

When I returned to the *schloss* I had to face Freya, who had missed me.

"Where have you been? Nobody knew what had happened to you."

"I felt the need for fresh air."

"You could have got that in the garden."

"I wanted to ride."

"You've been in the forest, haven't you?"

"How did you know?"

"I have my spies." She narrowed her eyes and for a few seconds I thought she knew about my meeting with Conrad. "Besides," she went on, "here is a clue." She picked a pine needle from my jacket. "You look really frightened. You are not what you say you are. You are planning a coup. That is why you are of independent means. Whoever heard of a governess who was not terrified of losing her post and being turned out on the streets?"

"You have," I said, recovering my equilibrium. "And here she is."

"Why did you go off without telling me?"

"You were fast asleep after your experiences as the belle of the ball, and I thought you needed your rest."

"I was worried. I thought perhaps you had left me."

"Foolish child!"

She threw herself at me suddenly. "Don't leave me, Anne. You mustn't."

"What are you afraid of?" I asked.

She looked at me steadily. "Everything," she said. "Marriage...change...growing up. I don't want to grow up, Anne. I want to stay as I am."

I kissed her tenderly. "You'll manage it all right when the time comes," I assured her.

"Will I?" she asked. "I am very rebellious and I would never tolerate mistresses."

"Perhaps there won't be any."

"That," she said firmly, "is how it will have to be."

"There is a saying in English that one should cross one's bridges when one comes to them."

"A very good one," she replied. "That is what I shall do. But I shall cross them in my own way."

"Knowing you, I am sure you will put up a good fight to get what you want."

"The trouble is that Sigmund seems the sort of person to get *his* own way. Does he seem like that to you, Anne?"

"Yes," I said slowly. "He does."

"Then it will be a question of which is the stronger."

"There may not be a contest. It is just possible that you will both want the same things."

"Clever Anne. You will be there with me. I shall insist. I shall make you my Grand Vizor."

"That is something you put on your head. I think you mean Vizier, and I am sure I should be most unsuitable for the post."

"We'll cross that bridge when we come to it," quoted Freya, almost smugly.

I laughed but I was thinking, What am I going to do? I must go. Yet he will never allow it. I shall stay. We shall live out our lives together...in the shadows perhaps, but together...as Francine and Rudolph did.

And I must discover who was the woman who planted flowers on Francine's grave. And perhaps more important than all, who was the child?

The King
of the Forest

Fortune favoured me.

In the early afternoon Freya came to me. She was pouting. The Graf and Gräfin wanted her, Tatiana and Günther to visit the Grand Duke.

"Well, what is so unpleasant about that?" I asked.

"I wanted to go for a ride with you."

"You can do that another time."

"I doubt whether we shall see him and we always have to stand on such ceremony. Oh, I wish I didn't have to go."

"It will all be over soon."

"I expect Sigmund will be there."

"Well, you will like to see him, I expect."

She grimaced.

I watched the party leave and immediately went to the stables. I had a free afternoon and within a short time was riding into the forest towards the lodge, and then on to the house I had discovered.

The woman was in the garden. I recognized her at once and called a good afternoon, asking her the way back to the town, which I knew very well.

She came to the palings and, leaning over, directed me.

I said, trying to hold her in conversation, "The forest is very beautiful."

She agreed.

"Is it lonely living here?" I asked.

"I don't notice it. I have plenty to do. I keep house for my brother."

"Just the two of you..." I murmured and wondered if I sounded both inquisitive and impertinent.

"Just the two of us and our maid and my little son."

No mention of a husband, I noticed, and my mind was beset by possibilities.

"I came past the lodge," I continued. "It seemed deserted."

"Oh yes, it is nowadays."

She had a frank, open face and she was friendly. Perhaps she relished a chat as no doubt she saw few people.

"Are you visiting here?" she asked.

"Not exactly. I am employed at the *schloss*."

"Oh?" She expressed interest. "My brother works there...for the Graf."

"I am there...as an English governess to the Countess Freya."

She was not extremely interested. "Oh yes, I had heard that there was an English lady there. And you rode out and lost your way?"

"One can do that easily in the forest."

"Nowhere more easily. But you are not far away. If you go back by the lodge and keep to the bridle path you'll come to the lodge cottage, and there is a road. You'll see the town from there."

"I shall know where I am then. The lodge looks interesting but rather dismal."

"Oh yes, it is never used now."

"It seems a waste of what must have been a very fine old place."

"Oh yes.... They used it frequently in the past for hunting, you know. You should be careful walking in the forest. Although it is mostly deer, there is the occasional wild boar."

"I thought I saw a grave...somewhere at the back of the lodge."

"Oh yes, there is a grave there."

"It seemed a strange place to find a grave. Why should someone be buried there and not in a churchyard?"

"Well, there was a reason, I think."

I waited but she did not seem as though she was going to continue, so I went on: "It seems well tended."

"Yes. I look after it. I don't like to see it overgrown. I don't think graves should be. It looks as though no-one cares about the person buried there if they are."

"It was a friend of yours, then?"

"Yes," she said. "You must excuse me. I can hear my little boy. He's awakened from his nap. You'll have no difficulty in finding your way. Good-day to you."

I felt I had mishandled the situation. I had discovered nothing except that she had known Francine and had been a friend of hers.

I would call again though. I had at least opened up a path where there had appeared to be nothing.

As I came back through the town I passed the inn where I had once hired a horse, and I decided to sit awhile in the *biergarten,* so I left my horse in the stable and did so. I think I wanted to talk to someone, and the innkeeper's wife had been very friendly.

She remembered me, and when she brought my goblet of *bier*—a speciality of Bruxenstein—she told me so. She paused and it was not difficult to detain her.

I told her I was now working at the *schloss.*

"I heard the Countess had an English lady to help her speak the language," she said.

"I am she," I answered.

"Well, do you enjoy it?"

"Very much," I replied. "The Countess is charming."

"She is popular and so is the Baron. It wouldn't surprise me if they put forward the marriage. It depends, I suppose, on the Grand Duke. If he recovers his health things will go on just as before, I suppose."

I agreed and said I found the forest enchanting.

"Our forests are famous in legend and song," she answered. "They say all sorts of things can happen there. Trolls, goblins, giants and the gods of old...some reckon they're still there...and some people have the power to see them."

"It must be rather eerie living in the heart of it. I passed a place today."

"Was it the lodge?"

"Yes, I did see the lodge, but I was thinking of a house...a small one in the forest...near the lodge. I wondered who lives there."

"Oh, I know where you mean. That would be the Schwartzes' place."

"I did see someone there. I asked her the way."

"That must have been Katia."

"Has she a little boy?"

"Yes. Rudolph."

"Does her husband work for one of the *schloss* families?"

"There isn't a husband."

"Oh...I see."

"Poor Katia. She had rather a bad time."

"That's sad. She seemed so very pleasant. I thought her charming, in fact."

"Yes she is. Life was cruel to her, though. But she has the boy and she dotes on him. He's a nice little fellow."

"I did notice a child. Would he be about four or five?"

"Yes, I suppose it must have been all those years ago. Rather a mystery really."

"Oh?"

"Well, who can say what happens in these cases. It seems a bit unlucky...that part of the forest...considering what happened at the lodge."

"You mean the murder?"

"Yes. That was terrible, that was. Some say it was jealousy, but I never believed that. It was someone who wanted Rudolph out of the way so that Sigmund could step into his shoes."

"You don't mean that Sigmund—"

"Oh—hush! I'd say it's all a mystery...and long ago now. Best forgotten. They tell me Sigmund has the makings of a fine Duke. He's strong and that's what we want. Listen." She cocked her head on one side. "I expect they're coming this way."

"Who?"

"The Graf and Gräfin with Sigmund and the Countess. I heard they'd been visiting the Grand Duke this afternoon. Sigmund will be escorting them back to the *schloss*. I'll pop out and watch."

"May I come with you?"

"But of course."

I stood with her and others crowded in the inn doorway, and my heart leaped with pride and fear as I watched him. He looked magnificent on his white horse, acknowledging the cheers of the people as he rode. And beside him was Freya, looking pink-cheeked, bright-eyed and very pretty. It was clear that the people liked her.

"Little duck," I heard someone say. "She's a charmer, isn't she?"

Then came the Graf and Gräfin with Günther and Tatiana. There were a few guards riding with them, colourful in blue and brown uniform with blue feathers in their silver helmets.

As I stood and watched, the hopelessness of my situation was borne home to me afresh, and I could see that there would be no real place for me in Sigmund's life. I would be his mistress, to be hidden away...to wait for those days which he could spare for me. And if there were children—what of them?

How could I do this? I must go away.

Oh Francine, I thought, was it like this with you?

When I arrived in my room one of the footmen was standing at my door.

He said: "I have a note for you, Fräulein. I was told to deliver it into no other hands but yours."

"Thank you," I said, taking it.

He bowed and departed.

I knew before I opened it who had sent it. It was written on blue tinted paper with the crest of the lions and crossed swords which I had seen before.

"My dearest," he had written in English, and then:

> *I must see you. I want to talk to you. It is unendurable that you should be so near and yet away from me. I cannot wait for tomorrow. I want to see you tonight. There is an inn just below the schloss. It is called The King of the Forest. Come there. I shall be waiting. Please. I shall expect you at nine. You will have dined then and can slip away.*
>
> *C.*

The King of the Forest. I had seen it. It was very close to the *schloss* gates. Could I do it? I supposed so. I could plead a headache, retire early and slip out. It would be unwise. It would be as it had been at the Grange. I must not go. Yet I thought of his waiting there. He would be so wretched. People like Conrad and Freya were used to having everything their way. They would have to learn that it could not always be so. And yet...I wanted to go.

But I must not, I admonished myself. Yet it was not possible to get a message to him. How could *I* ask someone to take a note to Baron Sigmund!

No. I decided I must go, and I must make him realize that I could not see him any more. I must leave the *schloss*. Suppose I went back to Daisy. That was not far enough. He would seek me out there. No. I would go and see him and explain that we must not meet again.

I managed to get away quite easily. Freya was a little absentminded. She had enjoyed riding through the streets with Sigmund and she had obviously been gratified by the cheering crowds. When I said I should like to retire early because of a headache she just said, "Have a good night's sleep then, Anne. Perhaps I'll go early, too."

So I was able to slip out without much trouble.

He was looking out for me and before I reached the inn he had joined me. He was in a dark cloak and black hat like any travelling businessman, but although I had seen many men dressed exactly like that, nothing could prevent his looking distinguished.

He held my arm tightly and said: "I have engaged a room where we shall not be disturbed."

"I have come to tell you that I must go away," I said.

He did not answer, but pressed my arm more tightly to his side.

We went into the inn and up a back staircase. I thought, This is the way it will always be—always in the shadows. And suddenly I did not care. I loved him and I knew I should never be happy away from him. What was the old Spanish proverb? "Take what you want," said God. "Take it...and pay for it."

It was a small room but the candlelight threw a pleasant glow over it, touching it with a romantic aura; but perhaps I felt that because I was here with him alone.

He pushed back the hood of my cloak and pulled the pins out of my hair and unruly as ever, it easily escaped.

"Pippa," he murmured, "at last. I have been thinking of you...dreaming of you...and now you are here."

"I must not stay," I began. "I just came to tell you—"

He smiled at me and took off my cloak.

"No," I said, trying to sound firm.

"But yes," he answered. "This is meant, you know. You can't escape it. Oh, Pippa, you have come back to me... never to be parted again."

"I have to go," I insisted. "I should never have come. I thought you wanted to talk to me."

"I want everything," he replied.

"Listen," I went on. "We have to be sensible. It is different now. That other time I did not know who you were. I was carried away. I was quite innocent... inexperienced. I had never had a lover. I thought we should be married and live... as married people do. I was as guileless as that. It is all different now. This is wrong and I know it is."

"My darling, these conventions are made for the convenience of society—"

I interrupted: "That is not all. There is Freya. I have grown fond of her. What would she think if she saw us now? It is wrong—dreadfully wrong. And I must go."

"I shall not allow it."

"It is for me to decide."

"You can never be so cruel."

"I understand that I am still naïve and that you must have been in many similar situations."

"I have never loved until now," he said. "Isn't that good enough?"

"Is it really true?"

"I swear it. Now and forever I love you—and you only."

"How can you know what you will feel in the future?"

"As soon as I saw you I knew. Didn't you?"

I hesitated and then I said: "Perhaps for me I knew it would be so, but for you it would be different. If I went away you would forget me."

"Never."

"There would be so many in your life to compensate for any loss you might feel because one woman rejected you."

"You won't understand. If it were just for myself, I would be ready to throw everything aside."

"All the shouting and the cheering. It means something to you. I watched you. I was on the porch of an inn when you rode by with Freya. I saw you. How you smiled. How you pleased the people, both of you, and I know how they pleased you. It is something you do very well because it means so much to you."

"I have been brought up to it in a way," he admitted. "But

I never thought all this would come to me because of Rudolph. I was just a branch from the tree. If Rudolph had lived—But, my dearest, what of that? Let us make what we can of life."

"No. I must go. I shall return to England. I think it is the best way. I shall go to my Aunt Grace and try—"

He had thrown my cloak aside and his arms were about me.

"Pippa," he said, "I love you and the time is short—for now. But we are going to be together through the years."

"And your life...and Freya's...?"

"I will work something out. Please, my darling...let us be happy...now."

My lips said no, but the rest of my body cried, Yes, yes. He was irresistible to me and he knew it and I knew it.

There is no excuse. I make none. We were just carried away by the force of our passion. Neither of us could think beyond the fact that we were alone together in this room.

And it was as it had been at the Grange. There was nothing else but our love and our need of each other. I could hold out no longer and I lay in his arms half tearful, half laughing, ecstatically happy and pushing away the cloud of guilt and apprehension which would eventually settle on me.

Then I was lying quietly with his arms about me and he was tracing his fingers over my face as a blind man does.

"I want to know every part of you so intimately that it is part of myself," he murmured. "I must carry the memory of you when I am not with you. I have already found a home for us. Not far from the town...in the forest...a delightful little house which we shall make our own."

I was brought to earth suddenly from the Olympian heights by a vision of the hunting lodge—dark, gloomy, haunted by ghosts.

"It is on the west side of the town," he went on. He meant that the town would be between us and the hunting lodge. "I will show it to you and we shall make it our home. I shall be there every possible moment. Pippa, I would to God it could be different."

"I will never do it," I said. "I cannot. I am filled with shame. Can you imagine what is like being with that child...that dear innocent child. I have grown to love her...."

"I am the one you love, remember?" he reminded me. "No-one must stand in the way of that."

"But I cannot stay with Freya...after this."

"Then come to our home in the forest."

"I must think about it. I cannot decide. I cannot imagine what I could say to her. What would her feelings be? She will be your wife. I shall be your mistress."

"It is not like that," he said.

"How else can it be described? I don't think I can do it. Not with Freya. Even now I feel despicable. The other day when she was feeling particularly affectionate she kissed me...and I returned her kiss. The horror swept over me. I was posing as her friend when all the time I was betraying her. I thought: This is the kiss of Judas. No. No, it would be better if I went home. I could go to my Aunt Grace, I could look round and make a new life...perhaps somewhere well away from Greystone Manor."

"You are staying here. I shall not allow you to go."

"I am free. Remember that."

"No one is free when he or she loves. You are shackled too, my darling. For the rest of our lives we belong together. Accept that, and you will see that it is the only way."

"The only way is for me to leave."

"That is unacceptable to me—and to you. If I were but free to marry you I should be the happiest man alive."

"There is no way."

"Unless we discover a new heir. If only Rudolph had married...."

"He did marry."

"Oh, the entry in the register. It wasn't there, was it? We searched. If only there had been proof of his marriage and there had been an heir. If we could bring forward that heir and say, 'Here is the new ruler of Bruxenstein' should the Grand Duke die."

"He would be only a child."

"Children grow up."

"What would happen? There would be a regency, I suppose.

"Something like that."

"And you would be the Regent?"

"I expect that is how it would happen. But I should be free. Kollenitz would not want an alliance with a Regent. I daresay they would want Freya to marry the heir."

"The difference in their ages would make that out of the question."

"They would not be greatly concerned with such matters. There have been more incongruous marriages for the sake of the state. Suppose she were some ten years older, that would not be considered a deterrent. After all, I am eight years older than Freya. But we are wasting time on suppositions which are wide of the mark. We have to accept what is. I shall have to go through with this ceremony with Freya. I shall have to get an heir. When that is done, so is my duty. But I am not letting you go, Pippa—never, never, never. If you ran away I should come after you. I would scour the whole of England—the whole of the world—and bring you back."

"Against my will?"

"Dear, dear Pippa, it would never be against your will. All your resolutions would crumble away when we were together. Haven't we proved that twice?"

"I am weak...foolish...immoral...I see that."

"You are gentle, loving and adorable."

"You have no right to tempt me."

"I have the right of true love."

"What a fool I am! I almost believe you."

"You are foolish not to believe me entirely."

"Is it really so, then?"

"You know."

"I believe I do. We are two people caught up in an unusual situation. I wonder if it has ever happened before."

"It happened to your own sister," he said. "Not exactly the same...but Rudolph could not have married her."

"Why not?"

"Because he was destined for Freya."

"But he had never gone through that betrothal ceremony which was tantamount to marriage."

"It is true. But he knew he must not marry without the approval of the Grand Duke's ministers. Darling, forget it. Make the best of what we have. I promise you it will be a great deal."

"I must go now. It is late."

"Only if you promise that we will meet again soon. I want to show you the house we shall have. I want you to come here tomorrow night. Will you do that?"

"I cannot. How can I get away like this? It will be noticed. Freya will suspect."

"I shall be here tomorrow at the same time. Dearest Pippa, please come."

I put on my things and he came out with me almost to the

castle gates. The guards looked at me oddly, and I wished I could still the wild, exultant happiness which enveloped me, swamping my fears.

I did not know how I was going to face Freya. If she talked about Sigmund I should be very much afraid that I would betray myself. She was observant and she knew me so well. She would surely guess something had happened.

Strangely enough there was a change in Freya since we had come to the *schloss*. She seemed to have become older, more withdrawn, obsessed with herself. Before, I believed she would have immediately noticed that my behaviour was a little unusual.

Fräulein Kratz had recognized the change in her.

"She is quite inattentive at her lessons," she complained. "I think coming here and seeing the Baron again and realizing what the future holds has turned her head."

"It is enough to turn anyone's head."

"She will not concentrate on anything for long and she is continually cancelling her lessons. It is very hard to exert one's authority. What do you think, Fräulein Ayres?"

"It is different in my case. It is not like a set lesson. We just talk English. We don't have to sit and study books, although I do like her to read in English."

"I suppose one must accept it."

"I should, Fräulein Kratz, and in any case it does give you a little free time."

She admitted this was so. The same thing applied to me— which, to my relief, I found that very afternoon.

I saw her briefly for the midday meal. She was dressed for riding and looked very pretty in a light navy habit which set off her fairness to perfection.

"I am going riding this afternoon, Anne," she said. "I daresay you will want to do the same or go into the town."

"Whatever you wish, of course."

"Oh no...not that. I can't go with you. I have to go with Tatiana and Günther."

My heart leaped with pleasure, for this would give me a little time to carry out a plan of my own.

"I hope you enjoy it," I said.

"I'm sorry you can't come with us."

"Of course I understand. Enjoy your ride."

She threw her arms round my neck. "Have a pleasant afternoon, dear Anne."

"I will amuse myself."

"And we'll talk a lot in English...tomorrow or the next day."

I went to my room and put on my riding habit. It was early afternoon when I set out for the forest.

The plan had come to me when I had awakened that morning. I was going to see the woman who had tidied Francine's grave. I had the strong conviction that she knew something and if she did I must find out what it was. I had been very interested in the child. Why not? It was a wild supposition, but at least his name was Rudolph. Why should a boy of four be made to kneel at a stranger's grave? What if that little Rudolph was the child of whom Francine had written to me? If I could prove that Francine had been truly married, if I could find her child, then that little boy would be heir to the Duchy. He would come before Conrad. I saw now that when I had come to Bruxenstein to solve the riddle of my sister's life and death here, I might also have been finding a solution to my own problem.

Perhaps my imagination was working too strongly; perhaps I was looking for too much simplification. I could but try; and I was going to with all the ingenuity I possessed.

As I rode through the forest past Gisela's house to the hunting lodge I was thinking of the previous evening, of Conrad, the wild demanding passion that consumed us both and robbed us of all awareness of everything else. How could I, who had always considered myself to be a fairly honourable sort of person, allow myself to be carrying on this passionate affair with the affianced husband of my pupil? I could not understand myself. I seemed different from the Philippa Ewell I had known all my life. I only knew that I must be with him. I must give way; I wanted above everything else to please him, to be with him forever.

I tethered the horse in the usual spot and walked round the lodge, past the grave and toward Katia's house.

As I came into the thicker part of the forest just past the lodge, I heard the sound of a horse's hoofs. I stepped back from the rather narrow path and waited for the horse and rider to pass me.

It was a man and strangely enough he looked familiar to me.

He stared at me as he passed. He was walking the horse as he must along this bridle path. He inclined his head in a form of greeting and I responded. Then I passed on, wondering where I could possibly have seen him before. People came in and out of the *schloss*. Perhaps he was employed there.

In any case my mind was too full of other matters for me to waste my thoughts on a mere stranger. I came to the house. It looked quiet. Deliberately I opened the gate. I was on a porch in which potted plants grew. There was a knocker, so I knocked.

Silence and then the sound of footsteps. The door opened and Katia stood there. She stared at me in surprise, not immediately recognizing me as the woman who had asked the way.

I had rehearsed what I was going to say and I said it.

"I wonder if I can speak with you. There is something very important I have to ask you. Will you allow me to?" She looked bewildered and I went on, "Please...it is very important to me."

She stepped back and opened the door wider. "I have seen you before," she said.

"Yes. The other day. I asked for directions."

She smiled. "Ah...I remember now. Please come in."

I stepped inside the hall, noticing how clean and polished everything was. She opened a door and we entered a pleasant room, simply but comfortably furnished.

"Please sit down," she said.

I did so. "I realize this may seem very strange," I said. "But I am very interested in the grave of the lady who was murdered with Baron Rudolph."

"Oh?" She was faintly alarmed. "Why...why do you ask me?"

"Because you knew her well. You were fond of her. You look after the grave. You take the little boy there and you clearly respected her."

"I take my little boy with me because I could not leave him behind. He is sleeping now. It is the only time I have to do anything in the house."

"Please tell me about your friendship with the lady who was murdered."

"May I ask why you are interested?"

It was my turn to hesitate. Then I made a sudden decision, because I saw it was the only way in which I could hope to get the information I wanted so badly. I said, "I am her sister."

She was quite taken aback. She just stared at me in astonishment. I waited for her to speak, then she said, "Yes, I knew she had a sister...Pippa. She spoke of her so—lovingly."

Those simple words touched me deeply and I felt my lips trembling and the words began to rush out, "You understand then. You know why I must—"

I saw at once that I should have discovered nothing of importance but for the fact that I had told her who I was, for the relationship between us had changed suddenly.

I went on: "I saw you tending the grave. I saw you and the little boy kneel together. I knew then that you had loved my sister. That was why I decided to talk to you."

"I did not really believe you had lost your way," she said. "I knew there was something."

"I believe my sister was truly married to Rudolph."

She lowered her eyes. "They said she was not. They said she was his mistress."

"Nevertheless there is proof somewhere...."

She was silent.

"Tell me about her. She lived here in the lodge, didn't she? You must have been a near neighbour."

"It was her home. You see, she could not be received at the *schloss*. The Baron had his duties. He came when he could. He came often. They were very much in love and she was such a happy person. She laughed all the time. I never saw her sad. She accepted the position. I am sure the Baron Rudolph escaped to her whenever he could."

"Tell me how you knew her."

"My father was alive then. He and my brother were in the employment of the Graf von Bindorf, as most people are hereabouts, either with the Graf or in the household of the Grand Duke. My brother Herzog is still with the Graf. He goes on missions for him. He is not here very often."

"Yes," I prompted.

"A terrible thing happened to me. It was in the forest. I was young and innocent, you understand. It was terrible. Nobody could know unless it happened to them. There was a man. I think he had watched me for some time...because I had sometimes fancied I was being followed. And then one day... it was dusk..." She paused and looked straight ahead, reliving the horror, I imagined. "He was one of the guards at the Grand Schloss. He caught me and dragged me through the trees and then..."

"He raped you."

She nodded. "I was so frightened. I knew he was one of the guards... I thought they would not believe me... so I said nothing. It was like a nightmare and I thought it was over and I must forget... But then... I found I was to have a child."

"I am so sorry for you."

"It is over now. These things fade. I do not think of it so much now. It is talking of it brings it back. My father was a very religious man, you understand? When he knew, he was horrified, and..." Her face puckered and I could see in her the poor defenceless girl she must have been at that time. "They didn't believe me," she went on. "They said I was a harlot, that I had brought shame on the family. They turned me out."

"And where did you go?"

"I did not know which way to turn and I went to her—your sister. She took me in. It was not just that... it was everything she did for me. *She* believed me. Not only that, she said that even if it were true that I had agreed, it was not such a sin after all. But she *believed* me. She said she would have helped me in any case. So... she did and my child was born in the hunting lodge."

My heart was beating wildly. "Did she have a child too... at about the same time?"

"I don't know of a child," she said. "I never saw one there."

"It would be dangerous if she had had a child, wouldn't it?" I asked. "He would be the heir to the Duchy."

She shook her head. "There would have had to be a marriage."

"I believe there was a marriage."

"Everyone says there was not."

"Did my sister ever talk of marriage?"

"No."

"Did she say she was pregnant?"

"No."

"And your baby was born at the hunting lodge, you say."

"Yes. I was well looked after there. She saw to that. And when the baby came I stopped having nightmares. I couldn't be sorry for anything that brought him to me."

"And you loved my sister, did you?"

"Who would not love someone who had done everything... who had saved me from such a terrible fate as that which could have overtaken me. I was half crazy with grief and fear. I thought I was damned as my father said I was. She laughed at all that. She made me see that I was not wicked. She helped me to bring a healthy child into the world. She saved us both. It is something I shall never forget."

"And... because of all this... you tend her grave."

She nodded. "I shall do so for as long as I live and I am at hand. I never forget, and I don't want Rudolph to either. I shall tell him the story when he is old enough."

"Thank you for telling me."

"What are you looking for here?"

"I want to find her child, because I believe there was a child."

She shook her head.

"There is something I have to tell *you*," I went on. "The Countess and those for whom I work do not know my true identity. I am here as Fräulein Ayres. You won't betray me?"

"I never would," she said, with a rush of feeling.

"I guessed you wouldn't, and I had to tell you because unless I did I knew that you would not tell me your secret."

She agreed that this was so.

I told her that because I had inherited money I was able to come here. I said again that I believed fervently that there had been a marriage between my sister and Rudolph and that there was a child.

"You have your son," I said. "You will understand how my sister felt about hers. I want to find him. I want to be able to take care of him. It will be compensation for losing her. Besides, if he does exist, how can I know what sort of life he is having? I owe it to her."

"I understand how you feel. If there was a child... but..."

"I had letters from her telling me about him."

"She longed for a child, perhaps. I know she did. I remember her with my Rudi. Sometimes when people long for something they dream...."

It was the old explanation. Not Francine, I thought. Francine always had her mind firmly in reality. She had not been a dreamer. I had been that and yet I could not believe that in any circumstances I could have deluded myself into thinking I had a child, let alone writing letters about him.

I said: "I am very grateful to you and thank you for looking after my sister's grave. If you should want to talk to me—if you have anything to tell me—remember I am here as Fräulein Ayres."

She nodded.

I left the house then, not much wiser than when I had come, except that I had discovered the reason for her tending Francine's grave.

As I entered the *schloss* and was about to go up to my room I came face to face with Tatiana. She looked at me in the rather haughty way which was habitual with her and said: "Good-day, Fräulein."

I responded and was about to pass on my way when she went on: "The Countess is progressing well with her English, I believe."

"Very well indeed," I answered. "She is a good pupil."

Tatiana regarded me with a certain interest and I grew uncomfortable under it and wished I were wearing my glasses. I knew my hair was escaping from under my riding hat.

"I think she is afraid that you are going to leave her. She has mentioned that you are a person of independent means."

"It is true I am not obliged to work for a living, but I very much enjoy my work with the Countess."

"So her fears are groundless and you will stay until her marriage?"

"That is looking rather far ahead."

"A year…perhaps less. You know all the circumstances, of course. I believe you are very much in her confidence."

"We are as good friends as we can be, considering our positions."

She bowed her head, letting me know that she considered there was a big gap between our social positions.

Then she looked at me sharply and said, "It is strange, Fräulein Ayres, but I fancy I have met you before."

"Could that be possible, Countess?" I asked.

"Just, I think. I have been to England. I stayed in a house in the county of Kent."

"I know Kent well. It is in the southwest corner of England. I was there at some time. But it would be rather unusual if we had met and I am sure such an occasion would stand out in my mind."

I was alarmed that she might pursue the subject, but to

my great relief she turned away to indicate that the conversation was at an end.

I went up to my room with a wildly beating heart. For a moment I thought she might have recognized me, but I was sure that if she had she would have questioned me more closely.

It must have been about an hour later when Freya returned. I was surprised because I had understood she had been with Tatiana and Günther. She came into my room; she was flushed and smiling.

"We've been miles and miles," she said. "Günther and I and two of the grooms lost the rest of the party."

"You weren't lost in the forest."

"Not exactly. But we did go a long way."

"The Countess Tatiana was back a long time ago."

Freya smiled at me conspiratorially. "I don't much like Tatiana. I have an idea that she is always criticizing me. She is very much aware of her position and thinks I'm a bit of a hoyden."

"Perhaps you are."

"Am I? Am I? Do you know, I don't mind in the least if I am. You rather like hoydens, don't you?"

"I like you, Freya," I said rather emotionally. "I like you very much."

Then she threw her arms round me and, remembering Conrad and all that had happened, I felt wretchedly ashamed.

Later that night I thought of his waiting at the King of the Forest. He would be frustrated and bitterly disappointed I knew; but he would have to realize that he could not lightly continue with this deception, and even if it were easy for me to get away—and it was far from that—I must hesitate to do so.

It was very different considering all this in the quiet of my room—yes, very different from being swept off my feet by an overpowering passion which assailed my senses while it numbed my impulses of decency, while I fought in vain to resist. He must understand that when I could calmly assess the situation, I deplored it. I was ashamed to face Freya; ashamed to face myself.

I awoke that night and sat up in bed wondering why I was suddenly so wide awake. Then I knew. I had had a revelation. It must have come to me in my dreams.

The man whom I had met in the forest when I was visiting

Katia Schwartz was the same one whom I had seen near
Greystone Manor on several occasions. He was the man who
had been staying at the inn and who, I thought, had been
exploring our countryside. I had seen him on the way to the
church near Dover when Miss Elton and I had gone there to
look at the register.

That he should be here in Bruxenstein was a very odd
coincidence.

I could not sleep. I lay there thinking of everything—my
love passages with Conrad, my conversation with Katia
Schwartz, the germ of suspicion I had seen in Tatiana's
eyes ... and now the man in the forest.

The next morning a note was brought to me from Conrad. I
thought it was very reckless of him to write to me in this
way, for it was not inconceivable that the notes would be
intercepted, but I had already learned that when he wanted
something he would not let minor considerations stand in the
way of forging ahead to get it.

"My dearest," he wrote, and then:

*You will be able to get away in the mid-morning. I am
sending an envoy from the Grand Schloss with messages
to the Graf and instructing that he must be entertained
by them, including the Countess Freya. This will leave
you free and the envoy will remain with them until the
late afternoon.*

*Meanwhile I shall be waiting for you at our inn and
from there we shall go into the forest, for I have something I wish to show you.*

My love now and forever.

C.

I was both elated and alarmed, for I could see myself slipping farther and farther into an intrigue from which I should
be unable to extricate myself and which could have the most
dire consequences. So I was free because Conrad had the
power to arrange it.

In due course I arrived at the inn. I wondered how many
his disguise deceived. I should have known him at once; but
then perhaps that was because I loved him.

We had some food in a private room and I had rarely felt

so happy as I did sitting there with him, while every now and
then his hand would touch mine across the table. There was
a gentleness in him that day. He was protective. He was
planning not just a hasty encounter but our future.

He was all eagerness for me to see the house which he
planned should be our home, although I was protesting all
the time that I could never agree to deceive Freya.

"Come and see it for yourself," he said. "It's rather delightful."

"However delightful, it could not influence my convictions
that this is wrong and I should never be a party to it."

He smiled at me appealingly. "Let's pretend then—for a
while."

We rode together out of the inn yard across the town. The
sun was high in the sky and shone warmly down on us and
I thought for a moment, I will pretend. I will have this day
and carry the memory of it through the years to come.

As we rode through the town we had to pass through a
square where some ceremony was in progress. It was delightful. The girls and women were in the national costume with
full red skirts and white blouses with red flowers in their
hair, and the men had white knee breeches with yellow stock-
ings and white shiirts; their caps were tightly fitting with
long tassels that hung halfway down their backs.

They were dancing to the sound of a violin and we paused
to watch it for a moment.

I thought how lovely it was there on that perfect summer's
day with the people's faces shining with pleasure and contentment while the young people burst into song.

Then suddenly a young girl approached us. She was carrying a little bunch of flowers which she presented to me. I
took it and thanked her and then suddenly the people were
crowding round us and singing what I recognize as the national anthem.

"Sigmund!" they shouted. "Sigmund and Freya!"

Conrad did not seem in the least perturbed. He smiled and
spoke to them, telling them that he hoped they would enjoy
the day and what pleasure it gave him to ride among them
unceremoniously.

He had taken off his hat and was waving it to them. I
wanted to turn and ride off as fast as I could. But Conrad was
enjoying it. I knew that the approval of the people meant a

great deal to him, and seeing him thus I realized how fitted he was for his destiny...and how ill I fitted into it.

They crowded round us, and from one of the houses someone brought out several sheets which they knotted together and held across our path. They were laughing and cheering.

"Come," said Conrad, and he caught my horse and led me along with him. We rode up to the sheets and with a great sigh they were allowed to fall to the ground. We passed through the cheering crowds and rode on towards the forest.

"They liked you," said Conrad.

"They thought I was Freya."

"They were pleased to see us."

"They will know in time that I am not. In fact, I am surprised that they mistook me for her. They see her now and then."

"I think some of them knew. It couldn't be otherwise. Their first thought was Freya...and then when they realized you were not Freya, they pretended that you were."

"Surely not. What would they think?"

"They will smile on us. They do not expect me to give up the society of all other ladies."

"Ah yes," I said slowly. "They will smile and shrug their shoulders...as they did with Rudolph."

"Cheer up. It was an amusing incident."

"It seemed significant in a way. I can see clearly how well you fit your role."

"I have to accept it. I have to live with it. I have to see the country peaceful. There is no way out of that. The life you and I have together will have its drawbacks—I would not try to pretend otherwise—but we *must* be together. I refuse to consider anything else. We must take what the gods give us, Pippa...and enjoy it. Because it will be wonderful. I can promise you that. Just to be together...that is all I ask."

When he spoke like that I felt limp with pleasure. I was aware of my principles slipping farther and farther away and myself growing closer to my sensual desires which were, in fact, becoming a need. I loved him. Every time I saw him I loved him more. I tried to imagine life without him and I could not bear to look into a future so dismal that it sent me into the depths of depression; and to contemplate the life he was planning for us filled me with a wild exhilaration...albeit apprehension.

I knew I was going to fall heavily into temptation. If it

were not for Freya...I kept thinking; and then the enormity of what I had done overwhelmed me and I then thought: I shall have to go away. I dare not continue with this.

How beautiful the forest was! When the trees thinned a little I could see the mountains in the distance. They were covered with spruce fir and in the valleys I could see little houses huddled together; I could smell the smoke rising from those places where the charcoal burners were, and I took deep breaths of the pure mountain air.

"You like this countryside," said Conrad.

"I find it delightful."

"Here will be our home. Oh Pippa, I am so happy to have you here. You cannot imagine how I suffered when I thought I had lost you. I cursed myself for all sorts of a fool for letting you go. Never again, Pippa. Never again."

I shook my head, but he laughed at me. He was sure of himself, so confident that life would work out the way he wanted it to.

We rode on and were going uphill.

"Listen," he said, "to the sound of the cowbells. You will hear them through the mist. You will love the mist. There is something romantically mysterious about it. I used to call it the blue mist when I was a boy. It seemed always blue to me. You climb high through the forests and you walk into the blue mist...and then after a while suddenly you are in bright sunshine. I used to come here a great deal. This was one of our houses. Sometimes when it was hot in the town below we would ride up here and spend the day. Perhaps we would stay. We slept out of doors often. It's full of happy memories for me, but they will be nothing compared with what lies in store for us."

"Conrad..." I began. "I can never call you Sigmund."

"Please don't. Sigmund suggests duty. Conrad is for those I love and who love me."

"Conrad," I went on, "have you always had what you wanted?"

He laughed. "Shall we say I've always made a good attempt to get it—and if you really make up your mind, what you want often comes to you. Dearest Pippa, cast off your fears. Be happy. We are here together. We are going to our home. It is a happy house and we'll make it entirely ours."

The house was enchanting. It was built like a miniature

schloss with pepperpot-type towers at the four corners, and it was the size of an English manor house.

"Come," he said. "There is no one here. I arranged that we should be quite alone."

"Who would otherwise be here?" I asked.

"The family who look after it. They have a house close by. Father, mother, two sons and two daughters. It's an excellent arrangement. They provide the entire domestic needs. If we used it for a large party we sent on our servants to help."

"It's beautiful," I said.

"I knew you would like it. It's a favourite place of mine. That's why I thought of it. It is known as Marmorsaal— Marble Hall. You'll see why. It has a rather exquisite floor in the hall, which is the centre of the house really."

There was a gateway leading to the house, surrounded by low bushes. "We keep them low so that it is not too dark," said Conrad. "I don't like darkness, do you? Well, who does? There's something menacing about it. This is always a happy house—so we cut down the trees and planted those small flowering shrubs to look pretty and not shut out the light."

"There is an inscription on the gate," I pointed out.

"Yes, that was put there by one of my ancestors who lived here for a while. He was a ne'er-do-well...the bad boy of the family...so they sent him off here to live in the forest. His great hobby was hunting the wild boar. He wanted to be alone and resisted all the efforts of the family to bring him back into the fold. He had this inscription put on the gate. Can you read it?"

"'*Sie thun mir nichts, ich thue ihnen nichts.*' Don't interfere with me and I won't interfere with you."

"An excellent sentiment, don't you agree? No one will interfere with us, I assure you. This is our home, Pippa."

He unlocked the door and picked me up in his arms.

"Is it the custom in England, too, to carry the bride over the threshold?"

"It is," I answered.

"Then here we are, my dear one. The two of us...in our new home."

It was beautiful, I had to admit. The hall floor was covered in marble slabs of the most delicate shades of blue. I could not help exclaiming at their exquisite beauty.

Pictures hung on the walls; there was a large table in the centre on which stood a bowl of flowers.

He stood there holding me tightly.

"You like it?" he asked.

"It's quite magnificent."

"We are going to be happy here—that is the most important." And when he was there beside me I could believe it.

We explored the house. Everything was in perfect order. That would be on his instructions. I wondered what the people in the forest thought. They would guess that he was bringing a woman here . . . his mistress . . . and they would know that this was to be her home. They would smile and shrug their shoulders, as Conrad would say.

Should we go through life with people smiling and shrugging their shoulders? What of our children? What would happen to them? Perhaps already I was pregnant.

Oh yes, I had fallen a long way down the slippery slope and I was going to find it hard to climb back to the right way, the honourable way. And it was that. I only had to think of Freya's innocent face to know it.

Nevertheless I found myself exclaiming at the perfections of the house: the dining room with its long narrow windows and its beautifully embroidered chairs; that room which was meant to catch the sun like our solarium at home; the bedrooms which were not large by *schloss* standards but which were light and prettily furnished. From the windows there were views of the forest and the distant mountains. It was a beautiful house in a perfect setting.

"You like it?" he asked eagerly.

I could only say that it was quite lovely.

"And you'll be happy here?"

I could not answer that. I knew in my heart that I could not be completely happy—neither with him nor away from him—and I could not pretend.

"I will banish all your scruples. I will make you see this as the only way to live."

"One which has been followed by the barons and counts, grafs and margraves before you."

"It is the only way. We are fettered for life if we do not break free. You must understand that, Pippa."

"I wish . . . but what is the use of wishing, though."

"Though what?"

"Here, I could imagine anything happening. It is the land of legend, of Grimm and the Pied Piper. There is magic in the air. I feel that in this forest . . . anything could happen."

"We'll make our own magic. Come, be happy. Take what is given you. You love me, don't you?"

"With all my heart."

"What else matters?"

"So much, alas."

"Nothing that cannot be overcome."

"I could never overcome my shame at my disloyalty to Freya."

"But she is just a child. When she grows up she'll understand."

I shook my head. "I think that because I am the one, she might not."

"Forget her."

"Can you?"

"I think of nothing but you."

"You are such a practised lover. You say what I most want to hear."

"It will be the aim of my life to please you."

"Please...please, don't..." I begged.

He held me tightly against him. He was in an unusual mood. It was almost as though he thought that our being in the house like this was sacred in some way. It was almost like a ceremony.

I said: "Is it just possible that you and I could be two ordinary people, that you could be relieved of your responsibilities, so that we could marry and bring up children, and live normal lives?"

"If Rudolph had not died it could have been like that. But he died too young...without an heir."

I told him about my visit to Katia Schwartz and that I had let her know who I was. That did not alarm him in the least. He brushed aside possible danger.

"If only there had been a child and your sister and Rudolph had married...well, then we could start thinking on different lines."

"Would you want to marry me?"

"I want it more than anything in the world. If I could marry you instead of Freya I would ask nothing else."

"I have always believed that my sister had a child."

"Even if she had it would be of no consequence, as far as the succession is concerned."

"If she and Rudolph had been married it would."

"But they were not."

I was about to say that I had seen the entry...but he had seen with his own eyes that it was not there.

"That would make all the difference," I went on, "if they had married and we found there had been a child?"

"But of course. However much the marriage would have been disapproved of, it would still be a marriage."

A sudden wild hope was surging through me. It was the magic of the forest. It was the blue mist, the fir-clad mountains and the feeling that I was in an enchanted land where strange events took place.

So I gave myself up to the joy of being with Conrad in our new home. I had the strange conviction there that I was going to find what I needed.

When I arrived back at the *schloss* the envoy was still there. I was relieved. It gave me the chance to slip up to my room unnoticed. I was always afraid of seeing Freya immediately after my meeting with Conrad for I felt it might be obvious to her that something had happened to me.

I threw off my riding coat and sat on the bed, thinking over the past few hours, and my eyes strayed to my dressing table. It struck me suddenly that the little pot in which I kept my hairpins was not in its usual position. I looked at it without much interest and wondered when I had moved it. It was a trivial matter, but it did look a little strange as I had never before seen it out of place. I was lost in thought about Conrad—the mood I was usually in after having been with him, alternating between joy and fear. There were times when I gave myself up to dreams. I let myself imagine that Conrad and I were together and everything had turned out right for us. I pretended that I had found Francine's child and he was acclaimed the heir; Conrad was free and we married and lived happily ever after. Fancies...wild dreams...How could they ever come true?

I must change from my riding clothes. The envoy must surely be leaving soon and then Freya would come and tell me what sort of day she had had. She seemed to have grown up lately; I supposed that now she was getting closer to marriage, she was becoming interested in the politics of the country in which as Grand Duchess she would have a part to play.

I sometimes fancied that life excited her. Was she perhaps falling in love with Conrad? That would be the easiest thing imaginable for a romantic young girl.

I hung up my coat and took a dress from the cupboard. I took off the scarf I had been wearing and opened a drawer to put it away. I had several scarves which I always kept in the drawer with my gloves and handkerchiefs. It was strange, but the gloves which were usually kept below the handkerchiefs were on top.

Then I had no doubt that someone had been looking through the drawer. Why?

A cold horror had begun to creep over me. There was one drawer which had been locked and in which I kept the papers Cousin Arthur had helped me to get before I left England. They would reveal my true identity.

If someone had seen them I should be betrayed, for whoever found them would know that I was not Anne Ayres but Philippa Ewell—and they would remember that the young woman who had been murdered was Francine Ewell.

I searched frantically for the keys to the drawer. I had left them at the back of one of the other drawers behind some underclothes. They were not in their usual place. I unlocked the drawer and hastily searched. I found the papers but was sure they were not quite as I had left them.

Now I was almost certain that someone had been in my room, had looked for the papers and found them; and then had put the key back in the wrong place. In which case I was betrayed. Who would have done it?

My first thoughts were: Freya. I often felt she was suspicious of me. She had a mischievous way of regarding me. On more than one occasion she had said, "You are not what you seem!" and there had been a calculating look in her eyes.

Could it be that she had determined to find out and had gone through my drawers while she knew I was away?

I would soon find out.

If she had seen the papers, I should have to confess to her. I would tell her the whole story and I knew she would understand.

The thought that it was Freya was comforting in a way.

But of course it could be someone else.

The Discovery

There was to be a thanksgiving service in the cathedral in the centre of the town to celebrate the recovery of the Grand Duke.

Conrad was naturally very much involved with the arrangements and the Graf, the Gräfin, Günther and Tatiana stayed at the Grand Schloss for two days and nights to assist.

Freya and I were together during that time more than we had been lately and I was very wary of her, wondering all the time if she had seen the papers in my drawer. She gave no sign of having done so, which would have been strange with Freya. I should have thought she would have burst out the news of her discovery immediately.

She was a little quiet, it was true. However, I thought that was probably because her marriage was coming nearer.

We rode together into the forest. I avoided both the hunting lodge and the Marmorsaal; and she was in such a reflective mood that she allowed me to lead the way.

When we had ridden for a while we tied up our horses and stretched ourselves on the grass and talked.

"The forest is beautiful," I said. "Listen...can you hear the cowbells a long way off?"

"No," said Freya firmly. "I am so glad the Grand Duke is better."

"Everyone is. In fact, it is going to be a matter for national rejoicing."

"If he hadn't lived, I should have been married by now."

"Does that alarm you?" I asked cautiously.

"I'd rather wait," she said.

"Of course."

"Why didn't *you* get married?"

"For one very good reason, that nobody asked me."

"I wonder why. You're quite attractive."

"Thank you."

"And you're not very old—yet."

"Every day I get a little nearer to senility."

"So do I. So does everybody. Even Tatiana..."

"Why select Tatiana especially?"

"Because she thinks she is different from everyone else—like one of the goddesses."

"I know someone else who had similar ideas about herself."

"Oh, it was just the name with me. What's in a name?"

"'That which we call a rose by any other name would smell as sweet.'"

"Poetry again! Really, Anne, you can be the most irritating person. Talking poetry when I want to talk about marriage."

I picked a blade of grass and stared at it. I was afraid she would see the rising colour in my cheeks.

I said slowly: "Are you in love with...Sigmund?"

She was silent. Then she said, "I think I *am* in love."

"Well, then you must be happy."

"I am. Yes I am. Do you think I am too young to marry?"

"Well, it won't be for some time yet, will it? In a year's time you'll be of a reasonable age."

"I was thinking about *now*. How do you know you're in love? Oh...I forgot...you wouldn't know. You've never been in love and no one's ever been in love with you."

I was silent.

Then I said, "I think one would know."

"Yes, I think so too."

"So...are you?" I asked, and felt as though the entire forest was waiting with me for her answer.

"Yes," she said firmly. "I know I am."

Then she threw her arms around me and hugged me. She kissed me lightly. I put my lips against her forehead and even as I did so I thought: the Judas kiss.

I felt utterly depressed and wretched.

* * *

The thanksgiving service was to be held on the following
Saturday. They were decorating the streets of the town and
they had arranged pageants to halt the Grand Duke's progress through the streets, to assure him of their loyalty. There
was no doubt that the people very much appreciated their
Grand Duke.

Conrad, as the heir, would ride with the Grand Duke in
the grand coach, and they would be followed by other members of the royal household and nobility in their own carriages. The army would be out in full force and it would be
very impressive.

"I am riding with the Graf and the Gräfin," Freya told me.
"Tatiana is furious because she will be several carriages behind. Günther doesn't mind. He doesn't care so much about
such things. I don't think Tatiana likes me."

"Why shouldn't she?"

"Oh, she has her reasons."

"Well, do you know them?"

"The main one is she wants to be *me*. She would like to
marry Sigmund and be the Grand Duchess."

"What makes you think so?"

"I just know. I keep my eyes open, you know, dear Anne."

She looked at me quizzically and for a moment I felt sure
she had seen those papers.

"Tatiana is ambitious," she went on. "She hates being just
the daughter of the Graf. She'll make a very grand marriage,
you see. But Tatiana wants the most important one. That,
of course, is Sigmund . . . for she couldn't very well marry the
Grand Duke, could she?"

"Hardly."

"So she wants Sigmund, but he is betrothed to me, so she
hasn't a chance. Poor Tatiana."

"Do you think she is in love with . . . Sigmund?"

I wished I could stop myself always pausing before I said
his name.

"Tatiana is in love with one person—herself. It's not such
a bad thing to be in love with yourself. You never get disappointed, do you? And you always make excuses for the
loved one. It's the way to have a perfect love affair."

"Freya, you are quite absurd."

"I know. And you like me that way, don't you? Do you
think my husband will?"

"I expect so."

"Anne...has something happened to you?"

"What do you mean?" I asked in alarm.

"You seem different."

"In what way?"

"Well, in one way you seem to be looking over your shoulder as though you are expecting something awful to happen...and another time you look as if something rather wonderful *has* happened. It's very disconcerting, you know. It must be one thing or the other. You should make up your mind."

"You're imagining it."

"Am I, Anne? Am I?"

"Of course," I said brusquely.

"Perhaps I am fanciful. I must be in love myself. That makes people a bit odd, I think."

"I daresay it does."

And again I was wondering whether she had seen those papers.

There was another letter from Conrad.

"Dearest," he wrote,

When this thanksgiving business is over, I want you to leave the schloss and come to our home. Make some excuse to Freya, but come. When you are there we will make all sorts of plans. I'm so longing to be with you. All my love now and always.

C.

As usual his letters filled me with delight and apprehension, but as I looked at the seal on this one I had a fancy that it had been broken and resealed before it had reached me.

I wondered if that was possible. Conrad was reckless, I knew that. He had become so accustomed to having his own way and expecting immediate obedience that it might not have occurred to him that he could have a disloyal servant.

If someone had read that letter before it reached me, they would understand at once the relationship between us. Could it be Freya?

No. She could never keep such a matter to herself. But her recent conversations had set me wondering. Why had she talked as she had about love and marriage? It was almost as though her observations were full of innuendoes, that there was some meaning behind her words. Yet, her affection for me did not seem to have abated. She had said she was in love. Then if she had read that letter she must be jealous of me. But she showed no sign of it.

It was disturbing to contemplate that the letter might have been intercepted. I tried to tell myself that I had imagined it because of my guilty conscience, but there was also the indication that my room had been searched.

One of the servants knocked on my door and when I told her to come in she took a letter from her pocket.

"This was given to me to hand to you," she said, "and I was told to give it to no-one else."

I immediately thought of Conrad, but surely he would not have given it to a serving girl. When I looked at the writing on the envelope I did not recognize it.

"A young woman gave it to me. She said you would understand."

"Thank you," I said.

I could scarcely wait for the maid to go before I opened the envelope.

"If you will come to the house," I read, "I will show you something which I think you will want to see. Katia Schwartz."

I was tremendously excited, and I determined to go to the house in the forest as soon as I could.

It was not easy. Freya would demand to know where I was going and want to come with me. I could see nothing for it but to wait for the day of thanksgiving. I should be expected to be there, of course, but I could make some excuse to get away.

Freya told me that I was to ride in the carriage with Fräulein Kratz and perhaps two others.

"Dear Anne," she said, "I am sorry you have to ride with the governess."

"Why be sorry? It's my place."

"But you know you are...different."

"On the contrary, I am here as the English governess and it is only right and proper that I should be treated as such."

"I spoke to the Gräfin about it."

"You shouldn't have done that."

"I shall speak how and when I like."

"I know that, but it was unwise."

"Tatiana was quite angry. She said you were a governess and your place was in the carriage with Fräulein Kratz."

"She was quite right."

"She was not. You are my friend. I keep telling them that."

"Freya, you must remember your position."

"I do. That is why I let them know when I don't approve of something."

"I shall be perfectly all right in the governesses' carriage. It's very kind of them to let us *have* a carriage in any case."

"Now you are being humble. I always suspect you when you are like that."

"Suspect me of what?"

She narrowed her eyes. "All sorts of things," she said.

"What shall you wear for the service?" I asked.

"Something bright and beautiful. After all, it is a time for rejoicing, isn't it?"

"It certainly is."

The day came. It was warm and the air seemed filled with the scent of pines. It was always like that when the wind blew in a certain direction. I had grown to love it.

What a great occasion it was—and one of those when I realized more poignantly than ever the great gulf between myself and Conrad. What if I succumbed to his wishes? There would be many occasions when he would be attending some ceremony. And I? Where should I be? One of the crowd, I supposed. Or perhaps not present at all. That was not important really. I loved him enough to want to make his life as comfortable as possible, and if that meant taking an obscure role I did not mind that. And yet I found it sordid in a way, unacceptable.... I was still hovering between my need of him and something within me which was warning me to get away while there was still time, before I became inextricably enmeshed.

The Grand Duke looked remarkably well, considering the danger he had passed through. He acknowledged the cheers of the crowd with a kind of benign tolerance. Conrad was beside him in the carriage, looking magnificent in the uniform of a general of the army—two shades of blue with touches of silver and a silver helmet in which waved a blue feather.

Freya rode immediately behind with the Graf and Gräfin and the ambassadors of Kollenitz. She looked very young and appealing, I thought. The people cheered her and I was touched by her obvious delight in their displays of affection.

Children in national costume presented her with flowers and sang hymns of patriotic fervour while banners waved across the streets which were crowded with spectators.

Then we entered the cathedral and the service of thanksgiving began.

I was seated at the back with Fräulein Kratz and as I listened to the singing and the prayers and the sermon of thanksgiving delivered by one of the highest dignitaries of the church, the incongruity of my situation was borne home to me. Thus it must have been with Francine. When had she realized that it would be impossible for her to lead a normal happy married life with Rudolph? Had she ever attended ceremonies like this?

Fräulein Kratz was singing fervently beside me. "*Eine feste Burg ist unser Gott.*" I noticed there were tears in her eyes.

As for myself, I felt a great desire to get away. Here I believed I could survey the future clearly, and it seemed to me that I could only be an encumberance to Conrad. Our meetings would be surreptitious—"hole and corner" as Daisy would describe it. I must go back to England. I must slip away and hide myself. I could go to Aunt Grace and stay with her for a while. From there I could make plans, start a new life.

I wanted to get away, to be alone, to strengthen my resolve. If I were going to do what I saw now as my real duty I must not see Conrad again, for he unnerved me, he robbed me of my will power; he refused to look the truth in the face and tried to make life fit in with his desires.

The service was over. Freya and the royal party would now go back to the Grand Schloss where there would be more celebrations; and Fräulein Kratz and I could go back to the Graf's *schloss*.

It occurred to me then that now that the Grand Duke was well, Freya would not much longer be the Graf's guest. She would go back to the Grand Schloss to await her marriage, and naturally I should go with her. I tried to imagine what it would be like, living under the same roof as Conrad, and I could see that we were, with every passing day, heading towards a climax.

It was four o'clock when we arrived at the *schloss*. I

changed into my riding habit and without delay set out for the forest.

Katia was expecting me. She said, "My brother is at the celebrations. He has a high position in the Graf's employ. I thought you would come as soon as you could conveniently do so."

"Thank you. I have been all eagerness since I received your note."

"Come in. I will not keep you long in suspense."

I was taken into the room where I had been before. She left me for a few moments and when she came back she was holding what looked like a sheet of paper in her hands.

She stood looking at me with a strange expression on her face and she seemed reluctant to hand it to me, although I knew this was that which she had to show me.

She said, almost hesitantly: "You are her sister. You were frank with me. You could be in a very dangerous position...yet you told me the truth. I felt, therefore, that I could not withhold this from you."

"What is it?" I asked, and she put it into my hand.

As I looked at it I felt the blood rush into my face. My hands were shaking. It was there...as plainly as I had seen it before...the signature, the proof of the marriage.

"But..." I stammered.

"The sheet had been removed...very carefully. My brother arranged it and brought it back here."

"I knew I had seen it. I—I can't think clearly just now. This—this makes a lot of difference...It proves..."

She nodded. "It proves there was a marriage. I did not think there had been—until I saw that. She always called him her husband, but I thought that was just because she regarded him as such. But he was...you see. And I thought I owed it to her. That's why I am showing this to you."

I said slowly: "It explains so much. I had seen it...and then it disappeared. Sometimes I thought I was not quite sane. What do you know about it?"

"I know that my brother brought it back from England."

"Your brother—of course! He was the man I had seen. He had been following me...and after I had seen the entry he removed it. I...I don't know how to thank you. You can't realize what you have done for me. For so long I have wondered about myself even. Why—why should he have removed this entry?"

"Because someone was anxious to deny there was a marriage."

"You mean...the Graf?"

"Not necessarily. My brother is a spy. He could be working for several people."

I was silent. Someone who was eager to deny the marriage. Who? If they were dead, could it matter? There was only one reason why it could. That was because there must be a child.

I said firmly. "There is a child somewhere. He is the heir to the dukedom, because this proves without doubt that Rudolph and my sister were married."

Dazzling possibilities had come into my mind. I would find that child...love him as Francine would have wished me to. I could go to Conrad and say, "What we have longed for has come to pass. You are free. If we can find this child...If he still lives, you are no longer the heir. You can disentangle yourself from your commitment with Freya." This was like a dream come true.

I could not stop staring at the paper in my hand. It was like a talisman—the key to my future.

But the child. I must find the child.

She was looking at me intently. Then she shook her head. "I just thought you should know she was actually married. We can go no farther than that."

There was a slightly fanatical look in her eyes and I had the impression that she did not want me to look for the child.

She said: "I took a great risk in giving you that paper. My brother...and others...would kill me if it were known."

"He will know it is gone."

"No. He thinks it was stolen when he brought it back."

"How was that?"

"He came back from England to this house. It was in a case of his—a flat leather case which he carried around with him when he went abroad. He arrived home exhausted after a difficult journey. I admit I was inquisitive. I wanted to know the nature of his business because I guessed it was not just an ordinary mission for the Graf, who sent him all over the world quite frequently. I looked at his case and saw the paper. I knew what it was and that it concerned the friend who had been so good to me."

"Did you take it?"

"Oh no...not then. He had to go in [...]
schloss the next day, but before he did so it [...]
take his horse to the blacksmith to be shod. [...]
away I staged a robbery. I took the paper and [...]
things as well, so that he should not think that som[...]
broken in to get just that. I damaged the lock on the door an[...]
disturbed the place. Then I buried the leather case under the
inscription on your sister's grave. I gave him time to get back
before I returned, so that he should be the one to find the
place in disorder. He was almost demented. He said he would
be ruined. He raged against me and said I should not have
left the house unattended, to which I replied, how should I
know how important documents were. He never told me. He
did not speak to me for days after that...but it passed, and
I still keep house for him. Some of the things I took are still
buried round the grave. I took out the paper though after I
had met you and you told me who you were. I thought I should
give it to you."

"You have been very clever. It is one of the two things I
came to prove."

"There is no child," she said firmly. "But there is the proof
of the marriage."

"My search has brought me so far," I said. "It will carry
me on."

"Well, you know now. I feel a great relief. I owed it to her.
That was how I saw it. She had been so good to me. No one
was ever kinder...and in my time of need. I had to do that
for her."

"I am so grateful to you. Listen! Is that your little boy
calling?"

She nodded and smiled. "Yes. He has awakened."

"Go and get him," I said. "I love children and he is such
a bonny little fellow."

She looked pleased and went out; in a short time she returned with the child. He was sleepy, rubbing his eyes with
one hand and in the other carrying a toy.

I said, "Hello, Rudi."

"Hello," he answered.

"I have come to see your mother...and now you too."

He looked at me steadily.

"What's this you're carrying?" I asked, touching the limp-
looking toy in his hand.

"It's my troll," he said.

is that what it is?"

...oticed that one ear was soggy. I touched it gently, and ...ia laughed. "Oh, he's a baby sometimes, aren't you, Rudi? ...e's had that troll ever since he was a baby. He won't go to ...bed without it."

"My troll," said Rudi with a kind of contemptuous affection.

"He still sucks his right ear. It was his comforter as a baby and I suppose it still is."

I felt as if the room was spinning round me. Words danced before my eyes. What had Francine said? "He has a troll which he takes to bed with him." Didn't he find great comfort in sucking its ear?

I reached out and touched the child. I said, "My sister's son was called Rudolph...like this little one. She wrote to me about him...so lovingly. He, too, had a troll which he took to bed and found great comfort in sucking its ear."

She had moved a step away from me.

"So many children have them," she said sharply. "They always have something to suck...a toy...or a piece of blanket. It's natural. It's what they all do."

She was holding the boy tightly and regarding me with something like suspicion. I thought then: I believe he is the child. He is about the age. He has the name and the troll.

There was nothing I could do about it...now. So I said, "I suppose I should be riding back," and the atmosphere relaxed immediately.

I must find out, I was thinking. I must ask Conrad what we should do. We will work together in this. And if it really is so...could everything come right for us?

I touched her arm gently and smiled at her gratefully. "You cannot know what you have done for me," I said.

I had folded the paper and tucked it into the neck of my dress. It was not going to leave that spot until I had shown it to Conrad.

Then I took my farewells and with many thanks rode off into the forest. Katia stood at the door until I was out of sight, the sleepy boy held tightly in her arms.

I spent the rest of the night in a fever of impatience. I studied the sheet from the register again and again. I went over it in my mind—that first time I had seen it when Miss Elton and I had stood in the vestry together. I pieced all the evidence together and a clear picture began to emerge. The man who had followed me and watched from the graveyard had been Katia's brother, and he was there to destroy the proof of that marriage. I wondered a great deal about the churchwarden who had denied ever seeing me before. Of course he had been bribed. Katia's brother would have been able to offer him a sum of money which would have seemed enormous to him, just to deny he had shown me the register. I could imagine how he must have been tempted, and looking back I realized now that he had been a little too glib, a little too certain. I should have pursued the matter, tried to trap him, but I had been so shocked that I had been easily brushed aside.

And now here was the evidence in my hand.

I wondered how I could get to see Conrad immediately. I even thought of riding over to the Grand Schloss but I dismissed that idea almost as soon as it came, for I could not possibly do that without arousing the curiosity of many people. No, I must be patient and await my opportunity.

The next day passed. I guessed he was busy with the foreign visitors who had come for the thanksgiving ceremony, but I did receive a note in the afternoon. He wanted me to meet him at the inn.

I slipped away, not caring very much if I was missed. I had seen little of Freya all day. I believed she had been with Tatiana and Günther, but as I rode out of the inn I saw Tatiana near the stables, so I presumed they had returned.

Conrad was waiting for me in the dark clothes he wore for these clandestine occasions. He caught me and held me in an embrace even more passionate than before.

"I had to see you," he said. "We'll go to the room here."

"I have something to show you," I told him.

We went up the back stairs and when we were alone he kissed me in the familiar demanding way.

"I have made a great discovery," I said. "It can change everything for us." I drew the paper from my bodice. He stared at it, then at me.

"This is it," I cried triumphantly. "The missing sheet from the register. I did see it after all. Then, before I could show it to you, someone removed it."

He was amazed. He said: "But the churchwarden..."

"He was lying. Obviously he had been bribed to lie, by the man who took it. It is all so very clear to me now."

"Who?"

"I can even tell you that. It was Katia's brother."

"Katia...?"

"Katia Schwartz. She lives in the forest near the hunting lodge. She knew my sister. I discovered her when I saw that my sister's grave had been looked after. I trusted her and told her who I was, and she gave me this."

"It's incredible," he said.

"No, perfectly credible. Herzog Schwartz was spying for someone whose interest it was to remove that sheet."

He was looking at me oddly. "Who?" he said.

"I don't know."

"Pippa, you don't think *I* ordered it to be done?"

"You!"

"Well, if you are looking for a motive, who stands to gain most?"

"Conrad...you didn't..."

"Of course not."

"Then who could?"

"That is what we must find out."

"There is only one reason why it should be necessary to do it," I said.

He nodded. "If there was a child..."

I cried: "There *must* be a child. Why otherwise should Francine have told me that there was? Why otherwise should it have been necessary to remove that sheet from the register?"

He was silent. I could see that he was stunned.

I went on: "If we could find the child..."

"He would be the heir to the dukedom," he murmured very quietly.

"And you would be free, Conrad, to make your own life."

"If that child exists..."

"He *does* exist. He must. Someone wants to hide the evidence of the marriage. He must be here...somewhere near, perhaps. I am sure he is Francine's son and the true heir to the dukedom."

"We'll find him."

"And then?"

He took my face in his hands and kissed me. "You and I will have the freedom we want."

"And Freya?"

"She will probably have to wait until the boy grows up. How old would he be?"

"About four years old."

"A long time for Freya to wait."

"And you would be free, Conrad. But...Freya would be hurt."

"It would be no slight to her. It is merely that the positions of power would be changed. If we can find that boy, I shall be free to act as I wish."

"I think I have found the boy."

"What!"

"His foster mother will not want to give him up and I am sure she will lie about his origins. But I feel certain of it."

"What have you discovered?"

"It is Katia Schwartz. Poor woman. She gave me the paper out of gratitude to Francine. It will be hard if through doing so she will lose the child."

"You have seen the child?"

"Yes. He is the right age, fair-haired, blue eyes and his name is Rudolph, which I know my sister's baby was called. She wrote to me about him and this is rather vital, I think. He had a toy—a troll, she told me in her letter—and he sucked one of its ears for comfort. When I was at the Schwartz home I saw the child; he had a troll and it came out that he sucked one of its ears for comfort and had been doing so since he was one year old."

"I will have everything checked concerning the woman. I will find out every detail concerning the child."

"If this could be proved true..." I whispered.

He said with a little laugh, "I believe you are a witch. You come here in disguise...you discover secrets that have baffled everyone else. You enchant me. What are you, Pippa?"

"I hope I am the one you love. That is all I want to be."

Then we talked of how we would proceed and what we would do if we could prove that the child in the forest was indeed the heir to the dukedom.

"I should have to be here until he was of age," said Conrad. "It would be my duty to hold the dukedom for him and to help teach him how to govern. We should have to spend long periods in the Grand Schloss but our home could be Marmorsaal. Oh, Pippa...Pippa...can you imagine that!"

I could and I did.

He said, "I will set everything in motion tomorrow. It should not take long. Katia Schwartz will have to prove that the child she has with her is her own. If we get the answers we want, then we shall let it be known that Rudolph was lawfully married and had a son. That will be the best possible news."

It was about two hours later when I left the inn. As we were about to go Conrad said to me, "I didn't want to tell you before—I thought it would spoil our time together—but in two or three days I have to go away. It will only be for a week or so. I have to return with our guests from Sholstein. There are certain treaties I have to work out with them. When I come back, whatever happens, I want you to come to the Marmorsaal. No more dallying. Unless of course we find our heir, then we shall have a wedding. Instead of living together in respectable sin, we shall be together in openly virtuous convention...all that every subject in this dukedom could wish."

I could see that he took the matter more lightheartedly than I did and I was faintly disturbed. Would he regret just a little giving up that supreme power? Did it mean more to him than a regular union with me?

I thought he was the sort of man who could have been completely happy as long as I was there. My uneasiness increased. If an outsider had come in and been asked whose interest would be best served by hiding the marriage of Francine and Rudolph and the existence of their child, his answer would surely be Conrad's.

I shook myself free of such feelings, and reminded myself that he had been as eager as I was to find the child. He had kept the sheet from the register and said he would put it under lock and key, for it was unsafe for me to carry it around.

That had seemed the right thing to do when he said it. But I wished I could throw off my doubts.

It was two days before I saw him again, and he would be leaving the day after that. He came to the Graf's *schloss* unexpectedly when neither the Graf nor the Gräfin was at home. Freya was riding with Günther and a party. I think Tatiana was with them.

When I saw Conrad arriving my heart leaped. There was a great fluttering below because there was no-one to receive him. I heard him in the hall, putting them all at their ease with that affable manner of his which earned him so much popularity.

"Leave me," I heard him say. "I will amuse myself until

the Graf returns." I had started to come down the stairs and
he saw me. "Ah," he cried, "here is the English governess.
Perhaps she will entertain me for half an hour. It will be
good practice for my English."

I approached him and bowed. He took my hand and kissed
it, after the custom.

"Let us go somewhere where we can chat, Fräulein..."

"Ayres, my lord Baron," I said.

"Oh yes, Fräulein Ayres."

I led the way into the small room which opened from the
hall. He shut the door and laughed at me.

"For the life of me I couldn't remember your name. Darling
Pippa I know well...but Fräulein Ayres—she is a stranger
to me."

Then I was in his arms.

"It is unsafe here...." I said.

"Soon we shall be free of such restrictions."

"Have you found anything about the child?"

He shook his head dolefully. "There is no doubt that the
boy you saw was the son of Katia Schwartz. She was raped
in the forest, so we do not know the father's name. The midwife who attended her has been questioned. She tended the
birth of the child and looked after Katia afterwards. The boy
was healthy, named Rudolph and several people will testify
that he has been living with his mother ever since."

"But the fact that she knew my sister...that I found the
troll..."

"She knew your sister, yes. That has never been denied.
The troll is a common child's toy. Children all over the country have them...and I am told it is a custom for them to keep
them and even suck their ears and toes. No, it is clear that
Katia Schwartz's boy is her own."

"He must be somewhere else then."

"If he exists, we'll find him."

"How?"

"I can have discreet enquiries made. Depend upon it, if
that boy exists we shall find him, for without him the sheet
from the register is of no consequence."

"It is to me, even if we cannot find the boy, for it proves
that my sister was telling the truth. It proves that she was
not Rudolph's mistress but his wife. And if she was telling
the truth when she wrote of the marriage, it follows that she
was when she wrote of the boy."

"We'll find him."

We sprang apart suddenly, for the door had opened. Tatiana was standing there.

"I heard that you were here, Baron," she said. She was in her riding habit and had clearly just come in. "You must forgive us. It was most remiss of us not to be here when you called. What are you thinking of us?"

Conrad had stepped forward, taken her hand and kissed it as a short while ago he had kissed mine.

"My dear Countess," he said, "I beg of you do not ask *my* pardon. It is I who should ask yours for calling at such an inopportune time."

"The *schloss* is always at your disposal," she said. She was flushed and looking rather pretty. "It is unforgivable that there should be no one here to receive you."

"Fräulein Ayres has been doing the honours of the household." He turned to smile at me and I wondered whether Tatiana would notice the somewhat mischievous twinkle in his eyes.

"It was good of you, Fräulein," said Tatiana. "I dare say you have a great deal to do."

I knew what she meant. Dismissal. I bowed and went to the door.

"I sought the opportunity to improve my English," said Conrad.

"It is always so useful," murmured Tatiana.

As I went out I caught a glimpse of Conrad smiling at her.

I felt angry—ridiculously so. I seemed to forget that I was, after all, only the English governess.

I went up to my room. My euphoria of the last days had evaporated. The enquiries had come to nothing and Tatiana had made me realize how invidious way my position here.

It must have been an hour later when I saw him leave. I looked out of my window. Tatiana was with him. They walked together to the stables and seemed to be engaged in very amusing conversation.

I did not have an opportunity of seeing him again before he left for his week's trip. There was obviously no news or he would have found a way of telling me.

There was, however, a letter delivered to me on the day of his departure. It was the usual tender note, telling me that he was longing to be back with me and when he did return

I must be with him. The Marmorsaal was waiting and there must be no further delay. He was having enquiries pursued in what he called Our Little Matter, and if anything came to light he would let me know at once.

A day passed and then another. Freya was absentminded. She was extremely lively at one moment and the next seemed to be plunged in perplexity. I wondered how I could ever tell her about myself and Conrad. The more I tried to reason with myself, the more despicable my situation seemed. How could I say, "I am in love with your future husband. We are already lovers and plan to continue so, even after your marriage."

I should never have believed that I could have fallen into such a situation. I wished that there were someone in whom I could confide. I had been to see Daisy now and then and I was always made welcome and enjoyed playing with little Hans.

The day after Conrad left I did confide in her to a certain extent, because I felt that Daisy was the sort of person who had a natural gift for picking up information and for fitting it together to make the picture complete. She liked to hear snippets of gossip about the reigning family and although she was not on the spot, she did know what the people in the streets were saying, and it seemed a fact that all sorts of information seeped out to them and that they sometimes had a clearer picture than those of us who lived more closely to events.

So I found comfort in talking to Daisy. I had not told her about the recovery of the sheet from the register. I felt it was too dangerous to tell even her, but I did mention that I had met Katia, who looked after Francine's grave.

"That was a tragedy what turned out to have a happy ending," commented Daisy. "Poor girl...raped in the woods...and then blamed by that old father of hers. Really, some of these men want teaching a lesson or two."

"Did you know her, Daisy?"

"I've seen her once or twice at Gisela's. But people did hear about her."

"One would have thought she might have lost the child after such an experience."

"Well, the child saved her sanity, they say. When she got him, she changed. It was like it was all worthwhile...to get him. She's been a devoted mother ever since."

Hans showed me his toys, among them a troll similar to the one I had seen with Rudi.

I asked him about it.

"My trolly," he said.

"Do you take him to bed with you every night?" I asked.

He shook his head. He was a bad troll, he told me. He had to sleep by himself in a dark cupboard. He took his dog to bed... if he was good.

Daisy surveyed him with wonder. Her little Hansie! She could understand how Katia felt about her Rudi.

"Little 'uns," she said, "I dunno. They plague you a bit, mind you. Into everything, that's our Hansie. But we wouldn't be without him for the world. Hans says so too. Well, after all, Hansie was the reason he made an honest woman of me. Talking of weddings, I reckon before the year's out, we'll be having the wedding of the year. Things'll change for you then, Miss Pip."

"Yes, they will. I shall have to have made my decision by then."

"That's a fact you will. I hope you don't leave us. We've got used to having you around. I like to think of you up at the slosh. Hans says they think such a lot of you there. Well, Miss Freya does. I reckon she'll stay with the Graf and the Gräfin until the wedding. It don't seem right she should be under the same roof with her husband to be—even such a roof. Goodness knows there's enough of it! I wonder when that marriage will take place. There's talk, you know. They say Sigmund's got his eyes on someone else."

I felt myself flushing and I looked down and picked up one of Hansie's toys. "Oh...?" I said faintly.

"Well, Freya's not much more than a child, is she? What can you expect?"

"Did you...say...there was talk in the town?"

"Oh yes. Quite a bit of it. Well, he sees a lot of her and human nature being what it is—"

"Tell me what they are saying, Daisy?"

"Well, it's the Countess Tatiana. It seems he sees a good deal of her. People have seen them together. Very friendly. If it wasn't for this contract he's got with Countess Freya... You see what I mean."

"Yes," I said quietly. "I do."

"Whether there's anything in it is another matter. I reckon the wedding will go through all right. It has to. Politics and all that. We don't want no trouble about a thing like that. Sigmund would be the first to see it. I reckon whatever he feels about Tatiana, it will be Freya he marries. You seem very absorbed in that rabbit of Hansie's."

"It's pretty," I said.

"I think it's an ugly little beast. No accounting for tastes, as the saying goes. Hansie likes it, though."

I took my leave soon after that. I felt bewildered and deeply disturbed.

When I returned to the *schloss* Freya was not there. It occurred to me that during the last few days I had been so concerned with my own affairs that I had thought very little of her. Fräulein Kratz, however, felt the same. I told her that we must remember that Freya was now growing away from the schoolroom and we must expect her to evade her lessons now and then.

"It is certainly since the Baron returned and we moved to this *schloss* that she has changed."

"It is all very natural," I insisted.

My conscience worried me. Perhaps I should attempt to talk to Freya. Sometimes I wondered how much she knew concerning the gossip about Tatiana.

I saw her in the early morning, when she greeted me somewhat absent mindedly.

I said to her: "Freya, is anything troubling you?"

"Troubling me?" she asked sharply. "What could be troubling me?"

"I just wondered. You seemed a little..."

"A little what?" She spoke sharply again.

"Preoccupied?" I suggested.

"I have a great deal with which to be preoccupied."

"We have spoken very little English lately."

"My English is really quite good, I believe."

"It is certainly better since I came here."

"Which was, of course, the whole purpose of the enterprise," she said pertly. Then she put her arms around me. "Dear Anne," she went on, "don't fidget about me. I'm all right. What do you think of Tatiana?"

The question was so unexpected, as that lady was very much in my mind, that I was startled and showed it.

She laughed at me. "Oh, I know what you're going to say. What you think of Tatiana is of no consequence. It is not your obligation...your duty...to have opinions of Tatiana. But that doesn't prevent your having one—and I'll swear you have."

"I know very little of the lady."

"You have seen her. You have drawn your conclusions. I think Sigmund likes her. In fact I think he likes her a great deal."

"What do you mean by that?" I asked, and I hoped she did not notice the tremor in my voice.

"Exactly what I say. I'll tell you this. I am sure he would much rather be affianced to Tatiana than to me."

"What rubbish!"

"Not rubbish at all. There she is mature...nubile...Is that the right word? Beautiful...I suppose she is beautiful. Do *you* think she is beautiful?"

"I suppose she would be considered so."

"Well then. Isn't it perfectly reasonable of him to prefer her?"

"It would be very wrong of him to," I said with an air of shocked propriety which shamed me and made me feel a despicable hypocrite. "And," I added weakly, "I am sure he would be too...too..."

"Too what?"

"Too—er—honourable, I suppose, to consider such a thing."

"Anne Ayres, there are times when I think you are nothing but a babe in arms. What do you know of men of the world?"

"Perhaps very little."

"Nothing," she declared. "Just nothing. Sigmund is a man, and men are like that...all of them except priests and those who are too old to bother."

"Freya, I really think you are allowing your imagination to run away with you."

"I observe. And I am sure that I am not the one he really wants to marry."

"So you have settled on Tatiana."

"I have my reasons," she said darkly.

I could not help feeling that she did not seem greatly upset about the possibility, and yet at the same time there was a strangeness about her.

Klingen Rock

When I try to remember the events of that night even now they remain jumbled in my mind, but from the first it seemed to me that some hideous pattern was repeating itself in my life.

I think I awoke with a feeling of dread. Something strange was going on. I was aware of it as I came out of what was like a nightmare. Voices, running footsteps...strange unfamiliar sounds...and yet that horrible realization that I had heard it all before. And there it was...unmistakable...the acrid smell of burning, the smoke-laden atmosphere.

I was out of my bed in an instant and rushing into the corridor.

Then I knew.

The *schloss* was on fire.

I was stunned. Freya...dead! And in this most horrible manner. The fire had started in her room and there had been no hope of rescuing her, even though the conflagration had been checked.

That night seemed endless. Even after the town's fire brigade had departed and we were huddled together in the hall talking in spasmodic whispers, it seemed to go on and on.

What had happened? No one was quite sure, except that

the fire had started in the young Countess's room and she
must have been overcome by the smoke almost immediately.
There had been repeated attempts to save her, but it was too
late; no-one had been able to penetrate that blazing room.

I sat shivering with the rest, waiting for the morning,
thinking only of my bright pupil whom I had grown to love.

With the coming of the dawn it was realized that three or
four rooms—including that one in which Freya slept—had
been gutted, but because of the strong stone structure the
rest of the building was undamaged and only lightly scarred
round the scene of the fire.

Fräulein Kratz was beside me in the hall. She kept murmuring: "Who would have believed this.... She was so
young...."

I couldn't bear to talk of her. I should never forget
her...never forgive myself for having deceived her. Dear,
innocent Freya who had never harmed anyone...to die like
that!

I was desperately unhappy and at the back of my mind
was the thought of how strange it was that something similar
should have happened in my life before. I was taken vividly
back to that occasion when there had been a fire at Greystone
Manor and to the accusations which had been thrown at me.

I was shivering because there seemed to be some evil por-
tent here.

I lived through the next day in a nightmarish daze. There
was much coming and going at the *schloss,* and people talked
together in whispers. I shut myself away. I could not accept
the fact that Freya was dead. I had not realized until this
moment how deeply I had cared for her.

In the evening of that day Tatiana came to me. She opened
the door of my bedroom and walked in unannounced. She
looked haggard as I was sure I did. For a moment she did not
speak, but just stood looking at me.

Then she said: "So...this is your work."

I stared at her questioningly.

"I know everything," she said. "You were too complacent.
You thought you were so clever. I knew you were masquer-
ading as someone else. I know you are Philippa Ewell, sister
of Francine Ewell, Baron Rudolph's mistress. I suspected you
almost as soon as I saw you. I had seen you before. You broke
into the Grange, remember?"

"I came to look round. I did not break in."

"This is no time to consider the niceties of words. You are an adventuress. Like your sister. I have seen your papers."

"So it was you..."

"I owed it to the Countess to find out what sort of woman you are." Her voice faltered. "That dear innocent child... now...murdered."

"Murdered!" I cried.

"Do give me credit for some intelligence, Fräulein Ewell. I know who you are. I know a great deal about you. I know you tried the same trick on your own grandfather. We have friends in all parts of the world watching our interests. Your sister had attempted to make a place for herself here, so we were watchful of her connections. You thought the trick worked with your grandfather, so you tried it again here."

"I don't—"

"You are going to say you don't understand. But you do understand—perfectly. That poor old man died, didn't he? So why not the young girl? They were both in your way. You have the strongest possible motive now...as you had then. But is not easy to get away with murder the second time...even for one as clever as you think you are."

"You are talking nonsense...wild nonsense."

"I do not think so, and nor will others. It fits perfectly. You are looking for position and wealth as your sister did. She ended up dead in a hunting lodge. Where do you think you will end up, Fräulein Ewell?"

"I have no intention of being spoken to in this manner," I said. "I am not employed by you. My services, alas, are no longer required. I shall immediately resign from the household."

"Murderesses must pay the penalty," she replied.

"What is your accusation?"

"That you deliberately murdered Countess Freya in a manner which you had tried out before and which worked successfully then in the case of your grandfather. You are not going to deny that that gentleman died in a burning room?"

"I am not denying it, but it has nothing to do with this."

"Allow me to contradict you. It has everything to do with this. Your grandfather displeased you. He was going to turn you out...so that was the end of him, and I believe you came very nicely out of the matter."

"This is monstrous. My money did not come from my grandfather but from my grandmother. I had nothing to do with his death."

"I have my friends there. I know exactly what happened. He threatened to turn you out and that very night he died—mysteriously. Oh, I know nothing was proved against you, but suspicion was strong, wasn't it? He was in a burning room which did not burn quite long enough to destroy the evidence. You were not going to make that mistake twice. You made sure that the evidence in the case of our poor Countess was completely destroyed."

"You are talking wild nonsense. I loved the Countess. She and I were the best of friends."

"Do you think I don't know how much you wanted to get rid of her? You are an ambitious woman, Fräulein. You thought if she were not there—if Baron Sigmund were free from his contract with her—you would reign as Grand Duchess of Bruxenstein."

I stared at her aghast and she laughed bitterly.

"I know of those meetings," she went on. "I know of that tender little romance...."

I was afraid now. I could see it all fitting neatly together. I was reminded of the horror of those weeks at Greystone Manor when I had been under suspicion. I looked into Tatiana's malicious face and I felt the net closing round me.

It was true that if Freya were no more, I had a chance of marrying Conrad. But how monstrous that Tatiana could make such a suggestion! And yet when I looked at the evidence against me, I saw that I was in acute peril.

Conrad would believe in me, I was sure. I must see him. He would surely come now that this terrible thing had happened to Freya.

I could not think clearly. I could only try to fight off this terrible numbness, this sense of impending doom which had possessed me.

"You have been clever up to a point," Tatiana was saying. "But not clever enough. You were too trusting in some quarters. You came here because your sister came. You thought you would follow in her footsteps but more successfully. You were going to try to prove that she was actually married to Baron Rudolph. I suppose you thought that would give you some standing."

"She *was* married to Rudolph," I said.

She snapped her fingers at me. "You fool!" she cried. "Who do you think wanted Rudolph out of the way if it was not Sigmund and his friends? Sigmund has been too clever for you. He has told me of your cloying sentiment. I know of your affair with him, of course. He found it so amusing and he had to know exactly what you were doing. 'So easy,' he said, 'to lead the Fräulein to great expectations and to discover what she was doing at the same time. She is shrewd enough...but she has her weaknesses and I found them.'"

"I don't believe you."

"No. That was your weakness. Too gullible. But we are not here to talk about your amorous adventure with Sigmund. That is of no importance to him or to this case. You thought he would marry you when Freya was disposed of. Unfortunately for you, Sigmund was not what you thought—and in any case we knew too much about you. You cannot play the same trick twice."

"This is a nightmare...."

"Think what it must have been like for poor Countess Freya."

I covered my face with my hands. The loss of my dear little friend...the knowledge that I was discovered to be Francine's sister...the hints about Conrad which I did not believe...the terrible danger in which I stood—it was all becoming unbearable.

"You are under arrest," said Tatiana. "Accused of the murder of Countess Freya."

"I want to see—"

"Yes?" she mocked. "Whom do you want to see? Baron Sigmund is not here. Nor would he wish to see you if he were. Is there anyone else you would like to see—if you were permitted to do so?"

I thought of Hans, but I did not want to implicate him. The Graf was his employer. I thought of Daisy. But she was too close to Hans. Who else was there?

She was smiling at me contemptuously. "Do not search your mind," she said. "Save yourself the trouble, for it would not be permitted. Put a few things together. I am removing you from here for your own safety. When it is generally known that the Countess Freya has been murdered and by whom and for what reason, the people will not leave you to the justice of the land. They will take the law into their own hands. It could be that Kollenitz will demand that you be

delivered to them. I would not be in your shoes then, Fräulein
Ewell."

I cried out, "I am innocent of what you accuse me, I loved
her, I tell you. I would not have harmed her for anything on
earth."

"Get a few things together. My parents agree that we
should get you away to a place of safety until you stand trial.
Hurry. There is little time."

She went to the door and turned to look back at me ma-
liciously.

"Be ready in ten minutes," she said.

The door shut and I sank back into a chair. This was indeed
a nightmare. I must be dreaming. Not only was Freya dead,
but I was accused of her murder.

Within half an hour I was riding out of the town with a
company of guards. People stood about in little groups near
the *schloss*, talking in whispers. There was a hushed atmosphere in the streets. I could smell the smoke in the air. I
looked back at the *schloss*. The scarred wall stood out strongly
in the sunlight.

We left the town behind us and came to the forest. We
passed near the Marmorsaal and went on. We crossed the
river and started to climb. It was about mid-morning when
we came to the Klingen Rock. I remembered it from one of
my rides with Freya, when she had told me the story of the
Rock and the small *schloss* which stood near the mountaintop.

Prisoners had been kept here in the old days, and when
they were condemned to death, they were often given the
choice of throwing themselves down from the Rock into the
gorge below instead of facing execution.

I think I must have been in a state of shock because I could
not quite grasp what was happening to me. Yesterday I had
been free to ride through the forest, to go to my lover....Now
here I was, a prisoner—falsely accused of murdering one I
had loved.

I had lost my dear Freya—a tragedy in any circumstances,
but in this way...I could not grasp the magnitude of what
had happened. The loss of a dear one, the terrible suspicion
that had come to me and my vulnerability to face the dangers
which surrounded me.

We were climbing a rough road cut into the mountainside
and at length came to a gate, which was opened by a rough-

looking man who regarded me steadily from under shaggy brows.

"This the prisoner then," he said. And then to me: "Get down then. We've not got all night."

I dismounted and he took my horse from me, examining it, I noticed, with a keen eye. A woman appeared.

"Here she is, Marta," he said.

The woman took my arm roughly and peered into my face. I was dismayed by her hard, even cruel expression.

"Zigeuner!" she called, and a cowed-looking boy in ragged garments came running out.

"Take her up," said the woman. "Show her where she's lodged."

I followed the boy into the stone-floored hall and he pointed to a spiral staircase at one end of it. The stone steps were steep and the banister was a rough rope.

"This way," he said.

"Thank you," I answered and he looked surprised.

We went up for a long way, round and round until we reached the top of a tower. He threw open the door and I saw a small room which contained a pallet bed, a jug and basin on a rickety table, and a stool.

He looked at me helplessly.

"Is this...all I have?" I asked.

He nodded. He had taken the key out of the door on the inside. "I've got to lock you in," he said with a wan smile. "Sorry."

"It's not your fault. Do you work here?"

He nodded again.

"What's your name?"

"They call me Zig because I'm from the gypsies. I was lost and came here. It was more than a year ago. I've been here ever since."

"It's not very pleasant, is it?"

"There's something to eat."

"Will they keep me here?" I asked.

"They'll try to persuade you."

"To what?"

He nodded towards the window. "Mustn't stay," he said. "They'll dock me supper." He went out, shutting the door, and I heard him turn the heavy key in the lock.

What had he meant when he had said they would try to

persuade me? I went to the window and looked out. I could see the overhanging Rock and the drop down to the gorge.

I sat down on the bed. I was still too shocked and bewildered to think clearly. This was becoming more and more like a fantastic nightmare. I was accused and condemned without a chance to speak for myself. I felt lost—and a desperate loneliness.

Then from somewhere at the back of my mind came the thought: "Conrad will come for me. He will discover what has happened and come to save me."

The boy brought up some stew for me. I could not eat it. He looked at me pityingly as I shook my head and turned away from it.

"Better eat," he said.

"I don't want it," I said. "Do you have many people here like me?"

He shook his head.

"What have you done, Fräulein?" he asked.

"I have done nothing to warrant this treatment."

He looked at me closely and whispered: "Did you offend in high places, Fräulein? That's what they come here for."

He left the plate with me and the sight of the congealing fat on the top of the broth sickened me. I turned away and looked out of the window. Mountains...pines everywhere...the great craggy Rock and below—far below—the ravine.

This is madness, I thought. This is a bad dream. It was the sort of thing that happened when one strayed from the conventional path. Was that why people laid down rigid rules for society? Who would have believed that I, Philippa Ewell, rather quiet, not particularly attractive, could become the mistress of a person of great importance in a faraway country, and then be accused of murder and brought to this mountain castle to await trial...execution for murder.

What had happened at Greystone Manor when I had been suspected of causing the death of my grandfather was not to be compared with this.

I had strayed from the narrow conventional path. I might have married Cousin Arthur and then I could never have been in the position in which I now found myself. But I should never have known the ecstasy I had experienced with Conrad. I had chosen to live dangerously and now the moment had come to pay for it. Once again I thought of that old Spanish proverb: "Take what you want," said God. "Take it...and pay for it."

Both Francine and I had taken. Francine had paid with her life. Was I to do the same?

The day wore on. Darkness came. The boy arrived with a candle in an iron stick. When it was lighted it threw eerie shadows round the room, which looked more and more like a cell. He threw a blanket on the bed. "It gets cold at night," he said. "We're right up in the mountains and the thick stone walls keep out the warmth of the sun in the daytime. Don't say I gave you that. Say it was here, if they ask."

"Zig," I said, "tell me who is here?"

"The old 'uns," he said. "And the Big 'Un and 'er and me."

"The old ones are the man and woman I saw."

"They're the keepers of the Klingen Schloss. Then there's the Big 'Un, he's a giant and he'll be there if he's wanted. Not for you, I reckon—you're just a woman—and then there's 'er and she's his wife."

"So there are four of them."

"And me—Zig. I do the work and get my food for it."

"And who has been there before?"

"Some others."

"What happened to them?"

His eyes strayed to the window.

"Do you mean they were thrown from the Rock?"

"It's what they're brought here for."

"Is that what they intend to do with me?"

"Wouldn't have brought you here, else."

"Who is they? Whom do you work for? Whom do *they* work for?"

"People in high places."

"I see. It's a sort of politics."

"They bring them here so they can have the choice. Taking the leap or facing what they have to face. It's when they like to keep it secret and they don't want there to be a big trial and all that. It's when they want to keep things dark."

"What chance have I of getting away?"

He shook his head. "There's the Big 'Un. If you tried, he'd throw you over right away...and nobody would hear of you no more."

"Zig, I am innocent of what they accuse me."

"That don't make no difference sometimes," he said gloomily, picking up the plate of uneaten food and going out. I heard him lock the door behind him.

That night in the Klingen Schloss seemed an eternity. Lying on the hard pallet, I tried to bring some order into the thoughts that chased each other round in my mind.

Was it possible to get away from here? What I wanted most was to explain to Conrad. Would he believe me guilty? That was something I could not bear. It seemed the worst aspect of the whole terrible business. He knew how very much I wanted to marry him and that I could not happily accept the situation he was offering me and that dear innocent Freya stood in the way.

Could he really believe that I would kill her?

I could imagine how lucidly Tatiana would put her case to him. It fitted neatly enough. "She did it before," I could hear her telling him. "She murdered her own grandfather. She got away with that and she thought she would get away with this. Thank God I discovered her foul treachery. I sent her to Klingen. I thought it would save so much trouble if she took the leap. And she did, of course, when she realized there was no other way out."

But I would not take the leap. I would find some means of escape. I should be thinking of that now. No matter how impossible it seemed, there must be a way. I must get back to Conrad.

But what if...? No, I must fight off these doubts. They were more than I could endure. But they would persist. There had been rumours concerning him and Tatiana. What if they were true? Tatiana said he had amused himself at my expense. I remembered how lighthearted he had been, how he had tried to persuade me to go to the Marmorsaal. How much did I know Conrad? I knew that he was shaped like the gods and heroes of his northern land; I knew that the looks of an ancient hero were combined with the suave and charming manners of a modern prince. He was the sort of man who would be any woman's ideal lover. Was he too attractive? Was he such a delightful lover because he was such a practised one?

I was wasting time with these suppositions. I should be thinking of a plan of escape. If I could get away from here, take the horse that had brought me, ride away...Where to? To Daisy. Ask her to hide me? To Gisela? To Katia? I dared not involve any of them. I was in the hands of my enemies and held on the serious charge of murder.

And the evidence against me could be made to appear irrefutable. I had been in the *schloss* when the fire started; I had been conducting a love affair with Freya's affianced husband, and it was feasible to think that but for her I might marry him and in time become the Grand Duchess. What a maze of intrigue I was caught up in, and I could not find my way out of it. I had even come out here with a false name. I should be labelled *intrigante* and judged guilty.

Oh Freya, dear sweet child, how could anyone think that I could harm you! And Conrad...where are you? He would surely have heard what had happened by now. He would be the first to hear of Freya's death. He would come....He would surely come.

I could not forget Tatiana's words. Could it possibly be that *she* was the one he wanted? Had he really found the episode with me "amusing?"

Another thought struck me. He knew why I had come, that I was determined to prove Francine's marriage and that there was a child. If there was he would no longer be heir to the kingdom. He had said that was what he had wanted. But could it be true?

So the thoughts went round and round in my head during that long and terrifying night and with the streak of dawn in the sky I was at the window looking at the Klingen Rock.

It was afternoon of the second day. The minutes seemed like hours. I was faint with lack of food, I suppose, for I had not eaten since the night of the fire. I was so exhausted that I even dozed for a moment.

No one came to me but the boy Zig. His presence did offer some small comfort because he was clearly sorry for me. He said the descent was swift and you'd be dead before you reached the jagged rocks at the foot of the ravine.

I went back over the past. I could smell the sea and the beautiful flowers on the island. I could clearly remember just how the bougainvillea grew about the studio. I could see Francine assuring the customers of my father's genius, and my mother's bedside when we had all known such sorrow. I could hear my father's voice: "It's Pippa's song. 'God's in his Heaven, all's right with the world.'"

So I brooded—waiting, living, it seemed, in a world of

unreality, longing for that time to pass and yet fearing that the end of my life was very close.

Zig came in with another plate of stew and I turned from it shuddering. "Ought to keep your strength up," he said.

I believed that when he was outside the door he ate it himself. Poor Zig, I suspected they gave him very little to eat.

Who were these people? Servants of the Graf. Did he always send his enemies to them for disposal?

It was so quiet in the mountains that one heard sounds from a long way off. That was why I was aware of the approach of riders before I saw them.

I was at the window. They were coming to the *schloss*. It was a party of six. Conrad, I thought. But no! He was not among them. I could not have failed to recognize him. He would have stood out wherever he was. Now they were close I could see that it was Tatiana who rode at their head, and her companions looked like *schloss* guards.

I knew then that my doom had come upon me, for I was certain that Tatiana was determined to destroy me. She had judged me guilty and was going to make me pay the price.

I watched their approach. Their horses were taken and they entered the *schloss*. I waited tense, knowing that before long Tatiana would come to me.

I was right. I heard the key turn in the lock and she was standing before me.

"I hope you found your quarters comfortable," she said with a twist of her lips.

"You don't need an answer to that surely," I replied.

I felt reckless. I was going to die, but I would try to do it bravely.

"We have pieced the evidence together," she said, "and have found you guilty."

"How could you, without me there to defend myself?"

"There was no need for you to be there. The facts are evident. You had been meeting the Baron at the inn. He confirms this. You had made it clear that you hoped to marry him and that this would have been possible but for his contract with Freya. There could not be a stronger motive. And you tried it before with your grandfather. People are in your way and you eliminate them. Death is the penalty for murder."

"Everyone should have a fair trial. That is the law."

"Whose law? The law of your country perhaps. You are not there now. When you live in a country you obey that country's laws. You have been judged guilty and the sentence is death. Now, because of the people concerned this is an unusual case and it would be dangerous for you to return to be tried. It would create a situation of great uneasiness, possible war between Freya's country and mine. Freya was important and Kollenitz will want revenge for her death. They will want her murderess to be delivered to them. So I am offering you the choice."

"You are offering me the Klingen Rock," I said.

She nodded. "It will save a great deal of trouble...perhaps war. You will throw yourself down and we will send your remains to Kollenitz. They will be satisfied to know that their Countess's murderess is dead. Justice will be seen to have been carried out. We shall leave in ten minutes for the Rock and you will do what has to be done."

"I shall not do it," I said.

She smiled. "You will be persuaded to change your mind."

"I know what is meant by that. Is it on your orders?"

"Mine and others."

"And who are the others?"

"The Grand Duke, the Baron Sigmund, my parents. We are all agreed that it is the best way and the most humane for you—though murderesses do not deserve to be let off so lightly perhaps."

"I don't believe this. I believe it is your judgment and yours alone." She raised her eyebrows questioningly and I went on. "Because you want me out of the way as you wanted Freya."

"You should prepare yourself. It will not be long now."

Then she had gone.

I stood at the window. Death, I thought. The quick plunge and then...darkness. And Conrad? If I could see him once...if I could only hear him say that he had truly loved me...that he had no part in this...

But I should never see him again. I should never really *know*.

They were at the door. It was the Big One this time. There was a woman with him. They had pale shut-in faces displaying no emotion; just cold, aloof as though death was commonplace in their lives. Perhaps it was. I wondered how many they had thrown from the Klingen Rock.

I put on my cloak and the man went first down the stairs;

I followed and the woman came after. In the hall the company was assembled. This was my funeral. How many people are present at their own funerals? And all those who were present were my enemies...except the boy Zig who stood there with his mouth slightly open and real compassion in his eyes.

Out into the cool mountain air. It was breathtaking after the confinement of my prison. I noticed the little white edelweiss and the sheen on the tiny rivulets that fell down the mountainside. There was an intensity about everything, a clarity. Did I see it more clearly because I was about to leave it?

Tatiana's eyes were glittering. She hated me. She was longing for the moment when I should go over the edge of the Rock...down to oblivion...out of her life forever.

We rode for a short way, then we left the horses and took the walk to the top of the ridge. The grass grew sparsely up here and our footsteps crunched on the brown earth.

Then, suddenly silhouetted against the sky, right at the top of the ridge at that spot where I should have to stand to take my leap, stood a figure. It did not move. It remained stationary, facing us as we came along.

I thought, I am having hallucinations. Is this what happens when one approaches death? Then I heard the cry break from me: "Freya!"

The figure did not move. It just stood there. It was unreal. It had grown out of my fevered imagination. Freya was dead. I was imagining I saw her there.

I turned to Tatiana. She was staring ahead, her face white, her body shivering with fear.

Then suddenly the apparition, if apparition it was, started to move towards us.

Tatiana started to cry out: "No...no...You're dead."

Then she started to run and I saw her struggling in the arms of the Big One.

Freya was saying: "Anne...Anne...She was going to have you thrown over. Anne, what's the matter? Do *you* think I'm a ghost?"

Then she put her arms round me and held me to her. Shuddering sobs were shaking my body. I felt unable to speak, unable to control my feelings, unable to think of anything but that she was here...in some form...and that she had saved my life.

"Now, Anne," she said, "Calm yourself. I'm not a ghost.

I was only playing at being one. If you'll stop shaking I'll tell you what all this means."

She gave a shout and several horsemen came out from behind a ridge of boulders where they had remained hidden, and among them was Günther.

He said to the Big One: "Take my sister back to the *schloss*. We will follow."

"She looks terrible," said Freya. "Who wouldn't? I knew that was what Tatiana would do. Have Anne thrown over the Rock. But let's get her back now."

She would tell me nothing until we had returned to the *schloss*. Then she took me into the small room which led from the hall and made me sit in one of the chairs while she took a stool and sat at my feet. We were alone as she had insisted we should be.

"I didn't want anyone else here just at first," she said. "I wanted to tell you... all by ourselves. Günther will come in when I call him."

"Oh Freya," I cried. "I can't think of anything but that you are here... alive... when we thought—"

"Now, you mustn't get too emotional. Where is my nice calm English governess? Nobody was going to make me marry someone I didn't want to."

"You mean Sigmund?"

"I didn't want Sigmund any more than he wanted me. Why should we be forced into marriage? It's ridiculous. I refused to accept it. So did Günther. You see, Günther and I decided that *we* were going to get married. They would never have allowed it, so the only way to do it was to marry and then say, 'It's done!' Nobody could stop it then, precontract or not. We're married and have consummated the marriage, so there. Who knows? I might already be *enceinte*. I should think it very likely. So how could I marry someone else?"

"Oh Freya... Freya... you go too fast."

"Well, we decided to run away. I am sure Providence was on our side that night. What I did was make up a roll of clothes and put them in the bed before I left. I arranged the bedclothes so that it looked as though the Countess Freya was sleeping there. That was just in case anyone looked in and raised the alarm before we had a chance to get far enough away. Tatiana planned to come in, hit me unconscious, and then start the fire. I knew it as soon as I came back and heard what had happened, because she came in before I had gone.

I was sitting in my window with my dressing gown over my outdoor clothes, waiting for the moment to slip out, when my door opened stealthily. I kept behind the curtains so I was able to hide to a certain extent and I saw her creep to my bedside. She was holding a fireiron in her hand.

"I was sitting in the dark because I didn't want to attract attention...sitting in the window waiting for Günther to give the call from below that the coast was clear. I called out, 'What do you want, Tatiana?' She was terribly startled. She said she thought she had heard me call out. I told her I had not and asked what she had in her hand. She said, 'Oh, I just didn't wait to put it down. I was dealing with the fire in my room when I thought I heard you call.' Of course it was all very odd, but I had other things on my mind and I forgot about it. Soon Günther and I were on our way. We went to the priest and got married, and being married is rather wonderful, Anne dear, when you are married to the Right One."

"Oh Freya...dearest Freya..."

"No tears. I'm here. You're safe. This ridiculous case against you is over. You can't accuse someone of murder when there was no murder, can you? But Tatiana tried to kill me and would have done so if I hadn't run away that night to get married. You see how favoured I am. I am so happy, Anne. Günther is the most wonderful husband—far, far better than Sigmund would ever have been. Who wants to be the old Grand Duchess? I'd rather be Günther's wife...and think of the dear little babies we'll have, looking just like him...and some like me perhaps...for I am not bad-looking, am I? Günther thinks I'm beautiful."

"Oh Freya, stop," I cried. "Talk seriously. Did Sigmund come?"

"They were trying to reach him to tell him what had happened. Of course, when I appeared with Günther everything was thrown into confusion. They had all decided that you were the murderess and I learned that you had been taken away for your safety. You can imagine the consternation when I arrived. You can't have a murder without a victim. The Graf and Gräfin were horrified. You know why, don't you? They thought if I were out of the way Tatiana would get Sigmund. Then I appear. There has been no murder...and someone has been hustled away for her own safety. My dear Anne, who wouldn't harm a hair of my head, and only chastises me by making me learn those horrible old English words. Why the English couldn't have made German their language, I could never understand. It's so much easier, so much more reasonable."

"Freya, Freya, *please*..."

"I know. I run on. It's because I'm happy. I've got Günther and that's wonderful. And I saved you. Oh, Anne, I was terrified. I thought I would be too late. I knew she was the one. I understood why. You see, I had caught her before I went off. I knew she had come back. She had hit that bundle of clothes in the darkness....She wouldn't bring a light, would she. And when she thought I was unconscious she set fire to the bed. Then she blamed you for it. I heard you'd gone to Klingen and I knew then what she was going to do. So I pretended to be a ghost. She's very superstitious and I knew that would frighten her out of her wits. Well, it would, wouldn't it, to see the ghost of someone you thought you'd murdered? I did rather well, I think. And now she's confessed her guilt—or she will—and you and I will be together...."

I could not speak. I was so overcome with emotion.

We had been in the *schloss* less than an hour when Conrad arrived. He came galloping in at the greatest speed and when I was swept up in his arms I thought I should die of happiness. The transition from utter despair to the heights of bliss was too sudden. And when he held me at arm's length and looked at me as though he must take in every detail of my face to make sure I was really there, I wondered how I could ever have doubted him.

Freya regarded us with satisfaction.

"All is well," she said. "What a wonderful ending! Now I know what they mean when they said 'and they all lived happily ever after.' And to think that it is all due to *my* cleverness. Though I do admit Günther had a hand in it. Günther!" she called.

And there were the four of us, smiling, clinging together.

It was a wonderful reunion. I knew there would be difficulties ahead—and none knew that more than Conrad—but for the moment we gave ourselves up to the complete joy of being together, to a happiness which was the greater because of the fearful ordeal through which we had passed. Conrad told me he had been terrified when he arrived at the Grand Schloss and heard that Freya was dead and I was accused of her murder and had been taken to Klingen.

He then learned that Freya had married Günther. He had raced to the Rock, and until he had actually seen me, he had been in terror that he might arrive too late.

And he would have done, but for Freya.

"Oh Freya," he cried, "how can I ever be grateful enough!"

Freya beamed on us, looking like the beneficent goddess she had so delighted in imagining herself to be.

"I don't know why I should be so good to you when you preferred someone else," she said severely.

"As for me," he retorted, "you jilted me. You just ran off and left me."

"Nothing to what you did to me. Falling in love with my English governess. Never mind. I'll forgive you because I happen to like her quite a lot myself. And now I shall have to call her Philippa, which is very strange. I don't know how I shall manage that."

Dear Freya! She could not look beyond the moment, and as it was a very happy moment, perhaps she was wise not to.

Later Conrad said to me: "We must imitate Freya. We'll get a priest to marry us."

"You are still the Grand Duke's heir," I reminded him.

"I am no longer affianced to Freya. There will have to be dispensations and so on, but she has broken that contract irrevocably. I shall now marry to please myself."

"It may be the people will not like it."

"They must accept it or banish me."

"You are risking a great deal."

"I risk unhappiness for the rest of my life if I don't seize my opportunities."

We rode to the Marmorsaal with Freya and Günther and there we found a priest who married us.

"The deed is done," said Conrad with a laugh. "There can be no turning back now."

"I hope you will never regret it."

Günther and Freya rode back to the town with us, and we were able to slip quietly into the Grand Schloss. There I was presented to the Grand Duke and Conrad told him that we were married. Freya and Günther were present and the four of us stood before the old man.

He gave us his blessing although it was clear that he found the situation very disquieting. It was a most unorthodox way in which to behave.

He said with a smile, as he looked at Conrad with real

affection: "I can see I shall have to live a little longer until they've all grown accustomed to the idea."

He looked at me gravely: "I know," he said, "that you have been wrongfully accused and I know there has been a long-standing friendship between you and the Baron. You have come into a way of life which will have many difficulties. I hope your affection for your husband will carry you through them."

I kissed his hand and thanked him. I thought he was gracious and charming.

Later I talked with Conrad.

He said that his uncle understood the situation because he had explained it to him. Tatiana's ambition had been to be Grand Duchess in due course, and she had sought to achieve this ambition through marriage. Two people stood in her way: Freya and myself. So therefore she planned to be rid of us both at the same time. What had happened in England had been known to her family because they had been at the centre of that faction which had wanted to get rid of Rudolph and set up Sigmund in his place.

"There are always such intrigues going on in these small states and principalities," said Conrad. "I have always thought it would be a good thing if we could be joined as one great country—a great empire. We should be more prosperous, a world power. As it is we fight among ourselves. There are secret societies and continual intrigues. No one can accuse a single person of Rudolph's murder. It would doubtless have been carried out by a hired assassin."

"Perhaps Katia's brother."

"Very likely. He was close by and it would have been reasonable to choose him. But who can say? And in any case he could not be accused of murder for he would be acting on instructions as a soldier does. Your sister died solely because she happened to be there. There was no intrigue against her... unless there was a child of course whom she might bring forward. That's how it would have happened. It could happen to us, you know. Pippa, have you thought of the sort of life you are marrying into? You live dangerously here. It is a long way from your English village where the main cause for concern is the death-watch beetle in the church roof and who will be elected to the parish council."

"I know exactly what I am doing," I said, "and so did Francine. I wouldn't change it. It is what I want."

He said: "There is another thing. The people may not like our marriage. Kollenitz can't object because it was Freya who broke the contract. But the people here..."

"They would have preferred you to marry Tatiana."

"Not now, because Tatiana will not come out of her convent, I imagine. She will be nursed back to health there, for they will say that she needs it. And very likely she will take the veil. It is what happens in such cases. She was always unbalanced. Now I believe her reason has deserted her. It may come back...and then she will not wish for any other but the convent life. And for us...we have to wait, Pippa. We shall have another marriage ceremony...one with celebrations in the streets. I'm sorry, but you did marry me, remember. You have to face them. I think they'll like you...in time. How can they help it? They might even think it is romantic...charming. They are like that, you know. Freya has been forgiven. There were flowers and cheers for her when she rode through the streets. They have always liked Freya."

"I can well understand that," I said. "Freya is charming and young and fresh and natural."

"They like Günther too. The fact is they like romance, and the story of her running away with the one she loved has caught their imagination...as our story must do."

"Conrad," I said earnestly, "you *don't* wish that you could give it up, do you? It means a great deal to you...this country...."

I saw the dreamy, far-away look in his eyes.

He had been brought up here. He belonged here. I had to learn to accept that.

"God's
in His Heaven"

It was two months later when our ceremonial wedding took place, and I was almost certain at the time that I was going to have a child. The thought gave me confidence. My life was here, and the child I carried would be heir to the dukedom.

Conrad looked splendid. I was dressed in a white gown which was covered in pearls. I had never worn anything so grand. Freya assured me that I looked magnificent, every bit the future Grand Duchess. The Grand Duke's presence at the wedding gave it the seal of official approval, and to my astonishment I came through the ordeal well enough.

I rode through the streets afterwards in the carriage with the ducal arms emblazoned on it. I stood on the *schloss* balcony with Conrad on one side of me and the Grand Duke on the other, while the people cheered us.

Conrad was delighted. I had come through with honours; and that night I told him about the child.

My child was due in six months and I was living, as they said, quietly, at the Marmorsaal in the forest. I would take rides out in a small carriage which had been selected for my use, and because it was small and insignificant I could go out unceremoniously.

I had brought the young boy Zig into the household. I could not forget his kindness to me when I most needed it. His gratitude was moving and I knew I had a faithful servant for life.

I often visited Daisy, who was delighted with the way everything had turned out, and whenever I visited her she would be overcome with awe for at least five minutes before she forgot my new status and I became just Miss Pip to her.

And then...it happened suddenly and when I had no longer hoped that it ever could.

Gisela was visiting Daisy when I called unexpectedly. Daisy was in her usual temporary respectful flutter when she saw who it was, and ushered me into her little sitting room where Gisela's twins, Carl and Gretchen, were playing with Hansie.

"Now then...where can you sit yourself..." Daisy was fluttering round pink-cheeked and flustered, and Gisela was almost as bad.

"Oh, for heaven's sake, Daisy," I said, "stop it. I'm just the same."

Daisy winked at Gisela. "Now listen to her, and her the Grand-Duchess-to-be. And how are you today, my lady? How's the little 'un?"

"Exceptionally lively, Daisy."

"That's a good sign."

"Good but uncomfortable. And how is Hansie?"

"Hansie's a good boy...sometimes."

"And the twins?"

They stood up and regarded me solemnly and not without suspicion, for as children will they had caught the uneasy respect which their elders were feeling towards me.

"You know me," I said to Carl.

He nodded.

"So show me your new toys."

Gretchen picked up a furry lamb from the floor and held it out to me.

"He's very nice," I said. "What's his name?"

"Franz," said Gretchen.

"He's a lovely lamb."

The children nodded.

"They play well together—the twins and Hansie," said Daisy. "It's nice for Gisela to come up here and for me to go visiting her. It makes company."

I agreed that it was nice and it did.

"You wait till yours arrives," went on Daisy.

"We shall have all the bells ringing then," added Gisela.

"I've got a bell," Gretchen announced.

"I've got a fox...a little fox," added Carl.

"And what's his name?"

"*Fuchs*," said Gretchen.

Carl sidled up to me. "I call him Cubby," he said confidentially.

Everything seemed to stand still suddenly. He had spoken the word with a perfect English accent. I was immediately back in the past reading the letter I had had from Francine and which I could remember word for word because I had read it so many times.

"What do you call him?" I asked, and my voice seemed to be shrill with my sudden excitement.

"Cubby!" he cried. "Cubby, Cubby."

"Why?" I asked.

"It's what my mummy used to call me," he said. "Long long ago...when I had a different mummy...."

There was silence in the room. Gisela had turned very pale. Carl had picked up his fox and was saying, "Cubby...There's a good Cubby."

I heard myself say: "This is the child then. Carl is the child."

She did not deny it. She stood staring at me, her eyes wide and frightened in her pale face.

Gisela realized that there was nothing to be done but tell the whole story. She assured me that she had never done so before, because Francine had made her swear that she never would until it was safe to do so.

Francine had lived a rather lonely life in the hunting lodge waiting for Rudolph's visits. She had formed friendships with Gisela and Katia, and through Katia she had gleaned some inkling of the intrigues which were building up. She must have been aware that Rudolph's life was in danger, and when she discovered she was to have a child her fears had been doubled. Living obscurely as she was obliged to do, it was not impossible to keep her pregnancy a secret, but she had faithful friends in the two women, a priest and a midwife, all of whom lived not far from the hunting lodge. She and Rudolph determined to conceal the fact that she was to give birth to the heir to the dukedom until such a time as it would be safe to reveal it, and with the help of these friends she was able to do so.

The Grand Duke had been in ignorance of the marriage, for Rudolph had been afraid to confess to his father in view of the political situation and the need for the help of Kollenitz in dealing with it. There would have been trouble on more than one front if it had been known that Rudolph had spurned the alliance with Freya.

Thus the great wall of secrecy had been built up. Rudolph had been a charming man, but he was weak and as far as I could gather had always taken the line of least resistance to any situation. So he had kept his marriage and the birth of his child secret.

Once the child was born and christened Rudolph, the task was easier. At this time Gisela was giving birth to Gretchen, and it seemed a great stroke of ingenuity to credit her with twins.

Thus Francine had her own child close to her. She could see him every day; and the two children, Gretchen and the little boy, whom they called Carl for safety, were with her constantly.

Francine had hoped that Rudolph would confess to his father, but he put off doing so and finally, when the child was a year and a half old, there came that night when Rudolph and Francine were murdered in their bed.

Now Gisela went in great fear. She loved her adopted child and she knew that if it were realized who he really was, his life would be in great danger. Moreover she had sworn to Francine that she would not betray his true identity until she was sure he would be accepted for who he was.

It was strange that the child himself had made the revelation.

The Grand Duke listened gravely to the story. He then put it in secret to his ministers.

The verdict was unanimous. The law of heredity must prevail. The child in the lodge cottage was heir to the Duchy and must be educated and brought up with a realization of the duties which would one day be his.

It was decided that there should be no covering up. The whole story should be known. The marriage of Rudolph and Francine could be proved. There was the sheet from the church register, and the priest who had married them could be found.

The midwife and everyone who had played even the smallest part in the conspiracy of silence should be brought forward and the truth established.

It was a wild, violent and romantic story—but such stories were not unusual. The truth was plain and the people should know it.

Those days stand out in my memory as some of the strangest in my life. I can remember riding through the streets with Conrad in the ducal carriage with the Grand Duke and little Carl—now Rudolph.

The boy took everything for granted, as though it were the most natural thing in the world for little boys who had been brought up in lodge cottages to ride in a carriage while the people cheered him.

There was one thing that did upset him, however, and that was being parted from Gretchen; so it was decided that Gretchen should be brought to the *schloss* and that the two of them should continue to be together.

Gisela was beside herself with pride. She was also greatly relieved, because she said it was as though a weight she had been carrying was lifted from her shoulders. She had always been afraid for Carl, and to think of her little Gretchen living in a *schloss* and becoming something of a scholar and being with Carl—for she would always think of him as Carl—was something she had never dreamed possible.

It was a good day for her when Francine, the beautiful lady from England, had become her friend.

It is amazing how quickly nine days' wonders are forgotten. Within six months the story seemed to have become distant history, and a year later when the Grand Duke died, Bruxenstein had a Regent—Conrad—and a wife who, although she was English and had once been governess to the Countess Freya, was accepted as the Baroness, wife of the Regent. I had a son of my own by this time, whom I called Conrad after his father, and Freya, herself soon to be a mother, had been one of the sponsors at the grand christening.

I had come to accept ceremony as a way of life, and as long as I was with my family I was happy. I was relieved to be accepted, for after all I was not only the wife of the Regent, but the aunt of the heir to the Dukedom. To my surprise, during the last months of his life, I formed a friendship with the Grand Duke who, after the first shocks, was not at all displeased by the turn of events, since the country continued in peace and prosperity.

Freya was happy; Günther was happy; and Graf and Gräfin, whom I had never known very well nor understood, had slipped into a quiet acceptance of the state of affairs. That they had been involved in the faction responsible for the assassination of Rudolph seemed very likely. Whether they had even then had plans for marrying Sigmund to Tatiana or whether they had felt, as so many people seemed to have done, that Rudolph's rule would have been disastrous for Bruxenstein, I did not know. I had discovered that there were many stern patriots who believed that the death of Rudolph was preferable to a war into which weak rule might have plunged the country. It may well have been that the Graf and Gräfin had been among these. I did know that Sigmund had had no hand in Rudolph's death; in fact he had preferred the life of freedom he had had before the responsibilities of state were thrust upon him.

"It is in the past," was his comment, "and there is nothing to be gained by trying to unravel it...even if we ever could get to the whole truth."

And he was right, of course.

Tatiana remained in her convent. Whether she was indeed of unsound mind or whether she found it expedient to appear so was something else of which I was not sure. She had attempted to murder both Freya and myself, but as long as she remained shut away we were both prepared to forget what she had planned for us.

Thus the months slipped by.

When our son was two years old, Conrad and I took a trip to England. The Grange was made ready for our arrival, and it seemed so strange to go back there and see the row of cottages where Daisy's mother still sat outside on summer's evenings and could be seen pegging her clothes on the line.

Daisy accompanied us, which gave me a lot of pleasure, but we did not plan to stay long, for we hated leaving our children.

I stood and looked at the grey walls of the manor. It seemed different now, for there were children playing on the lawn. There were three of them—two girls and a boy.

These must be Cousin Arthur's children.

Sophia made me feel very welcome. She was clearly happy and I thought how extraordinary it was that Cousin Arthur, who had seemed to Francine and me quite impossible as a husband, should have turned out so satisfactorily for Sophia.

I was even more astonished when I saw Cousin Arthur. He had grown plump and he looked amazingly contented. He clearly enjoyed family life and I was astonished to see that his children were not in the least in awe of him. I wondered what he was like when he gave them religious instruction.

When I was alone with him he became a little embarrassed, as though he was trying to tell me something and didn't know how to begin.

I said to him: "Marriage has changed you, Cousin Arthur."

He admitted that it had. "I must have seemed insufferable to you and Francine," he muttered.

"You did," I agreed. "But you are like a different person now."

"I was a hypocrite, Philippa," he confessed. "When I look back I just despise myself. And that's not all. I have been really criminal...."

I laughed. "Surely not. What do you call criminal? Forgetting to say your prayers one night?"

He leaned towards me and took my hand. "I was afraid of poverty," he said. "I didn't want to have to eke out some poor living as a miserable curate, which is what I should have done but for your grandfather. I wanted Greystone Manor... I wanted it desperately. It came to me... but I didn't deserve it."

"Oh, nonsense. You have made it a happy place. The children are adorable."

"That's true," he said, "but I don't deserve my good fortune. I'm glad to have an opportunity of talking to you. I wronged you, Philippa. I was ready—But let me explain. I wanted Greystone Manor badly so I made myself exactly what your grandfather wanted so that he made up his mind that I should marry either you or Francine. We know what happened about that. Well, I didn't want to marry either of you. It was always Sophia for me."

"Oh, Cousin Arthur, if only we had known!"

"I dared not let it be known. Sophia and I had been in love for some time.... Then, she became pregnant. I had to do something. There came that night when your grandfather died. You had quarrelled with him and everyone heard. He was in an excitable mood. I thought that now he had lost all hope of getting you to fall in with his wishes, he wouldn't want to lose us all, and while he was in this mood was the time to tell him what I had done. So I went to his bedroom. I had confessed that Sophia and I must marry now. I shall never forget his face. He was in his nightcap and his fingers trembled as he grasped the sheet. He stared at me unbelievingly and then got out of bed. I think he was going to strike me. He came towards me and I put out my hands to ward him off. I don't know whether I pushed him or not. It all happened so quickly. He fell backwards and struck his head. I was panic-stricken, for I realized that he was dead. I didn't kill him. He fell. I saw that there would be a great deal of trouble. Everything would come out.... I had to think of Sophia.... I had to act quickly...."

"So," I said, "you set fire to the place."

He nodded.

"I should never have allowed you to suffer for it, Philippa," he said quickly. "If it had gone further... I should have had to tell the truth. But there was Sophia and the child she was carrying— You understand. If we could keep it quiet... if it could all blow over..."

"Even though suspicion rested on me."

"They never brought a charge. It was accidental death. It *was* accidental death and, Philippa, you were young... you went away. I felt no guilt—except where you were concerned."

My thoughts slipped back to those strange days. I remembered how kind, how unexpectedly sympathetic he had been to me. I could hear the shouts of the children on the lawn, and I gripped his hand.

I was suddenly very happy. I looked up and saw a blackbird flying high.

I said:

> "'The lark's on the wing;
> The snail's on the thorn:
> God's in his Heaven—
> All's right with the world.'"